Shadows in the Water

A Lou Thorne Novel

For Kevin

XO

Kory M. Shrum

KMS

Copyright © 2017   Kory M. Shrum

ISBN-13: 978-1542623872

Also by Kory M. Shrum

For Kimberly,

my compass

shadows in the water

Thus did I by the water's brink
Another world beneath me think;
And while the lofty spacious skies
Reversed there, abused mine eyes,
I fancied other feet
Came mine to touch or meet;
As by some puddle I did play
Another world within it lay.

—Thomas Traherne, "Shadows in the Water"

Prologue

No, no, no." Her daughter's hand shot out and seized Courtney's slacks. "Don't leave me."

"Jesus Christ." She tugged her pants from Louie's dripping grip and shoved her back into the tub by her shoulders. "What is it with you and water? It isn't going to kill you. You won't drown! And I have to finish dinner before your father gets home."

Louie's chest collapsed with sobs. "Please. *Please* don't go."

"Stop crying. You're too old to be crying like this."

Louie recoiled like a kicked dog, her body hunching into a C-curve.

God almighty, Courtney thought as shame flooded her. *What am I supposed to do with her?*

The illogical nature of your daughter's fear doesn't negate the fact her fear is very real, the therapist had said. Dr. Loveless must have repeated this a hundred times, but it didn't make these episodes any easier. The fat-knuckled know-it-all had never been present for bath time.

Most ten-year-old girls could bathe on their own. No handholding. No hysterics. No goddamn therapy sessions once a week. And somehow this was supposed to be *her* fault? Why exactly? Because she'd gotten pregnant at eighteen?

No. She did everything right. She married Jack, despite her reservations. He was too young, uneducated, and a dreamer. Triple threat, her Republican father called it.

She read all the pregnancy books. She quit her managerial position at the insurance company and stayed home with Louie, practically giving the girl her undivided attention for the first five years of her life. If she was guilty of anything, it was over-attentiveness.

But Courtney didn't believe for a second this was her fault.

It was *Jack's*.

Jack was the one who insisted on renovating the upstairs bath and then insisted his friend do the renovations. Three years. *Three years* it sat unfinished and oh no they couldn't go to another builder because Jack *promised* Gary the job. Jack and his misplaced loyalties. What did it get them? Bum friends who always borrowed money and *three years* with only the clawfoot bathtub to share between them.

Things worth having are worth waiting for, Jack had said.

This philosophy worked for a DEA agent like Jack, someone who had to track criminals for months or years, but Courtney had never been good at waiting. She preferred what her alcoholic father had called *immediate gratification*.

Within a week of switching from the shower to the clawfoot tub, Louie's episodes began. After three *long* years, Courtney felt she'd had more than enough. God, it would be wonderful to shove a valium down the girl's throat and be done with this. She wanted to. *God almighty*, she wanted to. But Jack had been firm about pills. Courtney loved Jack, but goddamn his self-righteous "drugs are drugs" bullshit. Any half-wit knew the difference between valium and heroin.

You will have to be patient with her, Mrs. Thorne, if you want her to get through this without any lasting psychological damage.

Apparently, the therapist didn't know a damn thing. The damage had *already* begun to show. Louie not only feared water now but dirt also. The child who used to come in at night covered head to toe in grass stains and palms powdered with pastel sidewalk chalk, now crept around as if playing a constant game of The Floor is Hot Lava. This morning, Louie had burst into tears when Courtney asked her to pull weeds from the hosta bed. Even after putting her in coveralls and peony pink garden gloves, the girl had whimpered through the task, ridiculous tears streaming down her cheeks.

Now, hands on hips, Courtney stared down at her hunched, shaking daughter. She could count the vertebrae protruding through her skin. She'd grown so thin lately.

It could be worse, she told herself. She could have a child with quadriplegic cerebral palsy like her book club buddy Beth Rankin. Would she rather have a kid who screamed in the bathtub three or four times a week, or a man-child who had to be pushed in a stroller everywhere and his shitty diapers changed and drooling chin wiped?

Courtney forced a slow exhale through flared nostrils and pried apart her clenched teeth.

"Okay," she said in a soft, practiced tone. "Okay, I'm here. I'm right here."

She knelt beside the tub and grabbed a slick blue bottle of shampoo off a shelf above the toilet. As she squeezed the gel into her palm, Louie still cowered like a beaten dog, head and eyes down.

"I'm sorry," Courtney said, her cheeks flushing hotly. "But it's hard for me to understand this fear of yours."

The girl's teeth chattered, but she said nothing. Only one of her eyes was visible from the slate of black hair slicked against her head.

Courtney massaged the soap into her hair. Thick white bubbles foamed between her knotty fingers, her skin turning red from the pressure and steam. Her gentle massaging did nothing to relax the girl.

"Isn't this nice?" Courtney asked. "I'd love it if someone washed *my* hair."

Louie said nothing, her arms wrapped tightly around her knees.

"You have to lean back now." She trailed her fingers through the gray water. "So we can rinse."

Louie seized her mother's arms.

"I know." Courtney tried to add a sweet lilt to her voice, but only managed indifference. Better than angry at least. "I'm right here. Come on, lie back, baby."

She thought *baby* was a nice touch. Wasn't it?

But Louie's chest started to heave again as her head tipped back toward the soapy gray water.

"Breathe, *baby*. The sooner we do this, the sooner you can get out of the tub." Courtney hoped the girl wouldn't hyperventilate. That would be the fucking icing on the cake. Dragging her wet body out of the tub would be hell on her back, and she'd already had her valium for the night. She'd risk taking another, but she knew Jack counted them.

As the back of Louie's hair dipped into the water, her golden eyes widened. Her fingers raked down Courtney's arms as she clung tighter. All right. It only stung a little, and it would be something to show Jack later when she complained about his lateness.

It was your turn for bath night and look what happened. She might even get away with a second glass of wine at dinner sans lecturing if the marks were red enough.

This made her smile.

With one arm completely submerged under Louie's back, buoying the girl, she could use her free hand to rinse Louie's hair. Thick clumps of soap melted into the water with each swipe of her fingers.

"There."

Louie's muscles went soft, her nails retracting.

"Not so bad, is it?" Courtney cooed with genuine affection now. "I love baths. I find them very relaxing."

Louie even managed a small smile.

Then the oven dinged.

"My ham!" Courtney clambered to her feet.

"No, no, no!" Louie frantically wiped water from her eyes and tried to pull herself into an upright position. "Don't! Please!"

And just like that, the hysterics were in full swing again. *Fucking Jack. I'm going to kill you.* "Breathe, baby."

Shaking suds off her arms, Courtney jogged toward her glazed ham and caramelized Brussels sprouts three rooms away. The sweet, roasted smell met her halfway. "The door is open, *baby*. Keep talking so I can hear you."

"Mom!" Louie screamed. "Mommy! It's happening!"

"I'm right here." She slipped a quilted oven mitt over each hand. "Talk to me. I'm listening."

The girl's escalating hysteria cut off mid-scream. For a moment, there was only a buzzing silence.

Courtney's heart skipped a beat. Her body froze instinctually. Her reptilian brain registering *danger* entered a mimicked catatonia. For several heartbeats, she could only stand there before her electric range, in her gloved hands, the oven mitts spaced equidistantly as if still holding the casserole dish between them.

Her eyes were fixed on a spaghetti sauce splatter to the right of the stove, above a ceramic canister holding rice. She stared without seeing.

Then a chill shuddered up the woman's spine, reactivating her systems. As her muscles cramped, she thought, *fear trumps valium*. She yanked off the oven mitts, throwing them down beside the casserole dish steaming on the stovetop. She jogged back to the bathroom, the silence growing palpable.

"Louie?"

The tub was empty. No shadows beneath the soapy gray water.

In a ridiculous impulse, she looked behind the bathroom door and then inside the small cabinet beneath the sink, knowing full well Louie couldn't fit into either space.

The bathroom was empty. "Louie?"

She ran to the girl's bedroom.

It was empty too. And the wood floor tracing the entire length of the house was bone dry. Louie's soft Mickey Mouse towel, the one they bought on their trip to Disney World two years ago, still hung from the hook by the tub.

She searched every inch of their house, and when she couldn't find her, she called Jack. When he didn't answer, she called again and left a frantic message.

He arrived twenty minutes later.

They searched again. They called everyone. They spoke to every neighbor and the police. If Courtney thought Dr. Loveless was a ruthless interrogator with his second chin and swollen knuckles, she found the authorities much worse.

"I didn't kill her!" she said for the thousandth time. "Jack, do something! These are *your* friends!"

For three nights, they had no peace. Courtney doubled the wine and valium, but it wasn't enough currency to buy sleep.

In the early morning hours, she would find herself wandering their house, wearing down a path between the clawfoot tub and Louie's empty bed. Sitting on the firm twin mattress, she would pull back the Ninja Turtle comforter hoping to find her underneath.

In her mind, she apologized for every frustration, every cruel thought. *I'll do anything— anything. Bring her home.*

The call came on the fourth day.

Sixty miles east of the Thorne's home in St. Louis, Jacob Foxton was interviewed many times by the police, but his story never changed.

His nieces were coming down from Minnesota for the Memorial Day weekend, and he and his wife were very excited to see them. They'd changed the sheets on the spare bed and stocked the fridge with root beer and Klondike bars. The pool was uncovered and cleaned, and the heater turned on. All that was left to do before their arrival was mow the yard.

I was cutting my grass, and she... appeared.

As the police tried to pin the abduction on the man, the lack of evidence made it impossible. Foxton had no priors, and a neighbor confirmed Foxton's rendition.

Billie Hodges had been washing her Chevy Tahoe with a clear view of the Foxton family pool. Like Foxton, Hodges swore the girl simply appeared.

As if from thin air.

After thirty-six fruitless hours, the Perry County Sheriff's Department was forced to believe Jacob Foxton had merely cut a left around his rudbeckia bushes with his squat red push mower and found Louie Thorne standing there, on the top step of his pool.

Naked. Soaking wet. Her dark hair stuck to her pale back like an oil slick. Foxton released the lawnmower's safety bar, killing the engine.

"Hey! Hey you!" He rushed toward her, clumps of fresh cut grass clinging to his bare ankles.

The girl turned toward the sound of his voice, and his scolding lecture died on his lips. It wasn't only her fear that stopped him.

It was the blood.

So much that a cloud of pink swirled toward the drain in his pool.

The girl's body was covered in lacerations, the kind he got on his arms and legs as a kid, hiking through the woods. A great many of them stretched across her stomach and legs and a particularly nasty one across her cheek.

She must have run through the forests of hell, he thought.

But it wasn't the scratches that frightened him.

A ring of punctures encircled the girl's right shoulder. A ragged halo from neck to bicep. Like some hungry beast larger than the girl had grabbed ahold of her with its teeth. Long rivulets of blood streamed down her pale limbs, beading on her skin.

"Honey." Jacob pulled off his T-shirt and yanked it down over the child's head. If she cared about the sweaty condition of the shirt, the grass stains, or Jacob's hairy belly, she didn't show it.

"Are you all right?"

"Is it still on me?" she whispered. She turned her face toward Jacob, but her eyes didn't focus. His mother called that *a thousand-yard stare.*

"Who did this to you, honey?" Jacob asked. He took her hands in his. The hairs on his arms rose at the sight of blood pooled beneath her nails.

"Jacob?" Called Billie from across the stretch of lawn between their two yards. "Is everything all right?"

"Call an ambulance," Jacob yelled. He saw the girl's mouth move. "What was that, honey?"

"Is it still on me?" she whispered again. "Is it?"

And that was the last thing she said before collapsing into his arms.

1

Fourteen years later

Lou unfolded the tourist map and eyed a man over the rim of the creased paper. A boxy man with a crooked nose and a single bushy brow stood on the harbor dock, smoking a cigarette. He draped an arm around a woman's shoulder while he joked with another guy twice his size, a hairy bear as wide as he was tall. The woman was a little more than a caricature to Lou. Big hair and a big mouth, made bigger by the annoying smack of bubblegum between her magenta lips. Her clothes were too tight in some places and nonexistent in others. *A Jersey girl*, Aunt Lucy would've called her.

Lou scowled at the tourist map, pretending to read about the seaport's attractions, and wondered if the girl under Angelo Martinelli's arm would feel half as cozy if she knew what a monster he was.

If Bubblegum Barbie was observant, she might have noticed Martinelli's penchant for leather,

Dunhill cigarettes, and pointy shoes. Maybe Barbie even suspected the Martinelli family was responsible for fueling the heroin problem in Baltimore. Hell, she probably tolerated this aftershave-soaked prick *for* the heroin.

Whatever Barbie thought she knew of the Italian draped over her, Lou knew a hell of a lot more.

She should. She'd been hunting Angelo since she was fourteen.

Lou looked away as if to read the street sign, her heart fluttering with anticipation. A steady pulse throbbed in the side of her neck and in her hands. She was thankful her dark shades and windblown hair hid her excitement. And grateful that Martinelli was too nearsighted to see the map tremble in her sweaty grip.

Her mind kept turning toward the future, when he'd receive a shipment at Pier C and insist on counting everything himself. Better yet, because he'd want to be discreet as to how much dope he imported, his security detail would be thinner. He'd invite enough muscle to get the job done. No more.

Lou wouldn't get him entirely alone. A man like Angelo was *never* alone. He didn't even fuck without an audience. She knew this because she'd considered the possibility of going O-Ren Ishii on his ass. Before fully exploring this option, Lou realized she'd forsake her vow of revenge and blow her own brains out long before trying to seduce a Martinelli.

Tonight there would be guns, of course. And the ones chosen for this evening's mission would be fighters. Perhaps a few even better than Lou herself.

And there was the water to consider. The harbor sparkled in the late afternoon sun. Looking at it made Lou's skin itch.

Angelo ran a thick hand through his oiled hair and tossed his Dunhill butt on the ground. He smashed it out with a twist of his boot and hooked an arm around Barbie's waist.

Tonight, she thought, as a swarm of tourists swelled on the pier. *I'm going to kill you and love every minute of it.*

Her sunglasses hitched higher on her face as she grinned.

Before Angelo could turn toward her and spot a familiar ghost in the crowd, Lou did what she did best.

She disappeared, not returning until well after dark.

By 2:00 A.M., all the tourists were in bed with

dreams of the next day.

Lou, on the other hand, wasn't sure she had another day in her. That was okay. She didn't need to see another sunrise as long as Angelo Martinelli didn't either.

Lying on top of one of the shipping containers, Lou had a great view of the docks below. Her forearms and body were covered in leather and Kevlar, but her palms were bare. The metal container serving as her lookout was warm under her palms, sun-soaked from the day. She was small enough to fit into the grooves in the top of the container, making her invisible to those below. Unless of course, Angelo arrived by helicopter.

Her body squirmed. Despite the pleasant breeze rolling off the deep harbor, sweat was starting to pool at the back of her neck beneath her hairline. Her feet twitched with excitement.

Death by waiting, she thought.

She was desperate to swing at something. She imagined certain animals felt this way during the full moon. Hungry, unsettled, itching all over.

Do it already, her mind begged. *Slip*. A heartbeat later she'd be standing behind Angelo. So close she could run her hands through his greased hair.

Boo, motherfucker.

Not motherfucker, she thought. Mother *killer.*

True, Courtney Thorne was hard to love. Her compulsive and domineering behavior, her impatience. Her tendency to chide and scorn rather than praise. Her face a perpetual pout rather than a smile.

But Louie also remembered how hard her mother had hugged her the day after she was found in Ohio. Louie had sat in the sheriff's office for hours, wrapped in a scratchy wool blanket consuming all the soda and peanut butter cups she could stomach until her parents arrived.

Louie! Her mother had cried the moment she stepped through the station's glass doors. Louie had only managed to put down her soda can and slide out of the chair before her mother fell on her, seizing and squeezing her half to death. She smelled like makeup powder and rose water. Like the old woman she would never become.

Courtney wasn't her favorite parent, but she didn't deserve to die either.

Louie's fists clenched at her side.

Angelo's men stirred on the pier. To anyone else, it seemed as if an innocuous few stood around, smoking, and talking. Apart from the hour, nothing suspicious there. But Lou glimpsed blades catching moonlight and saw the bulging outlines of guns under jackets.

Jackets in this heat were clue enough.

Cops stop patrolling the harbor at midnight. Lou wondered if that could be blamed on budget cuts, ignorance, or money from Angelo's own pockets. *A little of each*, she thought.

She'd almost succumbed to drumming her fingers on the shipping container when a car pulled into view.

The black sedan was like so many others Angelo had rented in cities where he'd done business before: Chicago. San Francisco, New York, Atlanta and now Baltimore.

As soon as she saw the car, she started to slip. Bleeding through this side of the world. *No. Not yet*, she scolded herself. *Don't fuck this up.*

She'd only have one good shot. One chance to catch him off guard.

Tonight she would finish what her father started so many years ago.

Someone opened the back door, and Angelo stepped out. He adjusted the lapels of his leather jacket. She took a deep breath and let it out slowly. Again. Because the sight of him was enough to make her heart hammer.

Angelo called out to someone in Italian, then pointed at the boat. "Ho due cagne in calore che mi aspettano ed un grammo di neve con il mio nome scritto sopra."

Louie only understood a little Italian and caught the words *two whores* and *waiting*. Enough to get the gist of his harsh tone and thrusting hips, and comprehend why the men leered. One whistled through his teeth.

Angelo cupped his hands around a fresh Dunhill. A flame sparked, illuminating his face. With a wave, Angelo led his entourage to the pier where the boat sat tied to the dock. The boat rocked in the waves, straining against its rope, like a tied horse ready to run.

As soon as Angelo placed one foot on the boat, then dipping his head to enter the cabin, Lou let go.

She bled through. One moment she lay on top of the shipping container, the next, she stood in the shadows beneath the cabin's stairs. Her eyes leveled with Angelo's heels. It was hot in the unventilated room.

Angelo Martinelli descended the stairs with a man in front and one behind him. Lou smelled the leather of his boots and the smoke from his cigarette.

I can grab him now, she thought. *Reach between the steps and seize his ankle like in a horror movie.*

Someone turned on the overhead light, and the interior of the boat burned yellow in the glow of the 40-watt bulb. Lou jumped back into the corner without thinking. An honest reaction to the sudden influx of light.

But her shoulder blades connected with a solid wall.

Heads snapped up at the sound of Lou searching for an exit that had been there only a moment before but was now gone.

She had only a second to decide.

She drew her gun, one fluid and practiced movement, and shot the overhead light. The 40-watt bulb burst, exploding in a shower of sparks. It was enough to throw them back into darkness and provide Lou with her exit. She slipped behind the stairs, then emerged from a narrow pathway between two shipping containers. Gunfire erupted inside the boat behind her. The ship strained against its rope again, and the wooden docks creaked.

More men came running, guns drawn.

She cursed and slammed her fist into the shipping container. So much for the surprise.

The chance to grab Martinelli and slip away

undetected was gone. As her target emerged from the boat, gun at the ready, the weight of her mistake intensified.

He was spooked. Now he looked like the horse ready to run.

He inhaled sharp breaths of salty air as he hurried toward his car in short, quick strides. Fifty steps. Thirty-five. Twenty and he'll be gone.

It was now or never.

Fifteen steps.

Ten.

The thick tint of Angelo's car might work to her advantage, but her timing had to be perfect. Her blood whistled in her ears as she counted his last steps.

3....2...1...

She stepped from the edge of the shipping container into the backseat of Angelo's car. The leather seat rushed up to greet her, bending her legs into place.

But it was her hands that mattered. And she had plenty of time to position them.

Angelo turned away from her, pulling the car door shut. She pressed her gun to his temple the second the door clicked into place.

The driver began to turn, pulling his weapon up

from his lap but he was too slow. Louie lifted a second pistol from her hip and shoved it to the back of his neck, to the smooth nape. His neck tensed under the barrel, shifting the gun metal against her fingers.

"Don't," she said. Her eyes were fixed on Angelo. "I have a better idea."

"You were not in the car when I opened the door," Angelo said. His tobacco breath stung her nose. "I'm certain of this."

"Imagine how quick I am with a gun." It was a bold bluff given her predicament. His men were abandoning the boat. Some were moving the heroin. Others were lumbering toward other vehicles. If even *one* of them got into this car, she was screwed.

She could produce a third gun, sure. But not a third hand to hold it.

"You were also on the boat." Angelo's eyes shined in the dark, reflecting light like the black sea in front of them. "Or one like you."

"That would put me in two places at once," she said. She arched an eyebrow. "Impossible."

The driver remained very still, his hands at the ten and two positions on the wheel. Lou didn't recognize him, but she doubted that she'd ever forget the thick stench of Old Spice turned sour with sweat. It made her head swim.

If he was new, he was probably uninterested in doing anything that would cost him his life. She'd have to test this theory.

"What do you want?" Angelo asked. He shifted uncomfortably. Lou had found her silence made men nervous. Or maybe it was her gun. Difficult to tell. "Money? The drugs?"

"Driver?" she said.

The driver didn't turn toward her or even make a small sound of acknowledgment.

"Do you see the pier?" she went on, eyes still on Angelo. One of his greased curls fell across his forehead, and one corner of his lip curled in a partial sneer. His cheek muscles twitched. "Beside the pier is a space between the guardrails. Do you see it?"

The driver remained mute. His shoulders remained hunched, eyes forward. It was as if he'd had guns pressed to his head before and had since learned how to keep even a single muscle from twitching.

Lou saw all this in her perfect peripheral vision, not daring to look away from the man she wanted most.

Angelo Martinelli. This close he was smaller than she'd imagined.

She smiled at him, the taste of victory on her lips. "Drive into the bay."

When the driver didn't move, she smacked the gun against his occipital bone. "If you don't do it, then you're useless to me, and I think you understand what happens to useless people."

If he refused to drive, she'd shoot them both. It would be messier. Riskier. But if she couldn't get Martinelli into the water, she wasn't going to let this opportunity escape.

Yes. If Lou had to, she'd shoot them both and drive the car into the bay herself.

"Make your choice, Martinelli," she said. His eyes were pools of ink shining in the lamplight.

The confused pinch of his brow smoothed out. The curling sneer pulled into a tight grin.

"Drive," he said.

Without hesitation, the driver put the car into motion, and the sedan rolled forward.

"Faster," Lou said, grinning wider.

"Faster," Angelo agreed. A small chuckle rumbled in his throat. He slapped the back of the driver's seat like this was a game. "*Faster.*"

The driver punched the accelerator, and the car lurched forward. As it blasted past the men on the docks, shouts pinged off the windows. Angelo's laugh grew more robust, pleasing belly laugh.

He's high as hell, she realized. *High as hell without any idea of what's happening to him.*

They hit a bump when flying past the guardrails and onto the pier. The wooden slats clunked under the car's tires.

In the wake of Angelo's mania, Lou couldn't help but smile herself. She didn't lower the gun. "You're crazy."

This proclamation only made him laugh harder, clutching at his belly. His laugh warped into a wheezing whine.

The thrum of the wooden slats disappeared as the car launched itself off the pier. The sharp stench of fish wafted up to greet them as they floated suspended above the ocean. Her stomach dropped as the nose of the car tipped forward and the windshield filled with black Atlantic water.

There was a moment of weightlessness, of being lifted out of her seat and then the car hit the water's surface. Her aim faltered on impact, but she'd righted herself before either man could.

Cold water rushed in through the windows, trickling first through the corners, filling the car slowly as they slid deeper into the darkness. It seeped through the laces of her boots.

"Now what?" Angelo asked. He seemed genuinely thrilled. As if this was the most exciting experience of his life.

"We wait," she said.

"She's going to shoot us and leave our bodies in the water." The driver's voice surprised her, higher and more childish than she imagined. No wonder he'd kept his mouth shut.

The driver could open the door and swim away for all she cared. "I don't—"

The driver couldn't wait for any reassurance. He whirled, lifting his gun.

Without a thought, she fired two shots into his skull, a quick double tap. His head rocked back as if punched. The brains splattered across the windows like Pollock's paint thrown onto a canvas.

She was glad she'd decided on the suppressor. Her ears would be bleeding from the noise if she hadn't. The smell of blood bloomed in the car. Bright and metallic. It was followed by the smell of piss.

Angelo's humor left him. "Is it my turn now, ragazzina?"

Water gurgled around the windows as the car sank deeper into the dark bay.

"No," she said, her eyes reflecting the dark

water around them. "I have something else for you."

2

Will you do it?

The question looped in King's mind. *Will you do it, Robbie?*

At the corner of St. Peter and Bourbon, Robert King paused beneath a neon bar sign. Thudding bass blared through the open door, hitting him in the chest. The doorman motioned him forward. King waved him off. He was done drinking for the night. Not only because the hurricane was getting acquainted with the pickle chips he'd eaten earlier, but because the case file under his arms wasn't going to examine itself.

Despite the riot in his stomach, he hoped the booze would help him sleep. He was overdue a good night. A night without crushing darkness and concrete blocks pinning him down on all sides. A night where he didn't wake up at least twice with the taste of plaster dust on his lips. Leaving the bedside light on helped, but sometimes even that wasn't enough to keep the nightmares away.

Drunk revelers stumbled out of the bar laughing, and a woman down the street busked with her violin case open at her feet. The violin's whine floated toward him but was swallowed by the bass from the bar.

King paused to inspect his reflection in the front window. He smoothed his shaggy hair with a slick palm. He could barely see the scar. A bullet had cut a ten-degree angle across his cheekbone before blasting a wedge off his ear. The ear folded in on itself when it grew back together, giving him an elfish look.

A whole building collapsed on him, and it hadn't left a single mark. One bullet and…well, he supposed that was how the world worked.

Calamity didn't kill you. What finished you was the shot you never saw coming.

He straightened and smiled at the man in the glass.

Good.

Now that he didn't *look* like a drunk, it was time to make sure he didn't *smell* like one. He pinned the file against his body with a clenched elbow and dug into his pocket for mints. He popped two mints out of the red tin and into his mouth, rolling them back and forth with his tongue as if to erase all the evidence. Satisfied, he continued his slow progress toward home.

The central streets of the French Quarter were never dark, even after the shops closed and all that remained were the human fleas feeding in the red light of Bourbon Street. The city didn't want a bunch of drunks searching for their hotels in the dark, nor did they care to provide cover for the petty pickpockets who preyed on them. There were plenty of both in this ecosystem.

At the corner of Royal and St. Peter, King paused beneath a metal sign swinging in the breeze rolling in off Lake Pontchartrain and wiped his boots on the curb. Gum. Vomit. Dog shit. A pedestrian could pick up all sorts of discarded waste on these streets. He balanced his unsteady body by placing one hand on a metal post, cane height and topped with a horse's head. The pointed ears pressed into his palm as he struggled to balance himself.

A fire engine red building stood waiting for him to clean his feet. Black iron railings crowned the place, with ferns lining the balcony. Hunter green shutters framed oversized windows overlooking both Royal and St. Peter.

The market across the street was still open. King

considered ducking in and buying a bento box, but one acidic pickle belch changed his mind. He rubbed his nose, suppressing a sneeze.

Best to go to bed early and think about all that Brasso had told him. Sleep on it. Perhaps literally with the photographs and testimony of one Paula Venetti under his pillow for safe keeping.

And with his gun too, should someone come in during the night and press a blade to his throat in search of information. It wouldn't be the first time.

Will you do it?

King supposed if he thought this case was hot enough to warrant a knifing in the night, he should've said *no*. He should remind his old partner he's retired. Brasso should find some young buck full of piss and vinegar. Not a man pushing sixty who can't have two cocktails without getting acid reflux severe enough to be mistaken for a heart attack.

The case file sat heavy in his hand. Heavier than it had been when he'd first accepted it. He clutched the folder tighter and crossed the threshold into Mel's shop, the lights flickered, and a ghostly moan vibrated the shelves.

A gaggle of girls looked up from their cell phones wide-eyed. Then they burst into laughter.

One with braces snorted, and the laughter began anew.

Mel's sales tactics may not be old hat to them, but King found the 10,000[th] fake moan less thrilling than the first. Funny how it had been the same with his ex-wife.

It's all about theatrics with these folk, Mel had said when she forced him to help install the unconventional door chime. *They come to N'awlins for the witchy voodoo stuff, and if you want to keep renting my room upstairs, Mr. King, you best clip these two wires here together. My old fingers don't bend the way they used to.*

And he did want to keep renting the large one-bedroom apartment upstairs, so he offered no further resistance to her schemes.

The store was smoky with incense. Ylang ylang. Despite the open door and late breeze, a visible cloud hung in the air, haloing the bookshelves and trinket displays full of sugar skulls, candles, statues of saints, and porcelain figurines. The fact that he recognized the scent spoke of Mel's influence on him these past months. If someone had bet him he would know the difference between Ylang ylang and Geranium two years ago, he would have lost the shirt off his back.

Apart from the four girls clustered by a wall of talismans, only one other patron was in the store. A rail-thin man with a rainbow tank top and cut-off jean shorts showing the bottom of his ass cheeks plucked a *Revenge is Love* candle from a wooden shelf. He read the label with one hand on his hip. When he scratched his ash blond hair, glitter rained onto the floor.

King's heart sank. Despite Mel's endless tactics, business was still slow. At ten o'clock on a Friday, this place should be packed wall-to-wall with tourists, ravers, or even drunks. Five customers did not an income make.

Behind the counter, a twenty-two-year-old girl with a white pixie cut took one look at the falling glitter and her nostrils flared.

Piper wore a sleeveless tank top with deep arm holes revealing her black sports bra beneath. A diamond cat earring sat curled in the upper curve of her ear and sparkled in the light of the cathedral chandelier overhead. A hemp necklace with three glass beads hung around her neck. Every finger had a silver ring, and a crow in flight was tattooed on her inner wrist. She managed to mask her irritation before Booty Shorts reached the counter with his purchase.

"$6.99." Piper slipped the candle into a paper bag with the *Madame Melandra's Fortunes and Fixes* logo stamped on the front.

Booty Shorts thanked her and sashayed out into the night. A glow stick around his neck burned magenta in the dark.

"I don't see what a candle can do that a hitman can't." Piper blew her long bangs out of her face.

"Why would you have someone else fight your battles for you?"

"I don't hit girls." Piper scoffed in mock indignation. "Anyway, my point is it's a waste of time sitting up all night with a candle praying to some goddess who doesn't give two shits about my sex life. Don't cry about your sour milk! Go get another fish! A cute, kissable fish who'll let you unsnap her bra after a couple tequila shots."

"Be grateful for the candle-burning crybabies," King adjusted the folder under his arms. "Unless you want to be a shop girl somewhere else."

Her nostrils flared. "*Apprentice*. I'm learning how to read fortunes. Sometimes I set up a table in Jackson Square and make shit up. People *pay* me! It's unbelievable."

"The Quarter is a dicey place for a young woman to be alone."

"*Awww.* I've always wanted a concerned father figure." She pressed her hands to her heart. Then she rolled her eyes. "Who said I was alone?"

"Were you with Tiffany?"

"Tanya," she corrected. "And *no*. We broke up weeks ago."

King rubbed the back of his head, leaning heavily against the glass case. "That's right. You left her for Amy."

"Amanda," she said. "Keep up, man."

He'd never been great with names. Now faces—he never forgot a face. "I'm sorry. How's Amanda?"

"She's—"

A teenage girl burst from behind the curtain, clutching her palm as if it'd been burned. Fat tears slid down her cheeks, glistening in the light until her friends enfolded her in their arms.

The velvety curtain with its spiraling gold tassels was pulled back again and hung on a hook to one side of the door frame. From the shadows, a voluptuous black woman with considerable hips emerged. Mel's kohl-rimmed eyes burned and an off-the-shoulders patchwork dress hugged her curvy frame. Gold bangles jangled against her wrist as she adjusted the purple shawl around her.

"Bad news?" Piper arched a brow, and King realized she'd begun to mimic Mel's dramatic eye makeup.

Mel crossed the small shop, and King straightened again. He hoped his eyes weren't glassy, and the mints had done the trick.

Mel stopped short of the counter and put one hand on her hip.

"Crushing hearts?" Piper asked, and she sounded excited about it.

Mel rolled her eyes. "I only suggested a book."

Piper frowned. "What book?"

Mel puckered her lips. "*He's Just Not That Into You.*"

Piper's grin deepened. "You're so cruel. Do you want me to talk to her? I'm *really* good with damsels."

"They're release tears. They're good for the soul. She'll wake up tomorrow and feel like the sun is shining, the baby bluebirds are singing, and—"

"—she'll be $80 lighter for it," Piper muttered.

"She'll be fine." Mel tapped her long purple nails on the checkout counter and turned her dark eyes on King. "You, on the other hand, you're in trouble. *Big* trouble."

King felt the sweat beading under his collar. He

resisted the urge to reach up and pull at it. It was the chandelier overhead, beating down on him. Or he could blame the muggy night. New Orleans was hot as hell in June. Sweating didn't mean a damn thing.

"You're awfully quiet tonight, Mr. King."

He shrugged.

Mel stopped tapping her fingers on the glass countertops. King noticed reflective gems had been glued to the end of her index fingernails. "I see a woman in your future. She's someone from your past. Pretty little white thing. Blonde. Big blue eyes. And she needs your help."

His ex-wife Fiona had brown eyes, and no one would have called her *a pretty little white thing."* She'd been nearly six feet tall with the body of a rugby player.

Lucy.

"Is this a real fortune, Mel?" he asked his tongue heavy in his mouth.

Mel wrinkled her nose. "As real as the booze on your breath, Mr. King."

He adjusted the file under his arm. "It's mouthwash."

"I've done told you when you signed your lease, I wouldn't let no drunk man in my house again."

King found it amusing when Mel's southern

accent thickened with her anger. Amusing, but he didn't dare smile. Mel hadn't wanted to rent her spare apartment to anyone, let alone a man. It had taken two weeks of wooing and reference checking to convince the fortune teller an ex-DEA agent was an asset rather than a liability.

"At least he's not an angry drunk." Piper tried to pull the file free from King's underarm. She bit her lip as she tried to peel the flaps apart and glimpse the contents within.

He slapped her hand lightly. "I'm not even buzzed."

Mel's eyes flicked to the case file then met his again. She arched an eyebrow.

King didn't believe in palm reading or fortune telling. Ghosts only existed in the mind, and he would be the first to admit he had a menagerie of malevolent spirits haunting him.

But despite what his mother called a healthy dose of skepticism, he believed in intuition. Intuition was knowledge the frontal lobe had yet to process. He trusted his instinct and he respected the instinct of others. No one person could see every angle. Shooters on the roof. Boots on the ground. You had to rely on someone else's eyes, and this was no different.

Did Mel sense something about the case Brasso brought him? About a witness on the run and the man hunting her? And this mysterious woman from his past…

Mel spoke to the gaggle of girls. "Who's next?"

Three hands shot up. Someone cried, "Me!"

Clearly, they were eager to have their hearts broken.

"Wait." King touched her shoulder, and she turned. "Were you serious about the woman?"

"I don't need to be a fortune teller to know there's a woman, Mr. King." Mel tucked one of the girls behind the curtain and met his eyes again. She looked at him through long, painted lashes. Candle flames danced on the walls behind her. "She's in your apartment."

"You let a woman into my apartment?" His heart took off. "There's a woman in my apartment? *Now?*"

Mel grinned and dropped the burgundy curtain.

"Good luck with your ex-girlfriend." Piper swiped at the floor with a corn husk broom, doing no more than smearing the glitter. "Hope you have better luck than I do with mine."

"I'll be okay." King stood at the base of the stairs, looking up at his dark door. "Probably."

3

The moment the water overtook the car, Lou made her largest slip yet. She took Angelo, the car, and the dead driver. She didn't know if this was her doing, or if some things slip through on the current of their own desire. After all, there were enough rumors. Ships found floating without people. The Bermuda triangle. Planes disappeared and were never seen again. No debris ever found. She wasn't so egotistic to assume she was the only one who could slip through thin places.

Once the dark water turned red, became a different lake in a different place and time, Lou kicked out the window and swam.

She surfaced beside the body of the driver. He floated face down in the water. His shirt was puffed up in places where the air had entered beneath his collar. The water of Blood Lake, always the same crimson hue, added a surreal dimension to the floating body. As if the driver floated in an ocean of his own blood.

A large splash caught her attention, and she paddled in a half-circle. Her heavy boots tugged at her ankles, making it harder to stay afloat.

It wasn't Angelo. He was moving slowly toward the shore, making poor progress under the weight of his leather jacket. He slapped at the surface of the lake, each clumsy stroke of his arm like an eagle trying to swim. She spun further to the right in time to see a large dorsal fin dip beneath the surface about ten yards away.

She didn't need to be told getting out of the water was a good idea. Blood in the water was sure to attract any predator, earthly or otherwise. The splattered brains on the sinking car's window was an added draw.

And she didn't have much time. The ripples of the creature's descent were already lapping at her breast bone.

She swam for shore in slow, controlled movements. Not panicked. Not like prey. Yet she expected at any moment to find herself jerked under. Each easy stroke toward Angelo was an act of self-control.

Yet she emerged from the lake unharmed. Her heart hammered, but her body was whole. Angelo inspected a cut on his hand. He hadn't been careful enough with the broken window he'd pushed himself through.

Lou watched him, waited for him to adjust to his surroundings.

Finally, he looked up. He made a small sound of surprise, and Lou followed his gaze toward the water. The body of the driver bobbed once. Then a harder jerk submerged all but the puffed shirt. A flick of a large grotesque tail covered in purple spines slapped against the surface. One more tug and the body was gone. Only ripples on the surface suggested an exchange had happened.

Angelo stared gape-mouthed at the sky, transfixed by the two moons sagging there. "We are dead."

Lou tried to imagine what this place looked like to him. What it had looked like to her on her first visit.

The red lake. The white mountains. The strange yellow sky. A black forest with short trees and heart shaped leaves. Incongruous colors that were so different than those of her world.

"You are a demon." He crossed himself and kissed a saint pendant hanging from a gold chain around his neck.

It was the smell of sulfur that made him think of Hell, no doubt. It hung in the air and would cling to her hair and skin until she bathed. She shook water off her hands. "This is not some Roman Catholic parable." *Though you will learn a lesson here*, she thought.

"Who are you?"

"Jack Thorne's daughter."

Angelo's eyes widen. "No. She hit the bottom of the pool and didn't come up."

I didn't *come up*, she thought. *I went down. Sometimes the only way out is through.* And Lou thought there wasn't another person on Earth who that could be more true for.

She remembered every detail of that night, of her father's final hours. As if those moments had been burned like images onto film, forever preserved in her mind.

On the last night of his life, Jack Thorne entered their Tudor house in the St. Louis suburbs. He stood there in the doorway, wearing his bulletproof vest and badge. He was an intimidating sight, over six feet tall and filling the doorway like an ogre from a storybook. His gaze was direct and cumbersome most of the time. Only when he smiled, and the lines beside his eyes creased, did the gaze feel friendly.

"I want to talk to you," he said.

Louie, twelve, had slowly lowered her book, mentally marking her place on the page, before looking up from the window seat where she sat.

Her father had laughed, his grin transforming his face. "You're not in trouble. Scout's honor."

He'd never been a scout, but that hadn't stopped him from hailing the three-finger salute.

He ruffled her hair before heading to his bedroom where he changed. She'd listened to him, to the sound of his holster buttons snapping open. The clunk of the gun being placed on the dresser. One boot falling with a thud to the floor. Then the other. The Velcro of the bulletproof vest ripping free. These were the sounds of him coming home, and they had comforted her.

At dinner, she pushed a piece of soft, over-boiled broccoli around her plate, and waited. She listened to her mother complain about her day, about her part-time job at the chiropractor's office.

"They don't even vaccinate their children," her mother sneered between sips of red wine. "Six children and no vaccinations. Haven't they ever heard of herd immunity?"

"Mmmhmm," her father said companionably and scraped up the last of his turkey and broccoli with a fork. The turkey was dry as sandpaper, and the broccoli was practically mush. But Jack Thorne ate it with the same relish he would have a 24 oz. Porterhouse because of his respect for the woman who made it. *Tasteless food never hurt anyone*, he'd told Louie once. *But cruel words do.*

"Dr. Perdy said, 'my children have never been sick.' I wanted to ask, 'do you know why, Dr. Perdy?' Herd immunity, *that's* why. And do you know how we gained herd immunity?"

"Hmmm?" her father prompted, as he was expected to. He sat back in his chair, unbuttoned his jeans and began reviewing his teeth with a toothpick.

"He's supposed to be a medical professional." Courtney finished her glass of wine. "A medical professional surely understands what could happen if we sabotage our herd immunity."

Her father took a swig of beer. "Do you want to do anything special this summer, Louie?"

Louie looked up from her broccoli and shrugged.

Her mother made a *tsk* with her tongue, a sound which she reserved to express her annoyance. In this instance, it was about her husband's unbuttoned pants at the table and his attempt to shift the conversation to their daughter.

Louie's showers usually ended with such a *tsk* of her mother's tongue and a complaint about her aching back. Other times, her mother would thrust the towel past the curtain and hold it there until Louie wiped the water out of her eyes and took it. She hadn't been allowed to bathe alone since she'd returned from Ohio.

"She should do summer school this summer," Courtney said with arched brows. "Her social studies grade was dismal! We need to get serious about this, Lou. You only have four years before you start applying to college."

Louie opened her mouth but caught her father's slight shake of the head. She shut her mouth and resumed her assault on the vegetables.

Courtney topped off her glass of wine and retired to the bedroom, with the cordless phone as she did every night. She'd call her sister, and they'd talk while watching the DVR recordings of her favorite soap operas.

As soon as the bedroom door closed, her father nodded toward the back door. "Last one out is a snot-covered Wheat Thin."

Louie wrinkled her nose. "Gross!" Any lingering hunger from her unsatisfying meal was squashed by this disgusting image. She pushed back from the oaken table.

Despite his playful attempt to put her at ease, her heart knocked wildly against her ribs and her legs dragged beneath her like two bags of wet sand. She wasn't sure if it was the prospect of going near the pool or the pretense of their conversation.

Her father turned to find her trailing reluctantly behind.

She closed the door behind her and stepped out into their fenced backyard. She skirted the kidney bean-shaped pool. Her eyes transfixed on the dark water. "What's wrong?"

"Come over here and sit with me," he said. He slipped into one of the poolside chairs and patted the seat beside him.

Her arms and legs felt ten pounds heavier, but Louie obeyed, inching toward him. Once they were knee to knee, he spoke up.

"I want to talk about the pool."

The pulse in her ears blocked out all sound.

"Stay with me, Louie," he said as she instinctively stepped away from the water. "I know this scares you, but it's important."

When she didn't answer, he put his hand on her shoulder, cupping the large scar encircling her upper arm and clavicle. Twenty-three stitches and months of physical therapy to combat the scar tissue which formed after.

"Louie, Louiiii. Oh baby," he sang. If he wanted her to smile, he sang mumbled nonsense from some '60s cover song. "Do you trust me?"

She did. But she only managed a small nod despite her father's pleasing baritone.

"Do you remember me telling you about Aunt Lucy?"

Her brows pinched together. "The one you named me after?"

"That's the one. I want you to go stay with her."

"You're sending me away?" She swayed on her feet. The shadows dancing at the edge of the motion lights pressed in on her, swiped at her neck and face with cold fingers. And the water—the godawful water—seemed to roll toward her like a hungry, anxious tongue, lapping at the sides of the pool.

"No, no," her father said, squeezing her shoulders. "Aunt Lucy can help you."

"Summer school," she blurted. "Mom said I—

"You don't need to learn about wars, Lou-blue. You need help."

"I'm sorry about—" Louie stammered. "I know it's not normal. I—"

"No, no, hey," he said. He pulled her into his

arms. She collapsed completely even before he kissed the top of her head. A whiff of beer burned her nose. She liked the smell. She wrapped her arms around him.

"This isn't a punishment. You haven't done anything wrong. Do you hear me?"

"I don't want to leave." Tears stung the corners of her eyes. Her fists balled behind his back. "Don't make me leave."

I only feel safe with you. She wasn't sure if it was merely his size or the steady calm of his presence. He wasn't reactive like her mother. He wasn't volatile in his responses—one minute pleased, the next panicked—he was even. Predictable. A cool, unmovable stone to rest her hot face against.

He grounded her in a world where she felt on the verge of falling through at any moment.

"Maybe Lucy can come here," he said, kissing the top of her head. "But you need to see her. I think she can help you. When we were children, she would disappear like you did."

She pulled herself out of his lap. Like her. Someone in the world like *her*. "Why didn't you tell me?"

An aunt. An aunt like me. "Why didn't you tell

me about Aunt Lucy?"

"I had to find her first." He considered the beer bottle as if the answer was hidden in the bottom. He looked up and saw the questions in Lou's eyes. "Aunt Lucy and I didn't always get along. I didn't believe her. I thought she disappeared for attention. I figured she liked scaring our grandmother half to death."

Louie cupped her elbows with her palms and chewed her lip. *An aunt. An aunt like me.*

"But I believe you," he said and pushed her hair out of her eyes. "And I don't want you to be afraid. When you're out of school this summer, we'll have three whole months to work on this. We'll figure this out."

"This isn't a trick?" Louie whispered, squeezing her elbow tighter. "I'm not being sent away to an insane asylum or something?"

"No," he said, firm. "Lucy wants to help. She thinks she can show you how to control it—"

Louie's voice bursts from her throat. "I'm not going in the water!"

"You can control it," her father said again. He pressed her hands to his beard, trapping them beneath his own. She loved this beard and thought it made him look very handsome. But it wasn't enough to soothe her blind panic. Not now. The pool seemed to swell in her vision.

"No." She tried to pull her hands away from his. "You don't understand. There are things over there."

He wouldn't let go of her. "You can conquer this. And I'll be right here."

Nightmares reared in her mind. A great yellow eye. Rows of stained teeth. Hooked talons reaching.

"Master this, Lou-blue. Don't be its victim." He cupped her cheeks this time and kissed the tip of her nose. "Promise me."

Gunfire erupted in the house. Their heads snapped toward the sound of it in time to see strobe lights flash in the bedroom window. The noise of a wine glass shattering on the floor wafted through the open bedroom window. No screams. Then the gunfire ceased, and the bedroom fell dark again except for the soft blue light of the television.

Seconds later, only long enough for her father to stand from the pool chair, men burst through the side gates into their backyard. A hand shoved aside a lilac bush. Petals the colors of bruises rained down on the lawn.

Louie saw a specter, a phantom illuminated by the motion lights. And that was all she saw before her father lifted her off the ground and threw her into the pool.

Her body hit the surface, and on impact, the air was knocked out of her, swallowing her scream. The cold water engulfed her, enclosed her limbs like tendrils of seaweed. Through the aqua distortion, she saw her father turn and run, his white shirt an ethereal target drawing the gunfire away from her.

But even as she tried to frantically swim toward the surface, screaming and reaching out for him, she felt herself falling through.

But she never forgot the face of the monster.

Angelo Martinelli. And here he was at long last.

"She's dead. We made sure."

"Sorry to disappoint you." She kept one eye on Angelo, but her attention was on the trees. She had only one reason for bringing Angelo here. *Where are you?*

"What are you looking at?" Angelo turned toward the trees and peered into the black forest.

Her shoulder burned. The warped flesh and old scar tissue was a reminder of the beast's stealth. Of its ability to appear suddenly no matter how quiet or careful she was.

It's close.

The dark seemed to ripple, and Lou had only a second to prepare herself.

A beast with skin the color of tar leapt from the trees. Angelo screamed the way she must have the first time she saw the animal. If it could be called an animal. Six legs with scaly feet. Pus-colored talons and eyes. A face and round belly could be mistaken for cute, as long as it didn't open its mouth and hurl its death screech into the sky. Or bared its double row of jagged shark teeth.

Lou put one foot in the water, making Angelo the closer target. His decision to scream and run only sealed his fate. She knew she should jump into the water. Slip through before the animal could catch her.

When she used La Loon to dump dead bodies, she never stayed longer than a minute. But Angelo was alive. She wasn't leaving until she saw him dead.

The beast's serpentine back contracted, black muscle stretching long as it lurched forward onto its anterior feet. Screaming louder, Angelo dashed for her as if to throw himself at her feet and beg for mercy.

"You can't run from it," she said. Her voice was weakened by her throbbing shoulder. Her old scars were alive again. "It'll catch up to you every time."

One snap of its jaws brought Angelo down. A

second tore open his belly, spilling his guts on the wet earth. The flesh stretched away from his rib cage, the scraps of leather jacket serving as inadequate protection.

He stayed alive much longer than Lou expected, long after his intestines erupted, spilling out of his abdomen as if spring loaded. Then his screams weren't much more than gurgling sounds. The water's edge grew darker, thicker with Angelo's gore.

Lou took a step toward the creature. Its yellow eyes contracted at the sight of her. The eyes, forward facing like the predators of her own world. Its lips pulled back in a recognizable growl.

Master this, Lou-blue. Don't be its victim. Promise me. The sound of her father's voice in her mind winded her. Her sweet father who was dead because of the man at her feet.

The beast's nostrils flared.

"Am I still prey?" Lou asked, and slid one heel behind the other. She assumed a fighter's stance and curled her fingers around the handle of her knife. "If you think so, then I still have business here."

Lou waited for the pounce. A lunge. The way it would rise on its hind legs like a fox.

But the beast didn't pounce. It regarded her with its

acid-yellow eyes and then much the way a hyena protects its kill, the monster seized one of Angelo's legs in its mouth and dragged his body into the woods to eat in privacy. It kept one great yellow eye on her as it went.

4

King found Lucy Thorne stretched on his red leather sofa, an icy glass of sweet tea balanced on her pale knee. Her body was ethereal in the moonlight coming through the open terrace door. It was if she'd never left him. In twelve years, the only discernible change was her hair. She wore it longer now. It fell over her shoulders and hung halfway down her back like a curtain. It had been pixie short, a cleaner version of Piper's style when he met her.

"Nice place you have here, Robert." Lucy put the glass of ice tea on a coaster, one of the many mismatched rounds of cardboard King had stolen from local bars. He had quite the collection. He worried she might notice how many bars. Or he *would* have worried if the top of her red sundress hadn't stretched across her chest, showcasing hard nipples. It was difficult to worry when faced with hard nipples.

She caught him staring and grinned. "The

pension must be good."

"I'm a kept man," he joked, heat filling his face. "I hooked up with the rich widow downstairs, and as long as I pleasure her when she calls, all my expenses are paid."

Lucy barked a short, sharp laugh. "I'm glad to hear you're putting your talents to good use."

Your talents. The words were like a cold hand on the back of his neck. If anyone knew anything about his skills, it would be Lucy. He'd never worked so hard to please a woman in his life.

It hadn't been enough to keep her.

Lucy ran a thumb down the side of her thigh, wiping up a glistening trail of moisture left by her tea glass.

He realized he was standing in his apartment staring down at her like an idiot and not because she was beautiful but because he wasn't sure what to do with the file. If he set it down, there was the chance she'd scoop it up. And while he didn't think Lucy had any connection to the Venetti case, and wasn't sent to steal the file from him, he also didn't know why she was here.

"Were you in the neighborhood?" *Or feeling horny? Please god, say horny.* He didn't mind being used for a night. He would brush his teeth first. If he could squeeze one last dollop out of his crushed tube.

Lucy's coquettish face tightened around the mouth and eyes. "Right to the chase. I like that about you. Who has time for banter?"

"We can banter," he said, trying to recover the ground he'd apparently lost. Her tone had changed the way a woman's tone always changed when he said the wrong thing. Was it because he kept standing over her? Did he seem hurried?

He went to the leather armchair in the corner and sat down. He tucked the folder between the rolled arm and the cushion wedging it there.

"No," she said, not bothering to hide her curiosity. She tilted her head as if in question at the folder. Was he giving the game away like a first-year rookie?

She looked away. "You're in the middle of something. So I won't keep you."

Keep me, he thought. *I don't mind.*

His aging and pitifully nostalgic mind accosted him with bright images of Lucy the last time he'd seen her. The way her long body had looked in the morning sunlight. She was naked, tangled in his sheets. When she smiled, he knew she'd caught him staring. She'd rolled over, exposing her breasts. On the small side but perfectly sized with dainty nipples the color of cotton candy. And Lord, what a carnival ride their lovemaking had been.

"You're less reputable than I remember," she said, her elbows balanced on her knees.

King blinked away his thoughts. "What?"

She took a drink of tea, crunching a piece of ice between her teeth.

"I—"

"Nothing damning," she said. "But you had such a hard stance on drugs sixteen years ago."

Her eyes slid to the Bob Dylan vinyl lying beside a record player. That's where he kept his weed and a half-used pack of rolling papers. How had she known about that?

"You searched my place?"

"A little snooping," she admitted with a coy smile. "I wanted to make sure you were still an okay guy."

"Okay is a low standard." She'd hurt his feelings. When was the last time someone had been able to hurt his feelings? "I haven't turned into a drug dealer or pimp. I don't torture animals."

His buzz was gone.

She frowned. "I'm not criticizing you. I'm only saying you seem less self-righteous than I remember. It's a good thing, Robert. I always thought you needed to relax more."

Says the tofu-eating yoga teacher, he thought. He said, "Only young men can afford to be self-righteous. At my age, you realize we're all equally fucked."

Lucy's smile tightened, and her gaze slid away toward the balcony. They're in the dark and yet he couldn't bring himself to turn on a light. He believed she would disappear if he did. He wasn't ready.

"You didn't come here to listen to an old man rant." His chest clenched. "Tell me what you need. You know I'll do it."

She looked up at him through her lashes. "What makes you think I want something from you?"

"The fact that you're here," he said. "And you're not the begging type. It's important."

"Or maybe I do plenty of begging these days."

He said nothing.

Lucy looked toward the balcony, her gaze growing distant. "Jack worshiped you, you know."

It was like she'd slapped him across the face.

Jack Thorne.

When King broke three ribs during a drug bust, he'd been asked to do a term teaching at Quantico while he healed up. Jack Thorne, with sandy hair and big brown eyes that made him look like a goddamn doe in an evening field, was one of his first students. But Jack was brilliant. Smart as a whip. A damn hard worker. And sharp instincts. When Jack graduated from his DEA training, King himself put in the request to have Thorne transferred to his department in St. Louis.

The years he spent mentoring Thorne were the best in his life. King had his balls back post-divorce and he'd thrown himself into his work without apology for the first time in his life. He'd always loved his job, but now the work had been great because he had this bright, smart-ass kid at his side. Pushing him. Challenging him. King had never felt so alive, and they had the success stories to prove it.

They were the golden years. Until Thorne and his attractive, if uppity, young wife got killed by the Martinelli family. Their deaths were on King. He was the one who'd given Thorne the bust. Asked him to do the press. Put his fucking face all over the goddamn media.

He wanted Thorne to take the credit, him and his pudgy partner Gus Johnson. Hoped the recognition would give him the promotion he deserved.

It got Thorne a medal and six bullets to the

chest.

The worst of it: Jack Thorne's name was trashed, dragged through the mud by anyone who could get their hands on it. Overnight, he went from hero and family man to master manipulator. The media found a more sensational, better-selling tale. The murder of Jack Thorne and his wife wasn't a revenge killing for Thorne's arrest of Angelo Martinelli's brother. It was gang shit gone wrong. Thorne had been aiding the Martinelli clan all along. He was a mole. A snitch. He betrayed his comrades and closest friends. And it hadn't been enough to play both sides. When he'd gotten too greedy, the infamous crime family lit him up like flashing Christmas lights.

It was all bullshit. The press and the department slandered a good man to save their own asses.

Lucy was talking again. "He said you got through to him in a way no one ever could. And you may have changed, but you're still a good teacher. Your students say so."

So she even knew about the occasional adjuncting for LSU's criminal justice department. She'd been digging. For what? "If you're looking for my references, there's a job. What's the job?"

Lucy worried her lip.

"Spit it out while I'm still riding the tail of my buzz. You know I'm very open to suggestion when inebriated." It was a joke meant to put her at ease, even if he couldn't ease his own dark thoughts.

In his mind, he bent down beside a black body bag. His shaking hand pulled the zipper tab to reveal Thorne's face. So young. So goddamn young.

A fly landed on the dead man's face, twitching its wings.

"Lou is just like him. Tough. Smart. *Too smart.*" She barked another laugh. "Stubborn. Determined. Focused. A complete disregard for authority."

King grinned. "Quite a combination."

"She's a challenge, but she is an achiever."

A letter of recommendation, maybe. King did the math in his head. Thorne's kid would be 25? 26? Too old for college so it would be for the force then. Perhaps she wanted him to pull some strings and get her a job in one of the safer departments. But if she were even half as good as Thorne, she'd be wasted on a desk job. "You want me to put in a good word with someone? That's no problem. I'm happy to help."

And he was. It didn't matter that the minute Lucy learned her brother was dead, she'd dropped

King like panties on prom night and assumed the mantle of guardian to the girl. It hurt. He'd missed her like hell for a long time too. Looking at her on his red leather sofa in the moonlight coming from the terrace he wondered if he'd ever stopped missing her.

He didn't blame the kid.

He'd lost Lucy, and it was his own fault. He hadn't gone after her because his guilt wouldn't let him. It was his responsibility for getting Jack killed and for not working harder to salvage the man's reputation when the whole fucking ship started to sink. Everyone took hits when Jack's loyalty had been pulled up and examined. He saved his own ass, and he knew it.

Louie would face her own problems in the force. Overcoming her father's reputation was only the beginning.

A cloud passed over the moon, and Lucy's face was hidden in shadow. Only her mouth shown, her teeth glowing in the light as she let go of her bottom lip.

He realized what she *wasn't* saying. No, *thank you*. No *that would be great.*

Not a recommendation then. "Is she in trouble?"

King's mind ran wild with the possibilities.

Drugs. Prostitution. Kidnapping. She'd been kidnapped by a new drug lord, and he would have 32 hours to bring her back alive. He sure as hell hoped not. He was no Liam Neeson.

Lucy shook her head. "She's not a victim."

"I'm a piss poor guesser." *And it's been a long night for cloak and dagger meetings*. He ran a hand over his head. He moved from the chair to the coffee table so he could be closer to her. Right across from her. The wood groaned but didn't break. He was close enough to smell her lotion now. She still smelled like sandalwood and peonies. He prayed she couldn't smell his pickle-booze breath. "This is going to take all night if you make me guess, Lucy. If you want to stay the night, I can think of better things we could be doing."

She flashed him a weak smile. "I want you to promise that you won't go to the police with this. Hear me out and if you don't like what I tell you then forget I said anything."

"Kids make mistakes." He immediately drew up a list of twenty or thirty of his own fuckups. Some of them committed in the last few months.

"Do you remember Gus Johnson?"

"He disappeared."

Lucy gave him a look. "And the crime family

who killed Jack and Courtney."

"Wiped out one by one," King said. "But they never found a body. Or a weapon."

Lucy's hard look lingered.

A pinpoint of surprise dilated in his mind, expanding into full-blown awe. "You're saying Louie's working with a team? She fell in with some mercenary group or gang—"

"No." Lucy shook her head. "Lou works alone. She's not…a people person."

"Lou." He laughed. "A girl named *Lou* single-handedly destroyed an entire crime family? You're fucking with me."

Lucy's face was disturbingly calm.

"When you took her in, did you send her to ninja school?" He couldn't believe this. There's no way she pulled off those jobs alone. When King himself had heard about the Martinelli's destruction, he assumed it was a rival crime family. There were enough of them out there, vying for supremacy. And he knew some thought Martinelli's iron-clad rule had gone on for too long.

If Lou killed even *one* of the Martinellis, she had combat skills. Intel gathering skills. Espionage. A fuck ton of guns. Not to mention balls, or in this case ovaries, the size of Texas.

How did she come by that training? Certainly not from her Buddhist aunt who wouldn't even eat a bacon cheeseburger for fear of the animals' suffering. Lucy wouldn't have even let the girl kill the flies in her house, he was sure of it. Unless she was carting the girl off to some shaolin temple on the weekends…which begged a lot of questions.

So how was she trained? How did she pull it off?

No *one* person had it all. It's the reason mercenaries often worked in teams. "Logistically, what you're saying is impossible."

Lucy's face hardened. "She's Jack Thorne in miniature, with Courtney's cold heart. And she got a little something from me too."

His humor dried up like a creek bed in July.

She placed the empty glass on the table and leveled her gaze on him. "Do you remember?"

"No," he said. Doors in his mind began to slam shut. Memories tried to surface, and he shoved them down with a rough hand.

"The night those men came for you…?" she probed gently. As if she knew he was lying to himself as well as her. "She's hurt. She's angry. I think Lou hunts these men as a way to pay homage to Jack."

"I don't know what you think I can do." He grabbed her glass off the coffee table and dumped the rest of the ice into his mouth.

"Give her a case, anything that'll help her see there's another way to use her abilities." Lucy slid off the couch and knelt in front of him. She took his free hand in hers and squeezed it. "Please, Robert. *Please*. I've tried everything. I've lectured. I've chanted. I tried to get her into yoga."

"Yes, that's how we tame all the would-be assassins." The empty tea glass grew warm in his hand. "Down dog."

It was Lucy's turn to pull at her face in exasperation. "If she keeps going on like this, she's going to end up dead, and she's all I have left."

You could have me.

"I promised Jack."

We all made promises to Jack we couldn't keep.

"It's too much to expect her to stop…" Lucy searched for a word. "…*hunting*. I can accept her nature but she needs guidance. Please."

So will you do it?

He knew his answer. He would do it. For Jack. For Lucy. And tomorrow he knew he'd tell Brasso the same thing. *I'll do it.*

And just like that King found himself with not

one but two jobs in less than twenty-four hours. Two faces from his past surfacing. What was it his mother loved to say? Some old proverb?

Trouble travels in threes.

What could he expect next?

King took Lucy's hand and squeezed it. It was as cold as a corpse's hand, sending a chill through his body. "When do I meet her?"

5

Konstantine stood in the alley with blood drying in the hairs on his arms. His chest heaved as he struggled to catch his breath. A wind rolling through the narrow alley hit the back of his neck and the sweat beading there. It itched, and when he reached back and raked his nails along his occipital bone, his fingers came away wet.

Now that the excitement was over, the .357 in his hand doubled its weight.

He pulled a purple rag from his back pocket and wiped his face and neck. Then he tucked the gun into the waistband beneath his black shirt and the cloth back into his pocket.

Konstantine turned away from the body and searched the alley. A gray cat with white paws washed its ears on a stone stoop. Otherwise, no witnesses. No allies either.

The bells of the Duomo began to ring, loud clangs vibrating through the city center.

Where the fuck are they? Konstantine looked up between the buildings but saw only the clear blue sky. Then a sound caught his attention. *Speak of the devil, and he appears.*

A red Fiat 500 rolled past the alley and then the brakes squealed. The car whined as it reversed, backing into the tight space between the two stone buildings where Konstantine stood over a dead man.

It backed over the cobblestones, tires bumping as Konstantine used his hands to direct the driver. *Left, a little to the right*, and then a fist. *Stop.* The brake lights flared red.

The doors on both sides popped open, and two men climbed out, one with obvious difficulty. The passenger had to grip the roof and haul his massive body out of the small seat. Once he'd cleared the door, his enormous belly flattened against the wall, causing him to sharply inhale until he could squeeze through. Calzone was what they called him, at least amongst the Ravengers. His mother, whom he still lived with, called him Marcello.

Vincenzo, the driver, was rail thin and his limbs twitchy like a rat's. He jerked himself from the car, stopped toe-to-toe with the body bleeding out on the stone walk.

"O Signore, what a mess," he whined and

turned his head away, puffing his cheeks. He grabbed a cigarette from behind his ear and a white plastic lighter from his front pocket. He didn't look at the body as he lit the cigarette, indulged in a slow drag, and blew the smoke skyward in a long dramatic exhalation. Then Vincenzo's eyes slid to the corpse again. "A fucking mess."

"You bitch like a woman," Calzone said. His fingers disappeared into one of his many chins, and the fat jiggled as he scratched himself. "Hurry up, I'm hungry."

"You're always hungry," Konstantine said, but he tempered the words with a good-natured smile. Now that they were here, filling the alleyway with meaningless prattle, the knot in his chest loosened.

Another squeaking sound caused all three men to freeze and turn toward the opposite end of the alley. An old man with a shopping cart full of plants shuffled past. He wore an enormous hat and round spectacles with thick lenses magnifying his surprise. The old man froze under their gaze and his mouth opened in question.

Then he saw the purple rags hanging from back pockets. The old man howled like a theatrical ghost and threw his cart into traffic.

Calzone started after him, but Konstantine

reached out and barred his path with a straight arm. Let the old man get away. What could he do?

Konstantine nodded toward the corpse. "You'll never get lunch if you waste any more time."

"You've got to be heading out too," Vincenzo said. He pushed a button on the Fiat's fob, and the trunk popped open. The interior was lined with a thick plastic, not unlike the kind one might place along the floor before painting. "Padre's asking for you."

Vincenzo's black hair fell into his eyes as he squatted down to grab the dead man's arms. Still stooped, he looked up at Calzone. "You gonna help me or stand there looking pretty?"

Calzone grunted and bent to grab the dead man's legs. The jeans slid up revealing cotton socks. One shoe, an American sneaker, wobbled, threatening to fall off. Then it did.

They dumped the body onto the plastic without ceremony, and the Fiat bounced under the weight before the rubber tires settled. Vincenzo was forced to pretzel the dead man's limbs into the trunk. Calzone had one enormous hand on the trunk lid, waiting.

"Hold up," Vincenzo said and scooped up the sneaker. "What do you think this is, an 8 or 9? I bet

I could wear these."

Konstantine turned in the direction of the fleeing man. He didn't want to watch Vincenzo strip the dead man of his shoes. And he wanted to wash his hands and face before seeing Padre.

"Well *arrivederci* to you too," Vincenzo called after him.

Konstantine didn't stop. He marched to the Piazza six blocks away. There had not been much blood spray from the gunshot, and what little there had been was hidden by his dark clothes and shoes. A thin mist of blood had dried on his forearms, but no one in the streets looked too closely at him. It could be the purple rag in his pocket. Or it could be the way he walked the streets as a man who was not to be deterred in any way. Shoulders high. Chin tucked and eyes hidden behind dark shades.

Three guys lingered on the cathedral steps, smoking. Only one, Michele, greeted him before he ducked into the church. At the nave, he went right and stepped into a modern bathroom with a faucet. He'd seen no one in the church at this hour. No one on their knees asking for forgiveness.

He washed up without looking in the mirror. If he could help it, he went weeks without looking at himself in the polished glass, afraid of what he might see.

He would find Padre Leo in the basement.

In the chapel, the urge to kneel before the Blessed Mother overwhelmed him like a rising choir. He kneeled, crossed himself, and kept his eyes lowered. He had no problems worshipping Mother Mary. The idea of a mother goddess rang true. Mothers were love. Peace. Fierce protection. It was the heavenly Father he could not believe in. There was no such man in his world worthy of such reverence. Except perhaps Padre Leo. But Padre Leo was only a man as flawed as the rest of them.

Konstantine ducked into a stone stairway leading to the basement. Unlit torches hung on the wall, long ago rendered obsolete with the installation of electricity. His boots scuffed along the steps until the narrow passageway opened to the lowest level.

Men stood in groups of three or four. Some were laughing, oblivious to Konstantine's presence. Others had placed their hands on their guns, eyes sharp.

He waved a hand, and they relaxed. Shoulders slumped. Breath exhaled.

"He's in there," said Francesco. His new buzzed haircut made his ears look twice as large.

Konstantine fell on heavy doors made of redwood and stained-glass windows. The brass handles turned, and the hinges creaked open under the weight of his body. Slowly, an inner sanctum was revealed. Straight ahead, a desk sat with high bookcases behind it. The wood of the bureau, doors, and furniture was all the same rich wood. Cherry perhaps. Or oak with a sangria finish. The room was messy, looking more like the enclave of a professor than the head of one of the most notorious gangs in the world.

But Konstantine's lord and master was not at his desk.

A deep, whooping cough echoed from the bathroom. The door stood ajar. From Konstantine's place on the dusty rug, an outline of a man hunched over the sink was clear enough.

"Padre?"

Leo opened the bathroom door, and his lips pulled back in a grimace. "Close the door."

Konstantine leaned on the heavy doors again, sealing them up in the enclave.

Padre Leo shuffled across the dim room toward the desk and collapsed in the high-back chair, a hacking cough shaking his thin frame. He held a purple, silk handkerchief over his pockmarked face.

It was a long time before Padre caught his breath. Konstantine kept looking to the bathroom, wondering if he should fetch a drink or wet rag.

"Should I—?" Konstantine began.

"No need," Leo said, his face red with exertion. "This will not take long."

Konstantine felt as if he had been slapped across the face. The man owed him nothing. If he had decided Konstantine should stand on one foot from dawn until midnight, it was expected he would do so without question or protest.

The muscles in Konstantine's back twitched. "I am not in a hurry, Padre."

The man wiped at his mouth with his purple silk, and it came away wet with blood.

"Are you okay?" Konstantine's heart hammered at the sight of blood. It always did.

The man smoothed bony fingers over his gray hair and gave a snide snort. "I am not. Or so the doctors tell me."

"Is it serious?" Konstantine asked. Then seemed to catch himself and the absurdity of the question. "It's none of my business."

Leo waved him off. "Drop the ass-kissing. Frankly, we don't have time for it. I need to make my wishes clear while I still have the breath to do so."

As if to emphasize this, he began coughing again. The sound was wretched, shaking the man like a toy in the jaws of a great dog. The cords in his neck stood out. Sweat gleamed on his forehead even in the chilled basement of the old church. The purple rag was darker still with his bloody spittle by the time he caught his breath.

As Padre drew in a few shaky breaths, he motioned for Konstantine to sit in the leather armchair beside the desk. Konstantine understood and obeyed. He pulled the .357 from behind his back when he sat and laid it on the desk, pointing away from his boss.

"As you can see," Leo said at last. "It is challenging for me to talk. In truth, it's difficult to do anything. I've stopped eating. I've stopped sleeping. It is too painful to lay down. Even my mattress hurts my chest. The doctors say I have a month at most."

"What could act so quickly?" Konstantine asked. A red-hot flood of shame washed over him, but per Padre's wishes, he didn't apologize again.

"It wasn't fast. It's only I can't hide my illness any longer." He snorted, threatened a laugh but then pressed one hand hard on his diaphragm to stop himself, as if the cost of laughing was too high a price to pay now.

Padre fell back against the chair. He slumped like a child at the dinner table. Konstantine sat up straighter as if to compensate.

"This organization is my lifeblood, Konstantine. I believe you understand."

"Yes, sir." Konstantine expected some important task. Some last command or dying wish. He would honor it as he had every other request from Padre Leo since he joined the Ravengers fifteen years before.

Leo's breath remained shallow. "I have bled and dreamed and built this empire from the ground up."

"I know."

"When I am no longer in this world, I want to know my legacy is preserved, my ambitions honored. Change of power is a turbulent time for any group, but the right man can make the transition easy. A steady hand can take the ship's wheel and steer her fine."

Konstantine's heart sped up. "I will support whomever you choose. If others object—" because Konstantine knew that no matter who was selected, someone would object. The most ambitious would see themselves supreme. Others would consider their loyalty to the Ravengers finished, their contracts terminated upon the death of the man who had recruited them. "If others object I will persuade them."

Padre wiped at his brow with his bloody rag, seemingly unaware of the blood he smeared across his forehead. Konstantine leaped up, wet his own cloth with fresh water from the sink and offered it to the man. Leo's fingers trembled when he took it.

"I will name you as my successor, Konstantine."

"Me? Why in god's name? I am no one."

"You want my reasons?"

He knew he had no right to ask them. And already the older man's face was burning red, his breath shortening again. Padre spoke anyway.

"You understand this new age in a way most Ravengers do not. You are strategic. You are futuristic. You are adaptable. Who better to leave my empire to? You do things with computers most of my men cannot even fathom."

Leo pulled up his dress shirt and revealed his left forearm. He placed the arm, belly up on the desk so Konstantine could see the tattoo clearly. Not that he needed to see it. Konstantine bore the same mark on his own skin. A crow and crossbones. The crow, wings spread as if in flight and the two bones crossed beneath.

"The raven is a symbol of longevity. Of intelligence and stealth. It is why I chose it as my emblem."

Only Konstantine did not see a raven. He saw a crow with blunt and splayed wings rather than a raven's pointed tips. He saw the small flat bill without its tuft. They called themselves Ravengers—a poetic condensation of *raven* and *ravager*. But Konstantine alone seemed to see the difference between the cousin birds. He knew that while a raven could live for thirty years or more, a crow was lucky to see eight.

"You have the global perspective and technological comprehension to take us into the new age. Furthermore, I trust no one else."

"Padre—"

"Would you reject me?"

"No." He did not hesitate. "Never."

"Because I have already contacted those people whom I believe will be most beneficial to you during the transition. I will give you their names, and I want you to reach out to them immediately and make your intentions clear. Despite your reservations, sound sure of yourself and your plans for the Ravengers. It is easier to support a man who is sure of himself."

Your plans for the Ravengers. Konstantine had none. His heart pounded. He wet his lips with his tongue but still found no way to express his thoughts.

"And here is where I ask something *truly* difficult of you," the man said, and he extended his open palm to Konstantine. Konstantine had not held the man's hand since he was ten and Padre Leo had invited him into the fold in exchange for his mother's immunity and protection.

Konstantine could only look at the open palm.

Padre Leo smiled. "Indulge a silly old man."

Konstantine took his hand.

"Be a Martinelli," Leo said, and when Konstantine tried to jerk his hand away as if burned, Leo clamped down on it. Surprising power pulsed through the old man's grip as if Death itself lent him his indomitable strength. "You have rejected your father's name, but I ask you to embrace it now."

"You ask too much," Konstantine said, yanking the way an animal might jerk if caught in a trap, ready to rip off its own paw to be free.

Leo did not let go. "The only flaw the Ravengers bear is their youth. They wait for us to be foolish in the ways young ones always are. We are democrats, not aristocrats. New money, not old. But you can bridge that gap, Konstantine, with the Martinelli name alone."

Be a Martinelli. But he could never. How could he bear the name of a man he despised?

"I know you hold no love in your heart for your father, but others do. And I have heard the loyalists are desperate for any link to the family they've lost. With Angelo's death, you are the last. *Use* it. For all they know, he groomed you himself. A bastard son is still a son. Be a Ravenger, my boy, but also be a Martinelli. There is no one to oppose you! And taking up the mantel of an old, distinguished line will offer opportunities for expansion and unification. I am sure of it."

Angelo's death. He had not heard. So it was done then. She had her revenge. Good.

"No one will oppose you," Padre Leo said as if trying to read his silence. Konstantine knew he was wrong, but he let the man hold his arm and make his demands.

"Power comes with benefits," Padre said, eyeing Konstantine in his stillness, measuring his silence. "With my money and your father's name, you could have whatever you desire. Is there nothing you can think of having for yourself?"

Yes.

He wanted *her*. The girl who'd appeared one night, curled in his bed like a kitten by a fire.

With Padre Leo's resources, he could find her. As a Martinelli, she might find *him*.

6

Lou bolted upright in her bed, head throbbing with adrenaline. She had the gun pointed without consciously choosing a target.

"You've never been a morning person," Aunt Lucy said, closing the closet door behind her and stepping into the studio apartment. "But this is a tad extreme."

Her aunt stood by the closet with two take-out cups in hand. A long skirt rubbed against her calves and the tops of her sandals. *Jesus sandals* Lou called them. Like Lucy should be trudging across the desert preaching love and forgiveness to anyone who would listen.

Lou lowered the gun to the soft coverlet draped across her legs.

"Where have you been?" Lucy shifted her weight to one hip. "It's been hard to track you down."

In the three weeks since killing Angelo, she'd

been restless. She'd hardly slept. Hardly ate. A pervasive feeling of loss surrounded her, like she'd forgotten something and couldn't stop searching for it.

But everywhere she searched, she only found violence.

Last night she'd ended up in a dive bar in West Texas, beating the shit out of six bikers in a parking lot. She'd only wanted one of them—Kenny Soren. But when his friend grabbed her ass, she'd broken his wrist instantly. Then introductions were made by all.

She looked down at the dark purple and rose colored bruises across her knuckles. A marble-sized pocket of fluid rest above her second knuckle. She'd obviously busted a vein.

Lucy's breath hitched, and her eyes slid away. "You need ibuprofen."

"I don't have any."

"Here," Lucy said and gave Lou one of the Styrofoam cups. When Lou reached to accept it, the aches and pains from last night made themselves known. She'd done something to her shoulder. It screamed when the arm extended. It was probably the baseball bat that'd come down on her shoulder blade. She raised her arm overhead, rotated it until the tension eased. Then her neck cramped.

"You need to do bhujangasana," her aunt said. She put her own coffee cup on the counter and went into the kitchen, which was really still the living room, and the bedroom given the studio design. Drawers opened and closed loudly. Ice rustled in the freezer. Then Lucy reappeared with an ice pack wrapped in a dishcloth.

Lou accepted the ice pack. Her aunt's cheeks were flushed, and her jaw worked furiously. And if Lou wasn't mistaken, a hint of wetness glistened near her temples, as if she'd quickly scrubbed at her eyes.

They wouldn't talk about Lou's injuries. Lucy wouldn't ask how she got them, no matter how much she might want to. Lucy had set this policy herself and the fact that she'd taken her tears to the other room was proof this rule had not changed.

Lou's stomach turned. "Bhujangasana. Is that what the kids are calling it?"

She swung her legs out of the covers and put her bare feet on the cool wood floor. She let her hand rest between her thigh and the ice pack as she drank the coffee using her free hand.

"It's yoga," Lucy said, her voice strong again. "Cobra pose."

Lucy laid on the floor in demonstration, belly down, and pushed away from the floor with her forearms. "It opens up your chest and shoulders and feels *so* good."

Yoga. Of course.

Lou had no idea why she thought her aunt would even suggest drugs for her aching body. As a child, when Lou got migraines, her aunt would boil her tea rather than fill her prescription for Sumatriptan. Lou would be an inch from a brain bleed, and Lucy would hand her a steaming cup much like the one she held now and say some shit like *all the love and none of the side effects.*

"Or!" Lucy said, her eyes widening and lips breaking into an *ah ha* grin. "You could do Thunderbolt, Vajrasana." She rose into a lunge, arms out in front of her.

Lou tuned out the woman doing yoga in her periphery and lifted the cup to her nose. She inhaled. The scent of roasted coffee shifted the whole world into focus. The harsh sunlight softened to a warm glow. Her aches seemed to relax with the rest of her body. She was wondering if this was how cocaine addicts felt after their first line of the day.

"Le Bobillot?"

"It's still there," Aunt Lucy said, her face

smashed into the wood floor as she held her next pose. "As charming as ever, though I see no one is adhering to the smoking ban. *Gah.*"

Sunlight streamed through the large windows and warmed the back of Lou's neck. She sipped her coffee and pictured the Paris café in her mind. A corner building across from a boulangerie. Round tables were evenly spaced in a row on each side of the door, so if a patron so wished, they could drink their coffee while watching the 13th arrondissement buzz around them. Across the way, an ancient church, beastly the way only churches in the Old World could be, rang gigantic bells on the hour.

A month after her parents had died, Aunt Lucy had brought her to this café. Bought her a baguette from the boulangerie across the street. She drank espresso from the tiniest cup she'd ever seen and nibbled her warm loaf. It was the first happy memory she'd had since her father died.

Lou stood, leaving the warmed ice pack on the bed and stretched her arms overhead. She was careful not to dump coffee on herself and then padded over to the window.

Aunt Lucy continued to prattle off yoga poses behind her, building her own flow. It was hard for the woman to stop once she began. Besides, yoga always calmed her aunt. The tension that had erupted between them at the sight of Lou's injuries had diminished, like a mist slowly dissipating from the room.

Lou kept her eyes on the window, on the pool glistening two stories below. The sparkling water surrounded a lush garden with white and pink roses twining the fence. Petunias in patio planters and a creeping morning glory reached for the No Lifeguard On Duty sign.

Stretching out beyond the pool and its walled garden was the St. Louis skyline. The arch cut the sky with a delicate whoosh. The river coursed behind it, shimmering like melted silver. A boat with a large red wheel churning at one end cut through the waters. People as small as ants roamed the boardwalk.

This was the way with Lou and her aunt. Together, perhaps even occupying the same space, yet with an undeniable distance. Sure, each tried to cross the barriers to the other's side, out of love or respect, yet never quite breaking the borders of their own worlds.

"What are you doing tonight?" Aunt Lucy asked. She was on her knees, looking up at her. The yoga flow had ended, and Lou's coffee was nearly gone.

Lou thought of Jimmy Castle.

She'd been in Texas looking for names. Names of anyone associated with the Martinelli crew. Pimps. Drug pushers. Traffickers. She'd weed out all the rats who'd served him, starting with the worst. Before she put a bullet in Kenny Soren, he'd blabbed about Jimmy Castle, a dealer in Dallas, an old-time peddler who still carried the Martinelli torch.

Lou intended to pay Mr. Castle a visit tonight.

"I'm busy." Lou kept her eyes on the St. Louis skyline, on the cars speeding from one end of the bridge to the other. A hand clamped down on her shoulder and turned her around.

"With what?" Lucy demanded. Her blue eyes shimmered with the threat of tears. "They're all dead."

Lou's skin iced and she put the empty Styrofoam cup on a cinder block serving as a bedside table. "How would you know? Is there some Martinelli bulletin board I don't know about?" She forced a smile. She was aiming for joviality, but came up short.

Lucy's lip trembled. "Your father gave you to me—"

Like a goddamn coffeemaker, Lou thought bitterly. She stared at the callus on the side of her thumb.

"—because he wanted me to keep you safe. He wanted you to live, and you're trying your damnedest to get yourself killed!"

They'd begun with the usual cold silence and now the argument. Lou's shoulders relaxed as the conversation turned familiar. She was on solid ground again.

Her aunt drew a breath, seemed to draw on some inner reserve and stilled herself. "I know you can't stop cold turkey."

Lou snorted. "As if I'm an addict."

Lou thought it was her one good quality. She'd never fallen prey to drugs or alcohol, no matter how deep she went into the underbelly of the world. Lou was her father's daughter in that respect. She could walk beside the derelict without succumbing to the temptations herself.

"Aren't you?" Lucy spat. "Normal people have jobs and friends. Relationships. You're too self-serving for that."

Lou flinched as if slapped.

Lucy grimaced. "I'm sorry."

"Self-serving," Lou repeated. *Self-serving* was

her least favorite word in the world. That's what the papers and media had called Jack Thorne. Self-serving. They claimed he'd forgotten his purpose. Forgotten his duty as a public servant. He'd turned *self-serving* in a quest for more money. More power. And this greed had gotten him killed. "Like my father."

"Those were lies," Lucy said. Tears broke the surface and spilled over her aunt's cheeks. "Your dad was a good man."

Lou turned toward the window so she wouldn't have to see those tears. She didn't overlook the fact Lucy was professing Jack's innocence, not hers.

And her aunt was wasting her breath. Lou didn't believe the slander printed on every front page in June of 2003, yet it still stung to hear even the suggestion Jack Thorne had been *self-serving.* Her mother? Without question. Lou loved her mother, but Courtney had been a cold and selfish woman. Every inconvenience was taken personally. Every mistake a personal insult.

But not her father.

"I'm at my wit's end. Every night you go out, you hunt down some criminal and—"

Lou's headache worsened the harder she worked her jaw. She turned when Lucy appeared beside her at the window.

Lucy reached up and brushed the hair out of Lou's face. "I want you to have a life."

"Because your life is *full* of people," Lou said, knowing it would cut her.

Lucy's hand fell away. For a moment, she looked unsure what to do with it. Then she settled for putting it on her hip. "I want more for you. I want you to be happy."

"That's the thing about happiness. It's different for everyone. What makes the executioner happy? You need to understand that's what I am. You preach acceptance. So accept it."

Her aunt reached up and pinched the bridge of her nose. Lou couldn't count on all ten fingers and toes how many times she'd seen her aunt do this. *Here it comes*, she thought. *All the patience is gone, and we'll jump right to the demands now.*

Lucy took a breath. "Your father had a friend, Robert King. He's a private detective in New Orleans. He's offered you a job. He thinks your skills would be useful for his current investigation."

Lou blinked. The conversation had gone in a direction she hadn't expected. She searched for purchase, hoping to pull herself upright again. But her aunt charged on.

"He's an old friend. And he likes to bend the rules like you do. I think you'll like him."

"I don't like anyone."

"He can be trusted."

"No one can be trusted."

Lucy pinched her nose again harder. "He's known about me and what I can do for sixteen years. He hasn't told anyone. *I* trust him."

And now he knows about me.

"Everyone needs allies, Lou. Even you," Lucy said, and it was her own father's words from long ago.

Lou understood what allies were. A big fat liability.

"He wants to meet at the Café du Monde, tonight at eight o'clock. Please be there."

Lucy marched toward the closet and stepped inside. Lou thought she was alone until her aunt reappeared and hurled a bottle of ibuprofen at her.

It hit Lou square in the chest before she caught it.

"And don't shoot him," Lucy commanded, before disappearing again.

Sunset was at 8 o'clock in New Orleans. She wouldn't show up to the café before 8:15. Maybe he wouldn't wait, and this whole situation would dissolve like ice in water.

Fine. She would indulge her aunt if only to buy her a month or more of peace before the nagging resumed. And by then, she'd have followed the Castle trail to new monsters in the dark.

A Martinelli was best. They slaked her hunger better than any other kill. And she had to accept the possibility she would never know peace, no matter how many men she bled dry.

But she had to start somewhere, and there *were* other demons in the world worth hunting.

7

King tore open three sugar packets and dumped them into a large cup labeled Café du Monde in curvy black letters. Beneath the words was a cartoon image of the café where he currently sat, a sienna-colored building with green awning and chairs.

Coffee and beignets, it promised.

And it delivered, as King had a generous portion of both spread before him on the table.

He showed up thirty minutes early. Not because it was his favorite café in New Orleans, but because he wanted time to look at his file again, and to think about what he might say to Lou.

Lucy hinted that while Lou agreed to come, she wasn't sold on the idea. It would be up to King to sell it to her. He had to admit, if only to himself, he *wanted* the girl's help. If he intended to follow through with the Venetti case, her ability would be an asset. He could also use the gun power and someone to watch his back. Getting around without drawing attention would be easier, provided the girl was as discreet as Lucy.

Lucy claimed Lou had Jack's sensibilities, his mind. What would King say to Jack to win him over? He tried to imagine a bloodthirsty Jack Thorne and what words could be spoken like an incantation to bring him back from the dark side.

Yet in practice, a conversation never went the way King envisioned. It didn't matter who the person was or the circumstances. People were the final variable, and he found success most often when he was willing to follow their lead.

He'd chosen the right place, at least. It was crowded enough, with light flooding the eating area beneath the green tent. A woman could feel safe here, speaking to a man she'd never met before. It had the added bonus of coffee and deep fried donuts covered in powdered sugar. And an attentive teenager walking up and down the aisles, sweeping scrunched straw wrappers and crumpled napkins into an upright dust pan.

Of course, King had the feeling Thorne's kid might not be into crowds, lighted places, or deep fried confections. If she mopped up the Martinelli family the way Lucy thought she had, she probably didn't need some overhead bulbs to make her feel safe.

By the time King polished off the third of four beignets, he knew she wasn't coming. The Jackson Square crowd was thinning. A human statue painted to look like stone stepped down from her crate at sunset and packed up for the night. The artists who'd laid their canvases against the iron fence, on display for the day's passing tourists, they were packing up too. They stuffed paintings into large black sacks and picked up the blankets or jackets they'd been sitting on. King watched one man rub his half-finished cigarette out on the bottom of his shoe before tucking it behind his ear for later.

People shuffled deeper into the quarter with thoughts of after-dinner drinks on their minds. King kept waiting even as the last of the orange faded to black, and the only lights were the artificial orbs overhead and the streetlights growing brighter as the world dimmed.

King thought of Brasso, the way he looked the night before, sitting across from him at the high-top table. A toothpick bobbed in his mouth as he twirled a coaster on the smooth wood. His bright face had glowed in the tiki lights, and his smiles had been too quick to come and go.

A witness has skipped out on a high-profile case. Find her, bring her back, and there's a big fat retainer in it for you. We need her. These women keep disappearing and she's the only one who's survived. We need her if we hope to can this bastard.

Not the most compelling case, if Lou was as half fire-forged as Lucy made her out to be. *We're going to look for someone* couldn't compare to *let's kill off the mafia.*

And there was Brasso's story itself.

You came all the way down here to ask for my help? King had asked, doing the St. Louis to New Orleans math in his head.

You're retired. You can take a lengthy road trip, and no one is going to ask you to account for your time. And you're the most trustworthy guy I know.

It was bullshit flattery and only made sense if Brasso believed there was a rat in the department, tracking his movement.

There was another reason why he would have said yes to about any request from Chaz Brasso.

Brasso's face had been the first he'd seen after three days in the dark. The hand that had grabbed onto his and pulled him from the rubble.

What the media would later call the Channing Incident, had been the worst days of King's life.

Eleven enforcement individuals had gone into a building for drugs and a mob boss, and only one had come out alive. King was beneath a set of stairs when the bomb went off, bringing down the Westside brownstone they were searching. For days he laid in the dark, trying to breathe, trying to stay alive.

At 8:30, King stood from his wobbly little chair and went to the pick-up window for another order of beignets.

When he came back to his table, she was there, at *his* table, as if she'd been waiting for him all along. He slid into the chair across from her. "Lou

Thorne?"

She nodded, and he sat the plate of beignets, coffee cup, and three sugar packets on the table. Then he extended his hand, noticing a smudge of powdered sugar on his fingers.

To his surprise, she accepted it, sugar and all. She shook it firm, but not too hard. She wiped the transferred sugar off her hand with a couple of sharp slaps against her thigh.

"And you're *Detective* King," she said.

King snorted. "Is that what your aunt told you?"

She stilled. "You're not a detective?"

"Not legally, no. I never was. I have the skill set. I was a DEA agent. I taught your old man at Quantico. Got him straight off the bus. He was brilliant. And a hard worker."

The girl's ears perked up at the mention of Jack. King filed this observation away as well. Then he kept on, riding this train for as long as the rails were.

"DEA agents do a bit of everything. Investigation. Undercover work."

He gave her a long look, waiting for questions.

Her brown eyes held his unblinking. Her face

was unreadable. She might be Jack's kid, but those cold, flat eyes were Courtney's and damn unsettling.

"You'd make a hell of a poker player."

She considered this comment without smiling. Then she leaned back in her seat, a slight arch to her back. *She's packing*, he realized. "Lucy said you want my help with a case."

Ah, there was Jack. Right to the point. No time for bullshit. Now to see if she had Jack's patience. He didn't know how long the kid had been at this game. She could've survived this long purely by coincidence.

"This is an interview, Lou. You can't expect me to hand over secrets about a high-profile case to a stranger. No matter what kind of past I've got with your aunt."

That got a raised eyebrow. So Lucy hadn't told her about the two of them. King wasn't sure if his feelings were hurt or if he was relieved. Surely she hadn't kept their brief but intense relationship secret because she was ashamed. Lucy once tried to get him to go to a naked hot yoga class with everyone's *bits* flapping in the wind. Lucy Thorne didn't do shame.

He saw Lou's curiosity now. She was looking him over with a different expression on her face.

"Ask your questions."

He took a long drink of coffee then began. "What kind of training do you have?"

"My dad taught me to shoot when I was a kid. He didn't want me to be afraid of guns or blow my own brains out."

King remembered this himself. A memory, warped with age, bloomed behind his eyes. "Maybe I saw you at one of the family picnics."

"There were a lot of people and a lot of picnics," she said, looking out over Jackson Square. She shifted in her seat.

She'd been a shy, forlorn kid, he remembered. All the other children had been little bullets of motion and chaos, running, screaming, laughing. And Louie had been at the picnic table with a book. When Lou disappeared, scaring the hell out of Jack, they'd stopped coming to functions.

However else she might have changed, the perfect stillness hadn't left her.

"Apart from guns, I know some hand to hand. I studied aikido and Uechi-Ryu."

"When you were a kid?" He sipped his coffee. He was trying to gage how much experience she had. Ten years? Fifteen? Of course, if she was hunting and murdering regularly, he supposed that would keep her sharper than most cops who sat behind desks eating fast food for lunch.

"I wanted my father's service weapon, but Lucy has a stance on guns in the house. So we compromised. She agreed to send me to the dojo when yoga didn't work out."

He couldn't suppress a grin. "Do you have your own gear? Vests? Concealed weapons?"

"Yes."

King imagined what kind of apartment this young woman had. Did she push a dramatic red button and walls moved away, exposed studs and an arsenal worthy of a Colombian drug lord?

"Ever been tortured?" he asked.

She glared at him. "I've never been caught."

"Do you have a boyfriend?"

Her teeth clenched. "Is that relevant to my job

duties?"

"In this game, if they can't catch you, they lean on someone you love. I've seen it enough it's cliché."

He thought she would shrug him off again, fall back on the false bravado today's youth relied on. But her face remained pensive. She was serious. God, she was too young to know this was serious.

Goddamn, Jack. I'm sorry.

Sorry for giving him the case and the credit. For painting the target on his back. But most of all he was sorry for this hardened kid left behind.

"Lucy is the only one they can lean on," she said at last. "And she can take care of herself."

He took another sip of coffee. "Yes, she can. And from what I've heard, so can you."

"Do you want my help or not?"

"I do," he said. He grinned and shoved one of the beignets in his mouth. Sucking powder sugar off his fingers. "So you want to know about the case before you say yes? It's dangerous."

She gave him a flat, humorless smile. "I appreciate a challenge."

"My old partner still works for the DEA. He's got a partial case built but not enough to charge or convict. A senator invites women out onto his boat, only they don't always come back. One woman took a boat ride into the Texas bay and barely escaped with her life. She agreed to testify against the senator, but then she disappeared. She's either dead or on the run. We need to find her and convince her we can keep her safe until the trial. Bonus round: We find even more damning evidence on this guy."

"Why doesn't your partner want to look for her?" Lou asked.

She asked the right question, without accepting something at face value. Questioning people and their motives was what kept you breathing. Maybe he could keep her alive after all.

King smiled. "Good question. It's because of who he wants to convict."

She waited for him to go on, her flat shark eyes never leaving his. It was enough to make his skin crawl.

"Most drug trafficking is a front. A way to generate funds for more ambitious projects. It's not unlike municipal bonds actually. And when you work within the law, you've got to follow the law. And powerful men like Ryanson always have the law on their side.

Lou arched an eyebrow. "Senator Greg Ryanson?"

King nodded, knowingly. "I know. Pristine public image. Philanthropist wife. His two daughters serve charities that make you feel all fuzzy inside."

"I saw the picture of Ryanson holding the baby panda."

"His eldest Emma runs the wildlife charity, and she isn't afraid to use dear old dad's face for publicity."

King slid the file across the table and watched her open it.

"But this is him, in the photos, and it's…" Her voice trailed off.

"Looks damning, doesn't it?" he agreed. "So we're going to dig deeper, starting with Paula Venetti. She was his girlfriend for a long time. If she's still alive, I want to interview her in person. We'll ask better questions and build on what she gives us."

"Leads," she murmured, her face still focused on the photos.

Like a fish to water.

"According to your aunt, we should be able to figure out if she is still alive fast enough."

Lou didn't smile. She flicked her eyes up to meet his.

"This case is a chance to expose a horrible man for what he is. Maybe save some lives," he said. But he didn't think she cared about the heroic shit one bit. "At the least, we might defund some horrible projects."

She pushed the folder back over to him but didn't answer. Her eyes were roaming along the square, taking in the crowds shuffling beneath the streetlights. It was late, but jazz music still played, and the tarot readings over shaky card tables were in full swing. Several cigarettes burned in the dark as peddlers and pickpockets watched the crowd with hungry eyes.

"I've only got one last question," he said, vying for her attention. "I'll ask it while you're walking me back."

She looked at him warily as he slid the folder under his arm and stood. They exited Café du Monde's congested patio, stepping out into the hot summer night. She moved through the crowd effortlessly, cutting the waters without bumping into the drunks or the beggars with their hands out.

She'd be a hell of a stalker.

They'd made it to St. Peter Street when he stopped her. "Your aunt seemed to think you were in some kind of trouble. Maybe it's too late to get out. That's why she asked me to hire you."

Lou leaned against a brick wall at the mouth of the alley. Most of her was in shadow, with only a square of light from an adjacent shop, a closed antique store, cutting across her face.

"She said you've been killing off the men responsible for your old man's murder." He waited for her to speak. When she didn't, he backtracked. "What?"

"I'm listening for a question," she said.

Smart-ass. King wasn't sure if she'd gotten that from Courtney or Jack. "Are you in trouble?"

"If you want a partner," she said, turning away from the lit mannequin in the window to face him. "Don't talk to me like I'm a victim. I don't need your protection."

"There's nothing wrong with accepting help," he said. He felt stupid as soon as the words left his mouth. He didn't know her. And the idea she needed help from this old man with a gut was patronizing at best. "I'm not going to sell you out. I'm just wondering if you're in too deep to surface on your own."

"You have your own problems, King."

He had no time to react before she pulled herself up onto her tiptoes and clasped her hands on the back of his neck. She brought her face close to his, and for a horrifying moment, he thought she was going to kiss him.

She was beautiful. No question. Her body was young and tight in all the ways his had gone soft. She had Courtney's full jaw and Jack's big eyes. Her slender neck gave way to sharp collar bones.

He tried to pull away, but the hand on the back of his neck tightened, locking him in place. Any illusion he had about how easy it would be to disentangle himself evaporated. His pulse leapt. She could snap his neck if she wanted.

She brushed her lips against his ear. "You have a man following you, and he looks like a professional asshole. What do you want to do about it?"

He plastered on his own fake grin, seeing his reflection in the shop window do the same. He hated the look of it. An old man preying on a girl half his age. *Less* than half his age.

Lou stepped away from him, placing herself entirely in the alley shadows. She was impossible to see. In darkness, the eye relied on movement, but Lou was perfectly still. Invisible.

"$300 an hour," he shouted. "That's outrageous!"

He heard her dry laugh.

King made a big show of patting himself down. Then he whipped his head up. "You stole my wallet! Hey, come back here!"

He pretended to chase her down the alley, stepping off the side street into the dark. He fumbled through the darkness until she took pity on him and took his arm.

"Get us a better view," he rasped. He was embarrassed how winded he was from shouting.

The world had been yanked out from under him.

His stomach dropped as if he'd reached the top of a roller coaster and was now sailing down the other side. He was falling.

Then they were on a balcony. They stepped away from the corner of a privacy wall, dividing the balcony for two separate units' use. Lou grabbed his arm and yanked him down, so they were hunched behind the iron rails. She pulled apart a nest of fern tendrils and peered at the street below. King did the same. His knees popped when he crouched, and already his lower back burned. He had little confidence he would be able to get up from this crouch quickly.

"Look," she said, still watching the street. The stalker entered the alley, then came back out. He threw up his hands, apparently angry he'd lost his target. Then he headed up the block, presumably to catch King further up.

"The question is, was he tailing you or me?" he asked.

She looked ready to dismiss him outright, but then she hesitated.

"No one tails me." She met his gaze, her eyes shimmery in this streetlight. "They're looking for you. Maybe they know your game for Ryanson."

If they did, that was damn fast.

He stood slowly, slipping back into the shadow of the overhang. He leaned against a dark window. As soon as he did, a light kicked on in the bedroom, and a woman shot straight up in bed, screaming. Lou grabbed his shirt and shoved him into the corner.

Another roller-coaster drop and they were by the river beside a streetcar stop. It was abandoned this late at night, the tram running only during reasonable hours. They were alone except for the homeless man sleeping beneath the bench, a brown bottleneck protruding from a paper sack inches from his face. He was snoring too damn loud to give a shit about what they were saying.

"God, how can you stand that?" he asked, one hand on his stomach.

"What?"

He described the feeling to her. "It's jarring."

"I don't feel anything," she said.

King wanted to ask more, part horrified, part fascinated by her strange gift, but she looked ready to run. He would've bet a twenty spot she had somewhere to be.

"Are you sure you want to work this case?" he asked. He ran a hand through his hair. Sweat had beaded along his scalp, and his palm came away damp. "If those men were looking for me, then this is hot. And it's only going to get hotter."

"Are you sure you want to work with *me*?" she countered. "You'll have twice as many enemies."

He smiled at that. He saw Jack standing at ease in the Quantico gym as King paced in front of the men and women with their hands clasped behind their backs, chins up.

Are you sure you want this job? It's not all party dresses and tea time. DEA agents die every day. Some hard ass motherfuckers roam the streets of America. He'd stopped in front of Jack Thorne, speaking to him for the first time. *Are you ready for them?*

Are they ready for me? Jack had asked.

"You're more vulnerable than I am," she said. Her lip pouted out when she was thinking. It was cute. "If anyone sees us working together, they might kill you thinking you were part of..." Her voice trailed off. "...of what I've done."

He considered this. It wasn't bravado. Lou wasn't blowing smoke up his ass or puffing her chest. She was stating a fact.

"You *are* in deep," he said.

Lou smirked, a cold, hard twitch of her lips. "I've no illusions as to how this ends. I know what happens to people like me. People like my dad."

People like me, he thought.

"Live by the sword, die by the sword," she said.

The skin on the back of his neck stood up.

She turned, giving the impression she was about to leave him there by the streetcar stop.

"You're right," he blurted out, hoping to stop her. He gestured around them. "I am vulnerable. But you'd save me a lot of time. It takes hours and hours to research and hunt. More if I have to fly or drive. I can't say you're not a preferable alternative."

Not to mention her skills. She'd spotted the men in the crowd when he hadn't. She was young. Sharp. And he preferred working with a partner than working alone. He always had.

She gave him another once over. "When do you want to go talk to Paula?"

"Tomorrow?" he asked.

She agreed to his suggested time and meeting place before she disappeared, leaving him alone at the deserted trolley stop.

He thought, *Lucy is going to kill me.*

8

As soon as she could, Lou ditched King and went looking for Castle. She made only a quick stop at her apartment for a wardrobe change, having left the heavy stuff at home lest the retired cop turn out to be a snitch for Aunt Lucy.

Sitting on the edge of her bed, Lou slipped her feet into black sneakers. Then she pulled her dark hair into a low ponytail and brushed her teeth. It was a waste of time to wash her face. She'd be filthy again by the end of the night.

Ready, she stepped into an empty closet and waited in total darkness.

When she rented this studio apartment, the very first thing she did was remove the four flat wooden boards serving as shelves within the linen closet. She swept the square of wooden floor at the bottom and wiped the corners of cobwebs and dust. A few short steps from her bedroom, from the bathroom and from the kitchen, she could reach this exit at a moment's notice.

Even with the three walls bare, it wasn't a large space. Only one other person could fit inside the closet with her, if necessary, and even then, it would be a negotiation of elbows and angles. Her shoulder blades shifted against the bare wall as she tried to focus on her target. She pictured him in her mind.

The cowboy coat he favored. His shaved head. The three vertical cuts in his eyebrow made by a razor. A prison tattoo of a devil fucking a woman from behind on his bicep.

She fed her intuition these markers, letting her compass zone in on the man she wanted.

Then she saw him, in her mind first, as the compass swirled inside her, orienting herself appropriately.

Castle marched down a nighttime street with his arm around a girl's waist. He had a Marlboro between his lips. And a white ten-gallon hat with a brown and gray pheasant feather protruding from one side of the cap. A gold ring on each of his pinkies, one bearing the crest of the Martinelli family. An ornate capital *M* and two dragons chasing one another head-to-tail around the letter. Ahead of the man was a bright flashing sign for a bar Lou recognized.

Downtown Austin then. Same time zone, so no problem there. Much hotter than St. Louis, but she didn't want to step out of the closet and change. She wasn't going to stay in the city any longer than she had to. She held the image of him in her mind as the pull intensified, the wire on her imaginary compass vibrating stronger.

She'd learned how to do this, strengthen the bond between herself and her prey before slipping. By twenty-four, her control had improved. She traveled with intention now. She could step into the full darkness and remain right where she was for as long as she needed. That had not been the case when she was a child. As a child, she was prey to the darkness. Whenever it wanted her, it could open its fanged mouth and swallow her whole. Sleeping at night was always a risk when the world was darkest and her mind most off guard. She couldn't count the number of times she'd laid down in her bed, safe in her aunt's Chicago apartment, only to wake up halfway across the world.

It was the same for water. She would never be like her mother, who'd enjoyed sliding into a hot bath with a book and a glass of wine.

She found this new development in her gift, the most useful advancement. Slipping blind had huge risks. No one knew what waited in the dark better than she did.

The girl at Jimmy Castle's side was a brunette in a tight, short skirt and five-inch heels. The night air in Austin was humid as hell and sweat had already begun to form at the back of Castle's neck. Even though she stood in a pitch-black box 800 miles away, Lou could smell his thick cologne and the cigarette smoke haloing his jaunty hat.

When her skin and limbs felt like they were on fire, she let go and slipped.

The hum of her apartment's refrigerator and whirling A/C were exchanged for the blast of car horns and a wall of heat. It felt like someone had thrown a blanket over her head and she was trying to breathe through its tightly meshed fibers. She stepped out from behind a dumpster, wrinkling her nose at the smell of garbage rotting in the heat. A cat hissed at her sudden intrusion, back arching. She hissed back, and it ran.

It was cooler in the alley than in the main drag, all lit up with its cars and stoplights and people on their phones. Little screens like sentient eyes burning in the dark. People were laughing too loud. Talking too loud. Trying to hear one another over the din of the throbbing traffic. Lou's eyes slid over the bodies, over the collective slithering movement until she found her target.

And there he was.

Lou leaned against the wall of a building and pretended to scroll through her own phone. It was turned off, but no one was looking closely. She stole glances at her target when he wasn't looking.

Castle stood on a corner with his arm around the brunette Lou'd seen in her mind first. Now she took in the details her mind's eye had missed. Penciled eyebrows. A mole on the cheek. The way she grinned at Jimmy over her cupped hands as she lit herself a cigarette. Lou had learned not to overlook or dismiss the girls she saw with her targets.

If she had to track someone in the daytime or slipped only to find herself in broad daylight, she'd have to rely on other skills to track her prey. And following their girls always proved easier. In her experience, Lou found that no one kept track of men better than their women.

Jimmy fist-bumped another man on the sidewalk before turning toward the entrance of the building she leaned against. A green awning reminding her of the Café du Monde illuminated the sidewalk and a doorman checking IDs. He grinned at Jimmy and slapped him a high five. More machismo bullshit. Then he waved Castle's group inside, bypassing the long line waiting to get into the club. A girl near the back groaned.

Lou turned and walked back down the alley, past the reeking garbage. She pressed herself into the deepest corner between the two buildings, shrouding herself in darkness. A heartbeat later, she was standing in a closet, listening to the hard *dhump dhump dhump dhump* of the club's bass.

The door flew open, and Lou barely had a moment to register the stockroom surrounding her.

"What the hell are you doing in here?" a bartender in a white shirt and black vest hissed.

Lou faked a slur. "Where's the fucking bathroom?"

The bartender grabbed her by the arm and steered her out of the closet. She resisted the urge to break all his fingers. Hurting him would draw attention to herself, and she worked best when no one noticed her. No one to remember her. No one with questions that could lead back to her.

Still holding her elbow, the bartender spun her toward the mouth of the hallway. The music was louder, and up ahead laser lights in purple, pink, and neon green shot through the air. "Go back to the dance floor then hook a right. Take the *other* hallway, and you'll find the bathrooms."

He slapped her on the ass and pushed Lou toward the dance floor.

She might murder him after all.

She slid through the dark searching for Jimmy. Her internal compass told her he was somewhere near the dance floor, on its outer fringes. She found him in a velvet booth with four girls and three men. They were doing shots and laughing like the world was ending.

Not the best place to grab him, but Lou was patient. She ordered a drink. She paid cash.

She sipped her virgin daiquiri and kept an eye on the man in the booth with his friends. His girls. Lou didn't mind being in the clubs. They were dark. And darkness was her element. But there was also a vibrancy to this atmosphere that she could appreciate. It wasn't unlike the vibrancy she felt in her little closet back home in St. Louis, or when she slipped through the thick shadows clinging to doors and buildings, or even a thick knot of trees.

No one needed to tell her the darkness was alive.

Anyone who'd spent a moment standing in a dark room knew. They could feel the energy along the back of their neck. Their pulse rose. Some primal part of them sensed creatures lurking just on the other side. Most people didn't slip through the thin membrane as she did, but they *knew* what was there.

Castle was on the move. The girls were scooting out in their tight skirts so he could stand. He had another cigarette between his lips even though smoking was forbidden in this club and all other watering holes from Boston to Seattle.

She watched him over the sparkling rim of her daiquiri as he exited the booth and moved toward the bathrooms, lit cigarette bobbing in the low light. The music thrummed in her chest as she watched him go. The crushed ice against her lips cooled her.

As soon as he ducked into the hallway, she set her daiquiri down and glanced around the room for any eyes trained on her. The club was full of convulsing bodies, too drunk or high to be capable of coordination. No one watched her.

She was only another face in the crowd, and not even a very memorable one considering the painted peacocks with iridescent blue eye shadow and shimmery shirts on the dance floor. She cut through the crowd easily. Behind a booth much like the one Castle had vacated, she found a thin spot in thick shadow and slipped through. Then her hands were on the back of a stall door.

It was a single-room employee bathroom. Why would Castle bother to wait in the piss lines like everyone else?

The light flicked on as Castle entered the bathroom and locked the door behind him.

Castle's slurring voice hummed out of tune. He swayed before the porcelain, and after one precarious lean, his arm shot out and grabbed at the concrete wall to steady himself.

"Oops," he looked down at his pee-splattered boot.

Lou watched him through the gap between the stall walls. Castle's back was to her as he shook his dick over the basin. She made her move.

She grabbed him and twisted his arm behind his back, immobilizing him.

He wailed and fought her hold, throwing a blind elbow strike which she ducked easily, given the difference in their heights and his sluggish movements. Fortunately, she only needed to hold onto him for a heartbeat. She hit the light switch on the wall with one quick swipe of her hand and pulled him through the dark.

Once the fresh air hit her, she stopped clinging to Castle and let him tumble to the grassy knoll at the edge of the lake.

His drunk ass hit the dirt, and he cried out.

The crickets fell silent at having their concert interrupted. The other night sounds swelled, oblivious to their intrusion. So far into the wilderness, scuffles happened all night long. Beasts tearing apart one another wasn't newsworthy. So the night went on.

An owl hooted. A fish jumped up before belly flopping the surface of the water. Something on the opposite shore slid into the water, a silver trail cutting the surface behind it. Ducks maybe. She wasn't sure. Surprisingly, despite all her gifts, Lou's night vision was unremarkable.

She loved this place. A small placid lake in the Alaskan wilderness. The evergreens thick with snow. A caribou on the opposite edge darted away at their intrusion, but otherwise, perfect silence. Perfect stillness as snow fell from the sky. Standing in this snowy world of eternal night calmed her in a way no other place on Earth could.

And not only because it was the entrance to her dumping ground.

When she killed, she brought them here, got them into the freezing waters and slipped to La Loon. They were miles from anything. Perfectly secluded, in a world that was night for months on end.

It calmed her every time.

Castle pulled himself to his feet, clawing at the small of his back.

"Looking for this?" Lou asked, pointing his gun at him. A night bird cawed.

Castle stopped slapping his lower back, and his jaw fell open. "Oh fuck. It's you."

She stopped

He finally pulled up his pants. "You're Konstantine's bitch."

She grimaced. "I'm no one's bitch."

"No, you're her. I've seen the fucking pictures. I thought he was jumping at shadows and shit but look at you." He waved a hand up and down her body. "Oh fuck, are you going to kill me?"

She should've said yes. That was her intention. But she was hung up on the words *fucking pictures.*

"God, I'm too high for this right now." He ran his hands over his face. Then he dropped down by the lake and started splashing water on his face. His white cowboy hat with the fancy plume fell off his head and into the water. He fished it out and shook water off it before laying it aside. A strange expression seized his face. He was going to puke.

She lowered the gun. This was new. Usually,

when she came across a hired hand from the Martinelli drug ring, it had a predictable pattern. It began with threats.

There was the name calling.

The threat to kill off her family.

Too late, she'd said. *You've already killed them. I'm here to return the favor.*

Or some variation. It was all pretty much the same. These men weren't great conversationalists, with their limited vocabularies.

When they found her unmoved, they tried to strike first. Then she killed them and shoved their bodies and all the evidence into the water.

The end.

No one had ever recognized her before. Mentioned pictures before. Collapsed to their knees and started vomiting before the first threat was even made.

"Jesus fucking Christ. What did I ever do to you?" He sounded as though he would cry.

Lou lowered the gun even more. She kept the pistol cupped in her hands, ready to raise and shoot at any moment. She thought the best way to proceed in an uncertain situation was to check her facts.

"You're one of Martinelli's mules."

"What does that got to do with you?"

"The Martinellis are dead, but you're still selling. *Why?*"

He turned and heaved into the lake again. When he stopped vomiting, he added, "Like you said, I'm a mule. It's what I do. I gotta pay bills, don't I?"

"I don't like drugs."

"Fuck, then don't do them!" he said with a wild shrug. "I never held you down and forced you, did I?"

"Good point." Lou forced a smile. "I'll cut you a deal."

The man begged. Literally begged on his hands and knees. Hands clasped.

"You stop muling, and I won't kill you."

His Adam's apple bobbed in the moonlight.

"You don't like my deal, Jimmy?"

Jimmy ran his hands down the front of his pants. "Come on, man. Be reasonable."

She pistol-whipped him.

Castle touched two fingers to his bloody cheek. It swelled a dark purple in the moonlight. "If I quit I'm as good as dead. Konstantine will cut off my balls and stuff them up my ass."

"Ah, so that's the real reason. You have a new boss." Lou grinned. Why did pain compliance work so well? Hurt them a little, and they spilled their guts. "So who is he?"

Her pulse leapt at the idea of a bigger fish. A worthier opponent.

His bald head gleamed in the moonlight. His hat lay against one knee, and he studied it intensely. He said nothing.

Okay. Crime lords were all the same to Lou anyway. "He's another roach that'll run under the fridge when the light comes on. I'll get to him."

Castle's head snapped up. "He ain't no roach. He's Martinelli."

She raised her gun and shoved it between his eyes. "There are no Martinellis. I killed every last one."

"Missed one. And the things I've heard about him, you wouldn't believe it. Truly fucked up shit."

"And he has pictures of me?"

Castle tugged the damp hat back onto his head. "He sent them around. I thought it was a story to keep all the good little mules in line. But here you are, and you look like your fucking pictures."

Keep the good little mules in line.

Because they hadn't been in line. Lou saw the infighting herself. But she thought the chaos was the result of her murdering everyone in charge. She'd cut off the thumb holding them down, and now every dealer with an ounce of ambition was vying to be on top.

Of course, this Konstantine would have to be a bloody bastard. He'd never re-establish the pecking order or the fist of power his family had built with soft tactics. The clans and other crime families would eat him alive.

Alive. There was at least one more Martinelli alive. She couldn't help but smile. Grin like it was Christmas morning and she'd found a present under the tree, wrapped and ready for her. Before she could stop herself, she laughed.

"Get up," she said.

"Oh come on." Castle pulled himself to his feet. The sight of her jubilation intensified his horror. "Please don't fucking kill me. You want money? I've got—" His voice broke, and his face screwed up like he was going to burst into tears.

"Don't cry. It pisses me off," she said.

"Please."

"I'm not going to kill you."

"You're not?" Castle's face lit up.

"You sound disappointed."

"No, no!" he begged. "I'm not ready to die."

"Everyone dies, Castle." She stepped into the shadow of the tree and slipped, leaving Castle with wide, glassy eyes.

She didn't go far. Across the way, she peered from beneath a Sitka pine. He turned a circle, searching. He went to the tree where she'd been and looked beneath it as if expecting to find her there.

When he seemed satisfied that she had left, he lifted his hat and ran a hand over his gleaming, bald head again, before walking south, away from the moon-filled water.

She wasn't going to let him go far.

If he kept wandering his current direction, he wouldn't last two days. There was nothing but Alaskan wilderness that way.

And this place was sacred to her.

She loved it more than any place on Earth. It had taken her a long time to find one so perfect. Its silence. Its eternal night. The magic way the lake did not freeze with more than a thin layer of ice, no matter how cold it got. It told her the dark waters underneath were deep.

She wouldn't let him ruin this place for her.

She slipped through the trees, staying on his heels as he navigated the forest. Coyotes yipped nearby, catching her scent and no doubt Castle's. It didn't matter. As soon as he passed beneath the next shady limb, she was going to grab him.

The arm of a mighty fir tree stretched overhead. As soon as the shadow passed over Castle's body, she caught him. He yelped, as expected. And he was still howling when she dropped him on the sidewalk beside the downtown alley.

She ducked out of sight before he could turn and look for her.

Let him think she's a ghost. A boogeyman.

Power was only powerful when no one knew how much you had. It was better if they believed her invincible. She was in trouble if they realized how many limitations she had.

From beneath an awning across the street, she watched Castle clamber to his feet and turn in all directions. He peered into the dark alley, searching for her. Some of his friends called from the club's entrance, and he turned, wide-eyed and bewildered. He lifted his hat and ran a hand over his bare head.

Lou smiled. She could go straight to this Konstantine. Murder him outright. But she'd had nights and nights with no Martinelli in the world. And it had been cold and dull playing without a target.

Oh, he would die. Of course. But she would take her time with this.

Draw it out.

Enjoy every minute.

Run rat run, she thought, watching Castle disappear into the throng of sweaty parasites feeding on the night. *Take me to your leader.*

9

Lucy stood in Lou's dark apartment. One of the windows was open, and a light breeze blew through, rattling the blinds and mangling the slats. The moonlit sheets stirred, and a paperback opened face down, spine creased, ruffled in the breeze. Outside, a train whistled and huge iron wheels scraped against their rails. Horns blared even at this hour. God, how could she sleep with all this noise? Maybe she couldn't. Lou's bed was empty after all.

The moonlight falling across the bed between the blinds brightened the white sheets to an ethereal glow. It was rumpled the way Lou's bed was always rumpled, even as a child. Unlike Lucy and her brother Jack, God rest his soul, who made their beds first thing in the morning as their Nana had taught them, Lou could tumble in and out of a messy bed with little concern. If the sheets and blanket weren't in perfect alignment, who cared?

Lucy crossed the room and sat on the edge of

the mattress, a hard, unforgiving foam pad resting on a box spring. She exhaled and ran a hand over the coverlet and sheets, smoothing it. No girl. No gun either.

She was out hunting then. Did she do it every night? Every night that Lucy had dropped in unannounced, she'd found the bed empty, no matter the hour.

She stuck her hands under the pillow, still expecting to find a gun, but it was bare underneath.

Something like cardstock scraped the back of her hand. She frowned, her brows knitting together, and lifted the pillow. Nothing lay beneath. So she turned the pillow over in her lap and traced the fabric. Her fingers probed the pillow case and found it smooth until her nail snagged on a rectangle with soft edges.

Lucy slipped her hand into the pillowcase and grasped the edge of the card. She pulled it out.

Not a card. A photograph with a glossy image on one side and a cool white backing on the other, the kind developed in those one-hour photo labs found at most corner pharmacies.

Lucy's heart hitched. In the picture, Jack smiled up at her. His teeth were perfect, the product of braces he'd absolutely hated wearing for four years, but oh how they'd provided so much ammo for his tween sister. *Metal mouth. Brace face.* Or when she was feeling less imaginative, plain ol' *gummy dummy* worked. In her mind, Lucy could still see the little rubber bands, so many small bands, and the way he would shoot them at her, once catching the corner of her eye and throwing their grandmother into hysterics.

In the photo, Jack's hair was wet and falling into his eyes, and he had one massive arm around Louie. She was *Louie* then, no more than seven or eight years old and grinning at the camera, tucked into the crook of her father's big arm, one ear pressed to his chest. One of her front teeth was missing. But whether or not Jack would have submitted his own daughter to braces would never be known. He was dead four years later.

Their last visit burned in Lucy's mind.

You have to help me. I don't know what to do, Jack had said.

He was in head-to-toe black. Muscle shirt to combat boots, standing in the Walmart parking lot off Exit 133.

Help you? Lucy had said, spitting the words at him. *The way you helped me?*

On a warm July night, she'd seethed like the

boiling blacktop under their feet. Decades of anger crouched inside her, waiting to tear her treacherous brother apart.

I'd never ask you to do this for me, Jack had pleaded. *But Louie is scared out of her mind. She needs someone. And we both know I'm not that person.*

No, you're not. The only thing you're good at is abandoning the people who need you.

Lucy wished she could take those words back. *What if—as he lay dying he thought—*she squeezed her eyes shut and sucked in a tight breath. When she opened them, Jack was still smiling at her.

Louie's hair wasn't wet even though they were at the beach. Lucy understood why—*she never goes into the water.* Hadn't Jack told her that? *I try to put her in the bath, and she screams bloody murder. The therapist and Courtney are brushing it off as a phobia. There was even a word for it. Aquaphobia. But we both know it's more than that.*

But when she'd first heard of her niece's fear she didn't make the connection. After all, Lucy herself had never been able to slip through water the way she did through shadow. She couldn't imagine it was possible. Yet Lou did both, and the water didn't even have to be dark water. But from what

Lou told her, this mutation of their shared family trait did have its limitation.

Lou could slip in water, but she only went to one place. Every slip took her to *La Loon*. Their name for a strange place with a purple sky, red lake, and two moons. Lou could travel by water but always washed up on the shore of Blood Lake. And when she used the lake to return it was also into water. Never water to darkness. They didn't mix. If Lucy got into the car and drove north on I-80, she could only reach Chicago, not Paris. And it seemed the same was true for Lou's watery roads. She couldn't climb into her bathtub and pop up in the Atlantic Ocean. Perhaps her bathtub to La Loon, and then to the Atlantic Ocean, but never without that first stop.

Lucy worried about it. What was Lou's connection to that strange place full of monsters? Worse still, Lucy suspected that Lou had come to use it as a sort of dumping ground for the men she killed—and that notion frightened her more.

I'm sorry I didn't believe you, Lucy. I'm sorry I didn't protect you.

I didn't need you to protect me, she'd argued. And it had been a bold-faced lie. *I needed you there.*

There. When the darkness grew thin and

swallowed her up. *There*. When one by one she lost her friends and jobs because of her "delusion." When their own grandmother had called her a liar. A demon.

Think whatever you want about me, but please help her. I don't want her to feel alone.

Like me, Lucy had said bitterly.

Lucy frowned down at the photograph of her dead brother and rubbed her forehead. *I'm sorry, Jack. I'm trying. I really am.*

All the old blame rose, flared its cobra head and hissed. A cold voice enumerated her sins.

You blame Jack for abandoning you, for not being there when you needed him, and yet you weren't there for him either, were you? You could have saved your brother from those men if you'd been paying attention instead of fucking his boss.

She'd gone to Jack as soon as she knew something was wrong. She dumped King off at his sister's, and a heartbeat later crawled out from under a sedan in the driveway across the street. But she was already too late. Cop cars and unmarked SUVs lined the curb outside Jack's home. His two-story suburban house modeled after some quaint Tudor manor stood wide awake with all the lights in the house on. Dozens of officers passed behind the windows as they moved from room to room. Others clustered together behind the yellow tape.

Then she was across the street, lifting the yellow tape up over her head.

"Ma'am." A woman in a uniform held up a hand. "You can't come in here."

"Where's Jack? Is he okay? Where is he? Where's Louie?"

"I can't answer those questions," the officer said.

"What do you mean you can't answer my questions? Are they dead? Is my family fucking dead or not? It's a simple question!"

Her voice boomed across the damp lawn in the early hours. Across the street, lookie-loos were pulling back curtains, blue-red-white flashes dancing across their own homes. Several officers who'd been busy chatting with one another until that moment turned toward her. Lucy was about to storm away, slink around the side of the house, perhaps beneath the shade of a bush and slip into a closet. She had to get into the house. She had to see what was going on for herself.

Before she could, a wall of a man was coming across the lawn, his big boots stepping right through Courtney's begonias. He was calling her name.

"Lucy?"

Lucy didn't recognize his face until he stepped into the light.

"Detective Chaz," Lucy said and then realized it wasn't right. Chaz was his first name. But at that moment, she didn't give two chickens or a pile of shit about remembering his last name. "Is Jack okay?"

Brasso ran a pudgy hand across his brow. "I'm so sorry to be the one to tell you this. Jack is dead. His wife is too. It looks like a break-in occurred and they were both shot."

Lucy's guts cramped as if a massive fist had been slammed into it. "Louie—"

"We can't find her. We're looking. High and low, we're looking."

Tears streamed down her cheek for Jack, and surprisingly, for Courtney too, though the woman had never shown an ounce of kindness her—Jack's *insane* sister. Sorrow swelled, then the wave of it crashed down on her and under the sorrow, a chord of terror. *Oh god, where is Louie? Did she get out? She could have slipped through the dark when the gunshots started. Or god forbid, they took her. They took her and—*

Lucy whirled away from King's partner. "I have

to go."

Brasso started after her. "Are you sure you should drive? Hey, how did you know? Did someone call you?"

"Yes," she lied, saying anything to get him off her. "I came as soon as I could."

"That explains the lack of shoes." Brasso pointed down at her feet. He wet his lips and shuffled on his feet. "Who called you?"

"I'm sorry, but I have to go." Lucy was already jogging across the dark street toward the parked car.

"I don't have your number!" he yelled after her. "Why don't you give me your information so—" but whatever he intended to do with her information, she didn't hear. She was going down on her belly and rolling under the sedan.

He'll get it from King, she thought. *If he needs it.*

On her belly under the car, she heard a door open, heard someone say, "Where the hell did she go?"

She didn't wait to assure the owner she was no car thief. She slipped through the dark, desperate to find her niece.

Despite her night-long efforts, she didn't find Louie. She got a call from King the next day. Louie had come back to the house on her own, dripping wet. It would be months before Lucy learned why she couldn't find Lou despite all her searching.

Lou had been in La Loon, the one place where Lucy couldn't go. That strange world wasn't on Lucy's map. It could be Europa or in the Andromeda galaxy for all she knew.

And King. What a fuck up that had been. The first time she loved someone, and she threw him off the bridge like a discarded cigarette butt the moment life got hard. And what had been her excuse? *Louie needs me.* Bullshit. The truth, as she'd come to accept it after $5,000 in therapy and countless hours of self-reflection, was that she'd refused King out of guilt. She'd failed Jack. Failed his daughter. And she didn't *deserve* to be happy. And no matter how many self-help workbooks she read, or positive affirmations she recited while looking at herself in the bathroom mirror, she couldn't seem to make herself *un*believe this self-evident truth.

Lucy kissed the photograph and slipped it back into the pillowcase.

Think of all those years wasted, giving Jack the cold shoulder, and why? Because he hurt your feelings? Because he'd refused to blindly believe the wild stories you told him about your abilities? When

Lou tried to tell you about La Loon, how did you react? How did it feel? To know you were as close-minded as you accused Jack of being? He died with your words in his ear, Lucy. He died thinking he'd abandoned Lou as you told him he would.

Lucy tried to shake off this dark voice. The one which would have her drown in her own regrets and sorrows. Buddhism had taught her to embrace her sins. To forgive herself as a work in progress. To know she was perfect as she was, but there was also room for improvement.

On most days, as long as she didn't neglect her yoga, or chanting, or meditation, this personal mantra worked.

She had only one way to honor the memory of her older brother and his legacy now. Only one way to prove to the universe and herself that she loved him and forgave him, in death if not in life. She would do more than *show* Lou she wasn't alone. That she wasn't abandoned.

She had to keep her alive.

She stood, and her lightheadedness spun the room. A wave of nausea bubbled up into her trachea. She put one hand on her stomach and one hand on her head until it passed.

It was to be expected, she supposed, given her

condition.

This reminder of her body's frailty was a warning, a nudge. She would have to move fast if she wanted to make good on her promise to her brother.

She had to.

She was running out of time.

10

Konstantine walked from the Duomo toward his apartment as the lively summer day danced around him.

He loved Florence. With its cobblestoned town center and statues as old as civilization itself. Loved the stone walls, bridges, and ancient churches. Loved the river cutting through it as pigeons the color of sheet rock perched on buildings.

It was an old city built on the blood and corpses of men. Countless bones lay in the earth beneath his feet. Kingdoms rose, flourished, and fell. And it would be the same with his own empire.

Walking around the city made him think of his mother. While his mother had sold postcards from a squeaky cart she pushed around the city center, he would ask tourists if they wanted a tour for 5000 lire. He could get four or five takers a day during the low season and as many as twenty in high season, his sandaled feet wearing the cobblestones smooth before and after school.

His mother made enough with her postcards, keychains, and umbrellas. She had a sweet smile and bright voice. People liked her. And she let Konstantine use his money to buy treats from the countless vendors lining the streets.

When Konstantine did have money in his pockets, he spent it on koulouri and pide, Greek sweets that came from a shop by the Ponte Vecchio. He loved the koulouri and pide, but he also liked the immigrant shop owners' little girl. A dark beauty with big black eyes like polished river stones and hair like raven feathers. He'd discovered the shop with his mother, who favored it, insisting a Greek shop was incredibly rare in Florence, and therefore, should be appreciated.

Konstantine had loved the treats, but the girl was even better. He brought her little gifts. A two-scoop gelato, a frog made of blown glass. He'd buy his warm bread and then go down to the water with his treasures in his pockets, watching the gulls bob on the river Arno. Sometimes the Greeks, who were mostly amused by Konstantine's affections, would let their girl, Dica, go with him.

But when the lire were replaced with expensive euros, the Greeks closed shop and moved without warning. Konstantine did not even get to say goodbye. And not long after, his mother stopped pushing the postcard cart around the city center, and she accepted his tour money, more heartily than ever before. It would be much later before Konstantine understood what had actually chased his mother indoors.

Konstantine checked the time and realized he would be late if he did not hurry. On the steps outside the Uffizi, Asians posed with rabbit ears in front of the grand wooden doors. Teenagers with their tight jackets and scooters swerved around pedestrians, and the beggars lay prostrated, face down with their open palms cupped. A lovely girl in a sundress, no more than sixteen, stood outside his favorite gelateria, gobbling limoncello sorbetto with a girlish smile. She wiped at her dripping chin with a paper napkin as the breeze tousled her skirt.

Konstantine stepped through a portico into an atrium and courtyard. He passed beneath the rounded archway and ascended the old stone steps to his attic apartment overlooking the lush courtyard and fountain. Water poured through a cherub's mouth, his delicate stone fingers ready to play the lyre held up in his hands.

This courtyard always made him think of his

mother. Of the roses she tried to grow on the balcony of their apartment. When he was a good boy, his mother would let him watch the old black and white American movies in her bedroom.

He'd been watching *The Godfather* the night he decided to join Padre Leo's gang. It wasn't the glorified life of a criminal portrayed in the movie that had sparked Konstantine's interest. In fact, having watched the film about a hundred times, Konstantine was sure all gangsters died horribly, looking like bloody pincushions or with their brains sprayed all over everything.

But that night itself had changed everything.

Go into my room and watch your movie, amore di mamma. Let me talk to Francesca.

He knew she disapproved of *The Godfather*, Konstantine being only eight years old. But he also knew she hated to raise her voice in front of others. If he kept the volume low, she might not even hear him. If she caught him anyway, the punishment would be light given Francesca's presence. So he'd turned the movie on and pushed the volume all the way down until only one bar showed at the bottom of the screen. Oh, how thrilling childhood deviance had once seemed. Now Konstantine only felt such delicious panic when dumping a body into the Arno

River.

Fifteen minutes into the movie, Konstantine had wanted a drink. He went to the kitchen for water and caught a scrap of conversation between the two women. His mother sat at their bistro table with her head in her hands. Francesca was rubbing his mother's shoulders.

It doesn't have to be so garish as all that. No street corners in broad daylight, Francesca said. *Well, go on! He's waiting. Try to relax.*

His mother nodded and left the apartment, closing the door softly behind her.

Where's she going? Konstantine had asked.

Francesca paused in lighting her cigarette and turned to the boy. Her lips were pursed and her eyes wide. Then she forced a tight smile. *She went to my apartment to get something for me. She'll be right back. Go watch your movie.*

She was lying in that way adults lie, pulling a curtain to hide their adult world.

Konstantine returned to his movie having entirely forgotten about his thirst. And somehow, despite the rampant bloodshed and gun fighting on the screen, he'd dozed off. When he woke, the movie was off, the night was dark and quiet. Someone, his mother no doubt, had tucked him in tight. It took him several moments to realize it had been the sound of his mother crying that had woken him. Lying beside him, he could see the slender plane of her back beneath her thin nightdress. Her shoulders trembled.

Konstantine knew Francesca by reputation. Boys his age gossiped like anyone else. He understood then, with a child's clarity, what had happened. He visited Padre Leo in the basement of his old church the very next day.

It was easy enough to find him. All the boys in the city knew of Padre Leo and his small army. If a boy agreed to take a package across town without any questions, he could have a pocketful of candy and lire by the end of the day.

And by the afternoon, Padre Leo was sitting in his mother's apartment, drinking coffee and assuring her everything would be all right.

And it was, because Konstantine never saw Francesca again. And he never woke to the sound of his mother crying again. His mother was happy and safe. Until his father's enemies caught up to them.

Konstantine stepped into his apartment and an arctic blast of air hit him, like entering a meat locker. It was a pleasant change from his warm walk in the afternoon.

He opened his laptop with his thumb

recognition software. The screen whirled to life, loading his programs. He checked his watch again. His video conference call was in two minutes.

He arranged himself at the desk, adopting a relaxed posture purposefully. He turned on the camera to inspect himself. He made sure the lighting was right. A giant oil painting of a man with a sword raised high hung behind him. Otherwise, the stucco was bare and the room nondescript.

He could be anywhere.

Perfect.

He looked at the man framed in the video screen. His wavy black hair was neatly trimmed in the current style, short on the sides and a little long on the top. He left his mirrored shades on. He tightened his jaw to hide the fullness of his lips. He looked too much like a pouty little boy with his lips parted. He'd shaved that morning, but black stubble was already poking through. That was okay too.

Best not to look too polished, too refined. That sent a very different kind of message about the sort of man Konstantine was and how he would conduct his business.

The computer trilled with the sound of an incoming call.

Konstantine sat back in his chair and composed

himself. He placed his arms on the chair, clenched his jaw again and let it ring. *Best to never let people think you're too eager.* Wasn't it his beloved Padre who had said this?

"Hello?" he said at last. He liked the sound of his English. Accented, but not unpleasantly. In the movies, he would be the love interest of a beautiful woman who would love him for this voice, going wet between her legs from the sound of it.

The chat program opened by voice recognition and Julio Vasquez appeared on the screen. A cigarette dangled from between his lips, he sat back away from the screen as if to give Konstantine some room. As if the ocean and half a country weren't enough space between Austin and Florence.

Julio's hair was greased back, slicked against his head. He wore a black tank top, and hair protruded from everywhere. From under his arms, and from his chest, great black tufts of it. Julio was one of the men who Padre trusted. His open acceptance of Konstantine had been jarring at first, in the weeks following Padre's death. The way he performed duties without question. But now Konstantine was starting to appreciate the man's swift execution and efficiency.

Konstantine waited for him to speak. Men in

power never spoke first. It was beneath them. It was Julio's place to explain, Julio's place to ask for instruction. Not his.

"We've got Castle here." Julio plucked his cigarette from between his lips and exhaled blue smoke toward the ceiling. "He's got news about that bitch you're looking for."

Konstantine focused on the light behind Julio's head and the five-gallon paint bucket, orange with white splatters, overturned in the middle of the scene.

Konstantine considered correcting him. *She's not* that *bitch.* But it was too soon in his reign to start showing weakness. Infatuation counted as weakness in the eyes of most men. It was natural to want something and desire it. Having something you love within arm's length was stupid.

"Put him on," Konstantine said. He kept his tone even, checking his image in the box at the lower right of the screen. He looked a tad eager. He leaned back in his chair and straightened his spine.

Julio slipped out of sight, and another man appeared. He had a deeply pit-marked face and a tall, white ten-gallon hat on his head with a ridiculous feather jutting from one side. His eyes were glassy in the camera, either with fear or narcotics. The two men escorting him pushed him down onto the overturned paint bucket converted into a seat. The plastic scraped along the concrete floor.

"Hello, Mr. Castle." Konstantine laced his fingers. "How are you this evening?"

The man licked his lips and hesitated. His shoulder jostled when someone nudged him. Konstantine heard Julio say, "He's talking to you, dude. Don't be fucking rude."

"I'm good," Castle stammered and ran a hand under his nose. "How-how are you?"

"Fine," Konstantine answered with a smile. It wasn't a friendly smile. It was the smile he'd learned how to make from the gangsters in his American movies. His mother called it an I'm-so-hungry-I-could-eat-you-up smile. "I have heard something fascinating about you, Mr. Castle."

"Yeah, what's that?" Castle asked. He fidgeted, trying to get comfortable on the overturned bucket.

"Julio says you were kidnapped. By a woman."

"Hell yeah!" the man said, indignant. Relief was palpable on his face. Whatever he'd initially thought this conversation was going to be about, it wasn't about his woman. "She snatched me right out of the goddamn bathroom. Then we were in a fucking forest in the middle of fucking nowhere. It was cold.

I don't even think we was in America. Well, maybe Montana, some shit like that."

"Slow down," Konstantine said. His own voice had sped up with excitement, and he was speaking as much to himself as to the dealer. He took a breath and reasserted his self-control. "Mr. Castle, what you're saying seems rather remarkable. You expect us to believe you were kidnapped by a woman, and then magically transported thousands of miles away?"

He heard Julio and the others laughing.

Castle's mouth dropped open in outrage. "But it's fucking true! I swear it."

"Perhaps you need to sell more snow than you're using, man," Julio cackled like a hyena.

"Where were you when this happened?" Konstantine asked, measuring each word.

"Tito's place."

Julio bent down so that his face was visible in the camera. "It's a cowboy bar off 6th street. Up in Austin."

Konstantine flashed another one of his controlled smiles. "Mr. Castle, is it also true you only escaped because you, how did you put it, 'gave her the best fuck of her life'?"

Julio and the others roared. Julio slapped his

thigh and reached up to wipe tears from the corners of his eyes while Castle continued to defend his ridiculous story.

She would slit you, navel to nose, and leave you for dead before you even touched her.

Konstantine felt his anger rising. He let a controlled breath escape his nostrils, trying not to let them flare and give away his irritation. He would kill Castle for touching her.

She's mine, his brain whispered. *She's mine until the day she dies.*

"Settle down boys," Konstantine said once he felt he could trust himself to speak. "Castle may be a beast for all we know."

It was a cruel jibe and Castle's face crumpled, wounded. "I saw her. I swear I did."

"*That* I believe." Konstantine sat back in his chair. "So my next question is, why did she let you live? Every one of the mules she's taken has never been seen again. Yet here you are. Why do you think that is?"

Castle stiffened in his chair.

His reaction was a clue to guide Konstantine's questioning. He steepled his fingers. "Did you tell her anything?"

Castle didn't answer. His mouth hung open, and

his stained, yellow teeth gleamed in the computer's shitty resolution.

Julio smacked Castle upside his head. "Do you have enchiladas in your ears? The man asked you a question."

Castle set his jaw. "No. I didn't say anything. She grabbed me from the bathroom and dropped me off in the woods. She pointed the gun at me, I talked her down. Then she brought me back."

"You talked her down?" Konstantine grinned. How would one coax down such a creature? Whatever means necessary would be beyond a man such as this.

"Yeah, you know. I was fucking *nice*. I made her see she had the wrong guy."

Castle's cheek twitched.

"And who was the *right* guy?" Konstantine leaned forward and peered into the camera, seeing his face large in the small window within the chat box. "Me?"

"No, man, no." Castle was quick to rebuke. "I didn't say anything about you."

"Julio?" Konstantine said, part question, part call for attention.

Julio didn't even have to ask. The two men who'd escorted Castle in seized his shoulders, forcing him to sit still on the overturned paint bucket. Julio held a gun to his head while the others held his arms.

"Have you ever played the game twenty questions?" Konstantine asked. Sweat had begun to form on his brow, but his voice remained perfectly even.

When Castle didn't immediately answer, Julio slid the safety off the gun and chambered a round.

"Yes, yes!" he moaned. "Yes, every fucking body has played twenty questions. What about it?"

"I love twenty questions," Konstantine smiled. "I would play this game with my mother for hours, and she always indulged me. She was a very patient woman. Wasn't she?"

Before Martinelli threw her to the wolves.

"A fucking saint," he said, squirming beneath the pistol pressed against his temple.

"I want to play twenty questions with you now. But the version I play with you is going to be a little different than the version I played with my mother. With you, when I ask you a question, if you lie to me, Julio is going to blow off one of your fingers. If we run out of fingers, then we have your toes. Twenty in all."

Without having to be told, Julio moved his gun

to Castle's left hand. He pressed the barrel to the man's pinkie, holding it out to the side so the bullet could blast right through without hitting either Castle or the two men holding him.

Castle squirmed. "But I haven't lied to you!"

"Be still, or I might blow off your fucking finger accidentally, you dumb fuck," Julio warned. Sweat gleamed on the back of the Mexican's neck in the overhead light.

"And if we run out of fingers and toes, then we must find something else to shoot off. Can you think of anything else on your body which resembles a finger or toe?" Konstantine asked. The men, who weren't being threatened with a bullet, laughed.

Castle began to let out a high-pitched whine. "Come on, man. I haven't done anything."

Konstantine wet his lips. "Question one: Did you tell the woman anything about me?"

Castle hesitated. Julio pulled the trigger. The report crackled through the sound feed, and the black room momentarily lit up with light revealing exposed beams and rafters. They were in one of the unfinished condos then. Konstantine noted Julio's smart choice. It was as important to keep track of the honorable mules as it was of the naughty ones. Sometimes more important. The video lagged for a heartbeat then skipped, catching up.

Castle screamed. Blood gushed from the partial stump of his pinkie, pumping over his hand. He kept screaming as Julio moved on to the ring finger, grabbing the man's bloody finger as if the blood didn't disgust him.

Konstantine's stomach turned.

"Question two," Konstantine said, without looking directly at the blood. "Did you tell the woman who kidnapped you about *me*?"

"Yes!" Castle screamed. "Fuck yes. I might've said your name. But I swear to god I didn't say nothing bad about you. Not a goddamn thing."

"Question three. What did you say about me *exactly*?"

When Castle didn't answer after a few tense moments, Konstantine nodded to Julio. The gun went off again, severing the ring finger from Castle's left hand. The finger dangled in Julio's grip before it was dropped to the floor. Konstantine was thankful for his dark shades and the privacy they afforded him. He could close his eyes, and they would be none the wiser.

Castle's screams intensified. "Fuck man, I was thinking! I was fucking thinking!" Tears streamed down the man's face. It had become so red,

Konstantine had to remind him to take a breath or he was going to pass out.

"At the rate we are going, I don't think you'll live to see the end of the game, my friend. You're bleeding too much," Konstantine said. He managed to add a patronizing lilt to the end of his words.

"Don't shoot so fast," Castle begged. He wiped his snotty nose on his sleeve. "I got to think."

Ah, the begging. It came whenever they tried to slow down the pain.

"I can't think so fast with my hand hurting, man. It hurts like a bitch."

"Is that my fault?" Konstantine asked.

"No, man, no."

"I want you to try very hard to answer my questions as quickly as possible," Konstantine said. "I have appointments this evening. You wouldn't expect me to be late, would you?"

"No sir," the man said, spit clinging to his lips as he spoke. He looked like a bawling child, but he didn't yank his hand away from Julio as the middle finger was grasped and bent straight. Maybe Castle was not as stupid as he looked.

"So I'll ask again. What did you say about me exactly?"

"She told me if I didn't stop muling she was

going to shoot me, and I said I couldn't stop muling because you'd kill me."

"And then?" Konstantine encouraged with a little wave. He noted the spray of blood across the man's white hat.

"She said you were another roach or rat or something."

Julio raised his gun and pressed it against the middle finger on the left hand.

Castle's voice took off like a shot, rising fast. "God, I don't remember. An animal, some kind of animal that scurries. I swear to god that's what she said."

"And then?"

"I told her no, you were the new Martinelli. And she said there's no fucking Martinellis because she killed them all. And I said, no there was you. That's it. I swear on my fucking mother that's it. That's all she said."

His anger surfaced. His pulse throbbed in his ears. *The new Martinelli.* "And then she took you back to Austin."

"Yes."

Konstantine sat back in his chair. The new Martinelli. So that was why she'd cut Castle loose. No doubt she'd been furious at the idea of a

Martinelli living. Breathing.

After a moment he said, "Did she realize you recognized her?"

"Yeah," he said. He was looking like he might vomit. A sheen of sweat coated his face.

"Did she ask how you recognized her?"

"The pictures," he said without hesitation. He was going to pass out from blood loss, Konstantine realized.

"And then she brought you back," he said again, but he was grinning now.

"Yeah, man. I told you. She dropped me off outside Tito's place."

Konstantine's anger softened. *Tricky, tricky girl.*

"Julio?"

"Yeah, boss?"

"Please help Mr. Castle attend to his wounds. He has been very helpful. It would be unfortunate if anything were to happen to him."

The two men who'd been holding him down moments before now helped him up, slapped him on the back and escorted him from the room as if he were nothing more than a buddy who'd had too much to drink. Meanwhile, Julio barked orders to have the concrete floor hosed down and the fingers collected off the ground.

"Stay for a moment, Julio," Konstantine commanded before he terminated the call.

Julio pulled the overturned bucket up to the computer screen, the perfect height to frame himself in the camera. Two men discussing business. The blood-soaked bucket and fingers on the floor already forgotten.

"Make sure Castle doesn't die. I want him sewn up and back on the street tomorrow at the latest."

"You got it."

"She's going to track him. So we are going to track him too. Send a few men up from San Antonio, men Castle won't recognize, and have him followed. *Everywhere*. But don't be obvious. She will know we are onto her if she sees too many men standing around, obsessing over Castle."

"No problem," Julio said, slipping a new cigarette between his lips and lighting it behind a cupped palm.

"Should we give him his fingers?" Julio asked. "If we get them on ice, he can have them put back on."

"No," Konstantine said, his voice cold. "We are going to kill him, if she doesn't do it first. No need to go out of our way."

"She's only a girl," Julio said, scratching his hairy chest.

Konstantine grinned. "You have no idea what she's capable of."

She would come back for him. She would come for Konstantine and he couldn't be more excited. Even if it meant his death, he would see her again. And truly, she deserved her revenge. What his brothers did to her family, it was unforgivable. Why shouldn't she seek his blood in return?

"I started looking into her family the way you wanted," Julio said. He placed his thumb in his mouth and began to chew it. "It was Angelo's kill, like you said. But I'm hearing other shit too, man."

Konstantine leaned forward, unable to hide his interest. "Tell me."

11

At five past eleven, Lou stepped into her apartment. She'd only come back for a wardrobe change. She removed the machete from her back and switched to thin, efficient blades, easily concealed in her inner arms and boots. Their handles were sleek metal meant to keep the weight of the blade even if she needed to throw it rather than plunge it into her target's neck. Black metal would neither reflect the light nor draw attention to itself.

Killing, not intimidation, was the order of the evening.

She pulled four S&W blades from their hook on the wall and slipped them into place. Then she loaded six clips. Six was a tad much for a simple stakeout, but she'd only been expecting to meet her aunt's friend for coffee, and look how that turned out.

Someone was watching her. *Tracking* her.

It was a new sensation and unpleasant.

The part she loved most about her ability was the way she moved through the world. Like a ghost.

She blended into a setting, observed, took what she wanted, and was never seen again. And the men she seized, they never lived to tell the tale. Her anonymity was her greatest power, and she fully understood this. Even if she hadn't been raised in an age where starlets were displayed on magazine covers, and their sex tapes rampantly devoured, she would have understood this. His face and name had gotten her father killed after all. Even before the internet, five minutes on the television was all the Martinellis had needed to track him down.

Castle was the first man Lou'd let go since she killed Gus Johnson at the tender age of seventeen.

And the fact that this new Martinelli, *Konstantine*, had photos of her, shopping her face around, meant the number of men who could recognize her on sight was rising. And what the hell was his game anyway? He must want revenge for his murdered family. That was the only connection between them. And yet, she was certain she'd been careful. Left no witnesses. Konstantine shouldn't even have the smallest idea of who the hell he wanted revenge *from*. So where had she fucked up?

Fuckups happened, but they had to be cleaned

up. The only problem was, Lou was in a boat on the open sea. It was filling up with water, and she had no idea where the leak was.

That simply will not do, as Aunt Lucy liked to say in a fake and poorly rendered British accent, and probably misquoted from some old movie launched before Lou's time.

The moment Lou realized the not-detective King was Aunt Lucy's ex, she wasn't surprised. Aunt Lucy was too romantic. Of course, she would run to her ex, some man she probably still coddled a burning love for, and ask him to swoop in and save her wayward niece from self-destruction. The idea that a woman needed a man to help her do anything was ridiculous and five minutes with King was enough to tell her he was no saint on a white horse. His apartment reeked of marijuana. He had no food in the fridge. He was at least forty pounds overweight, and yet he'd gobbled those beignets like he hadn't eaten in three days, sucking the powdered sugar off his fingers with relish.

She loaded a magazine and then inserted it into the butt of her gun. She chambered a round. She didn't need some bored ex-cop to give her direction. She'd call her own shots, *thank you very much.*

She slipped the extra magazines into the pockets

of her cargo pants and the inside pockets of her vest. Again, it was a lot of ammo for stalking. But Lou felt the heat of the situation rising, and she'd rather be ridiculously over-prepared than ridiculously stupid. Besides, this was one of her father's vests. She ran a hand down the front of her chest over the Kevlar, and the muscles in her body went soft.

She'd had to sneak into their home to get it.

After her parents were killed, Lou returned to her house. Lucy had forbidden it, but Aunt Lucy couldn't watch her 24/7. The moment her aunt's snores turned soft and steady in the next room, Lou had slipped through and found herself in her house. Her *old* house.

The grief had welled fresh then, as her mind tried to sort through its options for reclassification: *my old house, my childhood home, my parents' house, where I used to live—*

She'd appeared in her room. The twin bed was there, and her covers rumpled. Most of her stuff was still there since they'd forbidden her from taking anything away from The Crime Scene. That's how they said it, as if in all caps, THE CRIME SCENE.

Lucy had slipped her back in of course, after a few hours, but only to get clothes. *Nothing they'll notice*, she'd said. But it wasn't enough. Lou knew the cops didn't give two shits about her books, clothes, or music. Her rollerblades with the one cracked wheel or the drawings she'd done herself and stuck to the wall with Scotch tape. She could've stuffed all her things into her camo backpack or her Hello Kitty suitcase, and they'd never question where the shit went. But she'd wait until Saturday for those, the day she was allowed to take what little was left of her former life.

Aunt Lucy was left with the task of going through her parents' stuff and determining what should be sold and what should be boxed up for Lou.

Sell it all, Lou had told her.

Because it wasn't all her mother's worthless shit that she'd wanted. All the throw pillows and doilies and ceramic vases and china figurines.

She'd wanted her father's things.

And she knew that's what the cops wanted too, so she had to be first. She went into her parents' bedroom and froze. Blood stained the mattress, one side of the sheets had been stripped back to reveal the mattress and the stain spread in an oval on her mother's side of the bed. The cordless phone was still on the floor where her mother had dropped it. And a glass of wine, with a thin layer of dried wine coating the rim, lay on the carpet beside the phone.

Her mind kept trying to put the two together, the overturned wine glass and the blackish stain on the mattress. *She spilled her wine,* her mind said. A lot of *wine.*

She'd torn her eyes away from it and went into her father's closet. Not her mother's, which had been the walk-in on the left, but the one on the right. She pulled the brushed aluminum handle, and the door came open with a *pop,* the frame sticking in the heat of summer.

She stepped inside and closed the door. The world wavered, threatening to pitch her through, but she turned on the light, and it became steady again. Her father's dress shirts were organized by color, Courtney's doing. At first, Lou could only run her fingers along the sleeves and feel the different fabrics. Mostly cotton. Some of them the flannel he loved.

She reached her arms out and squeezed the shirts into a giant ball and cried. They smelled like him and her mother's detergent, and she would never smell it again.

She had no idea how long she stood in the closet, sobbing into her father's shirts. But she took the flannel, still had it, though it fell to her thigh when she wore it. And she had to roll the sleeves up above the elbow. In addition to the shirts, she took two other things. Cut-resistant Kevlar sleeves which had to be resized later, but she'd found someone to do it. And his adjustable vest. Her father had worn it at the biggest size, the straps stretched fully extended. She wore hers at the smallest, with the Velcro overlapping. Before she grew up and found a use for her father's vest, she would wear it on the nights she couldn't sleep. She'd put it on, tighten the straps, and crush it against her. It didn't fit, but it was something of his. A poor substitute for his arms around her.

Lou blinked back tears and the St. Louis skyline came into focus, locking on the searchlight from Busch Stadium. A distant roar of loudspeakers and cheers swelled. There was a game tonight. Some man in a red and white uniform was dreaming he'd hit it out of the park.

Lou stepped into the closet hoping for the same.

When she stepped out of the closet, she was on a rooftop in Austin. She crouched in the shadow of a bigger building, standing tall beside the one she squatted on. The buildings were right against one another. She leaned one arm against the sun-warmed brick and watched the downtown strip below. From here she could see the evening in full swing. Women in fish scale or leopard print skirts prowled the four-lane boulevard. Men in jeans or leather stalking them or possessively holding onto their hips in a display of dominance. Cigarette cherries burned in the darkness beneath the pulsing lights, and music blared through bar doors, mingling with the sound of honking horns and squealing brakes on the street.

She could see everything from up here. And she could thank King for the idea. When he asked her for a better view of their stalkers, she knew what he meant immediately. She preferred to slip laterally. She could put real distance between herself and her attackers. It was easier to track from underneath, following the sounds of footfall through floorboards overhead. She had gone high for a vantage point, an idea she credited to King.

But it seemed perfect for her current predicament.

If Konstantine was looking for her and Castle was alive and spouting tales of his escape, he would put men on the ground. She had no idea if Castle had had time to talk yet. He could be dead for all she knew.

But he wasn't.

She pulled the scope from the front pocket of her vest—her father's vest—and lifted it to her right eye.

The boulevard was blown up to movie screen proportions.

It took her a moment of sweeping the walkway to find Castle. He still wore the tall white hat with feathers, making him an easier target. Tonight he wore jeans, black cowboy boots with steel toe tips and a black vest. A leather choker with a large turquoise medallion lay against his throat and bobbed up and down as he laughed.

He stood on the corner outside a bar smoking a joint and chatting with three men and two women. He showed them something in his hand, weaving some long, bullshit tale about his exploits no doubt. Some female conquest or a close battle won. She'd shadowed enough bars to know how men spoke when they were together in large, hungry groups.

Castle's audience bent down to look at something close, and then suddenly, they jumped back. One of the women shrieked. Her friend beside her clutched her arm, laughing, but the laugh was hollow. Pure fear.

When one of the men looked aside, creating a gap in the circle, Lou saw his hands.

They were empty. It wasn't what he held that was the spectacle. It was the hand itself. Two fingers had been severed from Castle's left hand.

She adjusted the scope.

Thick black stitches knotted the skin together. The flesh was torn, puckering between the black twine. A home job. And the fingers hadn't been severed cleanly with a knife.

Had Konstantine ordered they be torn off? Brutal.

But the wound was fresh, no doubt, as Castle had had all ten fingers when she dumped him on the avenue the previous night.

So Konstantine moved fast.

She lowered the scope and tried to think. Why would they sever the fingers? To send a message? Because he was angry? Because he hadn't captured her himself?

Perhaps.

Yet if he'd wanted his dealers to capture her, he would kill Castle and send a stronger message. Give them a strong motivation to come out of this alive, should one of them find themselves at the wrong end of her gun.

No, he must've wanted something else.

Lou lifted the scope again and started searching the walk for tails.

It was hard to tell who might be following

Castle as he stood on the sidewalk showing his war wounds to his friends. The tails would only move when he moved. And if they were following him to find her, she had to be careful of her own movements.

If she moved when Castle moved, it would draw attention. Like prehistoric reptilian beasts, her movements would attract their eyes and bring her into sharp focus.

She would have to confine her actions to slips, sticking close to the shadows.

Castle's phone rang, and he fished it out of his back pocket with his good hand. He used his thumb to mash the button to take the call. After receiving some instruction, he returned his phone back to his pocket and nodded down the street. Castle wrapped the pinkish white gauze over his hand as he walked. He moved in her direction, his face hidden behind the large brim of his hat as he focused on his hand. His group kept him encircled in a cozy knot as they walked.

In the scope, she could see the blood splattered across the brim of his hat. A grim reminder a lot could happen in twenty-four hours. Castle had lost two fingers. A shiver ran up her spine. What would happen to her by the time the sun rose on the next day?

She kept her arm pressed to the side of the warm brick building. Unmoving, only her eyes tracked Castle down the sidewalk.

A group of drunks bumped into Castle's front line and another man shoved them off. The belligerent drunk's eyes going wide when a knife was pulled and pressed to his throat. The victim looked like a bleating goat from where Lou stood. His eyes wide and lips blubbering. But the man with the knife let him go, laughing.

Lou wanted to put her knife to his throat and see how he liked it. In her mind, she moved this mule to the top of her list beneath Castle. She killed Martinelli mules in order of importance. Who moved the most dope? Yank the biggest fish out of the sea, and the ecosystem collapses. She had to keep these objectives in mind. What would she do when Konstantine was dead? The listlessness would not overtake her a second time. And King's pathetic interest in witnesses would never be enough to stimulate her or put her skills to good use. No. Rank the mules. And perhaps she would have something worth doing once this was all over.

Movement caught her eye.

The moment Castle and his group walked

beneath an awning, a shadow emerged from the alley one block up. She marched up the street in platform heels the color of bubblegum and a black skirt barely covering her ass. Her breasts were falling out of the front of her denim shirt, which looked like an ordinary garment, though molested. The sleeves had been rolled up above the elbows. The bottom had been knotted above the navel rather than buttoned correctly.

She wobbled down the street on thin legs, a cigarette burning between her fingers.

When Castle stopped to smash out the butt of his cigarette, she stopped. She shot a look across the street and met eyes with a man leaning against a light post, pretending to look at his phone. His face was aglow in the light of the screen. He made a nod toward Castle, and the girl started teetering after them again.

At least two tails then. But Lou figured where there were two tails, there were more. A horrible thought bloomed in the back of her mind. She tore her eyes from the ground and looked up. She searched the windows and balconies of the buildings for eyes.

Her heart sped up as she counted. Two. Three. Five. *Seven* pair.

Two men sat on a balcony with beers balanced on their legs, the picture of casualness if not for the perfect synchronicity of their heads turning toward Castle. Three were watching from the windows of two different buildings as he passed. One leaned down and spoke into a phone.

Her heart pounded in her ears.

She'd walked right into a shark den and hadn't even realized it.

There were too many men on Castle. She'd greatly underestimated Konstantine's interest in her. She needed to get the fuck out of here.

She looked into the window directly across from hers at the man speaking into his phone. The room behind him was dark and his face as translucent as a ghost, reflecting the light from the boulevard below. He scanned the rooftops. His eyes two buildings to her left and moving in her direction, his head did a slow, dramatic turn that made her heart hammer even faster.

She shrank against the building and slipped through this side of darkness.

The world solidified again with her in her closet, heart pounding. She sucked in deep breaths and tried to steady herself. Had the scout seen her? Had someone else watched *her* while she was all doe-eyed over Castle?

"Fucking stupid!" she punched the inside of the closet. Anger rose inside her.

The fear never lasted in her experience. This old familiar hate would always draw itself up, its head opening like a cobra hood, flaring to life around her. Hate she understood.

Konstantine thought he was smarter than she was? Thought he could overwhelm her with his muscle and use her own tricks against her? Because Castle had been her trick. She'd cut the rat loose and sent him running, hoping it would lead her back to the den.

Instead, the wolves came out, looking for her.

If he dared to use her trick against her, she would repay him in kind. She could slip to him right now if she wanted. Fall right through the closet and pop up wherever the bastard was hiding and cut his fucking head off. *Hunt this!* she'd say as his slit throat gurgled blood all over her hands and forearms. *Here I am, you fucking cunt.*

Easy girl, her better judgment began. The leash on her anger tightened. Her father's voice echoed through her mind. *Stay with me, Lou-blue*.

The anger broke on the shore like a wave. Each wave that followed less angry than the one before.

She saw his beautiful face. Felt his scruffy beard under her small hands, remembered the way it would tickle her nose when he kissed her. How he would lift her whole body off the ground when he hugged her.

She hadn't had one of those great encompassing hugs in sixteen years.

Stay with me.

"I can't," she whispered in her dark closet. Her chest ached. "They sent you somewhere I can't go."

12

Are you sure this is the right finger bone?" King asked. He looked at the disconnected phalanges in his cupped palms and frowned. The plastic rolled in his palm as incomprehensible as the entrails of some gutted animal. "They aren't matching up."

Mel placed one hand on her hip and glared at him. Her voice rose. She'd reached the limit of her patience and no more questions were to be asked. "You have these bones in your own fingers, don't you? Can't you figure it out?"

Her lipstick was a dark purple today, the color of bruises or rotting meat. And every time he looked at her, his stomach turned. He kept his eyes on the mess in his hands.

"I've never seen the bones in my fingers," King countered. "Fortunately."

Why did assemble-yourself projects have to be so goddamn complicated? The only easy part had been the one-piece jaw, which snapped into place and hung from the base of the skull. Every other step in this endeavor was like pushing a boulder up an oil-slicked hill.

"This skull face is so awesome." Piper leaned forward and adjusted the hood on the skeleton. Every time she leaned toward the skeleton, the ladder beneath her wobbled and King's heart hitched.

His emotions warred. He was both furious she might touch the skeleton in a way that'd decimate his hard-earned progress, and simultaneously fearful she would fall off the rickety ladder and break her neck.

"Can't you be careful?" King snapped, uncomfortable with the tight whine of his voice.

Piper ignored him. "It's going to scare the bejeezus out of the customers."

"Are you sure that's what you want?" King asked, looking from the finger bones to Mel hopefully. "You don't want people to run screaming from the shop, do you?"

"I'm tellin' y'all. Spooky foo sells! Since I installed the door chime—"

"Mel, that isn't what spooky foo means," Piper interjected.

"—since *we* installed," King said, seizing the

ladder as it started to tip.

"Sales have gone up by 200%. This guy here is going make it even better."

"200%?" Piper snorted, righting herself. "So what? $50 this month?"

Mel cast her a sharp sideways glance. "Perhaps you haven't seen the full vision yet." The fortune teller reached behind the skeleton and flicked a switch on his back. "Piper, go on outside and then come back in."

Piper descended the ladder and King was grateful for a chance to let go. His arm ached from clutching its rails. A warm breeze followed Piper into the shop as she strolled in, and King became aware of the time. Morning was nearly over and he hadn't made any of the phone calls he'd intended to make on the Venetti case. But he'd promised Mel he would help her with this skeleton and he couldn't duck out before he'd finished, no matter how strongly the case file called to him from his coffee table upstairs.

A shriek blared through the shop and King fell back, dropping the ladder. It was as if someone had grabbed a cat and swung it overhead, helicopter style. No. *Five* cats howling in fear and fury as the skeleton's jaw dropped down low enough to accommodate an infant. The eyes burned bright red. Twin bulbs shone in their sockets.

King's body flushed with adrenaline. An immediate tremor seized his hands.

Then the sound ceased, the jaw closed, and the red lights dulled to a flat black.

For a moment, no one spoke.

"That's—" Piper searched for a word, eyes wide, one hand on her chest.

"Perfect!" Mel clapped her pale palms together.

"Shocking," Piper said, licking her lips. "Uh, what's the return policy on this thing again?"

"We're not returning it. We're going to move it closer to the door," Mel said, her face lit up with her excitement. She practically danced from foot to foot.

"Okay but you better add some good health insurance to my work benefits package. Every time this thing goes off, I'm sure I lose a decade of life. By the end of the week, I'll have gray hair."

King pointed at the gold Mardi Gras beads hanging from her neck. "Did you have those a moment ago?"

Piper grinned and wagged her eyebrows. "Nope. I just got them." She jabbed a thumb over her shoulder at the street beyond the windows as if this explained everything.

Mel's excitement dimmed. "Must I remind you that while you work for this establishment, you must maintain a respectable reputation? This isn't Bourbon Street."

Piper pursed her lips. "I know. I don't get paid enough to forget it. And haven't you ever heard of gender equality? Or I think your generation called it 'women's lib'? Bottom line: I'll show *what* I want, *when* I want."

King shoved one finger bone onto the peg of another, trying to arrange them from smallest to largest. This must have upset the skeleton because it emitted another toe-curling shriek.

Once Mel's shoulders dropped away from her ears she said. "It has a 60-day return policy. But we won't need to return it, because we're going to see sales skyrocket."

"Oh, so we're going to make $100 a day," Piper huffed. She rolled her eye. "Sounds magical."

King felt Mel go still beside him.

"Pippy, go to the back and see if we have anything that'll go with this."

"What goes with a plastic skeleton?" Piper snorted, twirling her newly earned beads between her fingers.

"Look around," Mel said. But King heard the

hard edge to her voice despite the simple instruction. And he thought it was no coincidence Mel wouldn't look at the girl as she spoke.

Piper disappeared down the aisles toward a door marked Employees Only to the left of the curtained nook where Mel dispensed fortunes.

"You all right?" King asked. He hoped he sounded nonchalant, but he didn't. As he shoved the stump of a hand onto its wrist, the force and irritation with his task bled through.

"God help me, I love that girl, but sometimes..." her voice trailed away. King thought she was finished, but Mel's voice came hot and fast on a fresh wave of anger. "I mean, does she think I'm *trying* to tank my business? Does she think I've got nothing better to do than let this place eat me out of house and home?"

"She's a kid," he said. "She doesn't realize what she's saying."

And this is my home too. Even though he'd only been in the city for a few months, it *was* home. He had a breakfast place which served buttermilk flapjacks and the best eggs hollandaise, with a thick yellow sauce he could mop up with a salty biscuit. He had his coffee place. They knew not only his name but to put four sugars and a creamer on the counter with every order. What would horrify Mel, he knew, was his first-name-basis with a few of the bartenders at local watering holes, and he knew what drinks they did best. Kevin made a smooth dirty martini. Hank was a master of whiskey sours. Gemma made an unbeatable gin and tonic.

And there were the places themselves. The quiet streetcar stops. The steps outside the aquarium and Spanish plaza, a quiet place perfect for an afternoon stroll-and-sit. And he could have a beer there too.

All of this on top of the place where he put his head every night and the balcony from which he said goodnight to the world.

"You could raise my rent," he said and gave her a nudge with his shoulder.

Mel stilled beside him. She considered the face of the skeleton with the same intense stare she gave young girls with their smooth palms in hers. What did she see in those black sockets? The dark glass of the unlit bulbs shining in the dim light around them.

"We're gonna be all right," she whispered to the boney man. "Life is all about cycles. Up and down. The tide in and out. We're down and out now, that's all. When I saw this broken shop, I knew I could make her fly. I believe it, Mr. King. After these ten years, for better or worse, I still believe it."

Her eyes were glistening and wet when she met his gaze again.

Hurricane Katrina swallowed up the city and spit her out the other side, and many of the shops and businesses in the French Quarter were damaged. Fresh from a divorce with money in her pocket after a hefty settlement, Mel bought the place on the cheap from a couple of northerners who had neither the interest nor the patience to deal with FEMA or the insurance company in order to rebuild. One breaking dam was enough for those New Englanders.

And King couldn't help but wonder if she'd seen something of herself in the boarded-up shop. Hollowed out, half-drowned in an ugly divorce and nowhere to go but up. She had to remake more than these four walls. She had to rebuild a life after thirty years with a man who drank too much Johnny Walker and couldn't tell a punching bag apart from a jaw bone.

"I'm going to have to let Piper go. At least for a while. I can cover her this week and next, but after—" Mel's voice hitched in her throat. She sucked in a deep breath through flaring nostrils. "It's gonna break her heart."

The muscles in King's chest tightened. "Don't

do that. What do you pay her? $10 an hour? Twenty hours a week?"

"There about."

"I'll cover her. I can get her to do some of the little jobs for my case." King's offer was out of his mouth before he could consider what he was saying. But he was right. He *could* cover her. Brasso had hired him as a freelancer to find the Venetti woman, and he'd added the open-ended plus *expenses clause*. Piper could be his *plus expenses*.

He wasn't sure how long he could draw out the case, but if he could ease Mel's financial burden for a while, he'd do it.

Mel's black hawk eyes narrowed and her lip curled. "Out of the cast iron and into the blaze!"

"Not dangerous work," he said, pretending to be wounded. "Photocopying. Googling. Maybe a few innocuous phone calls."

King hated making phone calls. He'd pay anyone to do that unpleasant task for him.

Mel worked her lower lip, chewing off a great deal of the purple lipstick. "She'll love it. Any excuse to be nosey as hell."

"I'll talk to her if you want," King asked with raised eyebrows. "Or she doesn't even have to know I'm paying."

"No, I'll talk to her," Mel said scratching at an elbow absent-mindedly. "You know she's here morning and night. Yesterday I gave her a shift from 10-2. So, I had enough time to run to the bank and pick up a shipment from the French market. Then at midnight when I was taking out the garbage, I caught her sitting on the curb across the street, smoking a cigarette and playing on her phone."

King didn't add anything to this. He wondered what Piper's home life was like. The girl lived with her mother, he knew, but this wasn't unheard of for a twenty-year-old. Young women came by the shop asking for her. Never boys, or men. Mel didn't mind, because sometimes they bought candles or incense. But the fact remained these girls weren't meeting Piper at *home*, or at least, he didn't think so. And King's nose told him there must be a reason.

The door banged open behind them, and their conversation ceased. Mel and King turned in unison, reluctantly pulling their gaze away from one another, and saw Piper's butt first. White jean shorts cut off mid-thigh and halfway through an almond-colored birthmark. Then the rest of her came up, and she straightened, smiling.

She wore oversized sunglasses, a feather boa the color of wine, and a red and yellow foam finger with Loyola Wolf Pack printed on it. She shook her hips in time with her pumping arm while humming the basketball team's entrance tune.

"How's this for our slender man?"

Mel's eyes met King's. "She's all yours."

13

The line was quiet.

"Well?" Konstantine urged. He tried not to let his desperation for answers seem too obvious. He feared it was too late for such caution.

"Nah, it's nothing," the lookout said at last. "The roof is empty."

Konstantine's disappointment fell like a weight against his shoulders. His phone beeped. The number was blocked, but he knew whose voice he would hear when he answered.

"Report to me in an hour," Konstantine said and terminated the call. Then he switched lines. "Hello?"

"Konstantine? Mr. Konstantine?" An American voice with an exaggerated drawl responded immediately. His name was like rocks in the man's mouth. Kon-stan-teee-nnna. Horrible. Who taught him how to speak?

"Yes? Who is this? How did you get this number?" Konstantine hoped his irritation was authentic. He was disappointed his crew had not spotted the girl, but he wasn't surprised. He knew what she was and how difficult it would be to snare her. He hoped the trap he was laying for this caller proved more fruitful.

"I've heard your name around, in certain company. I hear you are a man of many talents, Mr. Konstantine. I'm looking to employ those talents."

Good. The bait Julio had placed worked.

"I am a busy man," Konstantine said, soaking his words with indifference. He dragged his fingers across his forehead and thought of the stakeout happening on the Austin rooftops as he spoke. It was difficult to switch the mind from one task to another. "Please skip the flattery and tell me who you are and what you want."

The man laughed. "Direct! I can appreciate that."

He told Konstantine who he was and what he wanted.

Konstantine's heart was pounding by the time the man finished.

"Are you still there?" the man drawled. "Did I lose you?"

"I'm here," Konstantine managed to say. He'd broken into a sweat and his shirt stuck to the high back leather chair in which he sat.

"After Colorado legalized marijuana, we have five other states trying to push the same bill," the man said. He spoke as if Konstantine should find this news horrific. "We've got to curb this as fast as we can. And it will be beneficial for your own enterprise, won't it?"

"We do not deal in marijuana," he said, digging deep for calm. He'd wanted the man to take the bait and he'd taken it. *Don't fuck this up now.*

"They'll legalize marijuana now and cocaine tomorrow and heroin the day after. It will be a *disaster*. Did you know they have clean needle exchanges on the streets?"

Konstantine knew of the same policy in the EU. Mitigating the spread of blood borne pathogens was more important to health departments than keeping drugs off the street.

"Come here, on my dime of course, and get the information we need. Information is as good as gold to these men. If we have the right information, we can swing the votes. We can keep the system running the way we like it. I'll make it worth your time. I promise."

This man was willing to pay a gross sum to protect his larger investments and wealth.

Konstantine thought Americans fretted over their money the way one worries over their children. They had no idea how much they truly had—or didn't—or where the bottom of the barrel sat.

So much of the world suffered from this illness. These men believed their money made them powerful. Omnipotent.

They sit on mounds of money and wish for more. But money makes a man lazy. Unimaginative and limited. Those who do without are forced to be clever, forced to keep their claws and minds sharp.

He had money from Padre Leo and a name from his father. True. But he would not let it weaken him. He eyed a more valuable prize than an unending bank account—true freedom. True and limitless power.

And once he had Thorne's daughter, it would be his.

"I do not have to come to America in order to do what you ask," Konstantine said, wearily. "I can produce information on these men here."

Silence on the line.

"I prefer to work with men I know. Whom I've actually seen," the man said. His tone set the hairs on the back of Konstantine's neck to rising. "And you should come to Texas so you'll have a chance to see how your stateside affairs are working. I understand you have contacts right here in Texas."

Julio had done his job well.

"I do," Konstantine said cautiously.

"Perhaps they would benefit from direct attention."

And if I came to America, did this hacking job for you, then I would have a chance to look for her myself. I could come to her.

"If this price is right, I will come," Konstantine said. He imagined the moment of meeting her. In a dark club, seeing her at the bar watching him, measuring him the way she had measured Castle. Would she take him there? Kill him in this winter paradise Castle spoke of? Would he learn firsthand what happened to Angelo and the others?

He knew encountering a leopard in the wild was a death sentence. But he still sought her out, convinced that if she only heard him out, she would know the truth of his vision. Of his plans.

"Can you come tomorrow?" the man asked.

"No," Konstantine refused. Outright. On principle. He agreed to board a plane, a private jet sent by the man himself, in three days and then terminated the call.

Konstantine turned his cell phone off and sat

back against the headboard.

Again, he saw her. Tight black clothing hugging her firm body. The way she looked up at him through her lashes. The glint of metal pressed to his cheek.

He reached up and touched the small scar under his chin. It was rough, catching on his fingernail. It was an old wound. The skin puckered into a line where no hair grew.

He would never forget what she'd looked like that night, the moment she stepped out of his closet and pressed a knife to his throat. The way she'd made his heart race.

She wasn't more than nineteen or twenty and it had been at least a year since he'd seen her last. This was the first night she'd appeared to him awake, and not as a sleeping doll in his bed.

The sight of her body so close to his, the smell of her sweat and skin. It gave him an erection. Then and now. Already his hand was on the button of his pants, undoing them, slipping a slick palm beneath the waistband.

Blood thrummed between his legs as he saw her lying beside him. Her hair fanned over his pillow. Her cheeks flushed with color as her brows knit together against dark dreams.

"I want you," he whispered to the woman made of darkness, the woman unfurling in his mind. As if admitting it aloud, he could summon her across the distance. But she did not come when called.

He would see her again. He'd find a way.

Unlike the lazy and greedy American, he knew true power when he saw it. And what was worth having was worth waiting for.

14

Lou paced her apartment. She felt the weight of her father's vest in one hand. She opened and closed it, mashing the Velcro together only to rip it apart again. The angry tearing sound soothed her. It soothed her the way the smell of beer on a man's breath soothed her. Remnants of her father's life still alive in the world.

Once when she was a child, her father had taken her to the zoo. She hated it. The large-eyed lemurs, the great wildebeests, and even the capybaras looked depressed to her. All the animals, which had once been free in the world, now confined to cages.

One animal had cut her deep.

Inside an exhibit, a black panther paced back and forth in front of the glass. It looked utterly exposed and vulnerable in the bright sunlight. Its big eyes followed her from beyond the glass as it walked up and down in front of people.

As she watched her pace back and forth in her

cage, Lou had begun to cry.

She was grateful for the full sunlight of the day. Her sympathy for the animal was so great she would have slipped into the enclosure.

That night as she lay in bed, the only thing keeping her from visiting the beast was the fear she'd be eaten alive. And she was too small to move the animal back to the South American jungle and keep all her limbs attached to her body as well.

But her heart hurt no less.

Now, as she walked back and forth in her apartment, opening and closing the vest, she knew exactly how the panther had felt.

Prudence her mind whispered. She knew she was being hunted, and the way the hunted survived was by hunkering down until the hunter walked past, unaware. Then when his back was to her—*pounce*. That was the moment to sink one's teeth and crush the skull.

Threat eliminated.

Hide her inner wisdom counseled, the part of her that had saved her skin so many times in the past few months. Hide and emerge only to cover her tracks. Because that was another consideration. If this Konstantine were half as smart as his predecessor—because of course the other

Martinellis had tried to find her—he would try to learn of her identity. She had no driver's license or government ID. She did not vote. She had no medical or dental records to speak of, if only because hospitals scared her. Too much bright light and not nearly enough shadows to hide in.

She had no phone number and no friends. The apartment was in her aunt's name with her aunt's billing information. All her bills were paid for automatically from the trust established by her father before his death. The fact that her father had life insurance and a trust established the moment Louie was born, told her he had doubted he would see his daughter grow to adulthood.

This thought alone broke her heart—or it would have if she'd had much heart left.

With only minimal public documents, would he make the connection between the murder of Jack Thorne and his wife and their surviving daughter?

And that was the problem, wasn't it? She couldn't predict how much this Konstantine knew and how accessible she was to him. He had pictures but perhaps not a name.

She knew he would be heavily guarded, like his brothers. So the idea of jumping right into his dark bedroom some night and killing him was suicidal.

Maybe she could *see* him.

She looked up at the lit skyline and smiled. She laid her father's vest down gently on her bed. Then she ducked into her closet and closed the door.

Her body softened in the darkness. The thin veil between this side of the world and Konstantine's thinned even more. It began to give, sliding out from under her. Her hand shot out and touched the grainy wood of the closet's opposite wall. She held this space, keeping her body rooted in place.

She heard sounds. A car honked. A bicycle horn blared in response. A dog was barking, and the bells of a church began to chime. She counted the toll—seven. She quickly did the math. Not America then. He was somewhere in Europe, in an industrialized city with a church old enough that the hour was kept by bell tolls—which hardly narrowed it.

He could be in Sweden, Poland or Algeria. Italy seemed the most obvious guess, given what she knew about his family, but it was dangerous to make assumptions when working with such a man. Only one thing was for sure.

Wherever he was, the sun had already risen over the horizon, and the shadows would be thinning. Tracking him openly in the daylight would be more dangerous than overtaking him beneath the cover of night.

Of course, if he was a world away, it meant Lou had more room to breathe than she thought. There was an ocean between them. And while Castle might have been heavily guarded and maybe most of the dealers holding the Texan line were off limits, for now, the world was a big place. The list of dealers she wanted deported to La Loon was fifty. *At least.*

He had mules in Chicago, Orlando, New York. And it was only one o'clock in the morning.

She grinned and placed her other hand against the closet wall, relieved to find a reasonable way to burn off steam.

She could accomplish a lot before dawn.

At 1:07, she grabbed Yorkie Hankerton off Michigan Ave where he'd been trying to finalize the deal between two sex workers and a tourist from Albuquerque.

Yorkie, with his chest swelled up and a hairy navel protruding from beneath a tight shirt postulated like a gorilla at the zoo. His back grazed the giant reflective bean in the Millennium Park and his mirror image mimicked his movements, mocking him behind his back. A shadow from the enlarged bean stretched out behind him, darkening the walk. The girls stood ten yards away on the corner, smiling, giggling provocatively until the tourist pulled out his calfskin wallet and began counting out bills in the chilly Chicago night. He looked up, money ready, and found the pimp gone.

The tourist circled the bean twice, $300 still clutched in his hand, but Yorkie was gone. The girls were clever, though. Before the man had the good sense to put his money away and slink off into the night for easier prey, the girls descended on him. One took the money. The other looped her arm in his, and the trio shuffled toward the river. Only one of the girls looked over her shoulder with a frown on her face.

At 1:47, Anthony Bortello stood on a pier in Baltimore. He was shaking with cold. With a cigarette balanced between his lips, he waved an arm in the air in a grand sweeping gesture, much the way a bullfighter waved his red flag in the face of El Bullo. A man driving a forklift carefully slipped the forklift's prongs into the two-way pallet. With a clank, it lifted over three hundred kilos of cocaine off the loading dock. With a great *beep beep beep*, the machine reversed and the pallet was carried toward the warehouse, toward the light emitting from the raised door.

Anthony heard the whiz of the next forklift accelerating toward him. He took this moment to lean against an empty transport container and relight his cigarette. He barely felt the hand on his shoulder before the dock and machinery disappeared.

At 2:23, Hank Kennedy was busy beating his wife. He'd come home to a dirty house and no dinner. Instead of finding her working hard on putting things right, he'd found her in bed, pretending to sleep. He'd yanked her from the bed by her hair, still wet from a shower, and proceeded to slap her across the face until she awoke screaming. She hit him back, slapping wildly until she saw who it was.

He'd cracked two of her ribs with a swift kick to her side as she tried to crawl away. She braced herself for a second kick, but it didn't come.

When Janie Kennedy looked up, only a woman stood there, bending down with Janie's cell phone in her hand. She pressed it to Janie's ear, and held it until the woman took the phone.

Then the bedroom was empty again, the silence

pressing in on her.

"911," the voice in her ear said. "What is your emergency?"

At 4:11, Tyler Pinkerton was in the shower, scrubbing at his eyes and hair with the dry soap provided by the hotel. It was dark out, and it would still be by the time he reached the opium farm in Gostan. But the workers started at dawn, and he wanted to be there when they did and get a proper count and gross product projection. Rinsing the soap out of his hair and eyes, he optimistically figured he could have the numbers run by lunch and spend the rest of the night in a little bar he'd come to favor. The waitress had big tits and made a habit of pressing those breasts to his arm as she leaned across the table to collect his empty bottles.

It was a bonus they didn't water down his drinks like some of the other bars in the most touristy districts.

He was smiling when he stepped naked out of the shower, thinking about the hard nub of a nipple trailing across his forearm.

He stopped smiling when a young woman clad in black, blood smeared across her cheeks and caked under her nails, stepped into the bathroom with him. And turned off the lights.

Lou stepped out of the closet into the pink dawn light saturating her apartment. She was naked and dripping wet. *I should hang a towel in here*, she thought as she crossed the hall to her bathroom. She flipped the switch, flooding the small room with artificial light.

She preferred the dark, without question. But she was exhausted and didn't want to struggle to keep her body on this plane, in this room with no windows.

She turned on the shower and climbed into the cold stream even before the water heater had a chance to kick on. Her limbs were beginning to stiffen and she would have to rely on the heat to loosen the overworked cords of her flesh again.

She wasn't worried about evidence.

Her cleanup process was more thorough than any on Earth.

She took them whole and unharmed to La Loon. The beast disposed of the body. And then Lou stripped and returned naked. The Alaskan Lake, her entry point, was always freezing, but never more than a stone's throw from a shadow leading home.

No clothes to wash.

No bullets to test.

No blood splatters to examine.

No body or weapon to find.

It was perfect.

If a witness saw a brief glimpse of a woman, how would they find her? And even if they did, they'd find evidence she was also a thousand miles away on the same night. How would they reconcile this discrepancy?

Reason would seal tight the small gaps in her dealings. After all, she had been in New Orleans earlier. There were witnesses to this. How could she also have visited Chicago? New York? Afghanistan? *And* Baltimore?

Impossible.

With her hair wrapped in a towel, so as to not dampen her pillow, Lou fell into her bed beneath the window. The sunlight was orange now, the color of the sherbet coated ice-cream she'd loved as a child. Summers all heat, sunlight, and the taste of Creamsicles in her memory.

A memory surfaced from its depths.

Her mother was bitching about dinner, something Lou hated. Cranberry dressing? And she'd heard the front door open. She heard the rattling box even before he called out to her.

She ran to him and found him grinning ear to ear, a box of Creamsicles pressed between his two great palms.

"It's cranberry surprise for dinner," Lou had said, or something like it. She remembered how her stomach turned on itself greedily at the sight of her favorite treat.

Her father had wrinkled his nose in sympathy and handed her the box. He gave her his customary welcome hug and whispered in her ear, *clean your plate, and I'll let you eat two*.

He put her on her feet and pretended to lock up his lips with a key.

A whistle blasted for the 606 Eastbound train, dragging her to the present. A steam engine honked on the river. And Lou's heart wobbled with heartache in her loft above the pool.

She knew peace only with another man's blood on her hands.

15

Paula Venetti rented a room in the basement of a record store in San Diego. During the day, she worked at a drive-thru. Burgers, milkshakes, and fries with banana ketchup, fast food for the eco-conscious consumer who dabbled in animal rights activism.

She and King gained two hours slipping from New Orleans to San Diego, and found themselves beneath an enormous tree on the edge of a parking lot. The streetlights overhead flickered on, marking the end of twilight. The drive-thru was spotlighted by these street lamps and it gave the impression a show was about to start and they'd arrived just in time to see it.

"Vegan fast food," Lou mused aloud, nodding at the sign. "Lucy would love this."

King remembered the first time he'd taken Lucy on a date to a steakhouse and had been affronted when she'd only eaten a few iceberg leaves with olive oil. Before that, he'd never even heard the word *vegan*.

"There she is," Lou said, giving a slight nod toward a woman framed in the drive-thru window.

Venetti was handing over a basket of fries to a kid with dreads, one of his feet balanced on a skateboard as he asked for ketchup.

"So she *is* alive," King said, his stomach settling.

Venetti was younger than King expected, or at least she looked younger than the age listed on her testimony. Of course, these men liked to run with younger women, didn't they? So why should it matter that Venetti was thirty years younger than the senator who'd courted her?

They approached Venetti with casual strides. Her strawberry blond hair was tied up in a Rosie the Riveter handkerchief. A black Marilyn Monroe mole had been penciled onto her face near her upturned nose. Her eyes were coated in thick green eyeshadow which made King think of mermaid scales shimmering beneath the surface of an ocean tide.

"What'll it be?" the woman asked, a pen gripped in her fist. Her Texan accent was strong.

"The facon-bacon cheezeburger and almond-vanilla shake, please," Lou said.

King looked at her, surprised. "You eat this shit?"

Venetti looked up from the order pad and arched an eyebrow. She said nothing, as if waiting for King to dig his own grave.

"You don't grow up with a Buddhist yogi and not develop a taste for vegetarian food," Lou said. "And I'm hungry."

"It comes with fries," Venetti said. "You can upgrade to sweet potato fries for $1.00."

"Regular fries. Add avocado to the burger, too," Lou added. "Thanks."

"And for you?" Venetti arched her perfect eyebrow at King. The flannel shirt rolled up to her elbows was a faded yellow with brown stripes. "Any of this *shit* for you?"

Lou snorted.

"Fries," King said. His eyes were roving over her exposed skin, looking for bruises. He saw none. "I'd love an order of fries, thank you. And a Coke."

"Organic cola okay?"

Lou's grin widened. "Lucy would *love* this place."

King's voice caught in his throat. "The cola is fine."

Venetti scribbled something on the notepad, tore off the sheet, and then clipped it to a string overhead. The paper whirled out of sight, pulled down the line by some imaginary force.

"That'll be $16.92," she said, and King fished a twenty out of his worn leather billfold.

"I can bring it out to you," Venetti offered and pointed at a picnic table on the grass beside the parking lot.

King sat first and Lou took her place opposite him. She was scoping the area. King could tell. She was doing a good job of looking like she was doing nothing at all. But when she leaned down to scratch an ankle, her eyes swept the perimeter. When she stretched her arms and then rolled her neck, she managed a full 360. Her eyes gathered intel in quick, nearly imperceptible glances. If King hadn't been less than a foot from her, he'd have never noticed her do it.

"So are you going to eat your fries and *organic cola* or are you going to ask her some questions?" Lou taunted. The bulb overhead grew brighter as the world darkened.

"The place closes in twenty minutes," King said. He couldn't stop staring at her. She stared right back with flat, black shark eyes. "When she brings the food, we'll tell her our intentions and then hope she sticks around after her shift."

"Is that the official protocol for interviewing witnesses?" Lou asked.

King found it difficult to gauge her emotions. Her face was expressionless. No happiness. No sadness. A perfectly serene face. And her tone lacked proper inflection. No hints of interest or boredom. Fatigue or curiosity. What was he supposed to do with that?

All the charm and normal effusiveness she'd shown toward Venetti was gone. He didn't like how she could turn it on and off again. Apparently, she viewed emotion only as a tool, to wield when necessary.

He tried to remember if Courtney had been like that. Cold. Unreadable. If her voice came out in a perfect uninflected tone…yes. He thought she was.

"You're staring," Lou told him, in the same steady voice.

"Sorry," King said. "I'm trying to read your emotions. It isn't working."

He hoped his honesty would throw her off guard.

She didn't even blink.

"I did a lot of interrogations for the DEA, I'm

pretty good with body language but I'm getting nothing from you. Even the involuntary stuff, what a famed psychologist called mini expressions. I thought I caught some excitement earlier but it's gone."

"I'm excited about my bacon cheeseburger," she said. With about as much excitement as someone who says, "I'm getting a kidney out next week."

"That's a lie." King glanced over his shoulder to the drive-thru, making sure Venetti wasn't walking up on him this very second. "All of it. The bacon. The burger. The enjoyment. *Lies*."

"I'm beginning to see why Lucy dumped you," Lou said.

"I'll have you know I ate all the tofu she cooked without a single complaint," he said.

Lou arched an eyebrow.

"Maybe *one* complaint," he said.

Venetti appeared with a milkshake in a to-go cup.

"Can I get a straw?" Lou asked. The normal cadence had returned, as well as the apologetic smile women often softened their requests with.

"Sorry, no straws. We have to think about the sea turtles."

King forgot all about Lou's body language.

"Sea turtles?"

"Yeah, the sea turtles. All the straws we use end up in the ocean." Venetti reached inside the black apron tied around her waist and pulled out a picture. She flashed it at Lou first and then King. A sea turtle was swimming around the ocean with a drinking straw stuck out of its nose. When she turned the photo over, it was the turtle having the straw removed, blood streaming from its nostril. "So sad, right?"

"Tragic," Lou offered, and King thought he saw real anger flash there, but it was gone before he could be sure. "Hey, do you think we can ask you some questions?"

Lou smiled up at her. Venetti shrugged. "Sure."

Lou turned to King and waved a go-on gesture.

"Ms. Venetti, my name is Robbie, and this is my—"

"Partner," Lou offered.

"We want to talk to you about Greg Ryanson."

Venetti froze. All the muscles in her body appeared to stiffen to statue-like rigidity. Her eyes went from casual interest to round half-dollars, dilating with fear.

Lou reached up and placed one hand on the girl's forearm. "Easy there. We aren't the bad guys."

"You can't," Venetti said. She was looking around and was none too subtle about it. "You *can't.*"

"Can't what?" Lou asked. King saw the grip on Venetti's arm tighten. Not enough to cause real pain, but it was a good grip. Venetti wasn't going to cut and run, even if she wanted to.

"Did he find me?" Venetti asked again.

"No," Lou said, her voice low and steady. "And he won't because we found you first."

"Have you gone to the police?" King asked, sitting up taller.

"I tried. I wanted to be a witness. For Ashley and Daminga…they deserved better." She fell silent, probably as the memories of Ryanson began to surface. Then she said, "but the police are on *his* side."

"Why do you say that?" King prompted gently. He'd pulled a thin pad from his pocket and had a pen in his hand. He was ready to collect any golden nuggets falling out of this woman's mouth.

"I was halfway through the interview when I realized I was fucked. I was talking to a spy. I don't know why I should be surprised. He owns everything."

A spy.

"But how did you know?" King asked, his hand still hovering above the notepad. Thoughts swirled and collided in his mind, but nothing cohesive yet. He'd need a minute to put the words on the page properly.

"Look at you!" Venetti said. She jabbed a finger at King and his little pad. King began to pull back reflexively. If she didn't like the pen and paper, he would hide it. He'd simply memorize what she said and make notes later. He'd done it before. No amount of nodding or soft smiles reassured the naturally paranoid. "You're writing down what I'm saying."

"I haven't—" King began.

But Venetti shook her head. "The man who interviewed me didn't write down anything. And he kept telling me to lower my voice. And when he said he needed to call his superior to get the okay to proceed, I watched him dial the number. It was *Ryanson's* number. I should know because I've memorized it. His and my mother's in case I ever got into trouble but didn't have my cell phone on me. Fucking pathetic, I know, but it's true."

"You ran," Lou said.

"Why do you think I'm here?" she asked. She waved at the fast food joint behind her. "I asked myself, where is the last place Greg would look for me? Last place in the *world*? A vegan fast food place in San Diego sounded about right."

"Good choice," Lou agreed. Her eyes were checking the dark around them again. Venetti didn't seem to notice.

"Right?" Paula said with a casual wave. "I didn't even know what the word vegan meant. I had to look it up."

"What did he look like?" King asked. *Who was the rat?*

"Medium height. Average weight. Dark hair and eyes."

Damn, King thought. *That was half the force, at least.*

"When I came to the station, a man asked me my business and I told them I wanted to report a murder. They were helpful until I said Ryanson's name. Then I was sent straight to the DEA detective. He wouldn't even give his name. What kind of detective or cop or whatever he was, won't give a name? Everyone else gave me their name."

"You sensed their involvement," Lou said, chiming in again at the right moment and it was good one of them was focused on the momentum of the conversation because King was drowning.

Ryanson owned the DEA? And the local police department?

"It was smart to run," Lou said. She didn't look away from Venetti as if she knew doing so would break the trance and send the girl running again.

Venetti nodded. "I wasn't going to be another dead bitch at the bottom of the bay."

King could see Lou's interest was apparently piqued. "Does he kill a lot of girls in Houston and dump their bodies in the ocean?"

Venetti laughed, a hard cough-like sound. "Who knows how many of those bodies have been swept out into the Gulf of Mexico by now."

King saw a gleam in Lou's eyes. If he didn't find a way to reinsert himself into this conversation and take control of it, Lou might slip off and kill the senator before he'd had any chance to gather a single piece of evidence that'd be admissible in court.

He could hear himself saying *sorry, Chaz. But I took care of it. Or rather my new pet mercenary took care of it.*

"Yeah, he's a real piece of work." Venetti wrapped her arms around herself. "The fucked-up part was I really liked him, you know? Most of the girls were only interested in his money or the drugs. And we all thought he was handsome. But I thought he was sweet. How messed up is that?"

Lou gave him a sharp glare which King could read perfectly. *Any time you want to jump in, Mr. Detective.*

But he couldn't get over the idea a senator owned an entire police department and at least one DEA contact. There were always snitches, of course. But this was different. The infection was spread far and wide or Venetti was unlucky enough to have found the one corrupt cop.

He didn't think so.

The girl was talking again. "He was rich. He was gorgeous. He had this classy vibe going on that none of my exes had. And he liked to give gifts. Even when he was mad, he never hit me or anything. He was always ready to party. He made me feel like the only thing that mattered to him was that I had a good time."

"Until he tried to blow out your brains and dump your body in the bay."

"Pammy, order up!" A boy called from the window. It broke the spell. Venetti blinked several times and then went to the window for the two baskets. One with a bacon cheeseburger and fries and the other fries only. She went back a second time for a bottle of organic ketchup.

"How did you find me?" Venetti asked. She seemed to remember who she was and why she had run.

"We're not with Ryanson," King answered, finding himself on familiar ground again. He'd spoken to witnesses on the run before, and this fear was always the same. That if they could be found once, they could be found again. Therefore, it was time to go. "We're trying to build a case against him. We want to prosecute."

"Prosecute," she repeated the word. "That's the word they used in the station when I told them what happened. "The spy had asked, *do you want to prosecute?*"

"Do you?" Lou asked, taking a huge bite of her burger.

"What happened to Ashley was—bad. I'd want someone to do the right thing if it was me. But I don't see how dying is going to make it any better. Men like that always walk. The men with money and power—I'll never see the inside of a courtroom. They'll kill me first. My only choice is to keep running if I want to live."

"No." Lou's voice was a mountain. Insurmountable.

"If you know where I am then…"

"He doesn't know," Lou said. "Even if he found out, he can't get to you faster than I can."

Venetti turned to Lou then. She stared down at her, mouth hanging open. *Catching flies,* his mother had called it.

King was looking at Lou too.

"No offense, lady," Venetti said. "But you're crazy. You can't be faster. Nothing travels faster than money."

"Do you want to get out of here before ten or what?" the boy called from the drive-thru window after a couple in their Subaru drove off with their evening meal.

"I've got to help close up," Venetti said. "Stick around and I'll tell you what I know. But I can't testify."

They watched Venetti disappear back inside the squat, tangerine building.

"Twenty bucks says she runs," King said, chasing a handful of fries with his soda. It was flat, and the sweetness was off. But the fries were good. Of course, it would be hard to fuck up fries.

They ate in silence. King thought of his Plan B. He would take Venetti's statement. He'd get all the details he could on Ryanson and his wrong doing, and then he'd look for another girl. One who would testify against the senator. It might take them longer, but they could build the case.

But that isn't what Chaz is paying you for, a little voice said. *Chaz wants you to bring Venetti back. You're hooked, Robbie Boy. Better detach now or you're going to choke on this lure.*

When the boy stepped out at 9:45 and locked the door, Venetti crossed the parking lot toward them. Before she even reached the table, Lou was up on her feet, gesturing toward her, beckoning Venetti to follow her around the side of the building.

King started to rise, but Lou held up a hand in a halting gesture.

"We'll be right back," Lou said, her eyes were dark water in the light of the streetlamp, her skin a soft tangerine color. "Finish your drink."

They stepped behind the building, which was a soft gray in the colorless light now. The two women were out of his range of vision, and he didn't like it. But he'd learned long ago the best way to gain trust was to give it. Lucy had begged him to let Lou learn how to work a legitimate case, and he knew unless he wanted to buy a plane ticket back to New Orleans, he had only one way home tonight.

He'd reached across the table and begun to finish off Lou's fries when the two girls reappeared.

Lou's face was hard, unreadable. Courtney's cold glare firmly in place.

Venetti, however, was grinning, eyes wide and her hair blown back like a kid who's just exited the most exciting rollercoaster. Venetti rushed over to King and placed both hands on the picnic table, slapping them down like a player tagging home base.

"I'll do it! I'll testify." Her ecstasy was palpable and her words rushed out of her in one breathy exclamation. "What do you want to know?"

16

In the back room of the corner market where King liked to buy his late-night sushi rolls and vinegar chips, Lou and King stepped out from behind a crate of 7-UP bottles. Without a word, the pair opened the back door quietly and slid into the vacant alley, closing the door to the market behind them. On this side of the door, the exit was a smooth metal slab without a handle, looking more like the sort of steel plate one would hammer into their head rather than seal an entrance.

King placed one hand over his rioting belly and placed a forearm against the brick alleyway. He'd never get over the 90-foot-drop feeling. When he was sure he could speak he said, "You gave her your *phone number*. I don't even have your phone number."

"It's not a phone number." Lou turned over her wrist and pointed the black face of a wristwatch at King. She clicked a button and the hour changed. A world clock, he realized. Displaying her time via GPS, in military time. After another click, a bright green ZERO appeared on the screen. "No messages. If I have one, it will buzz. Then I go. Depending on the time of day or my situation, response time varies. But it isn't registered or traceable like a phone."

"How the hell did you get it?" he asked. He thought this question was better than: *who the hell would page you?*

"Aunt Lucy. I refused a phone and she wanted a way to call on me, in the event she couldn't..." she searched for the word. "Reach me any other way. I think she got it from Germany. It has a global SIM card."

"I want the number," King said, remembering the business card she'd given Venetti. "In case, I need to page you too."

Lou forked one over. He let go of the brick wall for support and accepted it with two fingers.

It was a slip of cardstock. Cream with black numbers. No name, only the 11-digit call number, including country code.

King frowned at the plain scrap of paper. "You're displaying a shocking amount of organization for the rough brute your aunt told me about. Rogue gunslinger. A vigilante with *business* cards. And you handled Venetti as if you'd interviewed a hundred girls before."

Lou's gaze slid away. She wasn't uncomfortable. She was searching the area again. King knew there was nothing he could say that would make this woman squirm.

"You weren't talking," she said when her eyes met his again. "We were there to ask her questions, and you kept shoveling fries in your mouth."

He barked a surprised laugh. "I was assessing the situation. And preparing my attack."

"She'd be packed and halfway to Sacramento by the time you stuffed the cannons, Captain."

"You milked her like a cow." He couldn't let it go. She was proving impossible to read and he didn't like it. "How did you learn to do that?"

He could read anybody. *Anybody.* All he needed was one meeting and a serious conversation. But trying to get a handle on Lou was like trying to hold water. The tighter he squeezed, the quicker she slid through his fingers.

"I did not milk her." Lou wrinkled her nose. "I don't waste time. Mine or anyone else's."

"Is that a personal code?" he asked, wondering if she'd written herself a manifesto somewhere, perhaps tacked up in her apartment.

"One I wish everyone subscribed to," she said. She was looking bored again and at least that part King had gotten right, because she stepped away from him and started walking. He had to jog a little to catch up.

They came around the corner and a wall of warm summer heat hit them the same moment as the bright French Quarter lights fell on their face and shoulders. They faced Madame Melandra's Fortune and Fixes. Lou didn't go inside.

She feels safer in the dark, he realized. Even the soft glow of Mel's chandelier and the flicker of candle flames in the window were too much. Thick shadowed alleys and obscured doorways were as comfortable as worn chairs with their coffee stains and ass cheek imprints to her. His eyes slid over the sidewalks of the crowded quarter. At this hour, it was in full swing. A lot of noise. A lot of bodies. But Lou didn't seem to mind.

"You took an unnecessary risk," he said. He lingered on the curb with her so she would not be forced to go in. "The fewer people who know about your talents, the better."

"She'll keep my secret," Lou said, letting her eyes wander down the street.

"How can you be sure?"

"Because she wants to live. And if she was the kind of girl who liked to talk, she'd be dead now."

King couldn't argue there. Talkers ended up dead sooner rather than later. Of course, he could think of one exception to this. Brasso's mouth ran like a steam engine, and yet he was as free as a wildebeest.

Lou flicked her gaze up to meet his. "Do you care what happens to her once you're done with her?"

He flinched as if slapped. Her black water eyes held the twin flames of the streetlight overhead. Her dark hair was haloed with a ring of gold. "I don't *want* her to die."

"Hmmm."

"Don't you believe some people should be protected?"

"Yes," she said. "Truly defenseless people. People who are preyed upon by the weak bastards looking to extort or abuse them. Capable people can save themselves. There are enough of the first in the world, why waste my time on the second?"

Certainly no hero complex, he thinks.

"Is that what you want to do now that the Martinellis are gone?" he asked. "Will you use your abilities to save the *truly defenseless*?" He used air quotes.

Her eyes bore into his. The gaze so heavy it made the hair on the back of his neck rise. For a moment, a crazy moment where his front mind clicked off and his reptilian brain slithered into the driver's seat, he nearly pulled his gun. He *wanted* to pull his gun. Maybe the air quotes were a bad idea.

She hadn't moved.

Her expression hadn't changed, and yet the overpowering sense of danger welled inside him.

Her voice was shockingly soft when she spoke. "I have to go. Your landlady is giving me the finger."

King turned to look into the shop and found Mel standing there in full gypsy garb, her braids pleated over each shoulder. She wasn't flashing the middle finger salute. She was making the sign of the cross, touching each bare shoulder then her forehead.

King turned back, ready to offer reassurances, serve as Mel's character witness, but he was alone on the sidewalk.

Lou was gone.

Mel's arm brushed his. "Who are you looking for Mr. King?"

"A girl," he said. "But I think you scared her off."

"That was no girl," Mel said and reached into the folds of her skirts. She pulled out a pack of Camels and lit one with her Bic. She dragged hard on the filter and then blew the smoke out of her nose, reminding King of those cartoon bulls he watched on Saturday mornings as a kid. "She was the angel of death."

The angel of death.

He didn't even argue.

His adrenaline had spiked under Lou's cold stare and now it crashed. His stomach hollowed out. His head buzzed between his ears.

He was starting to think he'd like to smoke a joint before he called Brasso and told him about Venetti. But maybe the call should wait until tomorrow altogether. Or even, the day after.

If he was too quick in his turnaround, Brasso might wonder how he managed to track a girl to the West Coast so damn fast. Finding Venetti and getting to San Diego should take some time for an old man with no leads.

And there was Paula's testimony itself. King wanted to chew on it for a moment.

"What are you playing at, Mr. King?" Mel arched an eyebrow and inhaled a second time.

An excellent question.

What *was* he doing? He wasn't an agent anymore. He wasn't even a private investigator. In Louisiana, he needed a license. His DEA experience would qualify him, and what knowledge he might lack in regulations he could easily acquire in a certification course offered by the Louisiana State Board of Private Investigator Examiners.

But he wasn't certified and he hadn't considered it before Brasso showed up with this case. Could he even call it a case? He was looking for a missing person. Was he a liaison then? That too required documents and clearance through special channels.

What are you playing at?

"I've taken up a hobby," he said at last. "I hear it is very important to keep yourself active once you retire, lest you die of boredom."

At least that was the truth, in part. Something about Brasso's request had sparked him. He was awake, engaged with the world in a way he hadn't been for the months since he'd left the bureau and headed south like a snowbird.

King often envisioned his mind as a police station. Rows of desks and men—all looking like King himself—working furiously. Each one processing a part of his task or problem.

Right now, one considered how to talk to

Brasso.

Another formed a list of all the reasons he couldn't simply turn Venetti over to his old partner.

He wasn't a search dog that could be put away once it'd found the cocaine hidden in a suitcase. He had Venetti, but he didn't have answers. He didn't have *closure*.

A third King-helpful voiced his concerns for Mel and Piper. What he was doing was dangerous. He'd known it the second the two men tried to tail him.

A fourth from an imaginary desk in his mind called out, *but what about paying the girl? If you cut this case short, how will you compensate her? How will you pick up the slack for Mel?* The longer King worked on the case, the more expenses he'd accrue. The more expenses the larger the burden he could carry on his landlady's behalf.

And it wasn't safe to turn over Venetti now. *He owns them*, she'd said. If he had Lou pack the girl up and send her to Brasso, she could very well find herself in the bottom of the bay after all.

All of this was his mind avoiding the biggest question of all.

Lou.

The angel of death.

He swam to the surface of his thoughts and caught Mel watching him through the haze of her cigarette smoke. Her lips pursed around the filter.

"Come on. Don't look at me like that, Mel. This is another source of income. We can hang a sign from the balcony, Robert King's Detective Agency. You can charge me commercial property rent, if you like. Steady income. Isn't that what you were hoping for?"

Mel dropped the spent cigarette and stamped it out with a fierce twist of her boot. "Hope is a demon, Mr. King. And don't you forget it."

17

Konstantine opened his suitcase on his bed and unpacked a stack of dress shirts. Then he removed the row of dress pants all the same shade of midnight. And in the third row, his underwear, socks, gray silk pajama bottoms and two pairs of sweatpants. He considered the contents for a moment, wondering if he should put them in the dresser provided by the hotel, or if it was better to leave his suitcase packed, in the event he had to leave immediately.

His computer pinged. He went to the desk and opened the chat program.

"Konstantine," he said, hoping there was no hint of the eagerness straining his muscles in his voice.

"Hey boss, it's me, Julio."

"Go on."

"We checked the surveillance for the club and think we found your girl. I'm sending you the pic."

Konstantine's heart sped up. "Sure." *Sure* was

casual enough. Neither eager nor indifferent, but ice slid down his spine. It was sheer force of will that kept him from shuddering.

Julio was one of Padre Leo's most trusted servants, and was recommended by the benevolent father himself.

The chat box pinged again, registering a receipt of the image Julio had sent. Konstantine waited for the rainbow wheel to stop turning and the fully downloaded image to appear.

A black and white photo popped up on the screen.

"Down in the left corner there's a woman by the bar," Julio went on though his face was hidden behind the expanded photo. "You can't tell, but she's looking in Castle's direction. And when he goes to the bathroom so does she."

He hadn't needed Julio to point her out to him. He'd spotted her immediately. The remarkable exactness between his imagination and reality made the hairs rise on the back of his neck. Her hair was shorter now, only shoulder length. A short ponytail pulled all the hair from her face. He imagined sliding a finger beneath the black elastic, and plucking the band out of her hair. The hair would fall across her thin, feline throat. It was so small he was sure he could wrap his entire hand around it.

He was sixteen when he first saw her.

He had killed his first man a week before and had barely slept. Instead, he'd toss for hours and when that failed to settle him, he would quietly leave the apartment and walk the city streets until exhaustion won at last. When he left, he left a note. He had not wanted his mother to get up in the night, see him gone, and worry.

It had been his mother's only stipulation. *At night he will be home in his bed, Padre Leo. You cannot imagine the terror a mother feels when the night grows long, and she doesn't know where her child is.* So Padre sent him home at sunset each day.

He ate dinner with her. He kissed his mother goodnight. And when her gentle snoring rumbled from the adjacent bedroom, he would be gone again, knowing Padre would have a job for him if he wanted it.

The night he saw Castle's huntress for the first time, he was also sleepless. He'd been lying on his back, reading a spy novel in bed, one hand under his head. His mother's snores caught up to him at the end of the next chapter. Then he was up, shoving his feet into his Adidas sneakers with their white diagonal stripes—nice, beautiful shoes. A gift from

Padre Leo. What better recruitment tool than a well-dressed boy? What kid didn't want the *cool* American clothes and expensive Swiss watches? All his boys were dressed to the nines.

He'd adjusted the waistband on his track pants and had turned to look for a T-shirt to pull down over his head.

And there she was.

A girl. In his bed. Thick dark hair fell over her cheeks and face in delicate strands. It cascaded nearly to her waist. Her arms and legs glowed in the moonlight coming from his high windows. Her lips were parted, split like a cherry. She was the most beautiful creature he'd ever seen.

His thighs pressed to the side of the bed, and he peered down at her. He was half certain she was a trick of the light. Somehow the moon had met his rumpled bed sheets and created this magic.

But her brow knit, and her hand kept opening and closing on her chest. The small movements of a living creature. Not a moonlight illusion.

He watched her, barely breathing until it struck him this was the way his mother slept. Fitfully, until she woke with a scream.

He reached out to touch her pale cheek. As soon as his fingertips brushed her warm flesh, the girl shot up in bed. A sharp intake of breath passed her lips. Her wide eyes searched his room.

He stepped back. He held up his hands in apologetic reassurance.

She squeezed his sheets to her chest as if she was undressed beneath it and Konstantine had been the one to intrude upon *her*.

It's okay, he said first in Italian, the language he used with his mother. When her brow creased deeper, he said it again in English.

He took a step toward her, and the moment he did, she rolled right off his bed onto the floor. The sheet went with her, pulled right off the bed—except it kept going. Something about it reminded Konstantine of a magician's trick with silk scarves and a hat.

He ran around the bed to the other side, expecting to help the surprised girl off the floor.

Only there was no girl on the floor. The girl and his bed sheet had both disappeared.

All that was left was a thick patch of shadow between his mattress and the closet.

Konstantine understood this about her. Especially now with his father and brothers dead, he understood she traveled by the dark. Somehow, she rode the darkness like a passenger train. And though she had appeared in his bed only four or five more times when he was young, he never woke her again. He learned his mistake there. If she woke, she ran. But if he was still and quiet, then he could watch her sleep. He could lie beside her, breath held until she winked out again. Enjoying her scent. Her warmth and how it radiated off her like the fire in Padre Leo's office. Sometimes she spoke in her sleep. Once she cried for her father, bright wet tears sliding from the corners of her closed eyes and onto his pillows.

"So it is your girl?" Julio asked.

"Yes," he said and realized he hadn't blinked since seeing the image. "Any other sign of her?"

Julio paused. "Not on camera."

Konstantine reluctantly closed the image so he could see the man's face. "What do you mean?"

Julio worked his lower jaw as he mustered the courage to give his boss the bad news. Konstantine waited, more out of fear for what might be said than patience.

"She was busy last night," Julio said finally. He slapped the back of his neck, crushing a mosquito. A smear of blood dragged across the man's neck when he pulled his hand away. "I've had reports coming in all day. We're missing a lot of mules."

Konstantine wet his lips and steadied his voice before speaking. "How many?"

"Nine," Julio said. "So far."

Nine.

She was angry. Obviously. The question was why. What had he done to piss her off?

"What do you want me to do, boss?" Julio asked. He'd begun chewing on the meat of his thumb.

Konstantine's appreciation for Julio swelled. He'd executed the task of finding the girl flawlessly. And now he wanted another job. The man's work ethic was admirable.

"Kill Castle," Konstantine said. "We don't need him."

Julio nodded as if he expected this. "And the girl?"

"Track her movements, if you can. But make no move against her. I will deal with her myself."

"When do you arrive?" Julio asked, his spatulate fingernails scratching at the blood drying on his neck.

"I'm already here."

18

Melandra turned over the first tarot card, the reversed Queen of Pentacles. A woman in dire financial straits. She rolled her eyes heavenward and cursed the spread forming on the glass jewelry case.

"Tell me something I don't know," she murmured to the worn deck in her hand.

She looked up and surveyed her empty shop. It was late afternoon, and the sunlight slanted along the topmost shelves as it prepared to dip behind the buildings. It was warm, collecting the heat from the June day between its walls.

The virtuoso was back, busking on the adjacent corner, and her song drifted through the open door along with the warm air. At least she'd gotten better, Mel thought. When the girl had begun to play on the corner six months ago, each note screeched like a cat with its tail caught in the door.

She hadn't had a single customer all day.

It was true magic shops had more appeal in the

nighttime hours, when people found it easier to believe in ghosts and voodoo and all that lay in-between. But she could usually count on *at least* a *few* tourists to stream in during the day. Coming or going from the gumbo shop down the street. Or sugared up on beignets from the square. Foot traffic was good in the quarter, and she had an exorbitant mortgage to prove it.

She kept doing the math in her head. She counted the purchasing customers needed to keep her shop afloat. How many palm readings? How many past life regressions? How many tarot readings? Or maybe someone would want a picture of their aura. She hadn't done one of those in a while.

If five people come in and buy one thing... but this was where her mind split. Would they buy the mix and match incense sticks? Ten for one dollar. It wasn't enough to pay the electric bill. *But let's say they bought a candle, ranging from $5.99 to $9.99...in that case I'd have to sell...*

Why do I do this to myself?

Calculations for sales that aren't happening is one way to drive yourself mad, she thought.

She was half mad already, she knew.

Here she was.

Alone on a gorgeous afternoon, reading her own fortune because there was no one else to peddle the truth to.

Oh that's not all, and you know it, she chastised herself. This was no mere reading out of boredom. She'd been itching to turn over the cards ever since that woman came to see King.

The ex-girlfriend, Lucy, was sick. That much Mel knew. As soon as she'd shaken the woman's damp hand, she'd known it. And whatever she had wouldn't be fixed by juju beads or a gris gris bag. Maybe Grandmamie could have taken the sick demon out of her, but Mel couldn't.

She didn't have that kind of power.

She thought of Grandmamie. They'd called her a faith healer in their little town outside Baton Rouge. A Priestess. The Mother or sometimes Mamie Blue Jeans because no matter how hot it got down in the bayou, Grandmamie wore blue jeans.

Mel could see her in her mind, her saggy breasts lying on a great round belly and balloon arms on either side as she raised a sweating glass of sweet tea to her lips.

"Mmm hmm," she said to the thickening twilight.

"Uhhh huhhh *what?*" Mel had asked, a stick

creature with dirt splotches head to toe.

"Can't you feel it, girl?"

Mel had looked out from their porch into the growing dark. The trees were crowded against one another, and the smallest of spaces between them were black as a cottonmouth's back. But she didn't *feel* anything. She heard the chickens cooing in the grass and the squirrels yammering in the trees. And a jay screeching off somewhere. She smelled the beans on the stove. She could taste the licorice in her mouth.

But no *feelings* of any kind.

"Change is in the air," Grandmamie said and turned to her. She smiled at her through the round spectacles sitting halfway down the bridge of her nose. "You got to learn how to feel change a'coming, girl. It don't do you no good to be numb to it."

Change came as a decree from the governor buying their land so they could run a highway through it.

Change is a'coming, girl.

"I know it," Mel said in her quiet shop because she'd done as Grandmamie had asked. She'd learned all right. And now she felt all kinds of things she wondered if she had any right to be feeling at all.

She flipped the second card and lay it perpendicular across the first. *This is what crosses me.* The five of wands glared up at her. A war party in full swing. Staffs slammed against one another and faces contorted in hate. Conflict. War.

"Because that's what I need," she sighed.

She flipped the third card, the crowning position, meant to tell her the atmosphere of what was unfolding.

Death. A hooded skeleton with a scythe grinned its bone white grin at her.

This was Grandmamie's deck, or it had been a long time ago. And she had a faith in these old worn cards that she didn't have for any others. She sold cards in the shop. Glossy, unbent pieces of commercial trash, most of it. Sometimes a deck arrived and Mel would get a feeling when she turned the pack over in her hand. Sometimes she'd put one of those decks aside for herself. But not even those decks compared to the one she'd inherited on her nineteenth birthday, two weeks before Grandmamie died.

So she believed in the power of her grandmother's cards, but that didn't mean she had to like what they said.

She put the cards down and rubbed her

forehead. "If you ain't got nothing nice to say, I best stop right there."

Before she could push away from the glass case holding protective amulets, the breeze rustled the deck. The black cards with gold trim fluttered, and an unmistakable pull centered in her chest. She looked down at the cards, expectantly.

She waited.

Mamie Blue Jeans had taught her more than how to feel change.

She'd taught her to listen.

She'd taught her how to treat snake bites and read clouds as well as bones. She'd learned a spider taking down its web meant rain was on its way.

So when the breeze flipped over the Tower card, she didn't dismiss it as coincidence.

Unlike Mr. King, Melandra was a believer.

She placed the Tower as the center piece and then flipped the next several cards, rounding out the spread. Longing. Danger. A secret. Lies revealed. Disease. And a man, face down with seven swords protruding from his bleeding back. Betrayal.

The swords gave her pause. It was the suit she associated with Mr. King. The King of Swords being he himself, the other cards from ace to ten, his journey.

She pressed the fingers of her right hand to the Death card and the two fingers of her left hand to her forehead. She closed her eyes.

First only darkness. Bland and flat. Then the darkness swirled like water, gained dimension, and a woman, pale as moonlight, surfaced. Her name— Louise. No. That wasn't quite right, but close.

Mel pushed deeper, following Louise into the water. Men dropped like offerings at her feet. A mound of bodies, broken and bleeding. Blood on her hands, up to the elbows. Smeared across her mouth and cheeks. She was eating…Mel pushed harder and saw…a heart. Louise held a heart in her hand and was eating it. And when she was done, she danced on their bodies, danced like the death goddess Kali on what little remained of them.

Mel let go of the card and crossed herself. "Holy mother of god."

"Holy mother what?" Piper said. She stopped short of the glass jewelry case and plopped her backpack beside the register. Her brow scrunched up. "Whoa, Mel, are you okay? You look like you saw the devil."

Piper leaned over the glass jewelry case and peered at the cards.

"Oh," she said, frowning at the cards. "Not the

devil. The *Tower*. And a dude getting stabbed in the back."

"Seven of Swords," Mel managed to say around her tight throat. She swore she could taste blood.

"And that means…" Piper began. She tapped the side of her head, a pensive gesture. "Wait. I've got this. The swords are about thoughts. Brain stuff. Seven is delivery. Arrival. So the arrival of brain stuff."

She didn't wait for Mel to correct her. She powered on to the next card.

"And the tower…" her voice trailed off as her face screwed up in concentration.

Mel gazed down at the tower silhouetted against a stormy sky. Noted the body twisted and falling through the darkness. "The end of life as we know it."

19

King sat on the balcony overlooking Royal Street. The ferns waved in a gentle breeze. The sweat on the back of his neck chilled and offered some relief from the heat of the day.

Sometimes when the heat was too much, his apartment felt too small. He had to open all the apartment windows and let in the breeze. And if that wasn't enough to loosen the crushing hold the walls had on his heart, he went out onto the balcony. The sunlight, the people, the elevation, and open space—that usually did it. With a melting glass of Mel's sweet tea balanced on his knee, he felt more than fine.

King reviewed his notes.

He reviewed everything Paula Venetti had given them, which amounted to five and a half pages in his tight script on his yellow legal pad. It was quite a haul.

As Venetti told it, on a warm night in late

September, she witnessed the murder of Daminga Brown. She also assumes a third girl on the boat that night, Ashley DeWitt, was also dead.

Or worse.

He was getting ahead of himself.

King took a deep breath and put down the glass of tea.

He settled back in his chair and laced his fingers over his belly. He closed his eyes and reconstructed the scene Venetti had given them.

He replayed it step by step, slowly. He wanted to see what questions arose. What needed clarification. He wanted to turn this puzzle over in his mind and see its shape clearly.

And doing so began with this step by step reimagining.

He saw Venetti stepping out of the shower and into her closet, selecting a tight red dress. He imagined how the thin material must have cupped the curve of her ass. Watched her remove a blue dolphin ecstasy pill from a cigarette case and dissolve it on her tongue. He spared no details. The water droplets dripping from the end of her hair as she combed it out. The floral design of the cigarette case.

It was pure imagination, based only on the

details the girl had provided, but it was incredibly effective in helping his mind see what the witness may have missed.

She was feeling better than good by the time Ryanson's private car turned up at her apartment. A silver luxury car, the lights reflected in the polished exterior.

Two other girls were already in the back seat, drinking and rubbing their bodies against Ryanson's. Venetti didn't mind. It was hard to mind anything when you were on X. She joined right in and started nibbling the red lipstick off the closest pair of lips, bucked against the hand slipping under her dress.

The group traveled twenty minutes from the Baybrook Mall area down I-45 to Tiki Island where Ryanson had his Rizzardi CR 50 docked and ready for their arrival.

They all got on the boat—Ryanson, two guards and three girls—joining a captain already on board. Seven in total. The captain took them out on the water until the lights of the city were like pinpricks on the horizon. Far enough away the music and loud voices wouldn't disturb other seafarers. Ryanson kept the cocaine and alcohol flowing. The captain, a gold-toothed man with a crow and crossbones tattoo, slapped Venetti's ass when she leaned over the rail with a bout of nausea. She wanted to slap him. Instead, she smiled.

There was only one rule on this boat: no matter what, everyone had a good time.

Venetti sucked in the fresh salty air, trying to steady herself. When she opened her eyes, she saw a light burning in the darkness. Not in the direction of shore, but in the direction of the unbroken horizon. She stared harder, trying to comprehend the floating orb bobbing in the night.

"What is that?" Venetti pointed at the light, and the captain left his hand on her ass as he peered around her to see for himself.

His hand fell away. "Sir? There's another boat."

Venetti could see it now that it was close enough to fall into the light of their own vessel. The boat was smaller but still beautiful. Venetti didn't have a better description. *I don't know boats.*

King didn't know boats either, but for this exercise, he imagined a sleek speed boat with wooden side board. It didn't matter if this was accurate. King was more interested in the men who'd boarded.

They had matching tattoos. It was some kind of animal and a flag.

Five men got off the other boat and came onto Ryanson's. King did the math in his mind.

Now we have twelve people who know what happened that night.

As soon as they stepped on to the boat, I knew we were in trouble. Ryanson's mood had changed when the fifth man boarded. He was wearing a pinstriped suit and hat.

Before anyone spoke the captain pulled a gun. One of the men put a bullet between the captain's eyes. The girls started screaming, a natural reaction to seeing brains spill across the deck of a boat, and the men turned those guns on the girls.

If you don't want to die, you better sit down and shut your fucking mouths.

All three women sat down on the padded cushions of the bench and shut their mouths.

Ryanson was pistol whipped straight away, as if to set the tone for the interrogation that was to follow. *Where is it? Tell me where it is. If you don't tell me where it is, I'm going to put a bullet in her head.*

Venetti looked away. The violence only made her nausea worse. When she could bear to open her eyes, she saw a scuba tank hanging on a hook beside her. She knew the tank would be heavy because she'd dived with Ryanson before. And she wasn't sure she could grab it and a buoyancy compensator before someone put a bullet in her head. But a little farther away hung a scuba tank with an *attached* BC.

I'm ashamed to admit it but I knew Ashley or Daminga would be shot, if I jumped overboard. But I didn't care. I wanted off the fucking boat.

Where the fuck is it, Ryanson?

Ryanson didn't answer, and Daminga's brains were splashed along the Rizzardi's deck.

The warm spray of blood and bone matter on Venetti's own feet made a scream boil in the back of her throat. But somehow she'd managed to swallow it down, until Ashley bolted. She was up and trying to throw herself into the water.

Two laughing men pulled her back into the boat. All eyes on her like predators attracted to movement. Venetti saw this as her only chance to escape. She leapt up, grabbed the tank with its attached BC, and rolled over the rail of the yacht.

A bullet grazed her shoulder, and the cut ignited in the salt water. White hot pain bit into the flesh of her upper arm.

With the tank, she dropped like a stone. She tried to equalize the pressure on her way down, but her limbs were sluggish from pain and fear. Then, at last, she managed to find the BC's release button in the dark water.

She stopped sinking and began to swim.

She held her breath for as long as she could, already swimming underwater toward the direction of the shore. When her lungs were about to burst, she took sparing sips of air from the regulator. She had no idea how much oxygen she had, because she couldn't read the air gauge so deep in the dark, nor see how far she was from shore. So she sipped and swam until she thought she was going to die.

She never thought she would make it, swooping her arms out in front of her in the pitch-black dark. She couldn't be entirely sure she was moving at all. She was certain sharks would get to her long before she reached shore. Her bleeding arm would attract them, and everyone knew they fed at night. And if not some underwater monster, then a bullet to the back of the head would finish her. But nothing took a bite out of her. No bullets came.

She surfaced and saw the lights of a distant pier. She finally made it to the pier and pulled herself out of the water, collapsing on the planks with shaking arms. Her whole body shook. She didn't dare check Ryanson's stall on the marina's far dock to see if he returned. She went straight to the marina's entrance and hailed a taxi. She cut in front of a line of patrons leaving a restaurant and commandeered the first cab.

People shouted. She didn't care. The driver took one look at her and didn't seem to care either. He pulled away without even asking her where she wanted to go until they were on the interstate.

Venetti didn't go home. Her body hurt. She was cold and wet. But she wasn't stupid.

She went to Merry Maids, a housecleaning business on the north side of the city. She convinced one of the housekeepers to enter her apartment and pack up her essentials—some clothes, jewelry, toiletries and a stash of cash all packed inside a pink backpack. The maid hid them in her cleaning cart.

Venetti hoped this act would avoid suspicion, since Merry Maids entered her apartment once a week anyway. They would only be entering the apartment two days early and they could be doing it for any number of reasons.

Before noon, she was on a bus from Houston to San Diego without looking back. She'd chosen San Diego at random from a travel guide. She'd been inside a bookstore café, eating a sandwich and an orange juice. She bought the bus ticket next door. Next thing she knew, she was in San Diego with a rented room and a job.

Venetti had done more than recount the traumatic event which sent her running for the West Coast. She gave them details about Ryanson's habits and connections, everything she could think of.

For all her faults, King thought as he surveyed the massive amount of information scribbled on his pad, *she's a good witness.* This was more than he would have been able to wring out of most witnesses.

Of course, he would have to do some fact-checking on dates and times to see if the girl's memory was as reliable as it was detailed. He also had his doubts that all the details were precise, given Venetti's own admission to drug and alcohol use.

But if Venetti's memory was half right, they had a lot to go on. And they had other leads. Ashley DeWitt for one. If she was alive, Lou would find her and they would have a second witness to interview. If it didn't pan out, they had the boat at Tiki Island. It could be swept for evidence. King knew the bodies were long gone, but it was hard to remove all evidence of a murder unless the murder was performed in a certain environment.

He wondered how Lou had managed to be so thorough in her own cleanups.

On second thought, he wasn't sure he wanted to

know.

King hoped DeWitt *was* alive. It was the men King was interested in and she would have spent the most time with them. He could set Piper on the task of researching the animal and flag tattoo. Who were they, and what was their interest in Ryanson?

Who was Ryanson working with and to what end? Either Ryanson was involved in a turf war or made a shady deal with a gang.

It was clear Ryanson hadn't been killed. His pretty-boy face was all over the news, as he was the face for Don't Legalize Marijuana in his party. So despite the hardballing from the pimp in the pinstripe suit, as King had come to call him in his mind, he'd survived the night Daminga Brown had not—how? With promises? Was a deal struck? How many pies did Ryanson have his thumbs in?

The fire escape rattled as someone from the street started to ascend.

King leaned over the railing fingers twitching above his gun. Piper was climbing up the ladder. He relaxed with a muttered curse under his breath. Less than two days on the job and he was jumping and starting like a rookie.

"Shouldn't you be opening the shop?" he grumbled.

"Mel sent me up. She said she's pimping me out to you." She paused on the ladder and looked up at him. "Is that right?"

"Yeah, come on up," King shuffled his papers in a way so that nothing important could be read at a glance. Then in a wave of paranoia, he turned the notebook over so only the cardboard backing of the legal pad showed and placed his cell phone on top, to pin it in place.

Piper appeared, clutching her side, chest heaving. "Whew! I think I deserve a Snickers bar. I'm so athletic!"

King arched an eyebrow. "You're too young to be out of shape."

"Not all of us have exciting jobs chasing bad guys. I pay my bills by stuffing candles into bags and sweeping glitter off the floor."

King remembered the glittered raver and grinned. "I knew he'd pissed you off."

She scratched the back of her head and then shrugged. "It's fine. I get it. Sometimes you've got to sparkle. So what bitch work do you have for me?"

"Do you have a problem helping an old man?"

"You're not old."

King compressed his lips. Of course, he seemed old to someone who was barely old enough to buy alcohol.

"Is Mel going to fire me? Is this like a *He's Just Not That into You* hint? She's been talking about that book a lot lately."

King tapped his pen on the folder. "She doesn't want to fire you."

"Yeah, but she might have to. It's been dead around here. And not the kind of dead that sells."

King gave a weak half smile. "Business is slow. It'll pick up."

Piper snorted. She pulled up a chair and plopped into it. "Man, you suck at lying. And I thought you already had help. I saw you walking around the Quarter with a girl the other night. Dark hair. All black clothes. She kind of has this strut."

King stopped tapping his pen. "Lou?"

"*Lou!*" Piper shook in her seat. "That's her name? Oh god, it's *cute*."

"What about her?"

"Is she your girlfriend?"

King snorted. "I'm not a cradle robber."

"She's an adult. It's not cradle robbing."

"You know, some men actually see women as partners, not sex dolls."

Piper widened her eyes in mock surprise. "I had *no* idea. So, if she's not *your* girlfriend, does that mean she's someone else's girlfriend?"

King burst into a grin and tilted his head. "Are you milking me for info?"

The grin was accompanied by red cheeks. "*Maybe*."

King crossed his ankle over his knee, not speaking.

"Don't set us up or anything!" Piper said, her face burning brighter. "I'm perfectly capable of orchestrating my own *accidental* introduction. I'm trying to get a sense of her availability."

"What if she doesn't like girls?" King asked. He bit back, *sorry kid, but I don't think she likes anyone.*

"Who cares! All the girls I slept with in high school were 'straight.'" She used air quotes. "And I get this very ambivalent vibe from her." Piper made a so-so gesture with her hand. "I don't think she cares about a person's gender." Her face lit up. "Maybe she's pansexual! I've never met one of those. It's kind of fascinating."

"Do you think you can help me with my investigation, or will you be distracted by the brunette with a gun?"

Piper sat up straighter. "She has a gun? On my god, that's *so* hot."

King wrangled Piper's attention long enough to

give her two tasks, both research-based, and a $50 bill for any expenses. "I don't want you to use your computer."

Piper waved the fifty between her fingers. "Paranoid much?"

"Paranoid is my default setting."

"Don't get killed and stuffed into a trash bag. Got it." Piper leaned forward. "Okay, but about *Lou*. Has she said anything useful?"

"Useful? Of course. She's very capable."

"Favorite food? Television show? Favorite color? It's probably black, which isn't technically a color. It's a shade, but let's overlook that for now."

King could feel a headache building behind his eyes. "We don't talk about colors."

Piper frowned. "What do you talk about?"

"Dead people, mostly."

Piper rubbed her chin. "Maybe a ghost tour then. It's half-off if you go during the day."

"She doesn't come out in the day. Pretend you're trying to woo a vampire."

Piper nodded thoughtfully, completely missing the joke in King's voice. "Well, the tours run until midnight."

"Piper," King said, rubbing his forehead. "When do you think you'll have this information for me?"

Piper's embarrassed grin returned. "Not sure. I've never researched street gangs before. While I'm gone, feel free to put in a good word if you have the chance. Play up my best qualities."

"Maybe Lou isn't interested in someone with *qualities*. She's interested in someone with a special skill set."

Piper paused at the top of the fire escape. She grinned. "Even better."

King listened to her descend the steps, the rattle of the latch and the slow squeaking groan as the ladder lifted and returned to its resting position.

The skeleton shrieked and ghosts howled as Piper reentered Madame Melandra's Fortunes and Fixes below.

Now to buy more time.

King picked up his cell phone and dialed a number jotted at the top of the yellow legal pad.

His old partner Chaz Brasso answered on the third ring. "Brasso."

"We found Venetti and verified her testimony," King said.

"You found her? Honest to god?" Brasso said. "Where the hell was she holed up?"

"San Diego. In a vegan fast food restaurant of

all places."

"There can't be many of those," Chaz said. "That was a quick trip! Did you fly out there?"

King's stomach turned, but the lie came easily. "Yeah. I'm still here actually. I won't get back until tomorrow morning."

There was silence on the line.

Then Chaz said. "So what did she say?"

20

Lou stepped into King's apartment and found herself staring at two wet ass cheeks. Not the smooth sculpted muscle one could find in the Louvre, which she wandered sometimes. But dimpled and hairy flesh.

As soon as she saw the naked man toweling his hair and whistling a tune to himself, Lou stepped right back into dark corner from where she'd entered the apartment, and disappeared again. This time, she emerged on the balcony outside the window and rapt a fist against the glass.

"King?" she called through the cracks.

"Just a minute!" She heard his muttered curse and the sound of bone knocking on something. He clipped his elbow on the sink maybe. Or his toe on the side of the toilet. He was too large for that bathroom. His knees must sit against his chest when he shits.

Loud footsteps rumbled through the apartment,

the glass windows trembling as he darted past the windows into the bedroom.

"Hold on!" he called again as if she'd given him any indication to hurry. She leaned against the balcony and scanned the streets below. The man who'd been following King, and she was certain he *was* following King, was on the street corner. He sucked on a cigarette, the cherry burning orange with his inhalation. A large hat hid his face.

She'd already pointed these men out to King. She wouldn't do it again. Hell, maybe King would get himself killed and she could stop this charade. Her aunt would be sad, sure, but Lou would have fodder for any future attempts at rehabilitation. *Because it went so well last time*, she would say, and that'd be the end of it.

The balcony door creaked open and King appeared, hair still dripping. "All right, come on in."

Lou squeezed past him into the apartment. He was in jeans but bare-chested. A gold chain hung in the nest of his chest hair, and his feet were bare. It was always strange to see men barefooted. And he had old man feet. Toenails gnarled and yellow. He pulled a white polo shirt down over his head.

"Thanks for knocking," he said with a tight smile. "You would've gotten more than you paid for if you hadn't."

"No problem." She let her gaze glide along the apartment's interior and the brick façade of one wall. The steam had rolled out of the shower and now hung in the air reminding her of European bars where smoking was still allowed.

Her hair began to curl at the nape of her neck and temples from the humidity. The smell of his musky shampoo or soap permeated the whole apartment. A male scent like cologne. The way it had smelled when her father had bathed.

There was also something fried and meaty, perhaps chicken, that'd been microwaved within the last hour.

King continued to ruffle his hair with the white towel. "Let me run a comb through this and we'll check on Ashley DeWitt."

"If she's alive."

"Yeah about that," King said throwing the towel over one shoulder. "Explain how it works."

Lou arched an eyebrow. "Well, if the air is going in and out and she has a pulse—"

"No, your, what did you call it? Compass? Has it ever led you to the wrong person?"

"That's why we'll begin with, '*Hello. Are you Ashley DeWitt?*'"

"You don't want to talk about your compass, I take it?"

The muscles in Lou's back stiffened. "No."

She didn't want to talk about waiting in darkness. How she could clear her mind and hear what was on the other side. Or car horns. Or church bells. She didn't want to talk about the way she felt pulled, like her legs were in a great river, and all she had to do was let go and be swept away with its current to some unfathomable shore.

Because the conversation would do two things. First, it would give King the very inaccurate belief that he had any right to her business. Aunt Lucy's approval or not, she didn't know this man. Lou had assessed that King was benign, mostly. But he was a man with mental issues and a gun. That wasn't the kind of friend she needed. Secondly, such a conversation would inevitably lead to where she'd gone and hadn't wanted to. La Loon, without question. But there'd been other times and places as well. And Lou didn't like to think about her compass as an intelligence of its own. Doing so forced her to consider an uncomfortable truth: she wasn't as in control of her ability as she wanted to be.

As a child, this was apparent. Every slip was accidental and seemingly unprovoked.

As an adult, she'd convinced herself she'd grown into it. *She* chose her locations and moved where she wanted.

But she knew a lie when she heard it.

"Do you close your eyes, click your heels and *badda boom?*" King asked. Obviously, he'd missed her subtle clues to drop it. "Do you need a picture or object or—"

Her jaw tightened. "It's not hocus-pocus."

He frowned. "I wasn't trying to insult you. I'm curious. How do you navigate?"

Her unease grew. There was something about having a question she'd asked herself said aloud to her.

"If it's some big secret," King said, looking slightly hurt. "Then forget I asked."

You don't owe him anything the cruel voice inside said. *Tell him to mind his own damn business.* "I don't know what to tell you." Her voice sounded cold even to herself. Never a good sign.

King arched his brow. "You don't know?"

"Can you ride a bicycle without knowing how you can do it?"

"Hogwash. Everyone can ride a bike. Not everyone can do what you do."

"Tell that to an amputee without arms and legs."

King shut his mouth.

"You might understand there's balance involved and the pedals have to be moving. Otherwise, it's more practice and instinct than anything else. This is no different." She felt stupid suddenly and that sent her itching to pull her gun. Fuck people and their questions. What did she look like? Their schoolmarm? If he didn't understand why the sun was orange instead of some other color, why should she have to explain why she could do the impossible?

She turned away from him.

"But is it like—"

"Ask Lucy how she slips," she said. *She'll have more patience.*

"You call it slipping."

"Yeah," she said, breath softer now.

"Why?"

"Jesus Christ, you're like a five-year-old tonight. Why? Why? *Why?*"

Lou considered slipping King to the top of the empire state building and then letting him drop. That would shut him up. She already felt hemmed in by Konstantine's hunt. She didn't need to feel hounded by someone's curiosity on top of it.

"Did you ever end up somewhere you didn't

want to go?" he asked, tugging at his shirt.

Oh, look. He'd reached the question on his own anyway. "You know the answer."

"Your dad didn't talk about your disappearance much, but I read the report." King stopped in front of her, buttoning the top of his shirt. "That's how I met Lucy."

Lou stopped imagining his demise. "You met her when I disappeared?"

"About two days after you came back, Thorne—your father—asked me to hunt her down. I did."

Lou heard her father's voice in her mind. She heard his sharp intake of breath as he lifted her and threw her into the pool before drawing the gunfire away from her. Asking her if she wanted to spend time with Lucy was only a courtesy. He'd already decided for her.

King pointed at the glistening scar tissue encircling her upper arm, visibly protruding from the edge of her sleeveless black shirt. The scars were faded now. Time did that to every wound, no matter how bloody.

She hoped.

"What took a bite out of you?" he asked as he slipped on his boots.

"I call him Jabbers. Or her. I haven't tried to lift its skirt to verify gender."

King snorted. "You named the thing that took a bite out of you. What was it? A wolf? Did you end up in the Michigan wilderness or something?"

"No," she said. She refrained from defending the wolves. Healthy wolves didn't attack humans. That was a misconception. Her heart hitched, and she stepped toward the window.

"I didn't mean to pry."

"Yes, you did." She didn't turn around.

He didn't argue. Instead, he said, "The night isn't getting any younger, and neither am I. Let's go."

Lou searched the room for a deep pocket of shadow. In the corner stood a television armoire weighing no less than two hundred pounds. It was ancient and was probably in the apartment long before King ever showed up. Otherwise, she had no idea how anyone got it up here.

A diagonal shadow stretched from the side of the dresser across the wall, thickest in the corner.

"Turn off the lamp," she said. And when King did, her hand was already on his arm, pulling him toward the armoire.

She paused a moment beside the armoire and

listened. Pressing her ear to the ground and listening, feeling the vibrations through her body like a snake.

Silence. Absolute silence.

"What's wrong?" King asked.

Instead of answering, she pulled him through the thin membrane with her.

The first thing to catch Lou's attention was the swelling cacophony of sound. Crickets rubbing their legs together and frogs belting songs from their bloated throats.

The moon was full and bright, eerie light stretched across an overgrown field.

Lou took a step forward, still holding King's elbow, and her boots disturbed soft earth. A dirt floor. No. Dirt. They stepped from the doorway of a...what? Barn? A building of some kind. She closed her eyes counted to five and then opened them again, allowing her pupils to dilate and adjust to the light.

Then she caught the smell. Soft hay. Earth. Animal piss.

Horse stables.

A paddock stood empty a few yards away. They'd entered from the corner of the dark barn, standing in an empty field. The dilapidated barn barely stood. Boards jutted in all directions like crooked teeth. The stalls were empty, their doors slung wide. Hungry black mouths hanging open, waiting to be filled. And an unlatched door swinging slightly in the breeze was like a tongue lolling in the mouth. Begging for its thirst to be quenched.

"Where the hell is this?" King asked softly. He stepped away from her into the moonlight washing the land. A field stretched in all directions, interrupted only by trees as a border. "Have you ever been wrong?"

"No," Lou said, anger rising in her chest. "She's here."

She closed her eyes and listened. A pull formed down her right arm, and she turned in that direction. Leaving her eyes closed, she followed the pull. She let it lead her. A sharper right and then a throbbing from her belly.

Then the smell hit her.

She opened her eyes. She stood in one of the stalls. Half of the stall was clotted with broken boards from the exterior wall having fallen in. The rest of the soft earth was covered in a mound of sweet hay. More white moonlight filtered through the broken boards, painting the hay silver.

"Shit," King said behind her.

She swept her boot over the hay, pushing

clumps to the left and right, inching closer and closer to the floor with each pass. Then her boot hit something hard. This time, it wasn't only hay turned over by the swish of her foot. A white bone revealed itself, its glow preternatural in the moonlight.

"So she didn't end up in the bay. But why would they bring her here?" Lou asked, bile burned in her throat. But these bones had been picked clean. Given the teeth marked on the bone itself, Lou guessed animals did the job for the killers.

"Where's here?" King asked.

"I don't know." Lou toed the bone with her foot. *It's the radius or the ulna*, she thought. She had no desire to uncover the rest of Ashley DeWitt to confirm this, or even to lean in for a closer look.

King left the barn, stepping back into the open night, raising his cell phone toward the sky. The bright blue screen blazed in the darkness.

"You probably won't get a signal out here," she said.

"Oklahoma," he said. He lowered the phone and pressed a series of buttons. It clicked, the recognizable sound of a screenshot being snapped. He waved it at her. "So maybe they killed her on the boat, and instead of dumping her in the bay, they drove her north and dumped her here."

"Or they didn't kill her on the boat," Lou offered. "Maybe she ran to Oklahoma, and they caught up." A darker thought surfaced. "Or they killed her on the boat but couldn't dump her right away."

King shrugged. "If she ran, there must be someone here. In Oklahoma, I mean. Parents. Grandparents. A sibling. Someone worth running to. And maybe said person heard an interesting story in the hours before she was killed. We should find out and talk to them."

"Or they're dead too," Lou said, stepping out of the stable. "I wouldn't have left the family alive if I thought she had talked."

King stared at her. "Any chance you can find Daminga's body? We might find usable evidence."

Lou closed her eyes and strained. But the needle spun and spun. Nothing.

"I think she's in the bay." And Lou couldn't slip into the middle of ocean.

A cold wind blew through the sagging building, and a chill ran up Lou's spine. She didn't like this place. She wasn't sure what it was. Not the corpse. But something. And she knew better than to question it. Her instincts about places were never wrong.

Lou reached out and grabbed King. One

sidestep into an adjacent stable, one with its rear wall still intact, and then they were in his apartment again, standing in his bathroom. The toilet pressed against the back of Lou's leg.

"That was abrupt," he said. He frowned at her. "We could have gotten pictures. Taken notes. I could have swept the barn for evidence. Tire tracks. Fibers. Anything."

"It wasn't safe to stay there," Lou said. "I need to go."

What she hadn't said was, *or run the risk of stranding you there*.

Standing in the darkness, she could feel her compass whirling. Had the barn been unsafe, or was it the pull of something greater that had triggered her?

Threaded tendrils of nervousness tugged on her arms and legs, whispering into her dark heart there was another place she needed to be. Another place she had to go.

She knew this feeling and recognized its meaning. And with understanding, the heartbeat in her chest began to thump unevenly, as if straining under the pressure of wanting to be in two places at once.

"Yeah, okay. I can do the rest alone," King said.

He shifted his weight. "Hey, are you okay?"

She didn't answer him. She gave herself over to the current and was gone.

21

When Lou woke, something was wrong. The light streaming from the high windows was purple. The sun was dipping low behind the trees, its last eye open on the horizon. Under her pillow, her fingers curled around her gun and found the metal warm from the feathers incubating it throughout the day.

She heard a noise again. A small sound jerked her upright, gun pointed.

"Two for two." Lucy placed a sandwich wrapped in glossy newsprint on the counter and stuck her hand into the brown paper bag again. She gave Lou a half-smile from the kitchen island as she peeled back the wrapper. "One of these days you're going to blow my head off and save me the trouble of worrying about you."

"Stop creeping up on me." Lou lowered the gun. The smell of red onions flooded the studio. Her stomach rumbled its response. When was the last time she'd eaten? She wasn't sure. Sometimes when she was working, she'd forget to eat. The task distracted her. It was only when she worried her weak limbs or unclear head would cost her that she bothered to make time for the inconvenient task.

The burger, she remembered. She'd eaten a burger at the vegan fast food place about twenty hours ago.

"What are you doing here?" Lou asked.

"Can't a loving aunt bring her niece a veggie loaf sandwich when she wants to? I got your favorite. Extra avocado, extra oil, and extra oregano. Come eat with me."

Lou thumbed the safety back on and disentangled her limbs from the bedding.

"Don't you get hot sleeping by the window?" Aunt Lucy asked. She nodded at a barstool by the island where she'd spread the sandwich on its wrapper.

Lou slid onto it, placing her gun on the counter beside the wrapper. It clanked heavy against the granite surface. "It's the best light in the apartment. I don't have to worry about waking up in Bangkok."

Aunt Lucy popped open a bag of chips and dumped them onto the paper spread beneath Lou's sandwich. BBQ. Her favorite. But Aunt Lucy was frowning. "Do you still slip in your sleep?"

"No," Lou said, stuffing three chips into her mouth at the same time. The oils began melting the moment they hit her tongue. The muscles in her back loosened. "Because I sleep by the window, in full daylight."

Her aunt plucked a chip off her spread and made a pensive sound. "I thought that was something you'd outgrow. I did."

"We've already established I'm different."

Lucy squeezed her elbow. "Different in the most charming ways, my love."

Lou arched an eyebrow.

"What did you really come for?" Lou knew the food was her aunt's way of disarming her. After all, if someone shows up with a pint of ice cream or a pan of tiramisu, it's hard not to welcome them with open arms.

Lucy put a chip into her mouth and said, "How is it going with Robert?"

"*Robert?*" Lou laughed, charmed by her aunt's growing blush. "I've been calling him King. Aren't cops last-name-only?"

Lucy gave a curt nod, conceding the point. "You're right. Your father went by Thorne."

Her heart fluttered at the mention of her father. Somewhere in her stomach a snake coiled tighter.

She could feel his scruffy cheeks against hers. The sound of his boots hitting the floor when he came home.

Lucy's voice yanked her back to the present. "What does he have you doing?"

Lou spoke around a mouthful of sandwich and wondered if they were moving toward the reason for this visit, or away from it. "Witness protection. We are making sure this woman's ex-boyfriend doesn't find her until she can testify."

Lou had to convince King that partial truth was better than an elaborate story. Lucy's bullshit meter was razor sharp. Always had been. Lying to her was fruitless and only got her into deeper shit. King seemed rather horrified by this truth.

The crinkles in Aunt Lucy's forehead relaxed. "Do you enjoy it? Or is this too boring for you?"

Lou sensed the trap in the question. If she claimed to *love* working with King, Lucy would be suspicious why. If she said she hated it, Lucy would also expect an explanation. And it wasn't just the lengthy discussion Lou was avoiding. It was the concern. Her aunt's worry turned her stomach and made her feel guilty. She could put down ten men in one night and not feel the guilt she felt when confronted with Lucy's stricken face.

Lou settled on, "I'm giving him a chance."

Lucy's shoulders relaxed. "Good. That's all I can ask."

Lou's gaze slid to the gun on the table, saw her aunt looking at it too, and moved it into her lap out of sight. "King said he met you right after I went to La Loon for the first time."

Lucy froze, a chip halfway to her mouth fell to the paper. "You're gossiping about me?"

Lou laughed. "Wouldn't you like to know?"

Her aunt couldn't hide her smirk as she licked her lips and then crumpled up the glossy newsprint, stuffing it back into the brown sack. Then she folded down the top, once, twice, three times, far too much consideration for a brown bag smeared with avocado.

"Is it true?" Lou pressed. "How you met?"

"Your father and I had a falling out in high school. I...took off. We hadn't spoken for about ten years when he figured out you were...like me."

What was your last fight about? Lou wanted to ask. But she didn't ask personal questions, not just as a courtesy, but because she didn't want to open that door. If you asked questions, you had to answer them too. Lou was uncomfortable with simple questions like: *What are you doing tonight?* The notion she might have to respond with something as personal as *It must've hurt when he rejected you* was unfathomable.

And truly, she didn't need to ask. Lou could piece together much of the story herself. Somehow Dad had discovered Lucy's ability, and his reaction wasn't good.

If Lucy loved her brother half as much as Lou did, of course it had hurt. The smallest admonishment from her father—*Lou-blue, I'm disappointed*—had wrecked her.

She sucked in a breath. "Dad was motivated to find you because I disappeared."

A statement, not a question. Less emotional entanglement.

"Yes. But he couldn't find me. So, he sent King. The rest is history," Lucy gathered up the trash of their lunch and began separating it for the recycling bin. Paper in one pile. Plastic in another. "How does he seem to you?"

Lucy bent under the sink to retrieve the blue recycle bin and frowned.

Fuck.

Her aunt pulled out a cardboard toilet paper roll. "This is recyclable."

"I must have missed," Lou said. No other

response would do.

"Well?"

"I'll work on my aim. It's dark under the sink. Sometimes the trash can and the recycle bin look alike." Not much of an apology.

She tossed the cardboard tube into the bin with a shake of her head. "No, King. How does he seem to you? Be honest."

She thought of his wet ass cheeks, caterpillar brows, and yellowed toenails. "Old."

Lucy's frown deepened. "He isn't old. I think he's very handsome."

Lou did not find King attractive, but she couldn't tell her aunt that. It would be like leaning into a stroller and informing the mother it was the ugliest infant you'd ever seen.

"He reminds me of Dad," she said instead. And she hadn't realized it was true until it was out of her mouth.

Lucy straightened slowly. "How do you mean?"

Lou felt the ice cracking beneath her and tried to ease some of her weight off the frozen lake of her mind. The wrong step and she'd be submerged. "They're a particular breed."

"Thrill-seeking know-it-alls, you mean?" Lucy smiled, and the muscles in Lou's back released.

"Stubborn to a fault and prone to tunnel vision. They can overlook something obvious if they've got an idea in their head. And blindness can get them killed."

Lucy placed a hand on her hip and turned toward the large living room window. Her face was pallid in the orange light, and the dark circles exaggerated, looking puffier than usual.

Had she been crying?

Lou'd rather be shot than ask. But she'd try to bridge the distance anyway. "Are you…"

"What?"

"Are you guys fighting?" Then seeing her aunt's confusion, Lou added, "You seem…disgruntled."

Lucy sighed. "You're right. I'm being too negative. He is kind. Loyal. And very brave. He's definitely a man worth his salt."

"Is that so?" Lou forced a smile. *We'll see about that.*

22

King went to bed not long after Lou left. Only he didn't sleep. He lay on his bed, staring at the bubbly nodules of the popcorn ceiling, and thought of the long white skeleton bone protruding from the hay. It wasn't the bone that haunted him. It was the way Lou had rolled it under her boot like a soda can on the street.

Her face had been unreadable. As cold and impenetrable as the creek behind his great aunt's house in winter. When she pretended, when she smiled or adopted a lilting tone as she had with him in the alley to throw off the man following him and again at the picnic table with Paula Venetti, it had seemed as if she had thawed in these moments. But he knew now it was a lie. The real Lou was the one who'd rolled a dead woman's bone beneath her boot and said nothing.

And it made him uncomfortable that after hours with her and a full report from Lucy, King had discovered little more. Lou was the hardest read he'd ever encountered.

Was she sociopathic? Maybe psychopathic?

King couldn't tell. Did she honestly feel nothing? Or did she have the cop face to end all cop faces?

No wonder Lucy had been desperate enough to contact him. Though Lucy's belief this was a phase had been a mistake. This wasn't the kind of chip on the shoulder they could eradicate with some positive energy and hours of therapy. They should have started working on Lou when she was younger. *Much* younger. They'd waited too long. Whatever Lou was now, that was what she would always be. For better or worse.

He understood it. And he had no idea how he was going to break it to Lucy.

Lucy—a whole other box of questions. *Why now? Why him?*

He could smell a secret there too but hadn't yet figured out how to ask Lucy the truth. How to press her right. He needed a better hold on the thread if he hoped to unravel the mystery of Lucy Thorne.

Maybe he could develop a plan if only he'd get a good night's sleep. As he lay in his king-sized bed, staring at the ceiling, he couldn't list a single thing he wanted more. He wanted to sleep, but the *walls*. The moonlight hadn't done enough to make the room feel bigger. Too many pillows crowded his face. He shoved them away, and when this didn't work, he turned on the bedside lamp.

The bedroom walls seemed to move back an inch. Better.

Maybe it was that he lay on his back. In the dark under a collapsed building, King had lain in this position unable to move. Perhaps the claustrophobia would abate if he moved his body into a different position. The act alone defied his feeling of confinement.

With a great sigh, he turned over onto his side. His folders and papers lay in an unorganized pile beside the bed. The corners flapped in the draft caused by the fan whirling overhead, a high-pitched wind buzzing in his mind.

At least the shop was closed, and the goddamn skeleton was no longer screeching downstairs. Once, a gaggle of girls must have crossed the threshold, because as soon as the bony guard screamed, a choir of wails followed. For a full five seconds, it was hysteria before the squealing was swallowed up by nervous, fretful laughter.

It was clear Mel had decided to keep the damn

thing.

A fly trap waved in the corner of the room before the open window. The ferns lining the balcony looked like silver-headed crones from his bed. He imagined counting the leaves on each tendril and his limbs relaxed. A welcome weight settled into his arms and legs, and they softened like butter left on the table after dinner, long into the night.

Almost, a voice thought eagerly. *Almost asleep...*

His breathing had just begun to slow when the blade pressed to his throat.

Lou resisted as along as she could, then she slipped. The pressure to do so had been mounting since she took King to the barn. Her internal compass wanted her to go somewhere, and it finally got its wish.

She crouched behind a sofa, her shadowed entry point, and listened. Someone was in the next room. The sound of a zipper unlatching its teeth caught her attention and then heavy objects bouncing off a mattress, the coils groaning.

Her heart sped up, and she pulled her gun. *Where am I?*

Slowly, she rose from behind the couch.

A hotel suite. The cream and rose furnishings. A window with the sliding curtains pulled aside.

An American city, but not one she recognized immediately. A Ferris wheel burned blue beside an interstate six or seven lanes wide. The blue Ferris wheel rang a bell. Before she worked it out in her mind, a door closed and someone began taking a piss.

She lifted her gun higher and crossed the room. On the other side of an archway was the bedroom. A suitcase was open on the bed. Suits lay on top of each other. A garment bag was unzipped, and slacks lay smoothed over the suitcase beside half a dozen shopping bags from high-end department stores. To the left of the bed the closed bathroom door drew her eye.

A line of light traced its frame. A toilet flushed. A sink ran.

The bathroom door flew open, and a man stood there. His hair fell into his eyes and across his cheekbones. Bright green eyes widened at the sight of her pointing a gun at him. She recognized those eyes immediately. She took him in, head to toe. The scruffy jaw. His bare chest and a tattoo snaking up one bicep. A crow and crossbones. Then again the beautiful eyes.

He said something in Italian.

Swore. In *Italian*.

She lifted the gun and fired.

The bullet bit the trim, tearing a chunk of wood away from the door frame and spitting it out onto the tile floor of the bathroom.

He flinched, pinching his eyes shut as wood chips pelted his face. But he pulled his own gun and fired two shots wildly.

Konstantine.

She understood her compass had taken her straight to him. The last Martinelli. The last thread to burn before her revenge was complete.

And here was her chance to finish him, while he was alone and defenseless.

Only two things happened at once.

First, the pull was on her again. Her inner alarm flared to life with its urgent throbbing. The same compass that had led her to Konstantine was now tugging her away.

Time to go, it said. *Time to go!*

The second thing that happened was she recognized Konstantine. She *knew* him.

She hadn't seen him in years, true. And he was a man now, his body thick and muscular, no longer the wiry limbs of a street rat. Only she hadn't known his name when they were children, when they met long before she'd killed her first man.

He'd grown up.

And she wasn't that girl anymore.

But this sharp recognition was enough to unmoor her, throw her understood and arranged world into chaos, and send all the important pieces careening across the floor of her mind.

She stumbled back into the dark living room into the thickest shadow coalescing in the corner of the chamber behind a sofa. Another bullet slammed into the wall beyond her head. She dove for the corner, slipping through the smallest of cracks.

Her heart hammered in her temples, giving the world an unbearable tilt. She expected the sanctity of her own closet. Somewhere to catch her breath before rounding back and finishing the man.

Only she wasn't in her closet. There would be no time for a costume or weapon change or a chance to wrap her mind around why the hell her compass took her to Konstantine at all. Why it had chosen him of the seven billion souls on the planet—then or now.

She brushed a wooden edifice six inches in front of her face. If this wasn't one of her closet's three walls, it was the side of King's entertainment armoire. Cherry wood, bright in a sliver of moonbeams.

A man cried out.

Another voice replied in a low and unfriendly tone.

King chuckled. "Go fuck yourself."

Lou tiptoed across the shadowed living room, skirting an industrial coffee table, and crept toward the bedroom door. It stood open. She pressed herself into the corner. She saw the overhead fan whirling and sheets the color of cream. King was on the floor with his hands tied behind his back. One of his eyes was swelling shut, a puffy purple bruise pinching the eyelids together.

Blood was bright in one corner of his mouth, and King kept flicking his tongue out to lick at the swollen, split lip.

The man with the blade stuck it under King's chin, forcing King to look up or have his throat sliced. It was the man from the alley.

She couldn't approach him without being seen because King had left his goddamn lamp on. *Who slept with a lamp on?*

You do, a voice teased.

Fuck this. Lou pulled the trigger. The bullet went right through one side of the man's head and out the other. Brains sprayed the wall and doused the white coverlet.

King froze, eyes wide and unseeing for several heartbeats. Then he turned and looked at her. "I guess he was right about only asking one more time."

She didn't laugh.

His shock dimmed when he saw her. "Are you all right?"

She was shaking. Not from fear like he assumed, but with anger. She'd been pulled into forced slips *twice*. Back to back, and then she'd put a bullet into a man's head without thinking, without taking them to her Alaskan lake. It was her first messy kill.

What the fuck is wrong with me?

Konstantine. That's what was wrong with her.

She'd woken in his bed nearly a decade ago, from the worst dreams about her father's death, and found him there. Cooing Italian. A face part wonder. Part desire. Part sympathy.

Why would her compass take her to Martinelli's son? Why would she go to him before she even decided on her path to revenge? And she didn't know who he was, at least not consciously.

You're Konstantine's bitch, Castle had said.

"Hey, Lou. Talk to me. Are you okay?" King asked again. His hands were still tied behind his back, but he was standing in front of her, grimacing down at her through his swollen eye.

"I fucked up."

He snorted. "You saved my ass."

"I don't shoot them on this side," she said through her teeth. She breathed. Focused on the floor under her feet. It wasn't actually tilting.

King frowned. He looked at the wall. "You couldn't have done it from over there. There's a wall in the way."

She touched her forehead, trying to find relief from the pressure building behind her eyes. Her right eye was thumping in her skull. "I don't mean this side of the room. I mean on this side of...oh god, whatever the fuck this is. I take them to a lake. I move them, alive to another place where I can leave them. No mess. No body. No crime."

"You have a dumping ground," he said. He puffed out his cheeks with an exaggerated exhale. "Of course, you do."

"I'll get rid of him," Lou said. It sounded pathetic to her. Like an apology. "I'll clean it up."

"Untie me, and I'll help. I know what they'll look for," he said as if he cleaned up crime scenes all the time.

She didn't refuse his help. She wanted this to be over as soon as possible so she could retreat to her St. Louis apartment and think. She needed to fucking think. There was too much bouncing around in her head as it was.

Lou pulled a blade from a forearm sheath and sliced through the zip cord binding King's wrists together.

King rubbed his wrists. "Thanks. After we clean this place up, we need to move Paula."

Lou arched an eyebrow. It was easier to do than form words.

King touched his swollen lip. "Because we're in deep shit."

23

Konstantine stood in the middle of the hotel with his heart racing. It was as if two hands had wrapped themselves around his neck and were squeezing. He couldn't draw enough air. Nor could he convince himself she was gone. So he stood there, frozen between the living room and bedroom, unable to move.

The gun trembled in his hands, the barrel jumping at the end of his sight.

The shadows didn't move.

His eyes roved the room as he went from switch to switch, turning on every light he could. The room filled with bright, cheery light.

She wasn't here. She wasn't.

Sweat trailed down the side of his face. The moisture on the back of his neck began to cool, and along with the queasiness in his guts, he felt ill.

Wood splinters from the bathroom's door frame stuck to his damp cheek like sawdust. It reminded him of the days he spent down by the harbor while men sanded the boats and bent soft woods into place. The air around the workmen had been thick with dust. The ocean blew it back from the harbor. So even if he kept his distance, he left with a sheen on his skin and clothes.

She'd gotten too close. And hadn't he just been thinking about her?

He'd been thinking about her almost nonstop for the last 24 hours. Ever since he'd arrived, he'd been playing scenarios in his mind on how such an encounter might go.

If only she knew my intentions, he had thought. *If only she could see and understand what I want.*

But he knew his chance would never come. She had no interest in hearing him speak. And yet, she'd recognized him. She'd hesitated. He was not mistaken about that. And she *missed*.

She never missed.

The moment he wet his lips they felt dry again. His whole mouth was dry.

Someone knocked at the door, and he fired two bullets into the wall.

"What the hell! Mr. Konstantine, are you all right in there?" a man called. Another sharp bang. "Mr. Konstantine?"

Konstantine went to the door and opened it.

Julio stood in a long white T-shirt which stretched to his knees, and sagging acid-washed jeans. The American's repulsive dress code wasn't enough to bring the world into sharp focus. He still felt as though he wavered on the edge of hysteria. All the adrenaline left him as it did when one was in a near collision. But he had no rearview mirror from which to gain reassurance. No method for looking over his shoulder and ensuring that the danger had in fact passed and he was in the clear.

"Julio?" he rasped.

Julio's eyebrows shot up at the gun. "You okay, boss? You look…like you need a drink."

"What are you doing here?"

"I told you I was coming." Julio slipped a bright yellow backpack off his shoulders. "I got information on your girl."

Konstantine kept glancing over his shoulder.

"Is—" Julio stopped and considered his question more carefully. "Is this a bad time?"

"No," Konstantine said, bringing his forearm up to wipe at his brow.

When Konstantine didn't move or open the door wider, Julio asked, "Should I come in?"

He could, but Konstantine didn't think he could

stay in this suite. "Is the lobby well lit?"

"Like fucking Manhattan. Why?"

"Let's go downstairs. We'll order some drinks, and you can show me whatever you want to show me. I need…" Konstantine wiped his sweaty palms on his pants. "I need to get out of this room."

Julio slipped the pack on again. "Sure." Then his eyes fell to the gun. "But do you think you should be walking around with that hanging out? I mean, there's a lot of security."

"Yes, you're right."

Konstantine grabbed a shirt from the bed, his wallet, and his room key before rejoining Julio in the hall. His movements were rushed and jerky. But relief washed over him as he stood in the bright hallway, securing the gun under his shirt, tucked into the waistband of his pants.

If Julio had any other critiques about Konstantine's behavior or dress code, he said nothing. He waited for Konstantine to adjust himself before he led the way to the elevators.

Julio had been right about the lobby. Despite the late hour, it was as bright as midday. The bar, however, was swathed in shadows. Konstantine took a long look at the black bar and its black stools. Then he gave Julio a hundred-dollar bill and asked him to buy him a gin and tonic. Konstantine kept himself planted on a white leather seat in the center lobby. His back was to a wall, which was fine if the early evening was any preview to his lady's intentions.

Konstantine watched Julio go to the bar with his yellow backpack still hanging from one shoulder and order the drinks. A girl in black and white dress slacks and shirt combo came out and talked to Julio for a moment. She looked over at Konstantine when Julio pointed at the chairs along the wall and nodded. She said something too, her pouty little mouth bobbing open and closed, but Konstantine did not read lips.

It was hard not to think of anything but her.

She had come.

She had come, and he was not ready.

He thought he understood her and how she worked. She was cautious. She always surveyed her prey, stalked her prey before moving in. He had not, quite obviously, expected her to appear so late in the evening. And in the intimacy of his bedroom—like old times.

What struck him most: she seemed as surprised as he was by this encounter.

A moment of shock registered on her face, rendering her a decade younger in a single flash. One moment she was the merciless angel of death, with her sharp blade severing spines without conscience. Then their eyes met, and she'd become the girl again. Innocent and wrapped in the shadows of his bed, with the thinnest line of moonlight across a milk-white cheek. Troubled by the dreams in her dark heart.

He pushed back these thoughts as Julio crossed the lobby, bouncing the sack across his spine, adjusting its weight for better placement.

"The girl will bring our drinks," Julio said. He sat in the chair opposite Konstantine's, so close their knees touched. "I left the bill as a tab, is—"

"That's fine," Konstantine interrupted. The muscles in his back twitched. It didn't seem to matter how soft the chairs were designed, how much they encouraged lingering near the bar and consuming one's fill. He was uneasy. "What do you have for me?"

"I've been looking for your girl," he said, yanking his computer and a notebook out of his bag. For a common American thug, Konstantine thought he was rather organized. If not for the black teardrop tattoo on his face, and the ink up and down his arms, most of which was representative of the unskilled lines of prison art, he could be mistaken for a school boy. A nontraditional student returned to get a degree. In nursing, maybe. Or computer programming. "I started with the father like you said. Got her name."

Konstantine's heart hitched. He imagined what name she might have. Alessandra. Vivianne. Something unmistakably feminine but also feline. But less European he suspected. Emily perhaps.

"Louie Abigail Thorne."

"Louie?" Konstantine's heart flopped. "*Louie?*"

The sing-song word was too sweet. The hardest edge he could find when he turned the name over in his mind was a cowboy quality like Louis L'Amour.

"Louie?" he asked again. "Really?"

Julio shrugged. "Americans name their kids all kinds of weird shit. They name them after fruits and colors too."

Konstantine opened his hand to accept the paper Julio thrust at him. A copy of a birth announcement. Newsprint photocopied.

Julio recited the information from memory while Konstantine read. "Born to Jacob and Courtney Thorne on June 17, 1992."

More papers were passed over. Transcripts. More scraps pilfered from public records.

"She didn't do so good in school. Lots of her

teachers made notes about her being 'distracted' and 'withdrawn.'" Julio snorted. "Like that's so bad. Teachers are the dumbest people I know. Too educated. Drop them in the desert, and they'd be dead tomorrow."

Konstantine was looking at a yellow sheet with the words *counselor evaluation* printed on the top. *Psychosis-neg. Depression-neg.* Then printed in a meticulous blocky script below, in a box marked *additional comments,* someone had written: *Displays anti-social behavior. Intelligence exemplary. Placement test suggested. Perhaps bored with coursework and children her own age.*

"Her aunt put her in one of those schools for gifted kids," Julio said, offering Konstantine more paper. "She did better in the gifted school."

Konstantine frowned at him. "Her aunt?"

"Yeah. Thorne had a sister. She took custody of your girl when her parents died."

"And after school?" he asked. He felt as if he could not get enough information on her. He wanted to know everything. He slid back a sheet and saw the photocopy of her driver's license. Sixteen years old. Eyes brown. Hair brown. Weight 130 pounds. Height 5'7.

What a bland description of such a magnificent

creature he thought, taking something and rendering it to measurements and scientific specifications stripped the leaves from the tree. He realized Julio hadn't answered.

He looked up. The barmaid was putting their drinks on the table on top of two cardboard coasters with the hotel's logo. She gave him a grin and wink when she placed his gin and tonic on the coaster. "Will there be anything else?" she purred. When she leaned forward, her breasts filled his vision, giving them a swollen appearance.

He instinctually pulled the photocopies close to his chest, shielding them. "No thank you."

Her smile faltered.

"Thanks," Julio said, poking the lime slice down into the neck of his beer bottle with a stab of his finger.

The girl wandered off looking more than a little dejected.

"After school?" Konstantine asked again.

Julio pulled back his teeth in a hiss, either from the sour lime or the question. "That's it."

Konstantine's heart dropped an inch in his chest. "Nothing else?"

Julio shook his head, his lips pressed into a thin line. "After high school, she goes dark."

Konstantine wet his lips with the gin and tonic, drawing a steady breath. To be given so much and so little was infuriating. When he felt he could trust himself to speak, he said, "Nothing."

Julio wiped a hand across his brow. "I think she let her license lapse. Or she legally changed her name. So, she's not registered in the system. She doesn't have any bills in her name. No phone. No utilities. She's got a bank account and some money, but it's managed by a financial advisor. Her address is a P.O. box in Detroit."

"That doesn't mean anything." Konstantine grimaced. "She could get to any P.O. box anywhere in the world."

Julio went on. "Yeah. If what you say is true. And her bank transactions are limited. She doesn't have any credit cards. Either her bills are paid by the guy who manages her parents' estate, or she pays cash. Her bank records show ATM withdrawals, but they are all over. In the last two years, which was as far back as I could go, she hasn't made a withdrawal from the same ATM twice."

"Which bank?" Konstantine asked. The gin and tonic balanced on his knee was starting to melt through his pants. Julio told him the name of the bank and Konstantine snorted. "They have ATMs on every corner."

"She doesn't vote. She doesn't work, you know, for money."

"And she has no family," Konstantine said. "No way we can get to her."

Julio smiled. "She has the aunt. There's an Oak Park address on file. The aunt *does* vote and pays her taxes. And she's got a lengthy medical record."

Konstantine reviewed the file and considered this.

Konstantine didn't know if he wanted to threaten the aunt. At the rate he was going, Louie— *Louie*—he would have to adjust to this name— would put a bullet in him quicker than he could ring the aunt's doorbell.

And he did not think he had the element of surprise any longer. Whatever surprise he had was used up in the hotel room this night. His next move would have to be quite bold to elicit the same luck. And yet, it'd be good to have leverage should she ever return.

He had to talk to her. Reason with her. He wanted something so small from her. Surely, if he asked the right way, she would give it to him. But how to approach her? How to present himself?

Perhaps it was best to follow through with the

first part of his plan. If he could expose the lies about her father's murder, and clarify the Martinelli involvement in his death, perhaps it will get through to her better than bullying or coercion.

If he delivered the *real* man responsible for her father's death, maybe she will help him.

Konstantine turned the rocks glass in his hand before lifting it and taking a sip. He met Julio's eyes over the rim. "Let's talk about the senator."

24

King was on his hands and knees beside the bed, scrubbing carpet cleaner into the rug with an old, torn up St. Louis Cardinals T-shirt. He drew breaths in and out of his nose slowly. Combined with the back and forth scrubs, it was like a meditation—until the pain set in.

"I'm too old for this shit," he groaned. He leaned back and placed a soapy hand on his low back. His knees creaked, and sharp pains shot all the way up to his hips. Pulling himself to standing, with the help of his bed frame, required a Herculean effort.

It wasn't until he dragged a sponge across the wall to mop up his attacker's brains, he realized Mel had never come up to check on him. And he could not recall the surprising *crack-boom* of a gun going off. Had Lou used a suppressor? She must have.

Who fucking cares? A voice said. *You're awake at three a.m. scrubbing blood out of the carpet and wiping brains off the wall with a kitchen sponge. Is this how you wanted to spend your retirement?*

Spending time with a would-be mercenary?

Hunting for corpses in Oklahoma backcountry?

Being knocked around and threatened for information?

He was sure none of the above was healthy behavior for a man hoping to see his 70th birthday.

King ran the sponge under the tap in the bathroom again until the water ran clear. Little bits of bone hit the porcelain. Part of the skull cap. His stomach turned.

His bed thumped as it was lifted and dropped.

"What the…?" He stepped toward the dark bedroom, but before he could examine the scene, the knock on the door came.

"King, good lord, what are you doing in there?" Mel's voice was raspy with sleep.

"Fuck." King stuffed the carpet cleaner and the sponges under the sink and hobbled to the door, his knees still stiff from bending.

Mel pounded on the door again. "Don't make me use my key, Mr. King."

"I'm coming, I'm coming." He hurried through the living room and kitchen to the door. He plastered on a smile before he pulled open the door, but smiling made his mouth hurt, and his lip split anew.

"What the hell you be doing in here?" Mel was in a purple cotton bathrobe, eyes puffy. "I'm an old woman. You can't be hanging pictures and rocking the bed at 3:00 a.m., no siree."

"I'm sorry," King said and wiped his damp hands on his pajama pants. "I didn't mean to wake you. I—" He was already searching the Rolodex of his mind for a lie that would suit this occasion. But all he could think was *I need to move the fucking bed so mine isn't flush with Mel's. You can probably hear everything through the thin plaster.*

"Oh my god, what happened to your face?" Mel elbowed herself into the apartment, staring up at him with wide eyes. "Somebody beat your ass?"

King knew what lie he'd have to use then. There was only one for his predicament. "I was having a nightmare. I rolled out of bed and smashed my face on the nightstand." He made a face, palm gesture with his hand, and followed it with his best little boy shrug of disappointment. He thought it was excellent acting.

"No, you got your ass beat," she said. "I know an ass beating when I see one. And I'm not stupid, so don't try to fool me. Were you in the bar tonight?"

King groaned. "Come on, Mel. Not everyone is

a goddamn alcoholic. Plenty of teetotalers get beat up. They fall out of bed and bash in their faces too."

Mel poked at his bruises with relentless fingers. He hissed and squirmed until she let go.

She sniffed. "What's that smell?"

"I don't smell anything," King said. And he didn't, but that didn't stop him from running a furious checklist of *possible* smells. Gunpowder. Blood. Brains.

Mel turned on the kitchen light, which revealed nothing more than the clean, unused kitchen. So, she turned on the living room light.

"I didn't know random inspections were part of our agreement," King said. His voice was an octave too high. "Do I need to say I don't consent to a search?"

She gave him a hard look, pulling her robe tight around her. "I heard a crazy sound. Sounds, and I smell something funky. Are you hiding something in here? Oh Lord, did you kill somebody up in my house?"

"No," King said, and he felt a muscle in his face begin to twitch even though it was the truth. *He* hadn't killed anyone.

But Mel didn't look convinced. And she was going into the bedroom.

"Hey!" King called out as she stepped into the room. "Stay out of there. I—"

His bed was in disarray. His sheets were crumpled and tossed about in a way that made one think of a pterodactyl trapped and thrashing with its great wings. The bed was also at an oblique angle. The footboard pointed toward the bathroom about ten more degrees than it did before King had answered the door. The nightstand too had been pulled away from the wall, its corner edge pointing into the room.

The rug was gone. Entirely *gone*.

Lou must have come back and yanked aside the furniture and taken the whole goddamn rug. There was a wet spot on the wall still drying, but there was no sign of blood or brain there. He knew if forensic scientists ever decided to come in and black light his walls, he would fail their test miserably, but he doubted Mel would even recognize the slight reflection on the wall as moisture, or imagine what sort of matter had been stuck there thirty minutes before.

King knew he'd never see his rug again.

"One hell of a nightmare," Mel said, her eyebrows arched, yet somehow more relaxed now.

"Oh you're not mad," he said with a huff. "Now

that I'm not a drunk with a bed full of young, beautiful women."

"Let's clean you up," Mel said and went toward the bathroom.

"That's all right," King tried to say, and his voice hitched. The first aid kit was under the sink with the sponge and carpet cleaner.

Nosebleed, he decided. He would tell her he'd bled on the rug and had tried to clean it up with the cleaner. When it hadn't worked, he'd given up and thrown out the rug.

That was pretty good.

Mel stood in his bathroom, pointing at the closed toilet seat. "Sit."

"No, really, Mel. It's so late. I don't want to keep you up, babying me."

"Sit. Down." She gave him a look that made his testicles recede inside himself.

He turned off the bedroom light and then squeezed past her and took a seat on the closed toilet lid. His knees were forced against his chest, effectively pinning him between the tub and wall, with Mel blocking the exit.

She gave him a smile. "You already woke me up. You got me up here and your face looks like shit. I happen to know how to clean a face. So sit there and keep your mouth shut."

King looked up at her from the toilet. The lid held him but groaned. He was sure the plastic snaps keeping the lid in place would pop, and he would slide off into the floor with about as much grace as the pterodactyl that had destroyed his bedsheets.

She opened the door beneath the sink, and he expected to see the half bottle of cleaning solution and a wet sponge. But they were gone. The torn-up Cardinals T-shirt was gone too.

Mel pulled a bottle of peroxide from beneath the sink and took the white cap off the brown bottle.

"Cotton balls are in the cabinet," he offered.

She found them beside an oversized bottle of Tums.

"You've got yourself in some deep shit, Mr. King. And if you ever want to get off this toilet again, you're going to tell me what's going on."

King looked up into her dark eyes. Even in her already dark complexion, the dark circles were noticeable, a slight pink color to the purplish flesh, gave their own impression of a bad bruise.

He wanted to lie. His instinct was to deny everything. Lou was purging the apartment of evidence, perhaps this instant. After all, hadn't he seen a shadow move behind Mel twice already?

Something dark darting across his blackened bedroom.

But when he opened his mouth to speak, Mel arched an eyebrow and cocked her head. It was a challenge to whatever he intended to say next as if she was prepared to dismiss his first story on principle.

And there was the matter of her safety. It had been her shop. Her apartment was in this same building. The man had come for King, but Mel had been close. Too close. And what would have happened if Mel had used her key to let herself in? Would the gunman have turned and put a bullet between her eyes, no questions asked? Would he have taken her hostage or used her against him?

He dropped his gaze. "I should move out."

Mel's arched eyebrow fell, knitting together with the other. "Excuse me?"

"The case I'm working—some men came looking for me," he said. "You could've come in here. You could've gotten shot. I can't have that on me."

She stopped cleaning up his face and her scowl deepened. "And how do you think I'll fare when they come looking for you and *don't* find you? Do you think a couple of pissed off thugs might not go across the hall and take it out on the first defenseless, old woman they find?"

"If you're old, then I've got one foot in the grave," King said.

"Two feet, I dare say," she replied and dampened a fresh cotton ball with peroxide. "And it's that girl's fault."

"Lou's got nothing to do with this," King said, feeling his anger uncoil inside him. Like a snake, it lifted its flared head.

"This trouble didn't show up until her auntie came asking for your help."

"Actually," he said. "The problems started when I accepted a case from Chaz Brasso."

Mel dabbed at the cut on his face. King would have bet good money that she was hurting him on purpose.

King hissed. "Easy there!"

"Are you a sixty-year-old man or a little boy," she wailed. "Sit still."

King gritted his teeth and looked up at her.

"What was in that folder you brought home the other night?" she asked.

King bat his eyes at her.

She exhaled. "I read the cards about this one. She's the angel of death, Mr. King."

"Don't start with the cards," King said. "It's hard to talk about something as ridiculous as cards after I got pistol whipped by—"

Mel slapped him upside his head. It wasn't vicious. But with his abused face, it hurt plenty. "Stupid cards. My Lord, show some respect, Mr. King. Don't get me started on *your* stupid. I've seen plenty stupid out of you for you to be insulting an old woman's beliefs. My views are as good as anybody's. Not one person on this rock knows what's going on. I *trust* the cards. I believe in them. They never lie to me. I might be too dumb or blind to see the message, but they don't lie, which is more than I can say for some ungrateful tenants around here."

King touched his tender scalp gingerly with his fingers. "Maybe. But you're wrong about Lou. She's been through a lot, and she's got issues. But she's not evil."

Mel placed a hand on her hip. "The angel of death isn't evil, Mr. King. But she also isn't someone we want to be inviting to dinner."

She tossed the pink cotton balls into a wastebasket wedged between the toilet and wash basin.

He wasn't going to placate her with hollow

reassurances. He hated the automated way some men did that to women. He could recall a night his mother had woken to the sound of broken glass. An intruder had busted out the back window, intending to sneak into the kitchen and steal everything that would fit into his pillowcase. His father had chased him away with a baseball bat and his big booming voice. *It's okay. Now, now. Don't be so worked up. They're gone. And they aren't coming back*, he'd told his inconsolable wife, patting her like a worried puppy.

Only they *had* come back when his father was out of town, and they'd cleaned out the whole house the second time. The room they didn't get to was the bedroom because she'd locked it. And when she heard them in the house, she'd pulled Robbie into the bedroom's bathroom with her and locked that door too before she called the police.

He remembered thinking his mother had been right to be scared. Afraid kept a person cautious. Afraid kept you *alive*. And so, he wouldn't give Mel any sugar-coated bullshit.

"I'm sorry," he said, holding onto her forearm. "I didn't mean to bring this on you. When I told Brasso I'd take the case I—"

"You knew it was trouble," she said, her lips

pursed. "Don't say otherwise, Mr. King."

"I wasn't looking to get anyone hurt."

"But that's the thing, isn't it? When you go looking for trouble, it's not yourself that gets hurt. It's the people who love you."

"I'll move out tomorrow," he said. And he meant it. He had no idea where he would go. But he would take his bullshit with him.

"You'll do no such thing," Mel said, closing the cap on the peroxide bottle. "You'll stay right here and be ready to clean up the mess you made!"

King frowned at her.

"The next time they come knocking, you better be here to blow their heads off."

"You can't possibly be okay with living next door to a guy who's got a big target on his back."

"Better to live next to you than with you." Mel gave him a small smile then. It wasn't a pleasant, loving smile. It was flattened out by her pity and remorse. "Don't make me beg, Mr. King. You know I can't afford for you to move out. And maybe I like having your ass around."

It was a damn sweet thing for her to say, in not so many words, that they were friends. And that she'd no sooner throw him to the dogs as she would throw herself.

He smiled. "This is the French Quarter. You'd have another tenant in no time. You can even raise the rent. They won't know any better."

"But then I'd have to trust someone new," Mel said. "I just don't have the energy for that, Mr. King."

I trust you.

A lightning bolt of recognition shot through King's mind, a searing hot stab of betrayal electrifying him. He swore and stamped his foot. "Ah, you fat *fucker*."

"Excuse me," Mel said, one hand on her chest. "Did a devil take hold of your tongue, Mr. King?"

"Mother*fucker*," he said again. He sucked in his belly and squeezed past her into the dark bedroom.

"Who?" Mel cried, coming up behind him. But both King and Mel stiffened in the living room. Mel bumped into his back when King made a sudden stop.

Chaz stood in the kitchen, front door open behind him.

"Hey Robbie," Chaz said over the black-eyed barrel. He centered the gun on King's chest. "Where's Chuck?"

25

Water ran over Lou's hands, staining the sink in her bathroom with pink droplets. She looked into the mirror and saw a spray of blood had begun to dry across her cheek.

Looking deep into her own eyes, she replayed the parts of King's conversation with his landlady. She thought the woman had seen her. In one moment between snatching the rug out from under King's bed and mopping the last of the brains off the wall, her eyes had fixed on her, where she crouched down in the dark beside King's bed.

But the woman's gaze had slid right over her. And the way she'd spoken to King in the bathroom while she fixed him up had been part-fury, part-care. It made her think of Aunt Lucy.

It made her think of her first kill.

"Blood?" Aunt Lucy had said when she saw her. She stood up from the kitchen table in their Chicago apartment. The tea cup had jumped, knocking a few drops onto the black lacquer tabletop.

Louie was shaking from head to toe. Her body was soaking wet. Red droplets chilled her skin.

She'd just stood in the kitchen, dripping as her aunt ran her fingers all over Louie's body. She was searching for a wound, for some evidence of the attack. When she found none, she turned Lou around and started on the angular plane of her back.

"It's not my blood," Lou managed to spit out between chattering teeth. "I-I'm okay."

Her aunt went still beside her. Her warm fingers withdrew. "What happened?"

"I had to."

"Had to *what?*" Aunt Lucy had taken a step back. "Oh my god."

"He deserved it," Louie said, shivering harder. Her teeth chattered.

"I don't want to hear it."

"He—"

"Shut up!" It was the first time Aunt Lucy had screamed. It had shocked Louie into silence. Tears threatened to spill over her cheeks as she replayed Johnson gasping and choking on his own blood.

Aunt Lucy looked at the red on her hands. Her face flushing, she turned and darted into the kitchen behind them. She scrubbed her hands beneath the hot tap. Louie watched her, her heart pounding.

"He's the one who betrayed Dad. Johnson was the reason—"

"Don't tell me! I'm serious," Lucy hissed. "No names. No, no *details*. Not another word!"

Louie chewed her lower lip, swallowing everything she wanted to say about Gus Johnson. How she'd lied about going to a graduation party. How instead, she'd spent hours in the basement of the public library searching microfilms for news of her parents. How the moment she'd seen Gus's face in the interview, she'd known he was guilty. He was the one who had sold them out to the drug lords so he could save his skin.

Gus himself had admitted this in not so many words.

The way the traitor's mouth opened, the eyes rolling up and to the left in preparation for his lie.

Louie hadn't let him get far. She'd pounced. He knocked her off easily, outweighing her by more than two hundred pounds. He'd raised his gun to shoot her.

All the rationalizations. All the excuses. All her justifications.

She wasn't sorry she'd buried her father's pocket knife into the crook of his neck. She wasn't sorry he bled to death on the shore of Blood Lake in La Loon. She didn't give a damn that Jabbers took care of the rest.

But the way her aunt had finally looked at her, her fingers bone white from clutching her sink so hard, she *did* care about that.

Aunt Lucy had the appearance of serenity, if not for those fingers holding onto the sink as if any moment a tornado was going to rip the ceiling off and carry her away.

"I want you to take a bath," Aunt Lucy had said. Her voice was even and low, almost too low for Louie to hear. Now she was the one shaking.

"But—"

"Get in with your clothes on," Lucy said, ignoring the interjection. She didn't turn away from the kitchen window as if the very sight of Lou was unacceptable. "Take them off and leave them somewhere. But not on *this* side. Go to that place. Leave everything there."

"Aunt Lucy—"

"*Everything*," she said, refusing to be interrupted. "Your shoes, your underwear. *Everything*. If you used—something—leave it. Do you understand?"

She hadn't wanted to give up her father's

pocketknife, the small blade she'd buried in the hilt of Gus Johnson's throat, but she also understood the danger in keeping it. A weapon, however sentimental, was evidence.

"Go on." Lucy had waved her toward the bathroom at the end of the hall. "Do it now."

Before Louie could protest, her aunt walked into the empty linen closet in their old Oak Park apartment and disappeared.

She didn't need to see it, to know her aunt had slipped.

The apartment had hummed with her absence.

Lou did as she was told.

She'd run a warm bath and then she'd climbed inside it, shoes and all.

It was three in the morning by the time her aunt returned. She wasn't sure where Lucy had gone. Her aunt had favorite places she liked to haunt just as Louie did. But Louie couldn't describe her immense relief when Lucy came back. That she'd come back at all—that had been something.

"Louie?" Lucy sat down on the edge the couch where Louie lay, pretending to sleep. The cushions creaked under her aunt's weight. She placed a hand on Louie's knee. Then as if she'd sensed the girl's reluctance to start a conversation, she squeezed the knee and said, "Talk to me."

Louie turned over. It was hard to look her in the eye, but Louie tried to hold her gaze. The grim lines around Aunt Lucy's mouth had smoothed over in the last few hours. And her brow was no longer pinched in anger. Now she looked sad. And perhaps a little scared.

"Did you take care of it?" Aunt Lucy whispered as if someone would overhear them.

Louie nodded.

"It was someone who—" Her voice broke. Her aunt looked up at the ceiling and sucked in a breath. Once she seemed composed, she tried again. "He was responsible for your parents' death."

Louie nodded. "The Martinellis got to him first, and so he sold out Dad to protect himself. He's probably the one who told all those lies about Dad too."

Her aunt nodded as if this confirmed her suspicions. "And are there others? People you plan to…" Her voice trailed off. "Don't tell me details. If I'm ever captured and tortured I can't say anything to incriminate you. I can't tell what I don't know," Aunt Lucy had said in jest. She smiled, and made it seem like a joke. Lou knew better.

And she knew the answer to her aunt's question.

Even before she began her hunt, her search, she instinctually knew that the murder of her family was part of a large and intricate web. After the research into Gus Johnson and the Martinellis, the world changed. The world she was taught existed dissolved. A new, more menacing world reshaped around her. She saw the strings, the puppeteers, and all the figures working in the darkness, controlling what people did and didn't see on the mainstage.

And who better to understand this truth than her? No one needed to make Louie believe there were *in-between* places. She'd traversed these herself. And she knew that in the darkness your senses deceived you. You couldn't trust what you saw, what you felt, or heard—you could trust nothing but the compass inside you, the one you're born with—a force that tugged and urged and spoke inaudibly —and her compass said the work wasn't done.

Yes, there are others. Angelo Martinelli and his brothers. Maybe their father too. And anyone else who had a hand in it.

"Listen to me," Aunt Lucy said, fighting for Louie's attention. "This is very important."

Louie lay flat on her back and gazed up at the woman.

"I know you must be so angry. *I'm* angry." Lucy swallowed before going on. "When I think about your father, I'm filled with so many regrets. There are so many things I wish I'd said to him. And about a million things I would have done differently. I'll never get that chance. We must learn how to live with this, Louie. You and me."

Louie's throat tightened and her eyes burned. She thought of her father, her last vision of him from the bottom of their swimming pool. His figure blurred and distant as she swam futilely toward him. If she had reached him—if she had pulled him into the water—

"If you are anything like me," Lucy went on. "You think you could have saved him."

"I could—"

"No," Aunt Lucy stopped her. "*No*, and that's my point. You couldn't have done anything differently."

"But—"

"I know you don't believe me now, but you'll see I'm right if you stop and take a minute to think about it." Lucy pressed her lips together, wet them, and then continued. "Your father would not have *let* you do anything differently."

Louie came up on her elbows.

"He pushed you into the pool, knowing you would escape. That's what he wanted. It was *his* choice. And he would sacrifice himself for you every time, no matter what you did differently. He made his choice, and we have to live with it."

"He deserves justice," Louie had said. *I deserve it.* "What else am I going to use my ability for? Why do I even have it?"

"Why?" Lucy repeated. Sadness pinched her brow. "Why do ET salamanders breathe through their skin? Why do tufted deer have fangs and eat meat? Creatures adapt to their environment. An evolutionary necessity here. A chromosome mutation there. *Why* you have it is to survive. And it's what your father wanted when he sacrificed himself to save you. He wanted you to survive."

He wanted you to survive.

Louie burst into tears. She wasn't sure why her aunt's words had affected her, but that small admonishment had cut deep. Her guilt soured.

"It's not too late to honor his wish," her aunt said, stroking Louie's hair and rocking her softly in her arms. "It's never too late to let it go. Promise me you'll try to let go, Louie."

But the image of Johnson's bloody lips was already burned into her mind. Louie knew it was too late to let go. Even at seventeen, she understood that when you're this deep, it's best to keep swimming or you'll drown. She'd survived her revenge. She'd taken out all the Martinellis who'd killed her parents one by one. And now there was only Konstantine left.

Konstantine.

Bright eyes. A man in a doorway.

The hot water scalded her hands to the color of raw meat and was now turning cold. She reached up and turned off the faucets, but she didn't move away from the sink.

But you'd gone to him before you'd ever thought about revenge, a voice reminded her. *Something else is happening here.*

She reached up and wiped the steam off the mirror, revealing her hard face.

Her compass whirled. Something was pulling at her again, urging her to step into the darkness and follow the current.

The one thing she trusted was betraying her.

And she did trust her compass. Even when she questioned La Loon and why she would ever be drawn to such a nightmarish place, she came to trust the result all the same. The universe—as her aunt would call it—knew her family would be betrayed, knew she would need such a place to do her work. Even as dangerous and violent as her first visit had been, it had been necessary.

And every jump ever since.

She trusted that voice. So why did she feel like she couldn't trust it now?

"No," she said to the woman in the mirror staring back at her. She wasn't going to let herself be pulled around and controlled. "*No*."

The compass trembled, telling her it was time to go. There was somewhere she needed to be.

Master this, Lou-blue. Don't be its victim.

Her resolve solidified at the sound of her father's voice in her mind and the feel of his heavy hand on her scarred shoulder.

The compass wavered.

"I'm not a victim," she said, clutching the sink. She held firm to the world around her. "I say where we go."

26

King stared into the gun barrel, into the gaping black eye of Brasso's gun. "You little prick."

Brasso gave a good ol' boy shrug. "What can I say, Robbie? You've always been a little too eager to see action."

"You didn't want me to build a case against Ryanson. You wanted me to find Venetti for him."

"You've always been good at finding things. I knew if I set you on her trail she'd turn up sooner or later. But I must admit, this was a quick turnaround, even for you." Chaz's eyes flicked to Mel, and King stepped to shield her. "Did you get your pet psychic to read her cards or something? I'd like to see what other tricks she knows."

Mel huffed. "Why don't you come over here and *pet* me and see what happens."

King said nothing.

Chaz's smile widened. "You always liked them a little mean."

King was desperate to turn his head, to look over his shoulder into the dark and see if Lou was there. She would come. She *had* to come. And when she did, she was going to shove Brasso's gun so far up his ass the gunmetal would press against the back of his teeth.

King laughed then. The tight sound softened into a hearty chuckle. The damn thing was, once he started, he couldn't stop.

Brasso's brow creased. "What's so funny?"

He couldn't say how hard the humor had struck him. At 59 years old, he'd been hit with the realization, *I'm waiting for a girl to save me!* He couldn't say it. Nor could he make himself stop laughing. His belly began to ache.

Mel arched an eyebrow. "Mr. King, I'm not sure this is the appropriate time to get the giggles."

Brasso raised the gun. "If you don't stop laughing, I'm going to shoot you in the gut."

The little boy voice Brasso used to threaten him made him laugh harder. It had sounded too much like *if you don't give me back my train, I'm going to tell Mom!*

Brasso, face furious, pulled the trigger and put a bullet through a cabinet door. Something in the cabinet, a glass or bowl because he kept both there, ruptured. The door popped open with the force and glass was vomited out onto the stove and countertop. Glittering shards cascading over the countertop to the tiled floor.

King stopped laughing, sweat prickling the back of his neck. "You really want to do this?"

"It's not personal," Brasso said with another shrug. "It's business."

King arched his brows. "Whose business? Ryanson's?"

Brasso didn't answer.

"Did you set me up just to kill me?" King said.

"No. I sent Chuck to find out what you *weren't* telling me, and when he didn't come out, then I came to see what the hell happened."

"Chuck didn't come," King said. Mel shifted beside him.

Brasso snorted. "Your fucked-up face says otherwise. Where is he?"

"I want you to say it. Tell me you're working for Ryanson." King watched Brasso's face, searching each micro-movement for answers he knew the man wouldn't give verbally. "Or is it someone else?"

"That's your problem, Robbie," Brasso said. "You ask too many fucking questions. I should've known you wouldn't find the girl and hand her over. You'd have to ask fucking *questions*."

King thought he would pull the trigger then. His face tightened, and the gun centered on his forehead. And King had time to think about two sets of brains hitting the walls in one night when he saw her.

She appeared behind Brasso, raising a cast iron skillet over her head. He kept his eyes on Chaz's, so the girl and the skillet remained in the soft focus. He hoped Mel was as unreadable as he was.

Piper brought the skillet down on Brasso's skull, and the man crumpled. The gun fell from his hand and didn't go off. But the clatter along the kitchen tile was as jarring.

Mel threw her hands in the air. "Sweet Jesus, Mary and Moses."

She placed his kitchen rug over the broken glass as if bloody feet were their priority.

"Is he dead?" Piper asked. She touched the hemp necklace around her throat. Her eyes were the size of half-dollars. "Oh my god, am I going to go to prison for killing a dude?"

King bent and pressed a finger to his throat. "He's not dead. And you won't go to prison."

King pulled out his cell phone and Lou's card. He punched in her pager number, and a robot confirmed his page. *Press # if this is an emergency*. King smashed the # with his thumb twice. The robot thanked him. He slipped the phone back into his pocket.

"What are you doing here?" Mel asked. She turned all her fury on Piper.

"Uh," she bit her lip. "I was going to give you this."

She tiptoed around Chaz's collapsed body and passed over a handful of printed pages to King. At a glance, it was the information he'd sent her looking for. Everything the internet could provide on Ryanson and his dealings.

He arched an eyebrow. "You always deliver info at 2:00 in the morning?"

Piper forced a smile.

King stuffed his hands into Brasso's pockets, searching for a phone. Keys. Anything useful. Clues that might let him know the true depth of this rabbit hole.

"Forget Piper." Mel turned her finger on him. "Who the hell laughs at a man pointing his gun at you?"

Piper snorted.

They both turned and looked at her.

"His *gun*," she said with a crooked smile. Then

she frowned. "Never mind. Who knew getting shot at made people so *grumpy*?"

"Why were you here?" Mel and King demanded in unison.

Piper held her hands out in front of her in surrender. "Oh, my god. *Calme-toi!* Okay. I was outside creeping. I admit it."

"Why?"

"I was hoping I could bump into King's friend."

They blinked at her. King slipped a hand into Brasso's pockets. Anything. He needed anything to go on.

Piper sighed. "You know. The girl."

"Why would you want to *meet* her?" Mel's eyes were twice as large as normal.

Piper pursed her lips and tilted her head. "Really, Mel? You can't guess."

"It's two in the morning," King said.

"*Puh*-lease!" Piper cried. "The bars aren't even closed. But then I heard the gun go off and so I wanted to check on you."

"You'll get your wish." King pulled a green poker chip, a folded piece of paper, and a pen out of Brasso's pockets. "She'll be here any minute."

Piper pumped her fist in the air. "I knew it! Good things come to those who wait!"

27

Lou's watch buzzed on the island countertop. She leaped off the sofa and snatched it before the third buzzy chirp. A New Orleans number flashed on the screen followed by 911.

King. No one else in New Orleans had her number.

She took 911 to mean *guns*. She threw open a closet. Not *that* closet, and grabbed a shoulder holster. She put it on and holstered her twin Glocks, one on each side. She put a Beretta in the thigh holster.

She was about to duck into *that* closet when the watch buzzed again. She stopped, hand on the cool handle. This number was from San Diego. Also, a 911 page.

The internal compass was whirling, trying to decide which situation was more dire.

"Fuck," she said and threw herself into the dark. She pulled the closet closed behind her.

It was the second time that night she appeared at King's to find a body on the floor.

She stepped into the kitchen with her gun in her hand. Three faces watched her. The landlady was here in her bathrobe, one hand on her hip. Her eyes were narrow. She even shook her head. The girl, the blonde with dark eyebrows and wide, glittering eyes smiled at her. She gave a little wave. Lou humored her with a *hey*. Then her eyes met King's.

She looked from King to the body, to King again. "You're worse than me." She meant the body count. For the last several years she'd thought she was the only one who piled bodies the way others piled laundry.

"Paula isn't safe," King said by way of introduction.

"I know," she said and tapped the beeper tucked into her pocket. "She just paged me."

"Fuck," King said. "We have to go."

The landlady's voice went high. "What about *him*?"

"I need to question him," King said. He cut his eyes to Lou. No one had ever looked at her that way before. Part apology. Part desperation. His lips pursed with a question, but when he looked back at the blonde who was still smiling, the question died on his lips.

Lou took a breath before saying. "You want to save Venetti or question the man? Even I can't be two places at once, King."

King mulled it over. He ran his hands through his hair as if this would help him prioritize.

Lou looked at the girl again, because it was hard not to. She was *staring*. And when someone's gaze was that heavy, you couldn't ignore it.

"What?" Lou asked, scowling at her.

If the girl sensed Lou's irritation, she was not discouraged. "I'm Piper. I'm King's assistant."

The landlady muttered something under her breath.

The beeper buzzed again. Frantic vibration rattled Lou's wrist. It was as if Venetti herself were frantically shaking it. "King?"

"Fuck," he swore. He hissed his disappointment through clenched teeth. "Go without me. Move her somewhere safe and then come right back. I'll need your help with him."

"Bye," Piper said with a pout.

Lou was already stepping toward the closet cut into the bedroom wall. Only when she entered the closet, she stepped out of the world. It spun like a slot machine. Another time and place lining up in the dark.

She would worry about what to tell King's friends later. Then maybe they wouldn't see her at all. She was hidden by the wall. It would be easy to say she'd exited through the bedroom and leapt down off the balcony. Like a cat.

Lou stepped out of the dark into a park. She frowned.

A sidewalk stretched in both directions. Lined with street lamps made to look like antique lanterns on black posts. Her eyes skipped from orb to orb. But the tangerine-colored spotlights were empty, and the trees on either side of the red brick path were still. Not even a cool breeze disturbed the leaves.

A woman screamed. "Help me! Please, somebody, help me!"

A gun fired. Not the enormous *boom-blam* of a handgun. It was the compressed sharp torpedo of a bullet passing through a suppressor. The tree ten feet to Lou's right exploded in a spray of wood chips.

She dropped into a crouch, pulling her gun as she went down. The movement to her left drew her eye. Paula tore past her, running at full speed through the trees. Another bullet struck a tree, another explosion of wood splinters sprayed out into the night. Paula screamed again.

Lou pivoted on her heels toward the source of the bullets and spotted her target. A man, lean like a starving cat, kept shuffling forward. His arm was outstretched, moving in a slow arc as he tracked the woman running through the trees. He wore a baggy black T-shirt that stretched to his knees and dark jeans. His breath came in strangled pants. Tattoos snaked around both arms and up from beneath the collar of his shirt. His jaw clenched as he pulled the trigger again and again.

Paula howled.

Lou put a bullet in his knee. He screamed as blood bloomed on his right leg. His other knee buckled and he went down hard. The gun clattered against the red brick walkway as his palms hit the dirt, breaking his fall.

He moaned and cursed as blood poured from a hole above his knee. His eyes met hers across the walkway, and he snarled. *Snarled*, like a jungle cat in a zoo.

Lou put a bullet between his eyes and the snarl softened to an open, slack-jawed *O*. The eyes went unfocused, rolling up into the back of the shooter's skull at the same moment he fell back onto the grass, limp. She noted the tattoo on his arm, before she ran in the direction of Paula's screams.

She found the girl leaning against a tree, crying. Light cut across her face revealing dirt smudges and sweat gleaming. Her hands were covered in dirt, too. She must have fallen at least once when trying to escape.

Lou grabbed her, and Paula whirled, a large blade flashing in the moonlight. Lou caught her wrist and took the knife away.

"Easy," Lou said, releasing the other woman's hand before she broke it. "Easy does it."

As soon as Paula saw her, all the strength went out of the arms that had been resisting Lou and visible relief washed over her face.

"Thank god," Paula grabbed onto Lou's forearms. "I've been shot."

"Come on." Lou pocketed the knife so she would have her hands free to carry Paula.

Lou pulled her to her feet, and Paula cried out. It was the arm Lou had grabbed. Blood oozed from the deltoid, and because Paula wore a cut-off flannel with no sleeves, Lou could see right into the wound as she pulled the arm. The fleshy mouth puckered as the skin was stretched, pulpy tissue jutting in all directions around the gaping wound. It hadn't been a clean shot.

Lou's stomach hitched, but she didn't let go of

the girl. She stepped left, away from the walkway lights and into the cover of the tree's shadows. In a heartbeat, they emerged from the closet of her aunt's Oak Park apartment.

The closet banged open, and Lou fell out into slivers of moonlight. She noted first the temperature change, the way the warm apartment differed from the cool night. Second, her aunt's surprised squeal.

"What in the world?" Lucy stood from the kitchen table and came forward, her mouth opening in surprise.

Lou had counted on this. Counted on the nocturnal habits of her aunt to work for them.

"Are you hurt?" Lucy demanded. Her fear had made her angry.

"I'm fine." Lou rotated her shoulders to alleviate the ache of supporting Paula's weight. "But she's been shot in the arm. Fix her up. She can't go to a hospital."

Lou handed Paula over as if she were nothing more than a bread basket. Paula didn't even protest. She went as easily from Lou's arm to Lucy's, as if forsaking one bit of flotsam for another in a turbulent sea.

Lucy eased her into the kitchen chair. "I'll get my kit."

Lou felt her pager buzz. King. No doubt he was wondering what the hell was going on.

"What have you gotten involved in *now*?" Lucy whispered as she shouldered through, her voice went high with panic. Again, twice in the same night, Lou found herself thinking of her first kill, of taking down Gus Johnson and all the blood that had been on her hands ever since.

"*You* got me in this," Lou snapped. Her eyes fell on the six or seven pill bottles beside Lucy's laptop on the kitchen table. Too many pill bottles. Lou couldn't see the names of the drugs because the type was too small.

Lucy placed a hand on her chest. "She's King's case."

Lou didn't offer an explanation. By way of avoidance, she pulled her gun, counted the bullets, and holstered again. She was searching for what to say. With an irritated hiss, she issued her last order. "Clean her up. Stay indoors. Keep the doors locked."

Her aunt's frown deepened. "Louie, this is too dangerous. God, why did I think I could trust him?"

Lou was already opening the empty linen closet, so much like the one she had back home. Aunt Lucy's closet smelled of lavender and cedar sachets. Lou's smelled of gunmetal and grease.

"Just keep your eyes and ears open." Lou paused with her hands on the linen door. She pulled the knife out of her pocket and shoved the handle toward Paula. "Don't hesitate."

28

Mel dragged a pleading Piper from the room, while King stood vigil over Brasso's unconscious body. Looking at the man turned King's stomach sour.

He tapped his service revolver against his thigh and sighed. "You ambitious fuck."

Because King had no doubt ambition was to blame for this. Brasso had become Ryanson's lap dog in exchange for money or promotions. Did he party on the same yacht the girls were thrown from? Expensive gifts? Luxuries above a DEA agent's pay grade? King tried to think back, searching every memory of his partner for clues. Suggestive conversations.

Brasso always had that *me first* way about him. He remembered a few luxury items. An Armani watch. A $1500 bracelet. But Brasso's first wife had been rich, the daughter of a man with a fashion empire.

King pried open the folded piece of paper he'd

found in Brasso's pocket. It was a rectangular sheet of cream stationery, with *Hotel Monteleone* printed in elegant script across the top of the page.

Beneath it, in Brasso's scrawl, was a series of numbers and letters. FLR-CDG 815-1005. CDG-IAH 1040-205.

He also had a pen from Huang's carry-out and a green poker chip.

He slipped these items into his own pockets as Lou reappeared.

King's heart jolted as if kicked by a horse when he saw her. "You got shot?"

She frowned at him, looking down at herself as if seeing all the blood for the first time. She met his eyes. "Not mine."

Nausea rolled over him. "Venetti?"

"Shot in the shoulder. She'll live. Lucy is cleaning her up."

King flinched at the mention of Lucy.

Lou clenched and unclenched her fists. "Decide what to tell her before she murders you."

He ran a hand through his hair. There was nothing he could say to Lucy that wouldn't provoke her wrath. She'd expected him to rehabilitate Lou. Help her find a better way of slaking her bloodlust, not launch a death match against a senator and a corrupted DEA agent. "Let's hurry then. I want to solve this before she tears me limb from limb."

Lou frowned at the unconscious man. "I'll dump his body in La Loon."

King swallowed. "Okay."

To his surprise, he hadn't realized until this moment he might have to kill Brasso. He had no desire to kill his friend, even if the fucker had been about two seconds from putting a bullet in him.

But as soon as he'd said it, he knew she was right. Killing Brasso was a real possibility. What was the alternative? Turn him over to the authorities? Maybe. But his leverage against Brasso, an active serviceman, was limited.

It didn't help that he couldn't explain himself as well as he'd like. If he found himself in a media maelstrom, how would he explain how he found Venetti? How did he get to San Diego? He would start to look as suspicious as Brasso and twice as fast. And King saw the destruction of Jack Thorne firsthand. Being the good guy didn't immunize you against public opinion or the consequences of that public opinion.

King said, "I think he was staying at the Monteleone. I want to check his room."

Lou frowned. "Do you want to investigate or

interrogate first?"

He hesitated.

She arched an eyebrow. "He isn't going to stay unconscious much longer."

She was right. Damn.

Lou's eyebrow arched higher as she watched him debate inside how to deal with his traitorous friend. "I have a place."

"What do you mean *a place*?"

"Somewhere to hold him where he won't be found and he can't escape."

A chill ran up King's spine. "No one should have a place like that."

She looked up at him through dark lashes. "I do."

"Fine," he said and bent to help lift the man. "We'll take him—"

She already had him up under the other arm, lifting. King tried not to gape at her. It was discrimination, he knew, to be surprised a woman was as strong as he was. And while he might not have controlled his gaping mouth as well as he could have, at least he had not said anything stupid like *how much can you lift?*

The fact that she'd pulled Brasso out of his arms and balanced him against her shoulder was testament enough. Brasso was 220 at least.

"Grab on to me," Lou said without any hint of strain in her voice. King reached out and placed one hand on her hip before realizing it was far too intimate, the feel of her taut core under his hand. He moved it up to her shoulder, inching his finger between her shoulder and Brasso's bicep.

She pulled him toward his armoire as if it wasn't there. He had a moment of disbelief when he thought she was going to crash right into the giant piece of furniture. It was dark. Maybe she didn't see it?

"Hey—" he began, but the word stuck in his throat. His stomach dropped, and he was riding down the impossibly high roller coaster again, his body caught in a slipstream.

Then the ground came, and his knees buckled, wobbling.

"Fucking hell," he groaned and stumbled away from her. "I'm never going to get used to that."

King let his eyes adjust to dim light. It was completely dark in this space. And it was a space. No more than eight feet by eight feet. And as King ran his hands along the wall, he knew it was made of metal. Ore, perhaps. The scent of rust was strong. There was no door. No window. No hinges of any kind. Lou had popped them right into a sealed box.

His panic rose. The walls seemed to move an inch closer to the center, ready to crush him flat. "Where are we?"

She didn't answer. She propped Brasso against a wall and a fan kicked on somewhere. King felt a stream of cool air pump into the sealed box, and he used the back of his bare hand to follow the stream. When he was right beneath it, he jumped, arms stretching up, groping for the vent, but he grabbed nothing.

"It's twelve feet up," Lou said.

"What kind of place is this?" he asked. The walls were moving in on him. He felt the familiar closing of his throat. Claustrophobia bit into the back of his neck.

"I'd tell you," she said, her hands clamping down on his arm. "But I'd have to kill you."

Another chill ran up his spine. He opened his mouth to say something funny, anything to lessen the tension squeezing his chest, but the rollercoaster drop came again. The world had been yanked out from under him, and he was falling through the dark.

His legs trembled when the ground reappeared.

Lou let go of his arm, and he wobbled even more.

"A little warning," he hissed. He ran a hand over

his face, but closing his eyes intensified the dizziness. Despite the nauseated waves in his guts, relief swelled in his chest. No box. No crushing claustrophobia. He ran a palm over his sweaty face.

Lou looked as steady as a 9-to-5 job with an employer-matched 401K.

"Why doesn't it affect you like this?" he asked. He would've asked her any question right then if it meant pushing the walls of his world out.

Lou shrugged at the mouth of the alley. She stepped back into the light and looked up and down the street. "Lucy would say, 'Why would a bird get motion sick when it's flying?'"

"Call me a penguin then," King said and stepped into the light.

The Hotel Monteleone gleamed. The imposing white building loomed with its textured surface and grand flags hanging on either side of the shining entrance. It was in the Antebellum style and looked like a horse and carriage would pull up at any moment, Southern Belles stepping out in their glossy gowns, fans waving in their white-gloved hands.

"Do you know his room number?" she asked.

"No," he sighed. The night air cooled the sweat on the back of his neck. "But I've got these."

He put the poker chip, the folded stationery, and Huang carryout pen in her open hand.

She scowled at him. "What the hell am I supposed to do with this?"

King frowned. "Can't you use your *compass* to find out where these things came from?"

She snorted and shoved the objects back into his hand. "You're confusing me with your landlady. I'm not psychic. I don't touch objects to my forehead and see the future. I'll slip and see where it takes us."

"Then how does it work?"

"Here's your warning." She pulled him back into the alley.

This time, King managed to suck in a breath before the rollercoaster dropped, but he was no less wobbly when they appeared inside a hotel room.

Double beds in golden coverlets and gaudy curtains. Far too many ruffles for King's taste and the overkill was intensified by the pinstriped wallpaper. He suspected he would have appreciated the wallpaper, maybe even liked it, had the décor been more neutral.

"This is a grandma room," Lou said.

King scanned the room. A laptop sat on the cherry desk with curved feet. The cover had a DEA sticker on it they'd all received at an annual conference a few years back. He plopped into the desk chair, the wheels sliding under him.

He opened the laptop and saw the screensaver. Brasso was on a beach, reclining in a lounge chair, his pasty white arms looking too vulnerable in the blaring sun. A drink the color of sunrise sweat condensation in his right hand. He smiled behind enormous sunglasses and an oversized hat.

"Do you know his?" Lou asked, her tone impatient. What? Wasn't he moving fast enough for her?

King huffed. "I have no idea. Wait. I can find out."

Lou unplugged the laptop and wrapped the power cord around it. Then she moved on to a black leather satchel, lying against the rolled arm of a chair. Papers jutted from several pockets, and from where he stood, King could see the tabs of manila folders, much like the one Brasso had given him, sticking out of the open mouth.

Lou threw the satchel over her shoulder. It was amazing, actually. The way she came into the room, quickly identified what was important, and rushed on. God, it reminded him of Jack's hawk eyes.

"Why the rush?" he asked.

She gave him a look he knew well. It was a look

his ex-wife had given him every time something came out of his mouth.

"He had friends. They could show up. Or your friend could already be awake."

All true but King thought it was something else too. Was it the light in the room? She was still, her movements calm in the shadows. But in the light, she couldn't move fast enough.

The black face of her pager flashed in the lamplight.

"Can you jump through your worm holes with technology without frying it?" After all, he'd had his cell phone in his pocket as he had slipped with Lou to San Diego the first time. He had not thought to ask or show concern until now.

She followed his gaze, glancing down at her wrist. "I've never had a problem with this."

"Isn't a computer a little more complex?"

"It's turned off. We'll be fine," she said with an air of irritation. "What else are we looking for?"

King wasn't sure. She tossed the satchel stuffed with the papers and laptop at him. It hit him in the chest, the corner of the laptop catching his ribs.

He harrumphed.

Because she wants her hands free, he realized. She can't get to her guns as quick as she liked, not bogged down by Brasso's things. The idea struck him again, the bizarre absurdity that he was traveling around with a young, beautiful woman whose primary concern was her weapon. Not having drinks with friends. No dancing or shopping, or any of the other strikingly feminine interests his wife had when he met her—at about Lou's age.

There was a sound in the hall. A cart on squeaky wheels rolled past the closed door. King and Lou both held their breath until the person whistling *Sunshine, My Sunshine* rolled right on by. King smelled boiled meat. Pot roast maybe. Or stew.

When she spoke again, her voice was much lower. "Are we done?"

He adjusted the computer against his chest. "Yeah. No. Check the safe." Something in his brain clicked into place. "If there's anything else, it'd be in there."

She went to a coat closet by the entrance and slid back the mirrored door. Wooden hangers hung waiting on a metal bar that ran the length of the closet. An iron sat in a cradle nailed to the wall. An extra pillow and blanket wrapped in protective plastic rested on the top shelf. The safe, a metal box the color of bullets, was open, the door wide. It was bare. Nothing but shadows inside.

"Let's go," King said. "Is Brasso going to be okay, if we go somewhere else first?"

He wasn't sure what the conditions for his cell were. Maybe they'd stuffed him in a furnace that would kick on and burn him to a crisp.

"He'll hold." She turned off the hotel lights and left King in pitch black darkness. He stood there, heart pounding, desperate for his eyes to readjust. A sliver of light from the Quarter poked through the side of the curtain, an inch between the fabric and the wall itself.

Then he felt her hand on his in the dark.

"Do you know where you want to go?" she whispered. Her mouth was hot on his face. "For the password?"

"Yeah," he managed, half-choking on the word. The walls moved in again.

The coaster dropped, and for a moment he thought he let go of the laptop in surprise. What would happen if he let go while they were in motion? Would the darkness gobble it up? Would the item fall into some space between one place and another, like coins between sofa cushions never to be seen again? Like the second sock that went into the dryer, but never came out again?

Then the ground was shaking. No, it was his

legs shaking beneath him.

His eyes focused on an illuminated sign hanging above a doorway. It was the Saint Louis DEA office. The two-story brick building looked like any other municipal headquarters. Square. Practical.

"What the—" he started. He hadn't seen this building since he retired and it hadn't changed one bit with its boxy exterior and rows of windows. The staggered positions of the blinds. Some down. Some up. Some at half-mast. They gave the impression of a man not quite right in the head looking back at him.

"Isn't this where you wanted to go?" It didn't sound like a question.

"I thought Brasso had transferred to a Texas office. But if this is where your compass took us..." He couldn't question her sense of direction. She'd found the gaudy hotel room on the first try.

"Will anyone be in there?" Her eyes measured the plain brick façade. A breeze blew her hair into her face.

"Not yet, but some of the guys get here as early as four in the morning."

"What about cameras?" she asked, swiping at her eyes.

"Not where we're going. It's an office, not a

pawn shop."

She pushed him back a step, beneath the thick limbs of an old oak tree, and the roller coaster took another hill. Then they were stepping out of a bathroom on the second floor. He knew this bathroom. It had been a year since he'd taken a piss in one of these bleached white urinals while looking at the off-white and teal alternating tiles. But he knew exactly where he was the moment he saw it.

The light flickered on as they stepped out of the stall. Lou pulled her gun.

"Motion-sensors." King pressed a palm against the top of her gun and pushing it down before she put a bullet in something. Can't be leaving a bullet behind in Headquarters. They could analyze it in the basement for fuck's sake and who knew what kind of trouble that would conjure. "It was part of the measurements enacted with last year's budgets. All the lights are motion-sensor. Presumably to cut down on electricity consumption."

She hissed. "I hate motion-sensor lights. Get whatever the hell you need and let's get out of here."

King took the lead, but before yanking open the handle, he grabbed a scratchy brown paper towel from the dispenser by the door. He used it to cover the handle as he yanked the door open. He doubted most of the unhygienic fucks he'd worked with had learned to wash their hands in the months since he'd left.

Propping the door open with a heel, he waited, tossed the brown towel toward a waste bin, and missed by a mile. Lou crossed in front of him, sweeping her gun over the hall. There was nothing in either direction. The lights overhead clicked on again, and he saw Lou's shoulders twitch. The hall smelled like a burnt burrito, the scent of someone abusing their microwave privileges. And the air was artificially cool from the overworked A/C.

"Hurry up," she said, squirming beside him. "We have to get out of here."

"Easy girl," he said. He led her right toward the door at the end of the hall. "We'll be quick."

King searched for little black globes protruding from the ceiling. There had been no cameras when he retired, but things could have changed.

His shoulders relaxed when he saw the smooth, white tiles above.

In the bright hallway fluorescents, the blood caked on Lou's skin and clothes was even more horrifying. Lou looked like a victim from a slasher movie, who had dragged herself out of some hellish pit toward safety after watching all her friends get hacked up. She had said it wasn't her blood, but no one would know it by looking at her.

Her demeanor was far more solid than any victim, though. In this movie of his mind, he wouldn't have been surprised if, at the end of the movie, it was revealed she had been the one who'd wielded the machete all along.

The door at the end of the hall was locked, but only until King fished some keys out of Brasso's satchel and started fitting them into the lock. The door popped open with the fifth key.

It creaked on its hinges as it swung inward. The office was dim, but the moment he saw it, he knew it was still Chaz's office. The desk was littered with sandwich wrappers and papers. Cardinals action figures were poised in a row at the front-most edge. Old paper cups with half-finished beverages were sweating rings onto computer printouts. The blinds behind the desk sat at half-mast, revealing the empty parking lot littered with symmetrical orange spotlights illuminating the pavement.

Across from the desk along the wall was a giant whiteboard. The last note scrawled in green sharpie was dated six days ago:

Brasso- Lieutenant wants to talk when you get back. Answer your phone, you fat cunt. -Stevens

So, he'd been out of the office for nearly a week. One week, hunting New Orleans, checking him out, baiting him with false cases and pulling his heartstrings for remembered glories.

The light started to flicker overhead as they stepped into the room.

Lou growled and slammed the butt of her gun into the plastic switch on the wall. Sparks shot out, and plastic pieces of the broken socket rained onto the floor.

King jumped back and swore.

Darkness fell over Brasso's office. The remaining light came from the orange spotlights outside.

"Jesus Christ. Was that necessary?"

"Yes," Lou said. The growl had not left her voice entirely. "I *hate* motion-sensors."

King took one look at her, the angry snarl marring her features, and let it drop. He wanted to argue that of all the rooms in the DEA headquarters, perhaps light would be useful in here at least. He'd like to see where he was looking. But as his eyes readjusted to the darkness, he realized perhaps that wasn't true.

Generous light the color of daylilies spilled across Chaz's desk from the parking lot outside. He relied on it as he bent down and reached a hand underneath. A momentary fear seized him as he stuck his hand into the darkness. He thought a hand would reach out and grab him, yanking him off to some godforsaken place.

But no cold hand of death grabbed his. His arm disappeared as if painlessly amputated by the darkness. He reached up and felt the underpart of the desk, his fingers running over the gritty pressed board until his nails snagged on the corner of a piece of paper. He gingerly felt around the corners, memorizing the edges before using his thumbnail to separate the tape from the desk's underbelly. *Thank god*, he thought. He was lucky Brasso was a creature of habit.

He sat back in his old partner's desk chair and read the baby blue post-it aloud.

"b00BiEs4Me," he said and snorted.

Lou arched an eyebrow.

King felt the heat rise in his face. He turned the post-it toward her so she could read it for herself.

"A mature guy," she said, nervously thumbing the safety of her gun on and off as she peered through the crack in the door down the lighted hallway. The lights flickered off to conserve energy now that no motion was detected. He could see something in her relax visibly as darkness overtook the building once more.

King removed the laptop from the backpack and powered it on. As soon as he was prompted, he entered the password from the sticky note.

"How did you know he would have his password taped under his desk?" Lou asked. Even her voice was softer now in the darkness. The strident irritation clipping her words had dissolved.

"We were partners for a long time," King said. He felt his throat tighten as if a beignet had gotten stuck halfway down and was threatening to either suffocate him or come back up. He swallowed again. *And he saved my life. Something about that really makes you pay attention to a person afterward.*

"How long?" Her voice dropped, soft.

"Fifteen years," he said. "He was my first."

"How romantic," Lou said.

He looked up and met her eyes, expecting derision or the bland sarcasm he'd been privy to before. But her face wasn't flat and unreadable. Her lips were turned up on one side. Sympathy.

"You were betrayed," she said, her face a perfect mask of seriousness.

He wanted to ask her what the hell she knew about betrayal. She was too young and didn't appear to have anyone in her life. She only trusted Lucy, and Lucy wouldn't squash a bug, on principle alone.

But then he thought of Gus Johnson. The way he'd acted in the days following Jack Thorne's death. Or hell, the way *he'd* acted in the days after Jack died.

"Louie," he asked softly. Darkness was intimate. You didn't shout in the dark. You whispered. You held holy deference as if you were in an inner sanctum. In the presence of some ancient primal force. A god, maybe. In this case a goddess. A goddess of the dark. "Did you kill Gus Johnson?"

"He betrayed my dad," Lou said, without hesitation. "He gave Martinelli our address."

"Jesus Christ," he said and ran a hand over his head. "You just confessed to murder."

"Did I? I don't believe I did." Lou asked with a hint of amusement in her voice. "I'm just stating facts."

He realized it was true. She had not filled in the gaps for him. She's said the exact thing she needed to say to let him know *of course* she'd killed him.

"All they ever found at his house was blood," King said. He remembered going to Johnson's house himself. He wasn't in homicide and had no business being there. But Kennedy was the lead on the case, and Kennedy had looked up to King since the academy. He knew Johnson was one of his old students and gave the older man his due.

He also knew the Johnson case was cold. Long dead in its grave. So dead, daisies were sprouting through the dirt annually. Unless King stumbled upon a bloody weapon or Lou confessed on tape, he had nothing that would reopen it.

And he found he didn't want to turn the girl in.

How the hell had she worked him over so thoroughly in such a short time?

"You wouldn't have been more than sixteen or seventeen when Gus…disappeared," he said, typing the password into the blinking white box. Then he waited for the main screen to load.

"Is that so?" She wasn't shutting him down exactly. The same humor was there, beneath the surface. He had nothing, and she knew it. She knew his best grab was nothing more than smoke and shadows.

"Was he your first kill?" King asked.

The smile on her lips flattened. She didn't answer. And in its way, it was an answer unto itself.

Yes, the voice said in the back of his mind. It had been her first kill. And if that was true then Lucy had truly tried to deal with this on her own, tried to rehabilitate the girl and keep her from going nuclear. She'd tried for a long time before caving and asking King for help. He did the math in his head because Gus had been dead for eight years.

But it also meant Lou had been out for eight years, hunting and destroying the Martinellis, and that was a lot of ammo to go through. A lot of bullets fired. King was under no delusions a person could be rehabilitated after that much killing.

She's too wild. King imagined himself breaking the news to Lucy. *I'm sorry.*

"What does the computer say?" Lou asked. She didn't look at him. Her gaze remained fixed on the hallway beyond the crack they'd left in the door.

King blinked, pulling himself back to the task at hand. The screen had several documents still up as if Chaz had been in the middle of something when he'd powered it down and walked away. Or he'd stepped away from the computer, and the screen had locked itself after minutes of inactivity.

It was information for two flights.

King opened the satchel and started searching for the scrap of paper he'd lifted from Brasso's pocket. He found the folded piece of stationary and read the numbers again: FLR-CDG 815-1005. CDG-IAH 1040-205.

He looked at the screen. Flight numbers.

"It looks like he was expecting someone," King said.

Lou came around the desk and peered over his shoulder at the laptop screen. "Who was on both flights?"

After minimizing two tabs, voila. Lists for each flight sat framed in the screen. "I'm the detective here."

"You're not a detective," she said. "You said so yourself."

"I'm the one with experience." He regretted saying it immediately. After all, if they were going to compare credentials, he knew how he'd size up in the body count. King only killed one man in his life, and it hadn't been intentional.

He stopped scribbling names. "There's only four passengers who were on both flights."

He showed her the list:

Sasha Drivemore
William Glass
Paolo Konstantine
Dominic Luliani

Her shoulders stiffened.

"See something?" He asked, his eyes running down the list again. None of the names meant anything to him.

"Yes."

After a full minute, he made an *out-with-it* gesture with his hand, waving it encouragingly in the air. "Secrets never made friends."

"Konstantine." Her face scrunched up as if she'd gotten a whiff of rotten meat. "He's Martinelli's son."

"Martinelli's son? I thought you killed all of Martinelli's sons?"

"There's one left."

"What the hell does Ryanson want with him?" King asked, more to himself than to anyone else.

A car door shut and they both froze.

King scrambled to his feet, closing the laptop and adjusting the leather satchel on his shoulder. He pivoted in the desk chair and peered out the window. A red Sedan sat parked beneath one of the orange halos.

A man in a brown suit with a green tie sauntered toward the building with a travel mug in his hand. King didn't recognize him. But at four in the morning, it was probably some young buck, recently hired, putting in the hours to get ahead.

King turned and stopped. He blinked twice, but the scene didn't change.

Lou was gone.

He was alone in the room, and down the hall, the motion-sensors began to click on.

29

Konstantine stepped off the sidewalk in front of his expensive hotel room and toward a black sedan pulling up to the curb. The car stopped, and he lifted the handle, but it didn't open. A man from the driver's seat exited the car and came around to open the door for him.

The door opened. *How strange American men are*, Konstantine thought. *The richer they become, the more they like to appear helpless. Unable to open their own doors or drive themselves. Cook for themselves. They evolved into entirely cerebral creatures who would do well to be plugged into giant computers, pumping their thoughts and decisions into a main-frame. Their bodies would remain motionless and out of the way while they exerted their real authority on the lives of others.*

Konstantine forced a smile despite his desire to open and close his own door. *When in Rome.* "Thank you."

The driver dipped his head in acknowledgment.

Konstantine slid into the car. The temperature shift was shocking. One moment, he stood under the blanket of Texas heat. The next, he was in the car's refrigerated interior. The enclosure gave the impression of a grave. A large box deep in the earth and surrounded by crawling things on all sides.

Senator Ryanson smiled at him from across the seat. He wore a gray suit with a red tie. The suit gave the impression of small rabbits Konstantine had seen as a boy. Vulnerable things which could easily be squashed beneath the tire of a car in the city center, if it had dared to dart across the cobblestone at the wrong moment.

"Mr. Konstantine," Ryanson said with a wry smile. It did not reach his eyes. "A pleasure."

The man reached across the seats and offered his hand. Konstantine knew the American custom and accepted it. The hand was frigid. A corpse's hand, fitting for the corpse box they sat in.

The car pulled away from the curb without instruction.

"I can give you twenty minutes of uninterrupted access to the HIA database," Ryanson said. Straight to business. "Will this be enough time to gather the intel we need?"

"Yes," Konstantine said. He did not care to elaborate. *More than enough to get what I want on you.*

"Once you link up," Ryanson said, the same false joviality puppeteering his features. "How long do we have before they know something is up?"

"It depends on the nature of their security," Konstantine said, his shoulders tensing against the leather seats. "The more security, the less time."

"As long as I'm on my party boat and celebrating by 6:00." Ryanson smiled again. This time, the smile was genuine. His eyes crinkled at the corners, and he shared a wide toothy grin with Konstantine before raising a rocks glass to his lips and drinking. Ice clinked against the rim, and Konstantine found himself staring at the water ring on the knee of his pants where he'd balanced the beverage.

"This is why I brought you here," Ryanson said with a grin. "Sponsored your visa, got you through customs. It was a small price to pay for such brilliance. You know we brought Einstein here too. Another political refugee."

And what about my brothers? What had you brought them here for?

He couldn't ask, of course. It was too soon to

give up the game.

And the American was babbling again. Konstantine wanted to look out the window, watch the streets and buildings go by. He marveled at American architecture. It all seemed so new. So infantile. Malformed like a child's building blocks. In his country, they built with stone and rock. They prepared for war, having a long history and the basic comprehension it *would* come.

Even the newest buildings in his country had perhaps a century or more on these chapels made of glass and electricity. Where would the Americans hide when the war reached their shores? Not in these glass giants so easily brought down by their own vulnerability and gravity.

It was moments like this when Konstantine thought of his mother. She had done nothing wrong. She'd caved to Martinelli's affections because to rebuke him would mean her death. But what had it gotten her? A heartless end. Another man who'd wanted to hurt Martinelli but couldn't reach him, hurt her instead. Like a lion grabbing the weaker gazelle in the herd.

As of now, he knew of at least one other woman who'd lost her life this way.

Louie's mother.

"Not a very talkative man," the senator said, and he did not bother to hide his sneer. "You know, in America, we would call that rude."

"I prefer not to speak unless I can improve upon the silence," Konstantine said and offered his best disarming smile. *And you are talking enough for the both of us.*

The senator's sneer softened. "You'll enter the HIA with me under the pretense of my personal bodyguard. When I begin to speak to Fenner, I will leave you by the door. It's customary, a sign that I trust him as we do our cloak and dagger negotiations. It's all about the Mexico trade agreement. As much as you might want to be privy to *that* conversation, I think we both know you have something better to do."

Konstantine acknowledged him with a nod of his head. He thought, *I wonder how she will do it? Will she put a bullet between your eyes? Or will she use a blade? Slowly? Enjoy it?*

"The door to his inner office is to the right, and the door to the hallway is to the left. Take the office door instead of exiting and you can work your magic." Ryan fiddled with his cuff link again. "I'll spill my drink when it's time to go."

"It's like a spy movie." Konstantine smiled.

The congressman tilted his head and smiled back. "I thought it was a clever idea."

You're an imbecile. Elected by imbeciles who do not know how you work against them. She will see right through you. She'll know you for exactly what you are.

The congressman went on smiling. "Regardless, this computer is on the HIA server. You'll be able to do what you need to do from there."

"And after?" Konstantine asked with a grin to mirror the senator's.

The congressman's smile turned wolfish. "Then I will take you out on my boat to celebrate. Have you ever seen the Houston harbor at night?"

"No," Konstantine said.

"It's beautiful. Absolutely to die for."

30

Lou leaned against the cool tree trunk, clutching the bark as if it were a great log in a wide river. Her compass spun inside her. One part of her wanted to go back to King. She saw him in the upstairs window, in the fat bastard's office, a sliver of light across his face as he searched the hallway.

Another part of her wanted to go to Lucy. Aunt Lucy needed her. Was it Venetti? Or was some greater, more venomous danger on the move? She couldn't be sure. A third part of her pulled again toward Konstantine. At last she'd put the name to the face. And once she'd seen him, her compass forever marked his direction. When she listened through the darkness of her mind, she could smell him, the thick musk of his cologne and the pulse of his heart in the back of her head.

Stay, she commanded her shaking legs. *Don't be the victim, Lou-blue*, her father said. His voice echoed in her bones as if he was beside her, cooing encouragement into her ear. As if he'd never left her. *Master this.*

"I'm in charge," she said. All her life she'd been a slave to this greater current.

No more.

I say where we go. Get King. Then my apartment.

Lou let go of the trunk and plunged through reality's fabric. She reached out and grabbed the back of King's coat. He still had his face pressed to the crack of the door, searching the hallway for his chance to escape.

He sucked in a breath when she yanked him away from the door, but whatever he was about to say was swallowed up by the black ocean stretching between two fixed points in time and space. When they stepped out, they were in her closet. King's enormous body squished hers. The closet was too small. Grunting, she squeezed through the door. Fresh air hit her full in the face.

Lights from the buildings along the river danced across her apartment floor. While cabs raced down wide boulevards outside, she crossed the room and removed a painting that hung on the brick wall. A replica of Picasso's "Girl with a Mandolin." She'd always loved this picture since the first time she saw it with Aunt Lucy in the MOMA. It was a perfect representation of her being.

A girl, all broken up, but recognizable.

That's what happens to me when I slip through the darkness, she thought. She split into pieces, fed through the cracks and reassembled on the other side.

She propped the painting against her shin and pressed three bricks on the wall. A click rang out. The façade popped out. She peeled back the edge of the brick, revealing a gray steel safe set into the wall. Lou entered her six-number combination until the safe also clicked open. She shoved aside the extra guns and stacks of cash and grabbed a handful of glow sticks. She also grabbed one of the guns and extra ammo—the kind that exploded when it hit its target, leaving more shrapnel in the body than could be dug out.

She'd slipped it off a table at a gun show. The dealer, a man missing one of his front teeth, the other half-dissolved in blackened decay, hadn't even seen her do it. She was in and out of the shadows before he could ask her to show ID.

"I thought you lived in a hovel," King said. He *was* enormous. A wall of a man in her studio apartment, craning his neck to absorb the details. "I sort of pictured an abandoned warehouse, maybe a mattress in one corner and enough guns and explosives hanging around to take over New York."

He must have seen her glare.

"But this is nice. Real nice," he added. "Not too feminine."

His eyes roved over her counters, the bare island, and the unused stove. Lou didn't think she'd turned it on once since moving in two years ago.

And if she was honest with herself, she would have been fine with an abandoned warehouse. She'd only gotten this apartment, filled it with home goods and hung art on the walls, so that Lucy would stop begging her to get an address.

King opened a cabinet and found her six water glasses. Another had her four bowls and four plates. The third, a box of crackers and a bag of ground coffee. The other cabinets were bare.

"A man could live here." He pointed at the Picasso. "Men love to have naked boobs on their walls. Even artistic ones."

"I don't want to live with a man." She shoved the guns, ammo, and glow sticks into a canvas bag.

King frowned. "I wasn't suggesting you needed a man. I'm commenting on the gender neutrality of the apartment."

"Get in the closet." Lou tossed him the bag. He doubled over when the sack hit him square in the gut. "We're leaving."

King squeezed himself into the closet and looked ridiculous doing it. His shoulders were hunched up to his ears as she slid in, trying to find a niche for herself. The door wouldn't close on the first try.

"Suck in," she told him.

He snorted. "I am! It's the bag."

"Suck in *harder*."

"You need a bigger closet."

"You need to lose ten pounds."

"That's unfair!" King said, creating another inch or so by angling his body deeper into the corner. "If I said that to you, I'd be an asshole. That's sexism."

Lou managed to get the closet door to click shut and then they were moving, exploding out into the other side.

"Fuck," King said, bumping against the inside of the shipping container deep in Siberia. The cold of the container rushed in on them, raising the goosebumps on her arm.

Lou shoved her hand into the canvas sack, fingers searching until she felt the plastic tubing of one of the glow sticks. She snapped it in half and shook it. Orange light filled the shipping container. She handed the stick to King.

"What's this for?" King held the light over his head. From that angle, the tangerine glow illuminated the whole container. Chaz Brasso's dark liquid eyes blinked open in a slow, dazed sort of way.

She handed King three more glow sticks, keeping one for herself, and gave him the gun from the safe along with a full magazine. "Interrogate him. I'll be back."

"What?" he said, panic rising in his voice. "You can't leave me here."

"Lucy needs me," she said, closing the canvas sack and slipping her arms through. "Something is wrong."

His panic only deepened. "If you don't come back, I'll starve in some hole in the middle of fucking nowhere."

"A shipping container in Siberia," she informed him.

"A shipping container!" he exclaimed. "In fucking Siberia!"

"I'll be right back. Hide the stick under your shirt. Wrap your coat around it. Come on. I need a shadow."

When he didn't move, she plucked the transparent tube from his fingers and shoved it into his pocket. Then she was gone.

31

Lucy ran the once-white washcloth under her kitchen sink. Red ribbons of Paula's blood dripped down the back of her hand and into the metallic basin. She watched the blood swirling down the drain with all the intensity of an old crone reading entrails, looking for a way to save her village from an impending drought.

And she hurt like an old crone. The burning in her chest. The swollen and aching feet.

The blood made her think of Jack. Blood always made her think of Jack.

When he was dead, and Louie was missing, she'd gone to the morgue under cover of night. She remembered how cold the place had been as if stepping into a meat locker. Except this time, the carcasses weren't hanging from the ceiling on hooks, waiting to be hauled down by some butcher in a stained white apron. This time, the flesh was tucked neatly away in drawers, like the kind one might pull open at the bottom of a stainless steel refrigerator to retrieve a soda or a beer.

Except one of these drawers had held her brother.

She'd pulled open the drawer and slid him out.

He was pale and naked on the silver slab. They had not done the autopsy yet, for which she was grateful. But his chest was still a mess. Nine bullets had punctured the flesh, leaving behind nine puckered black holes. Some were misshapen, and Lucy imagined the morgue attendant inserting snipe-nose pliers into these wounds and digging out the bullets for the cops. They'd need them for their investigation, she was sure. If they intended to hunt the killer, that was. She had doubts. The way they smeared his name, his *good* name, she suspected the cops as much as the disgruntled drug dealers.

Lucy reached out and touched her brother's ghostly pale face. Tears spilled across her cheeks as she placed a hand on the unmoving chest. "I'll look after Louie." She'd promised him. "I'll do my damnedest to keep your baby alive."

She'd been certain, that night in the morgue, the killers who'd murdered her brother would be back for Lou. Much like the ancient Romans, after running through the soldiers with their swords, they dashed the babies' skulls against the hearth for good measure.

"I'll keep her safe," she said again.

I'm sorry, Jack. She thought now at her kitchen sink, watching the years stretch out between now and then. *I didn't do half of what I promised you.*

"Lucy?" Paula said.

The girl's voice pulled Lucy from the daydream of her dead brother. She looked down and saw that she'd wrung the washcloth until the water ran clear. Her knuckles were scalded red by the water still running.

She turned off the faucet. "I'm sorry, what?"

"Can I have another Coke? I don't know what's wrong with me, but I'm so thirsty."

"Sure. Bottom drawer." Lucy nodded at the fridge to her right.

Paula flashed a weak smile, either because her mood had not improved despite the passing danger, or because her swollen and purpling face didn't allow her to smile.

The stainless-steel drawer slid out, and a gust of chilled fog escaped into the kitchen. Instead of a drawer full of soda cans, Lucy saw Jack, chest full of black bullet holes.

She threw the rag in the sink. "Why don't you

take some Tylenol with that?" she said. "Your face must hurt like hell."

Paula gave another weak smile as she popped the cap on the soda can. "I'd love some Tylenol. I'd even take something harder if you got it."

The girl's eyes slid to the line of orange prescription bottles lined up on Lucy's table.

"You wouldn't want those," Lucy said and flashed an embarrassed smile. "They're not for pain."

Lucy never made it to the bathroom.

When she stepped out of the kitchen and into the living room, three men stood in her living room. Behind them, her apartment door stood open, revealing the dim hallway with a flickering bulb that the manager had promised to change no less than a hundred times and yet never found a chance to do it between fighting with his wife and NASCAR races on television.

All thoughts about Tylenol for the girl left her.

Lucy took in the three men standing there. How had they found her? How had they reached her so quickly? Lou had mentioned San Diego and a vegan drive-thru. But San Diego was a million miles away, and the men here couldn't possibly be the same ones trying to kill the girl.

"Lucy Thorne." The first man said, and he raised the pistol an inch in a sort of shrug. It wasn't a question.

So, she didn't answer.

"You wanna take a ride with us?"

"No," she said. It was a stupid thing to say, but it had come out of her mouth before she'd thought it through.

"Excuse me?" the first one said. His brow furrowed.

"No," she said, fighting to keep her voice even. "I don't want to take a ride with you."

The two men behind him laughed. It wasn't friendly rolling laughter. It was a short, harsh bark like a crocodile snapping at bait dangling two feet above muddy marsh waters.

"Even better," the one in front said and sucked at his teeth. Lucy's skin crawled at the sound. "I like it when they say *no*."

Would you *like to take a ride with us?* Only *you*. No mention of Paula. If they didn't even know about Paula in the kitchen, then this was something else.

Only they hadn't seemed that surprised to her.

A drawer opened and closed in the kitchen and at the same time three guns raised.

Lucy took a step back, her hand going to the

hollow of her throat. Her mouth had opened in a dramatic O, but no sound was coming out. Instead, all the air was going in a great panicked gasp.

"Is somebody here with you?" the man in front asked. His furrowed brow had worsened, his lips practically snarling.

She was going to say no, but Paula Venetti stepped out of the kitchen then and bumped into her back. When the girl saw the men with the guns, she shrieked, and she didn't stop shrieking.

"Shut the fuck up!" The first one said, but Paula didn't seem capable of shutting up. Lucy had to turn and clasp a hand over the girl's mouth. Paula trembled in her arms.

They were visibly confused. Each man's brow furrowed. The one in front shuffled his feet. His gun dipped.

But it was the one in the back, the smallest of the men, who spoke. "What is she doing here?"

"I don't know," the front man admitted. "But we'll take her too."

"But Chaz just wanted the one."

"It doesn't matter. We're taking them both."

Go go go, Lucy thought, her mind kick-starting. Her initial shock and panic and the erroneous connection between Paula and these men cleared away. She wanted to protect Paula, and she wanted to warn Lou, tell her not to come back to her place because someone was hunting them. Someone knew about her Oak Park home, and she should stay far away.

And Chaz… that name rang a faint bell.

But there were only three ways out of this apartment. One was the front door, now guarded by three men with guns. The second was a two-story drop to the street below, by either jumping off her balcony or tumbling out of a window. Either would surely end in a great deal of physical damage. The men would find it easy to haul away her busted body. After all, how could she protect herself if she had broken legs or half her brains spilled across the pavement?

The third exit was the closet.

She was already counting out the steps in her head, *eight*, maybe less if she took long loping strides.

She could yank Paula back into the kitchen, but it wasn't dark enough in there. Unlike Lou, who could slip in the barest of shadows, Lucy required full darkness. Dark so black she could hold up her own hand and not see it.

She wasn't sure she could reach the closet

before she got a bullet in the head. She couldn't get
Paula in the closet with her. The girl would collapse
on her shaking legs after the first step.

"What you looking at?" the man asked. His eyes
went to the closet. "You got somebody else in there
too?"

"No," Lucy said reflexively. She regretted the
words the instant they left her lips.

The man's brow deepened. "Donnie, look in
that closet."

Donnie sported a cleft lip. He looked at the
leader for a minute as if he wasn't sure he'd heard
him. When he gave him an angry look, he crossed
the room toward the closet as if it were the fire exit
in a burning building. Lucy became aware of a sharp
pain and looked down to see four red fingernails
biting into her arm.

She pried Paula's fingers off her flesh and held
her hand. The four crescent-shaped impressions
ached and burned, but this did not compare to the
discomfort of her hammering heart, which had even
surpassed her general unease.

The pressure in the room changed. Her ears
popped. The man opened the door and peered into
the closet.

"Where's   the   light   switch?"   he   asked,

uninterested in going deeper without light. "It's as black as an asshole in here."

Lucy didn't answer him. There was nothing to say. There was no switch. It was a linen closet that had had the shelves removed. She was sure if Donnie had reached up and touched the wall, all he would feel would be the even studs running horizontally, on which the shelves used to balance.

The thick outline of Donnie's body completely disappeared as he reached the back of the closet with his hand outstretched.

Lucy's ears popped again, and she thought she heard a sharp intake of breath.

"Donnie," the leader said.

Donnie didn't answer.

"Donnie!" he snapped. "Dude, what the fuck?"

But still, there was no answer.

The leader raised his gun. "What the fuck?" He punctuated each word with a jab of his gun, and Paula screamed in Lucy's ear, making her head split into two throbbing parts.

"I don't know," Lucy assured them, though she most certainly did, and the realization made her heart pound and ache with more panic. *Stay away*, she begged the inside of the dark closet. *Please god, Lou, stay away.*

Lucy held her hands up in front of her in the universal signal of surrender. She hoped that she would not get shot. Though if she was dead, perhaps that would be preferable than dealing with the difficult road ahead. A long and exhausting illness that was sure to strip her down piece by piece.

The leader considered the closet. His brows pinched together as if he was working on a challenge he had not encountered before. He was doing the math in his head, Lucy suspected. If he sent the other man into the closet, then it might be one against two, and while he had a gun, the odds were against him.

They need us alive, Lucy realized. Alive for some godawful reason. Torture. Or ransom. What did this Chaz want with them?

Chaz…Chaz… her mind searched for recognition but only conjured a body bag and the sight of flashing blue lights against a dark house.

"What's going on with the fucking closet?" he yelled. Confusion made him belligerent, as with most people.

Lucy raised her hands higher, she lowered her voice hoping she sounded calmer than she felt. "How the hell should I know? It's a closet."

"You've got somebody in there! Donnie!"

Donnie still didn't answer.

"Whoever the fuck is in there. If you don't fucking answer or send Donnie out, I'm going to put a bullet in these bitches' heads!" He pointed the gun at Paula who shrieked like someone had stuck her bare hand into a boiling pot.

I can't let them see you. I can't let them have you, Lucy thought, and even as her protective instincts rose, so did the obvious ridiculousness of her statement. *They have no idea what they are dealing with*, a darker voice said. She looked into the open closet, into the pitch black. She couldn't see Lou, but she could feel her there, on the other side of night.

She was one with the dark. More of a primordial force than a girl now, shrouded in a substance that they had mistakenly believed to be the absence of light.

But Lucy had always suspected that wasn't true. Naïve. Darkness was not the absence of light. It was its own substance. An organism that came in and occupied space like any other nocturnal creature in this world.

The gang leader had had enough of the game. He stormed across the room, gun raised, and shoved the barrel against Lucy's forehead.

That was his mistake.

The open closet door had been shielding him. Now his profile was in plain view.

He seemed to realize this a heartbeat after Lucy did. His eyes widened, and he whirled, gun raised.

Then his face disintegrated.

One minute, Lucy was struggling to keep herself between the gun and Paula. The next, half of his skull cap had been blown off. The ripe smell of meat, blood, and piss flooded her apartment.

She stared into glassy brown eyes with bloodshot threads running through the egg white orbs. She noted the acidic smell of his breath. Tobacco. The scar along one side of his jaw that came toward his mouth and pulled at the corner like a fish hook.

Then it was all meat and the white gleam of bone.

The other man who'd waited patiently in the doorway, as if his purpose was to block the only perceived exit from the apartment, jumped back. His mouth popped open in surprise.

Lou stepped out of the closet then, coming around the door with her gun up. The fat man with the oversized T-shirt turned toward her slowly.

He didn't get his gun up in time. Lou put two bullets in him. One in his throat and the other in his upper chest. His strong hand with its short fat fingers went up to his throat and clutched the wound. Blood spewed from between his fingers down over his hairy knuckles.

He started to raise his gun, but she shot him in the hand, and his mouth dropped open in a wordless cry. Only blood gurgled up.

Lucy had an overwhelming desire to cry then. Not because she'd witnessed three lives lost, but because of the absolute calm in Lou's face as she executed the task. She could have been turning on a television or checking her email. Or—god help her—doing something she truly *enjoyed*. Lucy was horrified to realize she'd seen this very expression on her own face when coming out of a deep and satisfying meditation.

Relief, she realized. When Lou killed, it gave her peace.

Lucy's heart was being crushed in her chest. She couldn't move. She couldn't speak.

Louie met her aunt's eyes. Her cheeks flushed red. "I'm sorry you had to see that. Had to see me—"

Lucy grabbed her and hugged her so hard, Lou groaned.

"Go somewhere safe," Lou wrapped her arms

around the smaller woman. "Keep moving until this blows over."

Lucy hugged her harder.

"I'll clean this up." Lou's voice was low and steady.

She put her hands on Lou's cheeks. So hot. On her brow. Blood came off on her hands, but she didn't care. She kept running her hands down the girl's arms and body looking for wounds, looking for fresh blood pouring out of some bullet hole. Lou had always been a stoic child, hiding her pain and fear when they went to the doctor or when she hurt herself playing. Once, when she crashed into a concrete barrier on her bicycle, she'd split open her elbow and needed six stitches. Most children would cry. Louie only said *gross*.

She suspected that tendency to hide rather than show pain had only deepened with her experience.

"I'm okay."

"Are you sure?" she heard herself say. Her voice went high, grew strident. "Maybe you were shot, and you don't feel it. Maybe—"

Lou cut her off by squeezing her hand a little harder. Not enough to hurt Lucy, but enough to get her attention. "Keep moving. I am not sure how big their network is, so try not to draw attention to yourselves, and don't stay in one place too long."

"Too long!" Lucy felt the pulse rising in her temples. "What's too long?"

"A day," she said after a moment of careful consideration. "One night per place."

Lucy touched the hollow of her throat. She could feel her heart pounding against her fingertips there as if it were going to leap out of her throat and fall to the floor.

Jack, she thought. *Oh god, Jack, what have I done? I sent her to King thinking...what had I been thinking?*

By taking Lou to King, she had hoped to cure a problem, not inflate it. Show her that there was a life worth building for her out there in the world. One where isolation and running weren't necessary. But she also did it because...because—

You're dying. You did this to give yourself peace.

But Lucy felt the tears streaming down her cheeks and the uncomfortable way Lou shifted away from her as if those tears carried the plague.

"I'm sorry," Lucy said. "Oh, Louie. I'm so sorry."

Paula tugged on her arm.

"Yes," Lucy said. "We should go. But we need

to pack clothes. We can't walk around with all this blood on us. We'll draw too much attention."

She was already picturing the dark YMCA showers in her mind. Both she and Paula could clean up without notice this late into the night. And once clean, move on to somewhere else. She had half a dozen vacation houses in her mind that stood empty this time of year. She wondered how she could package the idea to Paula, *an exciting tour of European closets!* An imaginary brochure read. And then how silly that seemed. She was exhausted, and her adrenaline had turned her mind on its head.

"I'll stay until you pack," Lou said.

And she did. She'd closed and locked the apartment door.

Lucy went into her bedroom and pulled a vintage suitcase from the top shelf of her closet, throwing in clothes, a toiletry bag, and cash into the hard case. Paula trailed her like a puppy at the heels, drawn to movement. By the time she'd returned to the intersection of her hallway and kitchen doorway, she found the apartment empty of bodies.

The blood and mess were still there, but the bodies and the guns were gone.

Lou stepped out of the closet, her hands and forearms slicked up to the elbow with blood. She saw Lucy staring and said, "I'll clean the rest. Don't worry."

Tears stung the back of Lucy's eyes again, and her throat threatened to collapse on itself.

Lucy reached up and cupped Lou's cheek. "Don't die."

First, her mind added. *Don't die* first.

Lucy Thorne didn't think she could bear it.

32

I'll be twenty minutes. Tops," Ryanson said, and he was saying it loud enough for the men in the other room to hear, but his eyes flicked left, toward a door. "Wait here until I need you. If I need you."

Konstantine did not move or smile or acknowledge him in any way. He remained standing in a foyer of an apartment until the senator had disappeared into the other room and another male voice joined Ryanson's in salutation. Their footsteps echoed the way they did in grand cathedrals back home. *Because their temples are the temples of commerce,* he thought.

Then the sound of chairs creaking and bodies settling in. Briefcase latches released. Someone cleared their throat.

Konstantine stood in the foyer where a magnificent crystal chandelier bloomed overhead. There were three doors: the one they'd entered from, the one Ryanson had exited from, and the last—a dark door to his left.

He waited for a guard to come and check on him.

A man in a red suit and black tie peeked at Konstantine minutes later. Then the guard disappeared again.

He still didn't move, but his eyes slid to the closed door again. He estimated how many steps it would take to reach it. He reminded himself why he was doing this.

When they came for his father, they took his mother instead.

In the middle of the night, men filled their house. They bundled up his mother and pulled a black sack over her head. So he wasn't surprised when they did the same to him. Their hands and feet were tied.

The stairs, the corridor and even the street outside their apartment were all familiar. He'd traversed these spaces so often he could do it with his eyes closed. But once the men put him and his mother into the back of a car, the familiarity was gone.

They drove forever. Or perhaps it was only the night that made the drive seem endless.

Then the cars stopped as suddenly as they'd

started. They waited. His mother tried to soothe him with reassurances. He didn't know what to say to reassure her.

Men were talking outside the car. They were shouting.

Then the doors were thrown open, and he was dragged out. He could smell the linden trees and the night air even through the sack. He heard his mother cry out as she was forced to kneel beside him.

The sacks were torn off.

The first thing he saw was the giant hole in front of him. It wasn't the perfect square usually dug for cemetery plots. It was crude and shallow, wider on the bottom and more narrow at top.

His father stood on the opposite side. He saw him clearly. His mother saw him too and at the sight of him, began to cry. She didn't beg for her life. She begged for Konstantine's.

Somehow Konstantine began to realize what was happening. This was a negotiation. They wanted something from senior Martinelli, and they were prepared to murder his lover and bastard son to get it.

Martinelli resisted, and they shot his mother. Konstantine remembers the look that passed over her face. She'd known death was coming but her mouth still opened in surprise. The sight of her pitching forward, nightgown billowing as she fell into the dark hole. Her gown seemed to glow in the bottom of the dark cradle, but her body had disappeared, swallowed by the shadows.

He did not remember what happened next. He didn't remember returning to Florence. Didn't remember being turned over to Padre Leo for safe keeping. He knew his grief had swallowed him, masticated him to bits and spit out another boy, months later.

None of that bothered him.

He had only one regret.

That he did not pay more attention to his mother's final moments. Consequently, he did not know where she was buried, didn't know how to honor her passing or make sure her bones were properly laid to rest. He could not honor her on her birthday, holidays, or the Day of the Dead.

Good women died at the hands of bad men.

He knew this was true.

But he could not accept his mother was alone in some Italian field, waiting to be found, waiting for a proper burial in a place where her son could visit often. He would make this possible as soon as he found her.

And he *would* find her. Lou would help him. Somehow he knew, Lou would reunite them at last.

When the guard peeked and disappeared for the second time, Konstantine darted for the office door. He reached it in eight steps.

It was an office. Unlit and silent. And completely and utterly dark as he slid the door closed behind him. But leaving it open was stupid. Anyone who walked by would know where he'd gone. But with the door closed, he had only the light from the computer to guide him.

He wasted no time rounding the desk and inserting his USB into the port. The laptop was already open, and three fish swam on the screen as if in an imaginary aquarium. Konstantine punched a series of buttons, and the password screen fell away. The air in this office was cool and the keys soft under his fingertips.

As he furiously typed, he imagined a series of bots marching out of the USB into the defenseless computer, sliding down these channels toward their battle stations.

He strained to hear the men talking. Listened for their booming voices vibrating through the walls, but heard nothing. For all he knew, they could be standing en mass outside the office door, ready to seize him, string him up and tear him limb from limb.

There was also the matter of the office itself. The *dark* office.

Konstantine's eyes kept slipping toward the thickest shadows in the corners of the room. Places where the walls seemed to breathe.

Any minute she would be there. She would appear, her face glowing in the darkness like Banquo's ghost come to choke him in his guilt.

But the shadows remained shadows. The darkness remained still.

And even if she did appear, he couldn't stop. He had to do this.

For his mother. And for Louie.

One did not approach a goddess empty-handed, begging for favor.

On the screen a green bar marking his progress filled. The task was done. He stepped out into the hallway, closed the door again without a sound, and assumed his same statuesque pose.

The guard checked him for a third time.

Konstantine's heart pounded in his ears so hard that he was certain if someone spoke to him, he wouldn't hear it.

As long as no one wanted to shake, he would be

okay. If he had to unclasp his hands for any reason, they would certainly notice the tremor in his fingers or the dampness in his palms.

But it didn't matter.

It would be worth it as long as he could complete the job.

Of course, this would be the hardest part.

How to stay alive long enough to deliver the truth?

33

King traced the small container for the hundredth time. Flecks of rust had wiggled beneath his fingernails, and when he tried to dig them out with another short nail, they were only wedged deeper. Now a sharp edge bit into the tender flesh and a line of blood filled the crescent moons.

"My head is killing me," Brasso whined as he pulled himself into a sitting position. And he made a ruckus doing it. His boots boomed against the floor, heels scrapping. And something was wrong with his arm. It lay across his lap, limp as a dead fish. But King couldn't remember anything happening to his arm. Unless Lou had done it.

Brasso rubbed the back of his head. "Did you give me a concussion?"

"No." King's tongue felt swollen. Either he'd bitten it and hadn't realized it, or it was his fear choking him. "You were hit in the head with a cast iron skillet."

"Jesus," Brasso said and touched the back of his head. "I should sue you."

"If you get out of this container alive, you do that." King's heart floundered in his chest.

These walls held no exit. No seam he could pry open. Lou had called it a shipping container, but unless the communists had tried to conserve money by not installing a door, it was an iron coffin.

His mind began a running list of everything that could go wrong.

What if Lou died? What if she was mortally wounded enough to make a return trip impossible?

Would he starve to death? Would Lucy come looking for him?

An air vent kicked on and air smelling like basement pipes filtered into the space. The air, no matter how dank, helped. He remembered what he was supposed to be doing.

He turned to Brasso and aimed his pistol. "Why did you do it?"

"What a stupid question." Brasso snorted and rubbed at his nose. "Why does anyone do anything? For the money. For the perks. If you want to start a conversation with me, Robbie, make it a good one."

"How much did Ryanson pay you?"

Brasso grinned. "A fuck ton. So much you'd

piss your panties if I told you."

"Your reputation is fucked," King said, "The moment I get back—"

"Oh come on, King, you're not going to out me."

"The hell I won't."

Brasso laughed. *Laughed*. "You won't. You know why?"

The walls were warping, moving in. This fucking orange light wasn't helping. It gave the room an off-kilter look.

"Because when I go down, I'll smear your name all through the mud with mine. I'll talk about how many cover-ups we did in our years together. I'll point my finger at you so hard you'll feel it up your ass."

The world shifted as if on a tilt. "They won't believe you."

Brasso laughed again. A great big belly laugh. "Oh, they'll believe. And you'll rot in a cell right beside me. And I'll sell out your old ass *again*, more specifically your asshole in this case, to the first young buck willing to give me a cigarette."

King punched him twice. The skin split across his knuckle bones before he caught himself.

He pushed back. He ran a hand through this hair

and resumed pacing. He threw one last punch. "Son of a bitch."

Brasso touched his face tenderly and hissed. "Yeah, yeah. You knew what *I* was. Like I've always known what *you* are, Robbie boy. The sanctimonious pratt who wants a gold star for every shit he takes."

King was going to kill him long before Lou returned, he decided. He would do it now, except the only thing worse than rotting in this container, was rotting in this container *with a dead body*. Everything was worse with a dead body.

"Thinking about killing me?" Brasso huffed. Sweat beaded on the man's forehead.

King shot him a look.

"Oh come on. I can read you like a stop sign. You're too predictable. Make you a little angry, and you want to shoot first and ask questions later."

"I was trying to decide if I wanted to eat you alive or dead."

"Ah, so we *are* stuck," Brasso said, his face pinched. "York all over again?

Mention of the collapsed building where King spent two whole days made his back clench. He was going to vomit. If he didn't pull himself together, he was going to do more than vomit.

"How long?" King asked.

In the orange light, Brasso's face looked slick with oil and his eyes shrunken in their sockets. "Twelve fucking inches. Why? You want to blow me?"

King didn't even flinch. He'd heard this dirty mouth for decades. "How long have you been Ryanson's fuck boy?"

Brasso's shit-eating grin flattened to a thin line. "Do you want to know that, Robbie?"

"Why wouldn't I?"

"It might change the way you view our relationship," he said. "The wife never likes to hear about the other woman. How happy can she be to learn her happy marriage included thirty years of infidelity?

King's stomach dropped. Not unlike the way it dropped when Lou pulled him through the thin fabric of time and space. But she had not returned. The only time he was falling through now was his own.

"How long?" he asked again, and he felt the muscles along his spine clench as if bracing for an impact.

Brasso pushed himself up even taller before falling back against the rusty wall. The walls gave a metallic pop that echoed through the container. "Do you remember the *talk* Bennigan gave me? I was gone for a whole day, and then I came back with my tail tucked."

For a minute, King didn't. He reached deep into the back of his mind but felt only cobwebs. A sensation of groping blind in the darkness. Then a lightning flash of recognition and his pulse kicked. "When I got shot."

Brasso was nodding. "You took a bullet and became a hero, and I got a goddamn lecture about not being where I was told to be...like a fucking five-year-old. Bad boy, little Chazzy. Mommie told you to come inside when the street lights came on, and you didn't listen and look what happened. *You* got a medal and were sent off to school the kiddies..."

And had the pleasure of meeting Jack Thorne.

"...and while you did your 90-day tour of Quantico, I was downgraded to a desk. Man, that rubbed my ass wrong."

King was waiting for the connection to be made.

Brasso wasn't done talking. "So when Ryanson rolled up on a white pony with a fuck ton of cash tied in a pretty bow, why would I say no? *No?* To more money than I'd ever make with the department? No to black-tie parties drowning in beautiful women who would blow their own fathers six ways to Sunday if you offered them one snort of coke, which by the way, is about as easy to come by in the DEA headquarters as an STD at Coachella."

King tried to count how many times drugs went missing between the bust itself and the evidence locker. Too many to count. But had he ever imagined that Brasso was palming the stuff himself? No.

"Thirteen years," King said. The shock was wearing off. After all, he knew it happened. How many cops or agents were in the pocket of this or that powerhouse? Most. Why? Because everything had a price. King knew full well that the price of his guilt was too high to be bought by anyone—but he wasn't naïve enough to believe that meant he had no price at all.

"Or maybe you think I should've said no to being fucking appreciated for my talents rather than kicked like a dog who pissed on the rug? You know what happened when I saved your life?"

King pressed his back against the metal wall as if to make the room wider.

"Nothing," Chaz said. "No medal. No slap on the ass. Just a that-a-boy, Chazzy. That-a-boy."

"If Ryanson wanted something overlooked, I took care of it. I pointed the hounds in another direction. Maybe evidence went missing. Maybe witnesses did. Enough misdirection to keep them off Ryanson's ass."

"So you betrayed the men and women who worked with you, to protect a rich bastard?"

Brasso rolled his eyes. "And you wonder why no one invites you to the parties, Robbie."

King ran a sweaty palm through his hair. This was all connected somehow. He knew it. But the pieces just weren't quite lining up yet. King still had more questions than answers: why did Brasso choose him? He could have chosen any number of private investigators to find Venetti.

He chose him so he could use him. Maybe even do away with him. If he could betray one friend, why not another? After King had delivered Venetti, maybe he was earmarked for a watery grave of his very own.

"Do you remember Gus Johnson and Jack Thorne?" King finally asked.

Brasso stopped smiling. "What about them?"

It was a strange reaction. The way one reacts if you say *I have a snake in this bag*. If King were an interrogator, he'd lean into that, press harder, and see where it took him.

He was a shit investigator, but he had to ask. "Right before he died, Jack was working a case. A *big* case."

Brasso's feral eyes didn't blink.

"This case was against a mayor. He thought this mayor was selling drugs and perhaps girls. He had bank records and a couple of witnesses. That case never saw the light of day because, *surprise surprise*, when Jack died, the bank records and witnesses and all the other bits of evidence disappeared. That was real curious, because even Jack's partner, Johnson, couldn't seem to find any of it. Or maybe he didn't look very hard."

King made a poof gesture with his left hand, the right still holding the gun, wide circles in the air before him.

"Are you calling me unoriginal?" Brasso taunted.

King wasn't going to let himself be distracted. "Did you know that same mayor went on to become a senator?" King heard the tremor in his voice. Felt the gun rattling against his thigh. The orange light in the container made his head swim. *If I don't take a breath, I'm going to hyperventilate,* he realized. *Breathe.*

Brasso still said nothing.

"But we all know the Martinellis killed Jack Thorne," King said. And he got the reaction he wanted. Brasso *relaxed*. "And we even know that Gus Johnson was the one who gave his partner up. Told the Martinellis where to look, even though Thorne had taken all the necessary precautions to keep his home and family off the radar."

"So then why are you telling me all this?" Brasso wet his lips and then cautiously met King's eyes. "I know you loved the prick. Thorne. The only time you stopped praising your ass was to praise his. But what's that got to do with me?"

King grinned. But it was a hard, curdled expression that made the muscles in his face twitch. "Because the more I think about betrayal, particularly *your* brand of betrayal, the more I wonder who wanted to put an end to Thorne's digging. After all, it wouldn't have been hard to convince the Martinellis to do it, if they already had revenge on their mind."

34

Lou stared at the blood-soaked carpet in her aunt's apartment and wondered where shit had gone wrong. She had a process. A clear-cut, no error approach to killing. Take them to her private Alaskan lake. Jump to La Loon. Kill them and leave their bodies for Jabbers.

No bullets. No casings. No gunpowder or evidence. No bodies. No blood. No witnesses, except maybe those from the point of abduction. But usually, she had enough counter-evidence to prove she was elsewhere. Enough improbability on her side to make people know she couldn't have been in both Milan and New York on the same night.

Therefore, officer, you are mistaken. That person you're looking for only looks like me.

With a sigh, she knelt on the rug and sprayed carpet cleaner onto the darkest spot. Then she took the scrubber to it, moving her hand in stiff circles the way her mother had taught her.

Of course, Lou'd never even been questioned by the police regarding a missing person. The people she yanked off the streets were the vermin in the gutters. Why the hell would the police even look for them?

Yet here she was, in her *second* trashed apartment this evening, furiously scrubbing at another carpet. Why couldn't Lucy get a rug? Rugs were easier to dispose of.

She stared down at the wet spot. No blood. Someone could have spilled a cup of water and was letting the carpet air dry. The walls and everything else had been wiped down as well. She threw the carpet cleaner and scrubbers into a bag and vacuumed the place. She spent extra time on the wet spots, trying to make sure no soapy spots dried stiff.

She stood up an overturned chair and straightened a crooked picture of Aphrodite in a tree pose on her aunt's wall above the Indian print sofa.

If this whole murder-revenge thing ever goes sour, she thought, *I could open a cleaning business specializing in blood. Kill your bastard husband and need help disposing of his worthless corpse? Lou-Blue is there for you! 555-7687*

She grinned and stepped into the closet and closed the door behind her. When she opened the door again, she was in her St. Louis apartment. The door hit a boot with a worn rubber shoe and stopped. She had to squeeze herself through the crack in order to escape the cramped space. Pink dawn was starting to sprout on the horizon, but her work was far from done.

She still had the bodies.

Four bodies and a spattering of other evidence—sponges, a torn T-shirt used as a rag, two bottles of cleaner, and a handful of bullet casings— she'd get rid of this too.

She dropped the bag of evidence and wet rags beside a black boot. Then she stepped over all the legs between her and her bathroom.

A giant tub sat in the middle of the tiled room. It was a puckered, god-like mouth waiting for her.

Lou bent and turned on the faucet. Measuring the temperature with the back of one hand, she used the other to plunge the stopper into the steel drain at the bottom of the tub. The tub was made for two people and deep enough to reach a grown man's shoulders when filled.

Lou filled it.

Then she dragged the body of one of the men down the hall. Not for the first time tonight, Lou was grateful that her apartment had no carpeting of any kind, only hard floors that could easily be wiped clean.

She stepped into the water with her shoes on and hefted the man up into the tub with her. It was hard. Dragging dead bodies around always was. They went limp and completely unhelpful when they were dead. Gravity enters the bones of the dead in a way it can't with the living.

But once Lou got enough of the big figure onto the lip of the tub, the momentum of his corpse dropped him into the water. She cradled his bulk against her like a lover. Then she tried not to feel any panic regarding the fact that she was going to pull a dead body on top of her in a bathtub, and should her ability choose to fail her now, she would suffocate under the corpse crushing her.

She took a breath and submerged herself, the corpse still hugged against her chest.

Her gift didn't fail her.

She felt the bottom of the tub soften and fall away and then it was gone completely. She kicked her legs for the surface of the water and broke for air.

She let go of the corpse and watched it sink without her. She knew she should drag a least one of the bodies onto the shore for Jabbers, a sort of offering in honor of their working relationship. But she had three bodies left to go. It could wait. She dipped beneath the surface and let the lake take her again.

The tub bottom solidified beneath her, and she sat up, sucking in more air. Black hairs from the dead man floated on the surface, and Lou made a note to scrub and bleach the tub when she was done. She wasn't concerned about cleanliness. Lou never bathed in this tub. She used it only as a doorway. It took too much energy not to slip that the idea of soaking in a tub for an hour was ridiculous. Her mother had loved to do that, with wine and a book.

But Lou would be exhausted after five minutes.

That's what the shower with its glass doors in the far corner was for. And it sat beneath a bright, beveled window for extra measure.

Her boots squeaked against the slick floor as she held onto the tub for balance. Water sloshed over her knuckles. But despite the discomfort of wet clothes clinging, she pushed on.

She dumped two other bodies, the full trio who had lay siege to her aunt's apartment, in Blood Lake. With each return trip through the tub, the water was a little pinker than the trip before. La Loon water clung to her hair and clothes. The tub was as red as blood when she climbed into it for the last time, with the body of the man who had pistol-whipped King, demanding answers to Venetti's whereabouts.

When she broke the surface of Blood Lake, Lou didn't let go of the body this time. Instead, she lifeguard dragged this corpse toward the shore until the silty bottom rose at an angle beneath her like a partially submerged boat ramp. Each step elevated her out of the water.

Dragging a wet corpse was even harder than dragging a dry one.

She didn't even have the corpse out of the water when the leaves rustled. Something thrashed through the thick jungle foliage on her right. It would be here in twenty or thirty seconds.

The two moons hung in the purple sky and Blood Lake was still in the quiet evening.

Of course, it was always a quiet evening in La Loon. Every time Lou had visited this strange place, the sky was the same color, the moons hanging in the same position. She had no idea if some version of the sun rose and set on this place. Perhaps this part of Jabbers' world was like Alaska. For months at a time, everything traveled the sky in the exact angle.

Lou realized she didn't have her gun.

A black face broke through the trees and

screeched. A mouth opened wide showing no less than four or five rows of long needle teeth the color of puss. A large white tongue lolled in its mouth, and the interior cheeks puffed, making Lou think of the cottonmouth snakes she'd seen as a child, hiking the woods with her father. Jabbers might be the same black-scaled, white-mouthed coloring of a cottonmouth, but she—or he—was no snake.

She had six legs with talons, curved nails that dug into the earth as she walked. Between the toes was webbing, no doubt useful in the lake spreading out behind her. But the talons made her think of gripping and digging in. Did she nest in the mountain range a mile in the distance? She imagined the beast waking in some cave each morning and climbing down to the water's edge, waiting for her offerings.

Jabbers darted forward, and Lou pulled her bowie knife. The beast stopped in its tracks and hissed, pulling itself up to its full height.

Lou took a step back away from the body, moving so that Jabbers could easily pounce on the corpse, as she'd seen her do many times before. Foxes hunted like that, jumped down on the frozen waters to get seal pups out from underneath the ice.

Only Lou wasn't sure it was necessary if the

prey was dead, served on a proverbial platter. They weren't going to put up a fight. But then again, if one has spent a lifetime putting a napkin across their lap before eating, one doesn't stop because the menu changes.

Lou was clear of the corpse and lowered the knife.

Jabbers pounced, coming down on her forepaws with a playful air of a puppy seizing a toy from its master's hand.

Though no one in their right mind could look at Jabbers and see a playful puppy. She was too terrifying with her slit eyes and teeth and the way her body contracted from shoulders to rump with each movement. She was a solid mass of muscle.

Lou heard a splash and looked out over the lake.

Fins cut the water, darting one way then the other, like fish on the Discovery Channel evading predators. Only these fins were far too large to belong to fish, and she couldn't imagine anything as large as a killer whale traveling in formation to protect themselves from predators.

Movement caught Lou's eye, and she whirled back toward Jabbers to find herself face to face with the beast.

Lou raised the knife instantly, but she was too

slow. The blade touched the underside of Jabbers' chin, and when it did, a grumbling sound came from its throat. Lou's arm tensed, ready to plunge the blade up through the beast's jaw and into its brain— if its anatomy remotely resembled the creatures back home.

Fucking stupid, she thought. *Fucking stupid for taking my eyes off you. Why in the world would you munch on a corpse with fresh meat so close?* Water drying on the end of Lou's nose began to itch.

Lou could smell her—smell corpse meat on her breath as her growl deepened.

Then her hind legs folded and she sat down on her rump. The long white tongue came out of her mouth and lapped lazily at the blood drying on her muzzle.

Not growling. *Purring*. Purring like a goddamn cat.

Immediately her mind flashed with news stories meant to warm over sappy souls. How lions came to love their masters, recognizing them, *hugging* them, jumping up and wrapping those large furry paws the size of a grown man's face around in a gentle embrace, even after years in the wild. How a tiger could not eat a goat that was put into its cage as a meal.

Lou had formed a shaky alliance with a creature straight from a child's worst nightmare, taming it with the corpses of her enemies.

But she had no illusions. She had a ragged scar on her shoulder that wouldn't let her make that mistake.

Lou took a step back into Blood Lake. Cool water lapped at her ankles, then the back of her calves. She held the knife out in front of her. Jabbers didn't mind. She lifted one taloned foot and began to gnaw at it, digging out the guts stuck in the webbing.

Lou dove beneath the water and wiggled herself out of her clothes. When she surfaced again, she was naked in the blood red water of her bathtub.

Her arms were shaking from overuse. Her head pounded with each heartbeat.

She pulled the plug and watched the water drain, leaving a pink ring in the tub. She bent beneath the faucet and rinsed her hair and body until the water ran clear. She smoothed a hand along the rim until all the pink droplets became white.

Jabbers' bright eyes and the smell of her corpse breath burned in her mind. That had been too damn close. Close and stupid. What was wrong with her? She'd never been this careless before. And Jabbers wasn't even her first mistake.

Konstantine.

She was still unable to explain the uninvited pull to visit Konstantine.

What do you want from him? She asked as she shivered, naked in the empty tub. *Your enemies are dead.*

Almost, her heart whispered. She paused with the comb in her hair. *Almost.*

35

Konstantine slid into the back of the sedan as the driver opened it. The A/C instantly began to cool the sweat on his neck as he took the seat opposite the doors, his weight against the partition. The small window was open, revealing an empty driver's seat. The senator followed him in, unbuttoning the jacket on his suit as he slid across the leather.

The door closed, and the car rocked gently to one side. The driver's shadow fell over them as he rounded the car, ready to reclaim the wheel.

Ryanson was clearly pleased. "That went well. Perfect. I can't wait to see what you've drummed up."

Konstantine handed over a USB indentical to the one hidden inside his boot.

"Any plans this evening?" The senator asked. His mood was bright and contagious. "A woman waiting maybe?"

Yes, Konstantine thought. And if she did not

find him tonight, she would find him the next, or the one after that. She was waiting all right. Waiting to slit his throat. He had to decide, while he had a chance, what to say first. His first words may be his last. So what could he say that would stop her?

Who understands you better? They were born of the same crime-ridden and violent world. They'd both lost their mothers. They both wanted revenge.

Too presumptuous, he decided.

I dream about you.

Perhaps too intense.

I only want one thing.

Too demanding.

"I considered visiting downtown Austin," he said. *Where she was last seen hunting Castle.* Her hunting ground. "There is a bar there."

"That's a shame," Ryanson said. He made an exaggerated pout with his lips. "Can't I persuade you to come out with me instead? I have a beautiful boat. Congress doesn't reconvene until Monday, and my flight isn't until Sunday night. I can bring five girls to make you forget about the one you miss."

Konstantine forced a polite smile.

"Ten girls?"

"No, thank you."

"You know, I don't like double-crossers," the

senator said.

Konstantine looked up from his lap and met the man's eyes. He noticed the shift in the man's tone, the change in the air's temperature.

"I have your man Julio in the trunk," the senator added. His eyes clung to Konstantine's, measuring him up.

Konstantine cocked his head. "Julio?"

"It took us a long time to crack him. Longer than I expected actually. He was very, *very* loyal to you."

Was. Konstantine's heart kicked his ribs, began thrashing in its cage.

"It's true that I planned to murder you both anyway. I don't like leaving trails," he said. Then his face brightened. "But when I found out who you were, hoo boy! You're a wanted man, Mr. Konstantine. Your father has—had—a lot of enemies. And Father Leo wasn't a favorite either. Unfortunately, you've inherited enemies on both sides."

Konstantine took inventory of the weapons on him. Two guns and a blade. Ryanson had the advantage of being by the door. And assuming the driver was loyal to him, he had a man at Konstantine's back. But he was still sure he could get to his guns before either of them moved.

"So I decided to have an auction. The highest bidder gets you and I'm spared the trouble of killing you myself. Win-win."

Konstantine's fingers brushed the butt of his gun the moment before a sharp pain pricked the side of his neck. He turned in his seat as the driver pulled his hand back through the partition. His fist clutched a syringe, the needle and a tube with the plunger completely depressed.

Konstantine reached up and touched his neck, felt a knot swelling under the skin. A drop of blood came away on his fingers.

He raised his hand up to strike out at the driver, but the partition slammed shut and his hands connected with the window weakly. All strength drained from his body, like water poured from a cup onto the floor.

"We'll keep it civil. Lots of guards. It'll be a bit of a sausage fest on the boat tonight, but I think it'll be fun nonetheless. Don't you?" Ryanson asked, leaning forward. He pulled a bottle of whiskey from the sideboard. He popped off the lid and poured the tea-colored liquid into a crystalline rocks glass. He cut it with water from the mini fridge. All his movements were slow and methodical as if he had no worry at all that Konstantine might reach out and attack him.

And he was right.

The backseat began to stretch and whirl around Konstantine. *I must not lose consciousness*, he told himself, as if his will would override the drugs coursing through his veins.

"You used me," Konstantine said and found he was smiling. Of course, he had been used. He couldn't even say that he didn't have it coming.

"No more than you used me," the man replied. It was *the man* because he could have been anyone now. The face and body blurred. A child's finger-painting done on a living room wall. His eyes couldn't focus on the light shooting through the windows. He was leaning forward. That much he knew because his face was inches above his knees. His body was a rock seeking a solid foundation in the jostling ride of the car.

"Close your eyes and when you open them, we'll be there. It'll be a party just for you." The voice elongated like a tape played in slow motion. The kind he used to have to rewind with his school pencils when the tape players ate the coffee-colored ribbons. He was such a tape now. Unraveled. Pulled apart.

The car hit a bump in the Texan road, and

Konstantine was pitched forward. He was falling. Falling through the darkness. And he lost consciousness before he ever hit the ground.

36

King counted backward from a hundred. When Lou still didn't appear, he counted forward to a hundred. The numbers trick was something he'd picked up in therapy during his divorce. He had not sought treatment after the Channing incident. They were told to, and medical leave was forced upon him. But he couldn't go.

The therapist he *did* see, with her horn-rimmed glasses and bangs that fell into her eyes, had insisted that human emotion could only be felt for ninety seconds. So, anytime he felt overwhelmed with anger and grief, his best bet was to stop whatever he was doing and to count to a hundred slowly, keeping his breath slow and steady as he did it.

It turned out that this particular therapy technique was not very efficient when used in a fucking sealed Siberian transport container.

Big fucking surprise!

After counting to one hundred the first time, he

didn't feel any less anxious than when he began. In fact, his anxiety grew like a black spider on the wall, larger and larger. The numbers seemed to be building toward something.

Something terrible.

"Can you sit down?" Brasso begged. "You're making me motion sick."

"The container isn't moving," King said through grit teeth. "You can't be motion sick."

"You're moving!" Brasso whined. "It's you moving that's making me sick."

King glanced at the thick orange rust coating his fingers, like a hand left too long in the Cheetos bag. It proved he had been tracing the inside of this container for a long time. Black lines ran up and down the wall where he'd completely rubbed off the rust. Breathing in these rusted particles was probably *wonderful* for the lungs too.

"What were you going to do with Venetti?" King asked.

"Not this again," Brasso begged. "Shoot me already."

No, he thought. *If I have to eat you, I'm going eat you fresh*, he'd decided. He'd already, in his mind at least, started calling the corner where Brasso leaned "the kitchen nook." And his eyes kept sliding to the opposite corner, which was slowly becoming the bathroom, as his bladder grew heavier and heavier beneath his belt. An uncomfortable burn formed inside his trousers.

"Answer me, or I'll shoot your foot," King insisted. He'd resumed pacing. Going from wall to wall helped. It reminded him of how much room he had.

"You know we were going to kill her and dump her in the bay. Don't play dumb."

King nodded absentmindedly. "What else?"

"I like daisies and when the girls touch my pee-pee. *Please* stop fucking *moving*."

Pressure rose suddenly between King's ears followed by a sharp POP as the pressure equalized. He turned and saw a girl form herself out of shadows, out of nothing.

"Get me the fuck out of here!"

The words exploded from King's mouth. Some wise, distant part of him noted, *I'm hysterical*.

Lou froze as if afraid to come closer to him. But then her hands were on him and—thank god in heaven—the shipping container dropped away. A clear, moonlit floor of his apartment rose to catch them. Only it wasn't moonlight. It was too purple.

King turned to his watch. 6:36.

Evening. He'd been in the shipping container all fucking day.

He had taken a lunging step toward her before he realized he'd done so.

She had already moved out of his reach.

"Don't you ever!" he bellowed. "Don't you ever leave me somewhere like that again!"

Lou's frown evened out.

"Do you hear me?" King said. He felt the cords on the side of his neck standing out. A vein in his forehead throbbed. "Don't. You. Ever."

He sucked in great gasps of air.

A panic attack. *I'm having a panic attack.*

He dropped to one knee.

Lou shifted uncomfortably. "Are you dying?"

He shook his head.

"Are you sure?" she asked.

He waved her off, pointing emphatically toward the bedroom. He made a motion with his hand hoping she understood. He sucked at charades.

She went into the bedroom. Drawers opened and slammed shut and then she returned with a red rescue inhaler. He swatted at it, knocking it into the floor before fumbling it up to his mouth. Pump. Inhale. Hold. Pump. Inhale. Hold. He breathed. Deep. Steady breaths.

He collapsed onto his ass, still clenching the inhaler in his fist.

The black spots and red sparks in front of his eyes began to disappear.

His palm holding the inhaler fell to his lap. The world came into focus. The throbbing headache didn't leave him, but the air was going in and out of his chest again.

He looked up, expecting to see her gone, but she stood there. Gun in her hand, watching him.

"You're hyperventilating," she said.

"You fucking think!"

"Use your inhaler."

"Where the fuck were you?" he asked when he felt like he could spare enough breath to ask a question. His lips were ridiculously dry. He reached up and wiped away congealed spit from the corners with his thumbs.

He was dehydrated and yet, ironically, had to piss like a racehorse. But getting off the floor was not an option.

"Men came after Lucy," she said in a steady voice, speaking the way one might to an enraged horse.

"What?" King said. The air was leaving him again.

"I took care of it," she said. "But it took a while. Lucy has carpet. No rugs."

"Lucy has carpet," he repeated. He was starting to see things now. The perfect steadiness in her hand. She wasn't thumbing the safety. And her clothes were clean and her hair was still wet from a shower, presumably.

"You're tired," he said. He snorted, absolutely surprised. "I thought you were like a fucking terminator. Send in a hundred bad guys, and you just say *I'll be back*."

She didn't smile. She didn't even shrug.

"Is Lucy okay?" His chest tightened again.

"She's on the move with Venetti. They'll keep moving until we finish this."

"Until we finish this," King said, his mouth was going dry again.

"Why do you keep repeating everything I'm saying?" Lou's brow scrunched up. "Are you sure you aren't having a stroke or—"

"You abandoned me in a *Siberian* shipping container and...and..." King searched for the next words.

"And he's claustrophobic," Mel said.

King turned and saw Mel standing in the archway between the living room and kitchen. Her eyes were lined in thick black makeup and golden bangles jingled on her wrist. How had she crept up on them without a sound?

Lou hadn't looked away from where King crouched on the floor with his inhaler. She'd known Mel had snuck in. Of course she did. The girl probably saw a whole spectrum of things that King couldn't imagine.

"What are you carrying on about, Mr. King?" Mel said. "I have customers downstairs. You can't be up here screaming and carrying on."

King ran a sweaty palm down his face. "I thought you wanted atmosphere."

Mel arched an eyebrow. "A screaming man upstairs isn't the kind of atmosphere I'm going for."

"Why are you claustrophobic?" Lou asked.

"He was buried alive for days. Ain't that right, Mr. King?"

"You should have told me," she said.

"Yes, because you look like the type who is very sympathetic to weakness," King said.

Lou flinched, and King wished he could take the words back. He'd been scared and angry, but he was wrong to direct it at her. That's what pathetic men do. But it was worse than that.

Lou looked like hell. She was too young for the

thick bags forming under her eyes. Dried blood had begun to flake off her skin.

"I'm sorry I yelled," King said. "You didn't know."

King looked to Mel, curious what she thought of this girl.

Mel crossed the room, palms turned over in welcome, like she was going to hug the girl. Lou was mortified. Her shoulders tensed, inching up toward her ears.

"You wouldn't know," Mel said. "But men are worse than children. They cry about all the wrong things. When they have a papercut or a cold, they act like the world has rolled over their legs and they'll never walk again. When they've been beaten half to death, they tell you not to fuss."

Sensing Lou's resistance to an embrace, Mel stopped short. Instead, she took Lou's shoulders in her palms and squeezed. Lou softened under the woman's grip.

"Priorities," Lou said with a pathetic smile.

"Speaking of priorities, you need sleep," Mel said. "It's written all over your face."

"We have a lot to do," Lou began. It was the opening line of an argument.

Mel's hand went to her hip, and her tone

sharpened. The harsh, bird-like Melandra that King knew returned. "Aren't you tired of carrying around dead bodies?"

Lou's lips twitched with the hint of a smile.

"They can't be light," Mel pressed.

The smile widened.

Mel arched an eyebrow.

King wasn't sure if he should get up or stay on his knees. "You two do what you want. You're both grown." Mel gave first, throwing her hands up and turning toward the door. "Just keep it down, Mr. King. You're not the only one trying to do business here."

The door shut behind her. Then the wall behind the stove vibrated slightly as she descended the stairs back into the shop. The ghoul by the door screamed.

King pulled himself to standing. Gratefully, Lou did not try to help him. He felt enough like an invalid, old man as it was. "You can have my bed," he began.

But when he straightened he saw that she was already stretched long on his red leather couch, one arm folded under her head and the gun, still in her grip, resting across her navel.

I'll have to wait to tell her about Ryanson, he thought. Because his bones ached and his head throbbed and the air moving in and out of his mouth wasn't nearly as smooth as he needed it to be if he was going to go in guns blazing.

37

Lou couldn't sleep. The cold barrel of the gun was a reassuring weight on her belly, but every time she closed her eyes, she saw blood. She saw a man's head exploding. Jabbers bloody snout ripping an abdomen, guts erupting as if spring-loaded.

Her aunt's wide and tearful eyes as she surveyed the carnage in her apartment. The carnage that Lou had brought to her door.

Lou sat up, listening to the dark. She heard nothing. She'd already taken two steps toward the large cherry armoire before she realized what she was doing.

When she placed her foot down again, silk shirts brushed her cheeks and the smell of a man's cologne lingered. She reached out and found the doorframe, and then the closet's handle.

She pushed it open, peering out into the room. It was a child's bedroom, two twin beds with spaceship sheets. Her aunt and Paula slept. Paula snored as loud as her father had when she was a child. A deep rumbling rattle in her chest, her head tilted back and mouth slightly open in the moonlight spilling through the open window.

Her aunt was curled on her side, facing Paula. She was on top of the sheets, her shoes still on.

Ready to go, Lou thought, and a wave of sadness struck her full in the chest.

How could I be so stupid? How could I think that what I did would never come back to her?

Lucy stirred in her borrowed bed. Lou understood it was some empty vacation rental in an offseason. The world was surprisingly full of them, rooms waiting to be filled. Some more stocked than others. Timeshare cabins and condos. Rentals or houses for sale. They could be found the world over.

I'll finish this, Lou thought, watching her aunt, so small and fragile, sleep the night away. *I'll make you safe again.*

She remembered all the prescription bottles lining the kitchen sill. A lot of bottles for a woman who thought love and tea leaves would cure all. Lou couldn't look at that truth yet, its significance. So she turned away and slipped back into the darkness.

When she stepped past the armoire into King's apartment, she couldn't bring herself to lay on the couch again.

She had better things to do. Like cut off Ryanson's hand and slap him across the face with it.

Before she realized it, Lou had paced herself right out of King's apartment into the stairwell. Only it wasn't a stairwell so much as an overlook. A railing created a partial hallway that ran waist high to the left. There was nothing right. When Lou looked over the railing, she saw only the store below.

The lights were on, and a girl was pulling the door closed and turning the lock.

Lou descended the steps as the girl picked up a broom propped against the wall. As she turned, she saw Lou and jumped. Her movement awakened the skeleton beside her, which also shrieked, a blood-curdling cry.

"God!" the girl said, stamping a foot. "I hate this thing." She bent and yanked the cord out of the wall.

Lou crossed the floor heading for the door. She would walk the block and cool off. Give King another hour or so of sleep before taking him into a firefight.

The girl stepped back into the wall, bumping her head.

Lou stopped advancing. "I'm not going to hurt

you."

The girl's eyes doubled in size. "Oh, I'm not scared. I was—"

"Moving out of the way of someone holding a gun."

The girl frowned. "No. It's not like that."

Lou didn't move. She was unsure what to do with herself. Why was she even down here?

She saw King in her mind's eye. Saw him collapsing to his knees and holding his chest. He went down the way a man who was shot goes down. Like how her father went down.

There you go, stupid girl. Be honest with yourself at least.

He's not my father, she thought.

No. And you don't need him to go after Ryanson. So why are you still here?

The girl standing with her back pressed against the door seemed to wonder the same question. "Hey, are you okay?" she asked. "You don't look so good."

Lou holstered her gun for the first time all night. Her eyes blinking open as if she were coming out of a dream. "I should fix this."

"No, I mean you look good. You just look..." she searched for words. "Stressed maybe? Tired? Like what was the deal with the guy in the apartment? The one I clobbered?"

Go alone. If something happens to you, it's just you. Venetti, Aunt Lucy, and King—they need to stay out of it.

As if on cue the compass inside her whirled to life.

Go, go, go, it murmured, tugging at her insides. *Before it's too late.*

Lou had turned away and hurried toward the velvet curtain. Surely it would be dark enough back there to slip to her apartment first and then—

She threw back the curtain and found Mel bent over a table peering at cards in the candlelight. A chubby guy in his mid-twenties looked up with wide eyes.

"What the fuck?" His chin wobbled in surprise.

Lou didn't have time to look for another exit.

"I'm sorry," she said to Mel. Before slipping in plain sight of the landlady and her customer she added, "Tell him I couldn't wait."

38

Lou took only five minutes to suit up. Three compartments from her secret vault were emptied. She brought five guns and the corresponding clips. She strapped two knives into sown-in slips designed for their enclosure. At last, her father's bullet proof vest hugged her as tight as his arms ever had.

And then she stepped out of a closet and into...what? A toilet pressed against the back of her leg and she put her hand down on the porcelain surface of a sink. A tiny bathroom then. She listened to the thin door for voices but heard only the low rumble of an engine. A car on a distant street? No. The floor swayed under her, back and forth. The gentle rocking of a boat and the slapping sound of rough waters assailing the hull. The scent of salt was sharp, burning her nose.

Ryanson's boat then.

No doubt the same boat Venetti leaped from with an oxygen tank, her last-ditch attempt to save her life. The question: why did she appear here now? Was Ryanson dumping more bodies? Killing more girls? Making shadier deals with the parasites feeding on the world's underbelly?

Her heart skipped a beat. She had hoped she would walk in on Ryanson alone. The good little senator tucked in his bed. A hop, skip and jump to La Loon, and then it was dinner time for Jabbers.

She'd clearly packed for more.

At the very least, he wouldn't go easy. He thought too highly of himself to roll over. And Lou knew in a distant kind of way that she could just as easily die tonight. It happened when you didn't expect it. She'd known this since watching her father die through a watery prism.

She supposed it didn't matter what Ryanson was doing here. Her intentions were clear. So whatever she was walking into—

So be it.

She eased open the bathroom door.

It was a bedroom. A giant bed with a mirror hanging overhead and a mirrored headboard behind it. Overkill. To the right were stairs leading up to a door. And voices.

So more than one man. More than one threat.

She ascended the stairs as slowly as possible,

one foot in front of the other, keeping a hand on the wall for balance. She would have to come out guns blazing, she knew. The deck would offer no cover, and if she intended not to have her head blown off straight away, she would have to use the door for protection.

But there was no time to fool with the hinges in the dark, popping the pins and creating a wooden shield that might prove as flimsy and pathetic as cardboard.

Keep low, she thought. The voice was her father's, and the sound of it made her heart constrict. She imagined him here behind her, the scent of him as he guided her. In her imagination, they were on the same team and about to bust a drug house. He was walking her through it. He had her back.

Duck down. Use the steps. Throw the door wide. Target. Shoot. Get as many as you can before the door closes. Track left to right, following the swing of the door.

She took a breath.

And threw open the door. She dropped as the door swung wide and banged against the opposite wall. All the guns came up. Five in all, from her vantage point. A man on the ground eye level with her was gagged and bound in front of a row of white leather benches, fluorescent in the light. A man with a power drill kneeled in front of him while Ryanson stood off to one side with a drink in hand, looking like a vodka advertisement, shades pushed up on his head and shirt billowing in the wind. On the other side of this door stood two more in the moonlight. Their skin shone as if polished.

They didn't shoot. Neither did she.

As good as her father's advice had been, giving up her cover when she could gather intelligence instead—she couldn't pass it up. So she remained frozen. Not a single muscle in her body twitched.

"What the fuck, Ryanson? You got a haunted boat?" the man with the power drill asked.

"No wonder it came so cheap," Ryanson joked, but she could hear the terror in his voice. The strong tremor to his words despite his insinuation that he had paid anything less than six figures for his beautiful seabird.

"Go check it out, Rick."

Rick was walking toward her when the cabin door clicked shut. So she stepped back into the dark and drew her knife. The wall behind her softened, and fell away.

When she slipped through, she was on the deck, beneath the white benches Venetti had described.

Lou surveyed the forest of feet. With one swipe, she cut through the boots of the man with the drill. He cried out as his Achilles' tendons snapped and he fell backward.

His back hit the deck hard, and he cried out. The drill clattered across the deck.

Someone bent down and looked under the bench, and Lou put a bullet into his brain and a second into the next lookie-loo. *There are more than five*, she realized. Some must have been hidden by the door. But she couldn't count them properly now either. They were jumping up onto the benches, out of her line of sight, like a gaggle of teenage girls escaping a mouse.

The bench above vibrated and at the last moment, she realized someone was running along it, positioning themselves above her so they could shoot her through the fabric and wood barrier from above.

She pressed her back against the undercarriage and slipped. The inside of the cabin with Ryanson's gaudy mirrors and throne bed reformed around her. The man who'd come to investigate the door, Rick, was running up the stairs toward the commotion. She shot him in the back of the head, and he stiffened, falling straight back like a tree.

Timber, her dead father said, and Lou smiled.

A bullet shot through the window of the cabin and sliced through her upper arm.

Her lips pulled back in a hissing grimace. Without thinking, she shot blindly at the window and wasn't sure she'd hit the gunner until she heard the scream and the splash of a body going overboard.

The water. She could sink this boat and take the whole thing to La Loon.

Only she was sure that the boat was designed *not* to sink.

She hunkered in the corner. The corner was dark, a potential exit, but also good cover. She tried to breathe through the pain of being shot, gather herself, count in her head how many more men she thought she'd seen—reassess her situation before commencing round two.

They were shouting on deck. Someone had looked under the bench, found nothing, and now they were spooked.

It would buy her a couple of minutes if nothing else.

I need to bring you down, she thought, imagining the boat sinking into black watery depths. *How to bring you down.*

Her strategizing was interrupted by another

round of bullets. Two hard knocks slammed into her vest, punching her into the wall. Then a third pierced her thigh and the knee folded under her weight.

39

King woke to Mel shaking him. "Get up you log! Get up! Get *up*!"

King wanted to remind her that he'd been shot at, beat up, and left in a Siberian shipping container all day. His chest still hurt from his attack and his throat was raw and burning.

It was hardly like he was a lazy bum.

Then his brain clicked on and registered the fact that Mel was the one shaking him awake in the dead of night. Not Lou.

King bolted upright so fast his forehead clipped her chin.

"Watch it!" she said, moving back.

"What's happening?"

"Your girl did a disappearing act, right in the middle of one of my readings. She said to tell you she was sorry but she couldn't wait. So I called your lady friend, and now there's a girl in my apartment and…"

"What?" King put one hand against his head. Then louder as if to shout over his blaring panic. "*What?*"

Lucy cupped King's bare foot in a strangely intimate gesture. It was as if she'd just appeared there, at the foot of his bed, materializing from the darkness as she did.

But her touch had a strong effect on him. King became hyper aware of the women beside him, of himself only in boxers with the chilly night air coming through the window, of the sweat drying in the fold of his neck.

"Lou went to kill Ryanson. Alone."

When King looked perplexed that Lucy knew the senator's name, she added, "Paula and I talked. She's in Mel's apartment."

"And this one!" Mel was pointing. "*This* one can disappear too."

Lucy gave a weak smile. "Secret's out, Robert. You have some explaining to do."

Mel touched her brow as if blessing herself. "You're going to sit down and tell me everything. At the very least, tell me what to say to Piper. She's inconsolable. She said all her unborn children are dying as we speak."

King pressed his fingers to his forehead hoping

his brains would go back inside his skull.

Their excitement and dread, playfulness yet resignation, King tried to absorb it, understand it. His mind pushed through the mania of their combined emotions and tried to focus on what mattered.

Lou took off. Alone. And she's doing it without knowing the truth.

"We have to stop her." King swung his legs off the side of the bed. "Ryanson ordered the hit on Jack. He orchestrated everything. If she murders him, the truth dies with him."

Lucy blinked several times.

"We could clear Jack's name," King said again. He tugged at the jeans on the floor. They didn't come up until Mel stepped off them.

Lucy offered him a shirt. "Let's go."

King's head snapped up "You're not going. No vegetarian Buddhists allowed."

Lucy threw the shirt into his face. "And how exactly do you intend to get to Houston without me."

King's heart kicked. Damn. She was right.

Guns. But Lucy would never take one. Mace, maybe. Handcuffs certainly. And a bullet proof vest for sure. He would have it all on her before they stepped out of this apartment.

King pulled on a boot and began lacing it. He glanced up at Mel, who still scrutinized him with an arched brow.

"If I come back in one piece, you and I will sit and have a nice long talk about all this," he told her.

Mel threw up her hands, and the gold bangles on her wrist jingled. "You're damn right we will. And what do I tell Piper?"

"Tell her not to underestimate Lou."

40

Konstantine fought against the grogginess saturating him. His limbs were heavy. His head felt as if it had doubled in size, rolling around on a neck that could no longer support it. The lights were too bright, and every sound struck him like a slap.

Then everything happened at once. The gunshots. The screaming. And suddenly a knife was in his hand.

He felt the blade brush his fingers. He scooted back until the blade was in his hand. The edge sliced his finger open, and a stinging fire shot up his hand. It sobered him, pushed back the drug-induced fugue.

He managed to pick up the blade again, gingerly this time now that pain forced him to be cautious. And he began working the blade up and down on his bonds. It was an awkward, slow process and all the while he could only watch the other men on the deck.

He hoped she had left, escaped in the confusion.

Half of the men were already dead.

When Ryanson caught Konstantine looking at him, he slid down onto the bench seat as if suddenly aware what a big dumb target he was, looming over the others. He sat with his knees folded against his chest, resembling a terrified boy. Konstantine thought he could reach Ryanson if he needed to— ten steps, maybe fifteen at most.

Konstantine's bonds snapped, and he darted to the nearest pistol lying on the deck, a few inches from a slack hand. He grabbed the gun and turned it on Ryanson. He would not be leaving this boat prematurely. Lou would have her father's executioner and the USB still hiding in his boot. He felt it, poking into the side of his heel and the knot in his chest released.

The cabin door burst open, and there she was, leaning heavy on the door.

Louie. She met his eyes but didn't see him.

There was too much blood.

Mio dio, he thought, *she's going to bleed out.*

Her right thigh was soaked with blood. It dripped like rain onto the top step. He could not tell if the femoral or the aorta were slit. Perhaps both. She had only minutes.

The last of Ryanson's men stepped in front of

her, and she blew them away like a child blowing dandelion seeds. Konstantine had never seen someone shoot so fast, with such precision, even in her weakened state.

She shot all the men huddled at the boat entrance in a small circular movement, pulling the trigger six times. Six bullets. Six bodies hit the deck. Then she pulled another gun with her other hand, and the body count doubled. Naturally ambidextrous or practiced, he couldn't tell.

When she pulled the third gun, she didn't shoot. Her eyes fluttered, and she slumped forward onto her hands. She dropped her gun.

The last two men, apart from Ryanson and himself, came around the corner.

She doesn't see them.

Konstantine put a bullet into each before aiming on Ryanson again. The two dead men fell at her feet as if prostrating to a queen.

In one fell swoop, she'd killed them all. *All of them,* except for Konstantine's minor two-body contribution. Traveling in and out in that way of hers.

Ryanson collapsed on the bench, surveying the carnage. He looked bewildered, unbelieving at the number of bodies on the boat deck. The blood that seemed to run from all directions, this way and that way depending upon the tilt of the sea.

Lou frowned at the dead men too. She looked from Ryanson to Konstantine, confusion screwing up her face, as if she'd forgotten what she'd come here for and was trying to remember.

Then she looked up and met his eyes. Her eyes focused despite the blood loss, and she saw him for the first time.

She recognized him. And lifted her gun to aim.

41

The boat rocked under Lou, unsteady, and her pounding headache didn't help. She was nauseated. But it was more than that. She'd felt this before—an alarming level of blood pouring warm down the inside of her thigh. If she didn't get the hell out of there and pump herself with a couple of pints of O-neg, she was going to become a permanent fixture in Ryanson's graveyard. Or she could jump overboard, sending herself to La Loon. A final offering for her faithful companion.

That was how it should be.

Ever since the creature had bitten her, shaken her, thrown her into the lake to die—they were one. They'd exchanged blood. The power of this arcane rite bound them together. Somehow this ravenous creature was her. It was a manifestation of her spirit. Her soul. Her shadow. It thirsted for blood the way she did. It knew only peace when she killed.

Horseshit, her father said.

His voice sharpened her mind, bringing her back from the edge of delirium.

She had to focus. She was almost done here. She just had to be strong for a few minutes more.

Bodies fell at her feet. *Forget them. Focus*, she said again. *Find Ryanson. Put a bullet in his brain.*

But it wasn't Ryanson who held her attention. It was Paolo Konstantine. A busted lip and bruised cheek made him more handsome than ever. And the fact that she found him attractive when she was bleeding to death pissed her off more.

"Konstantine," she said, her gun trained on his face. She wanted him to confirm it. Declare himself.

"Yes," he said in accented English. It was the kind of stupidly sexy accent that women went to movies and got all wet over. Her desire to shoot him increased tenfold. "And you're Louie. Louie Thorne."

And then like that, she had a third reason to shoot him.

Yet the gun trembled in her hand. Sparks danced in her vision, and she thought *goddamn, I'm going to black out.*

She was going to black out with the image of a teenage boy, with big beautiful cow eyes smiling down at her, purring Italian at her with a face full of tenderness. The first kind male face she'd seen since her father had died.

You need to elevate your leg, her father said. His heavy hand was on her back, and the weight of it was pushing her down.

"You need to elevate your leg." Her father's voice changed. Deepened. No, not her father. King. She was still on the deck of the boat, an arm's length from the cabin door.

"I heard you the first time," she said. Someone prodded the wound in her leg. She screamed.

"That looks horrible."

Lucy and King's faces solidified. They were both armored to the hilt. They had the sharpness of reality, unlike the warped delirium rolling her. Had Lucy entered from the dark cabin as she did? It didn't matter. She had to stop her mind from wandering.

Stay here, she commanded herself. *Don't you fucking black out.*

"We need a hospital," King said, prodding the leg again.

"She won't go to a hospital," Lucy warned. "She hates them. I'll have to pump her myself."

"Hates hospitals?"

"The light," Lou murmured. "All the light."

Speaking helped. It grounded her to a time and place outside her head. In the dark of her mind, the world was timeless, unformed. Everything existed all at once.

Lou seemed to realize that she was about to be transported, about to be taken away from her kill, and she raised her gun, centering it on Konstantine. His hands went up.

"What the hell are you going to kill him for?" King asked.

"He's the *new* Martinelli," she said. Her vision danced again.

"I'm Paolo Konstantine," he said. "It's true that Martinelli was my father, but he did not give me his name or a minute of his life."

"You're a criminal."

"You're the one holding the gun," he said with a soft smile.

The Glock shook in Lou's hand. *Why you? Why do I keep coming back to you?*

"Ryanson ordered the hit," King said behind her. But the hand on her shoulder was Lucy's. "It was Ryanson who wanted your father dead."

"Wait, what?" Ryanson said. He sat up straighter on his bench seat, making everyone aware of him again.

Lou turned her gun from Konstantine to Ryanson.

"I got the confession out of Brasso. He's the reason your dad's name got smeared all through the papers. And the reason he got shot and killed. The Martinellis were just the hired dogs."

Lou pushed herself up, forced herself to look at Ryanson. "It's a lie. I don't know what these crazy people are trying to tell you, but it's—"

He didn't finish before Lou was on him. She seized him with both hands and shoved. They tumbled into the black water. Hitting the water hurt. Everything hurt.

But Lou knew that if she was going to die, so be it.

She'd find enough strength inside herself for this.

When she broke the surface on Blood Lake, Ryanson was screaming.

Her limbs shook, threatening to fail. Her breath was labored, coming in pants.

But she wasn't looking at the half-drowned man she dragged toward shore. Her eyes were fixed on the beast waiting for them. She sat on her haunches like a poised cat, some ancient goddess prepared to accept the offering.

In ankle deep water, the senator finally stopped screaming. Seeing Jabbers had rendered him speechless.

"You like to have others do your dirty work for you," she said into the man's ear. She shoved him forward. Retribution rose to meet him. "So do I."

Epilogue

King put his dollar bills on the counter in exchange for a coffee and a plate of beignets. Then he shuffled from the service counter to the table beneath the green Café du Monde umbrella. Lucy sat at one of the tables in the July heat, eating pralines from a white parchment bag and sucking the caramel chocolate off her fingers. She grinned when he spotted her.

Her beauty was enough to kill him.

"Is this seat taken?" he asked, surprised, but happy to see her. She'd been absent in the two weeks since Ryanson's death. He assumed she was taking care of Louie because he hadn't seen her either. In his heart of hearts, he hoped this meeting meant there was more to their relationship. That perhaps they wouldn't disappear now that the case was over. Thorne women were hard to pin down.

But he also knew this might be goodbye. So he'd better say his piece while he had the chance.

"Please." She grinned and nodded toward the opposite chair. "A girl hates to eat alone."

"Not all girls," he said.

Lucy's smile softened. "Louie will come around. Give her time."

King squeezed himself into the chair. He put his coffee and fried donuts soaked in oil and powdered sugar on the table. They ate and let silence build between them. Fading sunlight sparkled across her face and the gray in her hair shined. He loved her more for those few gray strands.

"How long?" he asked.

She turned toward him smiling as if he'd said the magic words that she'd been waiting for. She waved a hand for him to go on.

King sighed, mustering the courage to say what he feared most. "I don't think it's a coincidence that you sought me out now. So how long?"

"That's the question, isn't it? Unfortunately, the doctors don't know. No one knows."

"Is it bad?" he asked. He'd stopped breathing.

"It's metastasized from my breasts to my bones," she said, sucking the chocolate off her thumb. "I've got anywhere from six months to twenty years."

He scowled, his appetite rapidly leaving him.

"Weren't they even a little specific?"

She plucked another praline from the white parchment back and studied it. King could smell the sugar from here. The sweet richness of the chocolate. "Most survive two or three years once their cancer metastasizes. Twenty-five percent can make it more than five years, and some hit the ten or twenty-year mark."

"You'll beat this," he said. It was a heartfelt wish as much as it was a declaration.

She spared him a weak smile. "We'll see. But I didn't come here to talk about being sick, Robert. I wanted to thank you for helping me with Louie."

He laughed. It was bitter. "You wanted me to be a positive role model. I think we can both agree I failed. Miserably."

She tilted her head. "You are a good man. I'm the one who needs work."

He barked a laugh. "How so?"

When she looked up at him through dark lashes, his heart fluttered. She said, "There's an idea in Buddhism that says nothing in this world is good or bad. It is only our thoughts that make it so. This is as true for cancer as it is for wayward nieces."

"It's good wisdom."

"Is that so?" she said, grinning. "If only I could

remember it."

She reached across the table and stole his coffee, sipping it with a mischievous smirk.

He'd never buy her coffee again if she always promised to drink from his cup like this. Despite her coquettish flirtations, the truth unsettled him. Metastasized breast cancer. His grandmother had died of that, and it had not been pretty. It was a long, hard road out of that hell. And he wasn't sure he had the strength to watch her suffer like that.

"I see this as a win anyway," she said, her tone light. "I don't think you realize how withdrawn Lou was when I came to you. One case with you and something has changed. If not in her, then in me."

"How so?"

"I have *hope*."

"Hope for what?" he asked, stealing his coffee back. He turned the cup so he could press his lips to the place she'd just pressed hers.

"I have hope that she'll find happiness. And if not happiness, then contentment. Peace."

"Then she is normal," King said, touching his foot to hers under the table. "Happiness and peace— that's what we're all searching for."

After a moment of surveying his empty beignet plate he said, "So can I go with you?"

Lucy arched an eyebrow. "To death? This isn't Romeo and Juliet, Robert."

He smiled, but it was a sad smile. "To the doctor. I'm sure you've got appointments and treatments." His face flushed. "I'm not saying you need me and maybe you don't even want me there…"

Lucy took his hand and squeezed it. "You're the sweetest man alive, Robert. Do you know that?"

Lou stood over Konstantine's sleeping body with a gun in her hand. He was bare-chested and laying on top of his sheets. Italy slept outside the window behind her.

She stood there and watched him, unsure for the first time in her life of what she wanted to do.

"How old were you?" Konstantine asked. His lashes fluttered open, and he turned his head to look at her. "The first time?"

She didn't even need to ask what he meant. She traced his lips with her eyes, full and pretty like a girl's mouth. She wanted to sock him in it, see the tender flesh split and bleed. Then maybe she would kiss it.

"I think you were fourteen or fifteen," he said,

smiling. "Am I right?"

"Your English is better." She still wasn't putting her full weight on her leg, but she didn't need to. Her shoulders, elbows, and hands worked. She didn't need her leg to pull the trigger and wipe the last trace of Martinelli off the face of the world.

He came up on one elbow and patted the empty bed beside him. "Would you like to lie down? For old time's sake?"

She raised the gun.

He jutted out his lower lip in an exaggerated pout. "Or are you here to put a bullet in my head?"

You're a Martinelli. You're a criminal. I want to kill you—But each statement sounded more pathetic than the last.

Instead, she said, "He never claimed you."

"No. To him, I was not his son. He only spared my life for the sake of his pride."

"Do you hate him?"

Konstantine looked away, and Lou's gaze slid to his neck. She watched the muscle move as he swallowed. Saw the throat jump with his words. "I hate what he did to my mother. She was a wonderful woman. She didn't deserve to be discarded that way."

Silence swelled between them. Finally, he

looked at her again. "Do you hate your father?"

"No," Lou said too quickly. She caught herself and in a controlled voice said, "Not at all."

Konstantine nodded. "I am sorry for what Angelo did."

Her finger twitched on the trigger. "Why did you go after Ryanson?"

Konstantine looked at the barrel for a moment and then he reached out, slowly, and pulled the gun forward, pressing it under his chin. If she pulled the trigger, it would blow off the top of his skull. Easily.

"I understand drive," he said. His eyes never left hers. "I know how hard it is to stop before a thing is done. If you need this, take it."

Lou pressed the barrel against his chin so hard it would bruise.

She waited. She waited for the rage to fill her up. To roll her like a wave and pull her down with it. But the fury never came.

Then he was talking again. And she was listening.

"When I saw you on the boat, dropping one man after another, I almost laughed."

She arched an eyebrow. "Do you find murder amusing?"

He snorted. "No. But Ryanson had called the

gathering an auction. Once he realized I was after him, he was going to sell me to the highest bidder. As a Martinelli and as a Ravenger, there were many bidders. But there you were, killing them all. It was...poetic. If I belong to anyone it's you. Of course, you should win any auction for my life."

She shifted her weight. The gun grew heavy.

"I am not your enemy," he said. "I believe we are drawn together for a reason. You came to me when you were dreaming. Did you dream of killing me?"

No. Her heart hammered. But the gun remained perfectly steady against his chin. She'd dreamed of feeling whole again. Dreamed of having someone who understood her as surely as her father did. Someone as steady and immovable as that mountain of a man. Someone to replace what had been taken from her.

And she still needed it—something to replace the revenge.

Her gaze bore into his, but she found no deception. She saw only dark eyes as deep as nighttime waters. An escape. Possibility.

"I wanted you to know the truth of Ryanson." He didn't push her gun away. Didn't try to pull her close. He laid there, belly up and vulnerable as he spoke. "I couldn't return your father to you, but I could give you the truth."

"The truth died with Ryanson."

Konstantine grinned. "Did it? We live in a new age, Louie. *Now* the truth cannot die."

Her battle-drum heart beat, relentless. The gun came alive in her palm again.

"What do you want in return?" she asked. Because nothing was without price, no matter how pretty the packaging.

"My mother," he said. His eyes shone. "I want to bring her home."

King had never seen the shop so busy. It was like a rave. Sweaty bodies were crammed in on one another. The place was alive with the excited chatter of amateur ghost hunters. News of Lou's disappearing act had spread through the quarter like a gasoline fire. Melandra's money problems disappeared in the rearview just as fast. And however heartbroken Piper might have been over Lou's disinterest, she seemed as chatty as ever. She showed a customer with a green Mohawk a voodoo candle with a wick where its penis should be. Piper said something and the girl laughed riotously.

All around the mood had improved.

King himself was there as crowd control, one enormous body to remind all others to behave. It was pretty much the only gig he had since Venetti was saved and the senator dispatched. Without Brasso, no one else was turning up to offer him the chase of a lifetime.

He wasn't complaining.

There was so much commotion in the shop he probably wouldn't have seen Lou if the movement hadn't caught his eye. He looked up and saw her on the landing outside his apartment. She didn't wave. Didn't call out *hello*. She stood there in front of his apartment door waiting to be acknowledged.

King shuffled her way.

Mel touched his arm as he pushed past. She followed his gaze.

"You going up to talk to her? Tell her that I'll give her $100 for every night that she does her ghost trick for me. If she says no, negotiate. I'm willing to go up to $500, but good Lord, don't offer her that unless you *have* to."

"I'm not sure she's interested in performing carnival tricks on demand."

Mel slapped his shoulder then shoved him in the direction of the staircase. "It doesn't hurt to ask! Tell her I'll be up until closing if she wants to stop by and negotiate. Anytime! Anytime is fine by me!"

King climbed the stairs to his loft and wasn't surprised to see that Lou no longer stood on the landing. He found her on the couch instead, scanning the first page of the *Louisiana Times. Hero Agent's Honor Restored,* the headline read. A picture of Jack smiling, two thumbs up filled the top half of the page.

"I was wondering when you'd turn up," King said. "Can I offer you a Coke? A beer?"

"Lucy wouldn't shut up until I came to see you," Lou said.

They were talking then. Good. He wondered if Lou knew about the cancer. If she didn't, she would soon enough, one way or the other.

King leaned against the doorway, looking down on her. "She's your aunt. She loves you. Though why she thinks you should waste your time on this old fool is beyond me."

Lou gave him a weak smile. "Maybe she feels pity for both of us."

King snorted, got a Coke for himself and returned to the living room. He sat beside her on the sofa with an empty cushion between them. They said nothing.

"What *did* you do with Brasso?" King asked, taking another sip of his Coke.

Lou smiled. "Who?"

King ran a hand over his face. "You *left* him there?"

"I gave him a one-way trip to La Loon."

King's eyes fell on the scarred shoulder in the moonlight. "That's the place where you keep your pet Jabberwocky." He was having a hard time understanding such a place existed. And even if seeing was believing, he thought he'd be okay if this one remained fantasy.

"And Venetti?"

"Enjoying her new life as a hotel manager in the Keys. But if you repeat that, I'll have to kill you."

He had no doubts she would kill him, if she wanted to.

He shook his head. "You know, when you jumped overboard with Ryanson, I thought that was it. The truth would die with him. No one was going to know what really happened to your dad."

Lou stilled on the sofa beside him.

"But lo and behold, your father is a hero again." King tried to read her face but saw nothing she wouldn't let him see. "Did you have anything to do with that?" he asked.

She didn't answer but her shoulders relaxed. The hard lines on her face softened. She looked ten years younger. How much youth was she hiding under Kevlar and bad dreams?

"All right, all right," he conceded. "Keep your secrets. But what will you do now? Your father is avenged. You've killed a lot of bad guys. The ones that are left are running like rats. You must be bored stiff."

"I'll think of something." She grinned and the resemblance to Jack struck him, a bittersweet blow to the heart.

"In that case, kid, come back anytime you want. I'm always looking for trouble."

Acknowledgements

Always so many people to thank...First and foremost, my wife, Kim. Her enthusiasm for my stories is the biggest encouragement. Many of the ideas my readers read and enjoy—they can thank her for their existence. If she had been even a little negative or dismissive, I would have put that story aside and moved on to something else.

Thank you to my Horsemen: Kathrine Pendleton, Angela Roquet, and Monica La Porta. You give every story the critical eye it deserves and because of that, you make the books better—and me a better writer. I hope I'm doing the same for you.

Thank you to the horde of volunteer proofreads who are always eager to jump in line for ARCs. We all know I'm a one-woman show here, and I rely on the generosity of those who are willing to help without compensation—except for my unending gratitude and an honorable mention here on the acknowledgments page. So this time around, thank you in particular to Claudette Bouchard, CC Ryburn, Andrea Cook, Rachel Menzies, Rebecca Shannon, Ashley Ferguson, Misty Neal, Joe Thomas, Rhonda Green Barron, Ben Rathert, Leslie

Church, Shelly Burrows, Julie Evans, Evonne Hutton, Sharon Stogner, Lisa Morris, Ashley Owen, Kerri Krauter, Amy Chadbourne Brown, and Wendy Nelson.

Thank you to The Cover Collection for this beautiful cover. And thank you to Hollie Jackson who will narrate the audiobook.

Thank you to every blogger—professional or amateur—who shined light on my work and anyone who talked about it to family or friends. Thank you for every review. Every review counts. It may seem trivial to you, the time it took to write your review, but it increases my discoverability and potential audience. You're vouching for me. You're giving me a spotlight. And that is priceless.

I also want to thank all the Jesse fans who read this. I began my publishing journey with Dying for a Living—a first novel that I wrote at the tender age of 25. I published it five years later…and many of you have been with me ever since. When I announced that I was writing a new non-Jesse series, you were overwhelmingly positive about it. You were willing to follow me into uncharted waters *again*. And that feels good. Really *really* good. I thank you for it a thousand times over.

Thank you to every person who took the time to say hello on Facebook, Twitter, Wattpad, or Instagram. To everyone who took the time to write me a sweet, thoughtful email or send along fanmail. You guys are remarkably good at sensing when I've hit a rough patch in the writing. More than once, your kind words pushed me back into the saddle. So thank you.

About The Author

Kory M. Shrum lives in Michigan with her wife Kim and her ferocious guard pug, Josephine. She's an active member of SFWA, HWA, and the Four Horsemen of the Bookocalypse, where she's known as Conquest.

She loves hearing from fans on Facebook, Twitter, or her website/blog: www.korymshrum.com.

If you like free stuff, be sure to sign up for Kory's mailing list, and be the first to hear about giveaways, and new releases. You can also follow her Bookbub page or Amazon author page for new release alerts.

And please leave a very, *very* appreciated review for this book wherever you can. Your voice matters to the author and other great readers like you.